The Lady
Adventurers Club

About the Author

Karen Frost is an LGBT fantasy author. Her "Destiny and Darkness" YA high fantasy quartet, published by Ylva Publishing, explores what happens when strong young women are thrust into the politics of a kingdom at war while monsters from another world are baying at the gates. Karen is also a pop culture pundit and blogger who writes about sapphic representation on the big and small screen. She lives on an island in North Carolina, which is pretty irrelevant to this biography, but there you have it.

The Lady Adventurers Club

KAREN FROST

BELLA BOOKS

2022

Bella Books, Inc.
P.O. Box 10543
Tallahassee, FL 32302

First Edition - 2022

Editor: Heather Flournoy
Cover Designer: Kayla Mancuso

ISBN: 978-1-64247-414-5

Acknowledgments

This book is a tribute.

It is a tribute to the astonishing female athletes and daredevils of the late 19th and early 20th centuries—like Camille du Gast, Marie Marvingt, Dorothy Levitt, and Hélène Dutrieu—whose names are almost totally unknown in America and other parts of the world but whose accomplishments challenge our ideas of what is possible for a single person to achieve in their lifetime.

It is a tribute to the intrepid female explorers and adventurers—like Gertrude Emerson, Alexandra David-Néel, Isabella Bernhardt, Mary Kingsley, and Florence Dixie—whose names don't appear in standard history books but whose travels were no less notable than that of their male counterparts.

It is a tribute to the women—like Geneviève Guitel, Édmée Marie Juliette Chandon, Marie Charpentier, and Marie-Louise Dubreil-Jacotin—who had to fight twice as hard as their male peers to be recognized in their professional fields.

And, of course, it is a tribute to legends like Annie Oakley, Bessie Coleman, and Gertrude Bell, whose names are still commonly spoken even a century later.

This book is also a tribute to the swashbuckling, supernatural Egypt of literary fiction—the imaginary world of mummy's curses, angry gods with human bodies and the heads of desert animals, and dastardly antiquities thieves—that has fascinated Western readers for centuries. At the same time, the real Egypt should not be mistaken for that imperialist, imagined fictional setting. In that setting, native Egyptians are all but erased from their own land and their colonizers made the heroes. One of the greatest injustices of imperialism is that even a century later, natives still are not the protagonists of their own stories. The real Egypt has an incredibly rich and interesting history, where the various invaders are just that—invaders.

Finally, this book is a tribute to the idea that women can be the heroes of their own stories, and that an ensemble of female protagonists can drive an action/adventure plot just as well as a single male action hero. Sometimes we must write the change we want to see and hope that in some small way, this helps to reshape the entertainment industry.

This book benefited from the help of many people. First and foremost, I'd like to thank Jen Montoya, who acted as the primary beta reader, tirelessly reading and rereading chapters to offer feedback. Never having used a beta reader before, I realize now the error of my ways. To any aspiring writers out there, I can confidently say that having a beta reader really does improve the quality of your writing significantly.

I'd like to thank Laure Dherbécourt, one of the sapphic author community's best kept secrets, for acting as a secondary beta reader and my French sensitivity reader, and Aimée, who also acted as a sensitivity reader. I am blessed to have made the acquaintance of each, and thank them for generously giving their time and attention out of the goodness of their hearts and love of the community. To the others who read drafts, acted as additional sensitivity readers, gave advice, or just listened to me prattle on about this book, thank you. That includes Elizabeth Jeannel, who was the first professional believer in this book and provided helpful feedback. If any individual who provided feedback doesn't see their suggestions or edits reflected in the final draft, mea culpa. I promise I meant to include it.

Books that transcend an author's own personal experience both benefit from and should use sensitivity readers. In the case of *The Lady Adventurers Club*, I did my best to leverage multiple sensitivity readers. However, everyone's life experiences and interpretations are different. An author could use a hundred sensitivity readers and still manage to misstep. Therefore, if any reader should find anything in this book to be insulting, demeaning, or negative in any way, I hope they will forgive the mistake as unintentional and part of a best faith effort.

The Lady Adventurers Club went through a long journey to find a publisher. I am infinitely grateful that Bella Books saw it as a story worth putting out into the world. I am also grateful to have had Heather Flournoy as my editor. It was a wonderful and uplifting experience, and every author should be so lucky to have such a warm, positive editor. To any reader who has read this book cover to cover (including this section, apparently), I'm glad it was worth reading and hope you will advocate for the continued publication of this type of book, since nothing is a given in the publishing industry.

As a final note, I hope that readers find the characters in this book—and to an even greater extent, the real-life women upon whom they're based—inspiring. If I learned one thing during the research of this book, it's that the only limits in life are the ones that we place upon ourselves. The world is full of opportunity for those who have the courage to go out and grab it.

Dedication

This time, this one is for me.

CHAPTER ONE

Anna

26 November, 1922
Luxor, Egypt

The candle flame flickered, buffeted by the cool air escaping from the tiny hole that had been made into the top left-hand corner of the tomb wall. On the other side, visible only through a peephole, was blackness dark as the nubile, naked body of the Egyptian goddess Nut, the Coverer of the Sky, She Who Holds a Thousand Souls. Archaeologist Anna Baring, seeing the darkness, whispered under her breath a prayer from the tomb of the Singer of Amun Henut-wadjebu: "O my Mother Nut, stretch Yourself over me, that I may be placed among the imperishable stars which are in You, and that I may not die." Then she whispered a second, more modern prayer, "Please let this bloody tomb have something in it." It wasn't eloquent and it wasn't directed at any particular god, but of the two it was the more heartfelt. And if any gods were listening, modern or ancient, hopefully they would grant it.

There was reason to be worried. In the last hundred years, sixty-two tombs had been found in the dusty, endlessly beige

Valley of the Kings. And every last one had been robbed centuries or—more commonly—millennia before, cracked open like mollusks, their contents slurped out by a relentlessly hungry, greedy world. Now Anna was standing at the threshold of the sixty-third. The odds of a different outcome were not just against her, they were almost impossible. Already, there were unmistakable signs this tomb, too, had been breached by grave robbers. If it *was* the tomb of the boy king, as the seal impressions on the wall bearing his cartouche indicated, it was likely just as much a dry, empty husk as the others; one more in a long line of disappointments.

Anna had had enough of disappointments. One didn't defy one's father's wishes and spend decades in the desert to have nothing to show at the end of it. One didn't spend nights lying sleepless in the Egyptian heat, give up friendships and comfort for nothing but endless rocks and dirt. There had to be something here. But what?

She hardly knew. The people who knew what an intact tomb looked like were in no position to say. They had turned to bone and dust long ago. All she had was imagination, and she was nothing if not grandly imaginative.

Despite the odds, a sort of electricity crackled in the air, filling it with heady, tangible optimism. Anna felt a certainty bordering on giddy madness. This was it. This was the untouched tomb she and Howard Carter had spent years seeking.

Their search wasn't only about discovery and science, persistence, and determination. It was about the majesty of the pharaohs and their unimaginable, impossibly vast trove of treasures. It was about the glory of the ancients and their unwavering belief in a second life beyond the grave for which they could bring—both literally and figuratively—the full panoply of their wealth. If the rooms on the other side of the wall were untouched, it would be the archaeological find of the millennium. Yes, she and Carter would be feted from Cairo to London, but more importantly, the world would see for the first time the full splendor of the Egyptian pharaohs. So much for the Louis XIVs, John D. Rockefellers, and Nicholas IIs of the world—this was the kind of unimaginable wealth that built pyramids out of sand. *This* was what she had given her life for.

She shivered with anticipation despite the heavy heat of the valley, her heart racing. She ached with a longing that set her skin on fire to know what waited on the other side of the wall. But she would have to wait. The honor of being the first to see what lay through that tiny puncture in the veil between modernity and antiquity went to the two men clustered tightly around it.

Carter, cutting the perfect figure of an archaeologist with his slicked-back hair, high-waisted gray wool trousers, and loose white cotton shirt, pressed his forehead to the cool, pale limestone. Although he had rolled his sleeves up to his elbows and loosened his bow tie, any pictures commemorating this moment would show the sweat that soaked his back and left dew in his thick black mustache. In Luxor, there was no escape from the heat, even dozens of meters underground. The man waiting impatiently beside him, impeccably dressed in a brown three-piece suit with matching fedora and cane, was their patron, the patrician George Herbert, Earl of Carnarvon. Anna knew this glimpse inside Aladdin's cave belonged to the two men by right, since Carter was the head archaeologist for the dig and Carnarvon the purse strings, but even so, she couldn't help feeling jealous. Hers would be the *third* pair of eyes to see whatever lay inside. She would have to wait her turn until they had drunk their fill of the glories within, and she was not a patient woman.

"Can you see anything?" Eagerness vibrated in Carnarvon's clipped and slightly nasal voice. As was true for Anna and Carter, this endless search for the fabled lost tombs of Egypt's god-kings had become his life's work. But unlike them, he had been losing faith. Until a few days ago, he had been ready to abandon the dig, to toss in the towel and let the valley keep its secrets. Then they found the steps to the tomb, and everything changed.

Carter said nothing. Anna's mood shifted instantly, a ship changing tack in the wind. Her chest squeezed tight with fear. Was his silence because he was considering how to tell them that what lay on the other side was nothing but shattered dreams and the corpses of scorpions? Was he pondering the valley's mocking curse—that every tomb found was fated to be empty? If all that awaited them on the other side of the wall was dust and potsherds, their years of backbreaking work, of endless hours sweating in the sun to find just one intact tomb of the pharaohs were for nothing.

Anna couldn't bear to think what she would do then. Would she abandon Egypt and go to England? Give up on everything that she had striven for in a pique of frustration and despair? Her blood may have been fully British, but she was born and had lived almost her entire life in Egypt. Egypt was her home. This land had understood her even when her own family hadn't. It had willingly opened its bosom to her axes and shovels, giving of itself selflessly. Yet if all her efforts had been for nothing, was that not a sign that even the earth here rejected her? If so, where did she belong?

She licked her lips, her mouth dry, and rubbed her palms against her hips to take away the sweat. She had to calm herself. All hope was not lost yet. There was no curse upon the valley. An intact tomb could still be found.

What may have been several lifetimes or only a minute later, Carter replied to Carnarvon's query about his view. "Yes, it is wonderful." And the awe in his voice revealed that whatever he was seeing, it was indeed breathtaking.

Anna took a deep breath, suddenly lightheaded. The air filled her all the way to the tips of her ears, and with it hope, joy, and relief. She was a firework, rocketing through the air, on the brink of an explosion. She was dizzy. She clutched the tomb wall, grounding herself.

Carnarvon took off his brown hat and ran its brim through his hands, looking down at it as though he didn't know how to react. His light brown mustache—which always reminded Anna of an excavation brush—twitched. "Then we've done it?" There was both uncertainty and cautious hope in his voice.

Half of Carter's face seemed to disappear into the hole, including all of his distinctive Roman nose and most of his lantern jaw. "It's too soon to tell for now. It could be a cache like the others."

Anna crashed back down to earth. What? No. Not a cache. Not again.

During the 21st Dynasty, Egypt's priests had moved dozens of royal mummies whose tombs had been robbed from the Valley of the Kings to a place called Deir al-Bahri. There, a single tomb had become the unceremonious dumping ground for some of Egypt's greatest pharaohs. By then, all of their funerary trappings—the gold, ebony, precious gems, alabaster, and ivory with which they'd been buried—were gone, their gold sarcophagi melted down. The robbers had been so vicious in their plundering they had even torn the wrappings off the mummies, dislocating and destroying limbs and faces as they'd tried to pry off the solid gold amulets that had been wrapped with the bodies to speed the dead to the afterlife. This sad cache had been heartbreaking enough. Then a second cache had been discovered in the valley. If the tomb in which they now stood was a third cache…

Anna had to fight against the desire to shove Carter aside and monopolize the view for herself. Surely he was being cautious. It couldn't just be a cache, not if he had seen "wonderful things." A cache wouldn't be wonderful, it would be soul crushing. For four years, she had lived in a mud-brick hut adjacent to his and spent almost every waking hour walking the burning sands of the valley, melting like candle wax in the relentless heat and fighting mosquitos at night. If the tomb was a child, he was the father, but she the mother. She couldn't bear for that child to be stillborn.

Abruptly, Carter spoke again, disrupting her thoughts. "There's gold. Gold, everywhere. Statues…beds…chests… alabaster vases…chariot wheels." His voice rose with excitement as he enumerated each item. "And another sealed doorway!"

He stepped back from the wall, bringing the candle with him. His face was flushed. Sweat dripped down the side of his face and into his mustache, carrying with it dirt from the plaster wall that turned to soft mud in the long hairs. "I think we may have done it. I think she may be untouched!"

He was triumphant, ecstatic, but Anna was still shell-shocked. In the space of minutes, she had gone from the top of the world to the bottom. Returning to the top now left her spinning. But also buzzing. The tomb was intact. They *had* done it!

Carter handed the candle to Carnarvon, then quickly widened the hole with a chisel enough that the two of them could look through at the same time, two children with their faces pressed to the glass of a candy shop. For an agonizing few minutes, they were silent. Anna ground her teeth, feeling as though she might shed her skin like a cicada. *How much* gold was there? Was the room positively filled with it? How big was the room?

"Extraordinary," Carnarvon said finally, leaning back and looking at his chief archaeologist. "Just extraordinary."

They stepped away from the hole and shook hands, overjoyed by what they'd seen. This was their victory, a shared moment of triumph for two determined, passionate men who had invested so much of themselves into this moment. Carter took Carnarvon's elbow to guide him out of the passage, already chattering about what steps needed to be taken in the next few days to secure the tomb. As he passed her, he handed Anna the candle with a nod.

She immediately rushed to the hole, pushing her body against the wall and threading the candle through to the other side. At first, she saw nothing. The candle swam in front of her eyes, the red-orange flame shimmying in the air like a belly dancer. Then, slowly, other shapes resolved themselves.

She was looking into what was almost certainly the antechamber, a sort of foyer that separated the passage from the burial chamber. And it was full of…*everything*. A row of three funerary beds stood along the wall across from her in the shapes of a hippopotamus, a cow, and a lioness. Their gilt paint caught the light of the candle and reflected it back at her, sparkling like gold in a mineshaft. Stacked on the floor around them were plain wooden chests and empty wicker crates. Piled on top and below them was, for lack of a better word, bric-a-brac: benches; small wooden tables; petite, ornate chests; ovular, white wood boxes; beautiful alabaster jugs in the shape of lily and papyrus plants; and an exquisitely wrought black-and-white chair with gold inlay.

A shiver ran up her arms and found a home in her heart. These objects hadn't been seen by human eyes for over three thousand years. Below the hippopotamus bed was a golden chair. It was hard to make out all of its delicate, gorgeous details in the dim, flickering light, but on the backrest she saw the image of a seated pharaoh and his wife, their skins the color of brown ochre. The armrests were the pale blue wings of a vulture wearing the double crown of Egypt. *Yes*, a voice whispered, electric with excitement. This *must* be Tutankhamun's tomb.

With effort, she tore her eyes away from it, forcing herself to keep looking at the items that filled the room. To her left, a golden chariot lay disassembled among a pile of wheels. To her right, two life-sized statues with gold jewelry and black skin faced each other. She gasped, a silent inhalation of shock and pleasure to see such large effigies of a pharaoh. Dust floated into her nose, and she sneezed. Once, twice. The air was close and rank after millennia of being cut off from the rest of the world, but it was the air of the New Kingdom. She was literally breathing history itself.

She withdrew the candle and stepped back, rubbing her nose. Her emotions swirled, overwhelming and exhilarating. This was a monumental, unmatched moment for archaeology and Egyptology. It was everything she had dreamed.

And yet...something was wrong.

She leaned against the wall, plain beige and bare of hieroglyphics, and tried to identify what it was. Hadn't there been gold in the tomb? Hadn't it been grand and awe inspiring?

No. And that was the problem. *These* were the treasures of a pharaoh? *This* was the sum of Tutankhamun's ten years of rule? It was true that for a moment, she'd allowed herself to be overcome by the emotion of seeing this intact tomb, but now that she reflected on what she'd seen, she couldn't deny a nagging, quiet undercurrent of disappointment. The chair aside, nothing else had been of superfluous craftsmanship and value. In fact, looking at the artifacts with an objective eye, they weren't terribly different from what had been found in the tomb of the nobles Yuya and Thuyu, who had lived only a generation or two before him and whose tomb had been robbed several times. The paint was often shoddy, and frankly, it was clear everything had been thrown haphazardly into the small chamber, piled together without any attempt at order or organization.

If she was honest, it all looked a little too much like her gran's study, full of oddities and curiosities but lacking grandeur. Even the gilt was chipping away at the edges, and not just due to age. Her father would have scoffed at the tomb's poverty and condescendingly called it "a bit of a mess." Even the walls, which for most other pharaohs had been covered floor to ceiling with decoration, were utterly barren. It wasn't picturesque, and it certainly wouldn't awe the tourists that flocked to the Valley of the Kings in the winter months.

She bit her lip, pushing back against her ambivalent feelings. She shouldn't rush to judgment. There would be more to see inside the tomb. There would be other chambers, including the burial chamber. Who knew what treasures could be piled around Tutankhamun's sarcophagus? And yet...

She considered again the small antechamber and the blank limestone walls of the passage. Clearly, the tomb had been carved for a noble, not a pharaoh. As she and Carter had suspected, Ay, Tutankhamun's successor, must have switched tombs with the young king and dumped him here with callous indifference. Had he stolen Tutankhamun's gold as well? The answer lay on the other side of that wall, but she had a feeling she knew it already.

Blowing out the candle, she strode down the passage, bracing herself for the bright sunlight that awaited her. It was midmorning, and already the heat was starting to build in the valley. In a few hours, it would be ungodly. She handed her beige pith helmet and the candle to one of the Egyptian workers, then climbed the steps back to the valley floor. As she patted dust off her shirt, not only Egyptian eyes, but curious European ones, too, watched her. Every year, thousands of Egyptophiles from all over the world flocked to Cairo, Luxor, Aswan, and the Valley of the Kings. All the tourists who happened to be visiting today had gathered to watch the opening of the tomb. Everyone knew the Egyptians had more gold than Midas, and it would be the story of a lifetime to say they were there when some was found.

But Anna didn't care about the stories they would tell back home and had no interest in answering the questions they shouted to her. She marched past, ignoring their cries with her chin held high, and headed to the tomb immediately next door. This was the tomb of Ramses VI (usurped, of course, from his predecessor, Ramses V). It had been looted long ago in antiquity, but she nevertheless considered it the most beautiful tomb in the entire valley. It had five corridors, three regular chambers, and a large burial chamber, all of which were intricately and breathtakingly decorated. It was one of the biggest tombs, too, with soaring, dramatic ceilings. It was a marvel of Egyptian engineering and artistry, a testament to the ancients' skill at coaxing beauty from rock. Unlike its neighbor, *this* was clearly and undeniably the tomb of a pharaoh.

Taking a deep breath and slowing her stride to an amble, she made her way through the corridors. When she came upon two Belgian tourists marveling at the painted scenes in sunk relief that lined every inch of the tall walls and ceiling, she vicariously shared in their awe. Although much of the paint had been lost in time, there were still more than enough flashes of yellow, blue, and red to know how majestic the white walls must have once been. Gods, slaves, and the pharaoh himself wove through every inch of Ramses VI's final resting place. Bitter frustration teased Anna's tongue. *This* was how Tutankhamun's tomb should have looked. *This* was the splendor of a pharaoh's tomb.

When she reached the burial chamber, she sat down on a shelf of half-carved rock and tilted her head back to look at the bright blue-and-yellow painting from the Book of Sky that ran the length of the ceiling. She felt lost. Ramses's tomb was elaborate, grand, and imposing. Tutankhamun's, on the other hand, was featureless, close, and underwhelming.

It was then she realized what was bothering her most. She had found the pharaoh she had spent years seeking, but somehow, unbelievably, he had turned out to be a pauper. The pharaohs were not poor. Amenemhat I, for example, had claimed to have built a palace decked with gold, whose ceilings were made of lapis lazuli. Ramses III's palace, meanwhile, was reported to have had a floor of silver and doors of gold and black granite.

And yet almost more treasure had been found in the tombs of regular nobles than she'd seen just now in Tutankhamun's tomb. His tomb, that plain cave, was an anomaly, a pale facsimile of what a pharaoh's tomb should be.

Her heart sank as she imagined what they would find in the rest of the tomb: pottery, wood statues, and low-quality jewelry. As an archaeologist, it should have been enough for her. Her discovery of an intact pharaonic tomb would forever be memorialized, and she and Carter would spend years cataloguing its contents. It should have been the discovery of a lifetime. But it wasn't enough.

She clenched her fists, resolve building in her. There were still four New Kingdom tombs that hadn't been found: Ahmose I, Thutmose II, Ramses VIII, and Amenhotep I. They were out there somewhere. One of them might have what she was seeking. Once Tutankhamun's tomb had been properly excavated, she would find it. She was destined to. Tutankhamun's tomb wasn't the end of her journey. It was only the beginning.

* * *

29 November, 1922
Luxor, Egypt

Three days later, they hosted the official opening of the antechamber, a luncheon for select members of Egypt's high society held at the head of the valley overlooking the tombs. Anna would have rather been knee-deep in potsherds and dried unguents, carefully documenting what was in the antechamber and wrapping it for transfer to Cairo, but this was an equally necessary part of their work: currying favor with the Egyptian Antiquities Department and other key British officials and expatriates. After all, both had the power to uplift or ruin their efforts. Half of archaeology in Egypt, Anna had learned, was having tea with the right people.

In point of fact, the antechamber had been opened two days before. After electrical lighting was set up, Anna, Carter, and Carnarvon had carefully tiptoed through the room, gently touching and feeling the boy king's funerary objects. It had been a transcendental, surreal experience to handle items no one else had touched for thirty-two centuries, and Anna would always cherish the memory. Nor had they seen just the antechamber. Behind the hippopotamus bed, they had encountered another plastered wall, indicating the presence of a secondary room. Carter had secretly taken a crowbar to it, creating a small hole through which a person could wriggle on their chest to see what lay on the other side.

Yet for Anna, this room only proved her initial instinct that the tomb was a mildly disappointing hodgepodge of royal trinkets. The annex was even smaller than the antechamber and filled with so many plain clay pots thrown together in staggering disarray that it would have been impossible to walk in it. Upended furniture was scattered between dishes, beds, stools, boxes, statuettes, chairs, and baskets. Carter believed the annex had been ransacked by treasure hunters soon after Tutankhamun's burial, but Anna disagreed. If thieves had indeed made it into the tomb, why hadn't they taken the glorious, extremely valuable golden throne in the antechamber? It seemed more likely Tutankhamun's tomb had been unkempt from the start. More disappointment.

This ambivalence about their discovery weighed heavily on her as she took her seat at the luncheon table. She was pleased that her years of effort would be rewarded by professional accolades and her name forever listed as one of the finders of the tomb, but she found she simply couldn't feel the same exuberant joy as Carter and Carnarvon. Where they saw a cave of entrancing wonders, she saw only a disappointing jumble of objects chucked into a heap by Tutankhamun's funerary team. It was a wonderful find, one well worth celebrating, but it wasn't the find she had dreamed of. She wanted more.

"Go on, Howard, tell us the story of how you found the tomb," Henry Morton said as tea sandwiches were served. Carter had invited the representative of *The Daily Express* to the luncheon specifically to document the tomb's opening. No other reporters had been invited. It amazed Anna how much Morton and Carter looked alike. They might have been brothers. Perhaps that was why Carter liked him.

Carter gave him a broad smile. "Luck, old chap."

Anna, who was seated near the head of the table with Carter on her left and Carter's assistant, Arthur "Pecky" Callender, on her right, stiffened with surprise. Luck? She blinked, trying to process this unexpected response but finding no way to. How could Carter call the discovery *luck*? Luck had nothing to do with the precise, mathematical method she had used to meticulously map out the valley floor. She had spent years narrowing down the search to the exact place—the *only* place—the tomb could be located. *That* was how the tomb had been discovered. Why hadn't he said as much?

Raising his glass of water and holding it aloft as though he intended to toast, Carter continued, "The Fates have a funny way of playing with us mortals. My water boy was poking with a stick at the ground as we worked. In this way, by utter coincidence, he found the first step. It was a mere four meters from the tomb of Ramses VI, as I had thought it might be. Indeed, I suspect the tomb survived intact all these years only because it was hidden beneath the rubble of the carvers of that tomb." Carter raised his thick eyebrows, adding a dash of the dramatic. "Yes, a stroke of luck is all that separated the end of our efforts here in the valley from the splendor that you will see before you today."

Anna felt the world constrict around her like a fist closing. She could barely breathe. What was Carter doing? What was this fantastical tale of water boys and Greek tragedies? Why was he lying about the process that had led to the tomb's discovery, making mystical and arcane what was practical and methodical? It was absurd.

She stared at him, aghast, but he only had eyes for the journalist. She looked to Carnarvon and Pecky, men who knew the real story, but neither of them reacted. They didn't so much as blink in the face of Carter's fable. They certainly didn't rise to contradict him. In their silence, they affirmed his lie as truth.

Morton took a sip of his red wine and chuckled. "A stroke of luck indeed. For all of us."

Morton and Carter, two peas in a pod. In a terrible flash, Anna could see the story writing itself in his mind. Dedicated archaeologist tirelessly searches for the lost tomb of the boy pharaoh for seven years, triumphantly finds it as patience (and Carnarvon's money) runs out. Water boy breaks open mystery hidden for three millennia. What a story it would be, an international sensation. It was the perfect struggle of man against nature, of luck trumping science. The press would fall over itself to re-create photos of Carter and his noble benefactor Carnarvon carefully breaking the seals and peering inside the tomb. They might even find a quaint Egyptian boy to re-create the imagined discovery of the steps.

She saw it all and her stomach turned. As the only journalist here, whatever Morton wrote would become irrefutable fact. Justice demanded she correct the account and claim what was hers by right, but to contradict Carter before their guests would be unthinkably gauche. Not to mention he was the head archaeologist and well-respected among the luncheon guests. It would be difficult if not impossible to challenge him, especially if Carnarvon and Pecky remained silent. In a dispute of her word against his, she had no chance of winning.

She opened her mouth, not yet decided what she would say, but before she could say anything, Pecky's massive, fleshy hand briefly touched her right thigh. It was only meant to catch her attention; he removed it immediately. When she looked at him, he shook his head subtly. "Let it go." His voice was low. The words were meant for her ears alone.

"But…why?" She felt like a balloon whose air had been let out. Why had Carter made up the story about the boy? Why had he left her out of it completely? Why should she allow his fabrication to go unopposed? And why would Pecky let this happen?

"Let him have his stories. It doesn't hurt anyone."

Didn't hurt anyone? Anna gaped at the giant, who towered over the other guests like a well-dressed ogre. What about herself? What about *her* contributions to this dig? Was she no one? Her credentials were almost as impeccable as Carter's own, and she, unlike him, had been born in Egypt. This was *her* country, not his. *He* was the interloper.

Dazed and shaken, she realized for the first time that Carter had failed to introduce her to anyone at the table, even though men like the Chief Inspector of Antiquities in Upper Egypt, Rex Engelbach, and the Department of Antiquities's Luxor-based representative Inspector, Ibrahim Effendi, knew full well who she was. She hadn't thought anything of it at the time since she had come to the luncheon late, but now she saw that to the others she must have seemed like just another invitee, a celebrant of the archaeologist's success rather than a participant in it. Carter had planned this, and Pecky knew it. The betrayal was stunning in its brazenness.

"What's next? When will the next wall be taken down?" Morton asked, continuing a conversation from which Anna was slowly realizing how fully she'd been excluded.

Carter pushed back his white fedora. Although he, like all their guests, was sweating in his light gray suit, he had elected not to remove his jacket. He must have thought it fit the image of a successful archaeologist. Pettily, Anna wanted to tell him that his black bow tie with white spots mirrored a little too closely his mustache and it looked as though he had two mustaches. He would always be an impostor among the rich patrons he was so desperate to impress.

"What comes next is a good deal of work. It will take months, if not years, to catalogue the contents of the antechamber and the annex. Every piece must be carefully documented." He smiled, full to the brim with self-satisfaction. She wished he would choke on it. "Eventually, we'll open the burial chamber and see the king himself. I cannot say when that might be, but I look forward to that day."

Anna no longer heard their conversation. Her ears were full of buzzing locusts. The world was spinning too quickly around her and it was all she could do to sit and take one breath after another. She fussed with her red-and-white-striped tie, then, still fidgeting, ran her hand through her thick hair. It was a luxurious, radiant red like paprika—or the red date of Egypt, the zaghloul—and she was terribly vain about it. Even now, in the valley's dry heat, it refused to be tamed. She, on the other hand, appeared to be completely subjugated by the traitors around her.

She felt as though she'd fallen into some alternative version of her life, in which she had ceased to exist but everything else had continued apace. How had she suddenly become invisible to people she had known for years? They knew the truth. They knew what she had done. Why did they not speak up in her defense? She stood abruptly and grabbed her hat, unable to remain a character in Carter's play a moment longer. Beside her, Pecky stumbled clumsily to his feet as courtesy required.

"Are you all right, Lady Baring?" Carnarvon asked from across the table, alarmed. He, too, was rising, attempting to play the gentleman to a lady he'd just wronged.

No, she was not all right. She was being erased from her own life as surely as Ay had tried to erase Tutankhamun, and Carnarvon himself was enabling that erasure. But there was nothing she could do about it, as Carter had anticipated. The corners of her mouth twitched, a pale attempt at a polite smile for the benefit of the people around them. "It's the heat. I've been out in it too long working. Do excuse me."

Without waiting, she turned and stalked away from the table. Her abrupt departure would be both noted and whispered about by the guests, but she was too angry to care. Fury drove her as fast as her legs could carry her, pistons fueled by injustice and hurt. As she passed the crowd of workers waiting at the edge of the valley, Ali, the dig foreman, separated from them and slipped into step with her. His oversized leather sandals hissed against the sand as he walked. He was a tall, thin man, with a dusty white gallabiyah and matching turban that set off the deep carob color of his skin. A darker circle on his forehead showed he was a deeply religious man. He was the opposite of the luncheon guests, with their European suits and hypocritical morals.

"Is the lady well?" There was genuine concern in his voice. Anna wished all men could be as honorable and genuine as him. *He* would never have betrayed her like Carter had. He would never even think of it.

Suddenly she was tired. The weariness went all the way to her bones. She rubbed her forehead. "I'm fine, Ali." Not really, but it was no use telling him the truth. "But *low samaht*, have Abdul pack my things. I'm going home to Cairo. Immediately."

Surprise flew across Ali's face, making his thin eyebrows jump. "But the dig…?" He looked back reflexively toward the tomb they had spent days excavating together.

Carter's treachery was more than professional. It was personal. Anna's nostrils flared as she realized for the first time exactly what the future held. By leaving, she was giving up any and all access to her own discovery. She would have to learn the full extent of what was in the tomb from the papers. She could never step foot in it again. It was no longer hers. But then, it never had been.

Ali peered at her, worried. "Miss Anna, you are not happy. Your face is like the monsoon. What can Ali do?"

Despite herself, she looked back at the luncheon, which had carried on as though she had never been there. In a way, she hadn't. Lady Baring the woman had been present, but not Anna the archaeologist. Even from this distance, she could hear laughter as Carter played the consummate showman. She ground her teeth. She had learned a powerful lesson, albeit not one she wanted. "Nothing, Ali. But *shukran*. You are a good man."

Ali gave her a shrewd look, perhaps intuiting the discord between his two archaeologist masters. Or perhaps he had overheard something, planning between Carter and Pecky, for example. "*Allah* is with you and will never deprive you of your good deeds. Do not give up, Miss Anna."

She gazed over the valley, which was bustling with dozens of tourists, and her lips puckered. Let Carter have this small victory. She would do what he hadn't. She would find a *real* tomb, with *real* treasure. Then let him feel how it is to have his name overshadowed.

CHAPTER TWO

Clara

May 13, 1923
New York City, America

Clara Pickering huddled under her black umbrella. To anyone else, the red brick building in front of her would have looked mundane and unremarkable, but she knew it was neither. From its face hung two flags: the American flag and a second flag, unclaimed by any nation, also in red, white, and blue. Two letters, E and C, were written diagonally in its center, bisected by a compass rose. These were the initials of the Explorers Club, and that meant this building was hallowed ground, a meeting point for the world's greatest adventurers and scientists, men of great learning and uncommon courage. The thought of entering such an august place was more than a little daunting.

It had taken no small measure of determination for her to even walk up to the Studio Building at 23 West 67th Street on the Upper West Side of New York City. The city was big and crowded, full of busy, important people who wore fancy clothes and smoked long cigarettes. Walking to the Explorers

Club, she'd felt like a tiny insect lost in the middle of a forest, overwhelmed by the dizzying motorcars and the endless waves of people walking in every direction. The city was too fast for her, too superficial.

With her free hand, she reflexively patted her pocket, feeling for the news article she'd carefully torn from the paper.

Secrets of the Pharaohs Revealed: Archaeologist Anna Baring to give lecture on recent excavations in Egypt to unearth the treasures of the world's oldest kings. 4-5 p.m. today at the Explorers Club, 23 W. 67 St.

It was such a small, unremarkable announcement that Clara could easily have missed it in the morning paper, but chance had brought it to her attention. Chance had played a role in other ways as well. It was only by coincidence she was in New York City at this exact moment. Had the lecture been even two days later, she would have missed it entirely.

Truth be told, she didn't know much about Egypt. She wasn't even certain she could identify the country on a map. But like everyone else in America, she had heard about the discovery of King Tut's tomb last November and she was intrigued. With nothing else to do, she thought she might as well come to the lecture.

A thin woman in a high-collared white shirt and long black skirt strode past, taking no notice of Clara. When she reached the door to the club, she closed her umbrella with a flourish, then crossed the threshold without so much as a pause. Clara should have followed her. Her effortless entry proved it could be done. But instead, she stayed rooted in place, half certain she would flee before she found the courage to go inside. She could shoot the button off a coat at fifty yards with one hand tied behind her back, and ride upside down under a galloping horse, but bravery and fear were relative.

Her world was laughing cowboys and cigarette smoke and rodeos and the sound crickets make at night. She didn't know about science and research and exploration. Those were things she saw in the paper, worlds away from all the places she'd ever been. She hadn't even learned to read until she was a grown woman already. She belonged inside the Explorers Club about as much as a fish belonged in a cloud, but she wanted to know more about Egypt, and the only way to find out more was to enter. If she didn't go, she knew she'd regret it. There would be no other opportunity. Adjusting the hem of her brown suit jacket, she took a deep breath, put her hand on the knob, and pushed.

The foyer she entered was warm and brightly lit by torch-like sconces set in the wall. Their fuzzy yellow light pushed back valiantly against the gray drizzle outside. Clara marveled at the inside of the building. In front of her was a sculpture of two rhinoceroses. On the wood-paneled walls around her were maps, portraits, and paintings of foreign lands.

To her right was a long wooden desk, at which stood a bald Black man in a tan wool suit. He looked up when she walked in. "May I help you, madam?" He had a strong accent, which Clara, who had never heard anything like it, believed might have been African.

She clutched the front of her jacket, reminding herself that the lecture was open to the public. She had every right to be there. "I'm here for the lecture."

She felt exposed to his dark eyes. She hoped he couldn't see the stains at her wrists or the mud that would never come off her boots. No matter how hard she tried, there was always a little dark dirt under her short fingernails, a taint of uncleanliness no amount of soap would wash away. But if he saw these things, he gave no sign of it. Instead, he nodded. "Of course. Would you wait in the members' lounge, please?" He pointed to the room across from him, on Clara's left.

She smiled weakly, feeling the smallest breath of relief that he had not seen her for the interloper she was and banished her from the premises. "Thank you, sir."

The wood-paneled lounge epitomized what she imagined the explorers themselves to be: exotic and boastful, sumptuous yet academic. The focal point was the large stone fireplace, which was framed on either side by curved ivory elephant tusks as tall as she was. A large brown globe, over a yard in diameter, sat to the right of the fireplace, and two statuettes of strutting Spanish soldiers were set on a table in the center of the room.

In front of the fireplace were a red leather couch and two matching armchairs. The woman who had passed Clara outside sat in the armchair to the left of the fireplace. Clara saw now that she had an extremely fine face, with a pointed chin, a delicate nose, and skin like porcelain. She wore black-rimmed glasses and a black bucket hat, under which her light brown hair was styled into a neat bun. A large, floppy black bow tie matched the color from her black skirt with her white shirt, whose sleeves puffed at the shoulders.

Clara thought the outfit was out of place in New York, where every woman seemed to favor the straight, sleeveless, loose dresses that flappers wore. Perhaps she was a visitor, like Clara. The idea gave her a brief spark of hope until the young woman—Clara guessed she was no older than thirty—stared at her with sharp brown eyes. Clara looked away, feeling uncomfortable.

A Black woman was sitting on the couch, her back to Clara. As Clara stepped farther into the room, she turned in profile to observe Clara's entry. She was a heavyset woman—not fat, but of broad frame and carrying a little extra weight that settled mostly around her middle. She was older than the other woman, likely somewhere above forty years old, although her face was completely wrinkle free. She was well put together in a red felt cloche hat and a stylish mustard dress.

She nodded to Clara. "Good afternoon."

Clara nodded back shyly. "Ma'am."

When the woman had nothing else to say, Clara moved to stand beside the long wooden table on the left side of the room. The windows above it overlooking the street had the appearance of church windows; when she looked out of them, the world was distorted and blurry. She realized the glass had melted with time. That was how old the city was—old enough even for glass itself to have lost its clarity. Where she was from, nothing was old. Everything had been hastily built a few years ago and could fall down again in the next few. No one had the money to build anything that would last.

She stood awkwardly at her new post, avoiding the women's eyes and waiting for other lecture attendees to join them. But no one else came. Several minutes later, a rotund man in a blue pinstripe suit and a straw boater hat entered the room. His pants were pulled a little too high above his waist, and combined with the hat, it gave him a slightly comic appearance. He raised his hands, showing short, sausage-like fingers. "Ladies, welcome!" His voice boomed, filling the space with sound. "I'm George Heye, president of the Explorers Club. It is my great pleasure to invite you all here today."

He held up a meaty index finger and gave them an earnest look. "You may not know, but this is the first time the club has opened its doors to female guests. This is truly a historic moment for us all. If you'll follow me, please, we can begin. Lady Baring is waiting."

Clara looked around, surprised. She couldn't believe she and the other two women were the only guests. For the last three months, the country had been wild with Egyptomania. A lecture about Egypt should have attracted dozens if not hundreds of listeners. The line should have been out the door. She pondered this mystery as Mr. Heye led them to the elevator and up six stories.

"Normally," he explained as he placed his hand on the brass door handle, "we hold our meetings in the Clark Room. However, this being a special occasion, I think the Trophy Room will be best. It's more"—he paused—"ah, intimate."

"Oh Lord, we're about to be shoved into a coat closet," the woman in mustard muttered.

She said it loudly enough that Mr. Heye must have heard, but he didn't react, and when the door opened, it was clear she couldn't have been more wrong. Clara gasped. The Trophy Room had been decorated to look like a safari lodge. The high wooden ceiling was painted the eggshell white of canvas, while slanted beams connected the walls to the center of the room like the supports of a tent. The taxidermied heads of more than a dozen animals—including half a dozen brown gazelles, two black mountain goats, an American buffalo, a reindeer, a black rhinoceros, and a walrus—ringed the reddish-brown oak walls. A slightly dingy stuffed penguin stood next to the black tile fireplace, which, like the one in the lounge, was framed by massive elephant tusks.

Clara was so distracted by everything she almost missed the woman already in the room. She had been standing with her back to the door, admiring the stuffed cheetah or perhaps the large African tribal mask on the wall behind it. Hearing the group enter, she turned to face it.

Clara was instantly dumbstruck. She had never seen a woman so elegant and striking in her entire life. Her fulsome red hair cascaded down her shoulders like fall leaves, a corona of brilliant color that brought out the deep green of her eyes. She looked as though the very next moment she might set off on an expedition through the jungles of Central America or on a camel ride through the Sahara. Her fitted khaki pants and white shirt rolled up to her elbows could only have been tailored for her specifically. They must have cost a fortune.

The woman's striking eyes skimmed over the group, and she smiled warmly. "Hello, friends." Her voice was rich and warm. It made Clara think of hot chocolate after a cold winter day. She spoke with sincerity, as though they were all old friends who were reuniting after a long absence and not five strangers.

Clara knew this could only be the archaeologist Anna Baring. Subconsciously, she shrank into herself. She hadn't expected the woman to be so young and beautiful, although she might have guessed she would be rich. She felt like a turkey in the presence of a peacock. She spotted a stain midway up the sleeve of her jacket and wished she could scrub it off. At home, no one would look twice. Here, it seemed to stand out like a sore thumb.

Anna's eyes traveled over the newcomers, quickly evaluating them. When they reached Clara, they flickered up and down, taking her in from toes to crown. Unexpectedly, her smile deepened. Clara dropped her eyes to the ground and wrapped her arms around herself, certain the archaeologist had seen all the ways she didn't belong. Although she'd worn her best outfit, the jacket was all but threadbare at the elbows and too bulky at the shoulders, having been meant for someone a size larger. Her shoes, too, were the rough boots of a woman who had worked since she was just out of diapers, not the fashionable footwear of—she realized with horror—an actual lady.

"Sit! Sit!"

Mr. Heye's cry was so sudden it caused Clara to jump. He motioned to the long wooden table in the middle of the room. Fourteen chairs were set at it; when they sat, the table would be over half empty.

"Is this all, George?" the archaeologist asked, obliquely acknowledging the disappointingly small audience. At the same time, her light tone suggested she didn't seem to mind.

Mr. Heye's face undulated with a pained grimace. "Yes, Lady Baring. I suppose the rain will have put people off. They'll be sorry to have missed it, I'm sure. I'll be hearing about it for months."

He wouldn't meet her eyes; he was lying. The streets, Clara knew, had been full. The inhabitants of New York hadn't been put off by a little rain. She wondered then how much opposition he'd faced inviting the lady archaeologist to the club. Given none of the members were here now, she realized they must be silently boycotting her presence.

The archaeologist clapped her hands together, then rubbed them. "No matter. Let's begin, shall we? And George, we're in America. Call me Anna."

"Yes, Lady—Anna." He gave an awkward semi-bow. "If you'll excuse me, I'm afraid I must leave you. Terribly sorry. It's bad timing, but we have a lion skin coming in today. The animal was shot by President Roosevelt himself years ago. He was a member, you know, before his passing."

Anna waved her hand, magnanimously accepting his apology. "Of course. We'll see ourselves out when we're done, shall we?"

"If you don't mind."

As Mr. Heye left, the four remaining women took their seats at the table, Anna at the head, Clara to her left, and the other two women to her right. Clara felt uncomfortable sitting so close to the archaeologist, but she hadn't had a choice. It would have been impolite to seat herself at the opposite end of the table, never mind that's where she would have preferred to be.

Anna tossed her glorious red hair behind her shoulder and gave the women a welcoming smile. "This is cozy, isn't it? I think some introductions are in order. There's no need for us to be strangers." She turned to Clara. "You are?"

Clara froze, terrified. She clutched at her jacket, her tongue stuck to the roof of her mouth. Anna's penetrating eyes were like spotlights, and she was transfixed beneath them. Working hard, she eked out an answer. "Clara. Clara Rose Pickering, ma'am." She winced. The twang of her accent sounded rough and inelegant compared to the smooth tones of the archaeologist, like a saw cutting wood. She wished she could swallow the sound so no one could hear it. It betrayed all the tumbleweed towns she'd passed through, the corn fields, the nights spent sleeping in tents or under the stars.

She hoped the archaeologist would move on immediately to the next woman, but to her dismay, Anna did not. Instead, she leaned toward Clara, her green eyes sparkling. "Clara Rose. How lovely." The intensity of her attention made Clara squirm. She tried to inch away, her hips shifting to the far edge of the seat. "Do you know what you look like? An actress. Have you ever considered it?"

Clara blushed. The rush of blood to her face was so powerful even the tips of her ears tingled. She looked down at the table and rubbed the back of her neck. She'd only seen a few movies in her life. The idea that she could be in one was unimaginable. When she looked up, the archaeologist was smiling at her. "You should. You have a face for it."

Clara had nothing to say to that, but to her relief, Anna didn't pursue the topic any further. Instead, she turned to her right. "And you are?"

The lady in mustard drew herself up proudly. "Eliza Law." Like Clara, she, too, had a cadence to her speech that spoke of distant Southern roots.

"Welcome, Eliza. And you?"

The third woman, who had taken off her hat and placed it carefully on the table in front of her, tilted her chin up as she answered. "Georgette Martin, *madame*." She had a thick accent that even Clara knew was French. The words sounded like water flowing over river rocks, elegant as the clothes she wore.

Anna beamed as though delighted to find herself in their company. "Wonderful. Well then, now that we're all friends, let's begin, shall we?" She dropped her voice and looked at the women conspiratorially. "The story I'm about to tell is of gods, men, and gold unimaginable."

* * *

True to her word, the tale Anna wove was full of jackal- and ibis-headed gods, kings from the Bible, and pyramids capped by solid gold that refracted the light of the sun like a lighthouse. When she finished, Eliza asked, "So what now? What's left now that King Tut's been found?"

Clara didn't miss when Anna's face twitched with some nameless emotion, but she smoothed the expression almost immediately. "Four New Kingdom pharaonic tombs remain undiscovered."

"And you are looking yourself for them?" Georgette queried, leaning forward with interest.

For someone who had spent years digging in the Valley of the Kings, it only made sense that she would be at the forefront of the investigation.

"Yes, but…" Anna sighed and ran her hand through her hair. For a moment, she looked tired. "It will take time. Excavation is meticulous, backbreaking work. Just look at how long it took to find Tutankhamun's tomb: fifteen years of digging in the valley. And sometimes it's all for nothing. It's possible to dig for decades and find only more rocks and dirt."

Clara could imagine Anna standing in the desert, a shovel thrown carelessly over her shoulder, her cheeks burned red as an apple by the fierce sun. She could imagine Anna anywhere, really. This was a woman who seemed capable of anything she set her mind to. If she was determined to find a pharaoh's tomb, Clara was certain she could do it.

"You looking for one in particular? One of the four tombs, I mean," Eliza said.

Anna stood and leaned against the table. The sun seemed to shine brighter against her face, or else it was lit by an internal flame of excited passion. "Yes, Ahmose I. He was the first ruler of the New Kingdom. He pushed the Hyksos invaders out, restored Egyptian rule over the whole of Egypt, and even campaigned into the Levant. He reopened mines and trade routes and brought prosperity back to the kingdom."

Clara wasn't sure what any of that meant, but it sounded impressive. Georgette cocked her head, her thin eyebrows pulling together. "But the newspapers said there were no more *pharaons* in the Valley of the Kings, *non*?"

Something akin to cunning crossed Anna's face, a sly expression that tickled the right corner of her mouth. "Ahmose isn't buried in the valley. At least, *I* don't think so. Ahmose stood on the divide between the Second Intermediate Period and the New Kingdom. The New Kingdom pharaohs were buried in the valley, but the pharaohs of the Second Intermediate Period were buried in a place called Dra' Abu el-Naga', a few kilometers east of it. I think Ahmose is buried there. That's why they've never found him in the valley." The triumph in her voice was matched by the smug expression on her face. "And since most archaeologists consider Dra' Abu el-Naga' a dusty old necropolis not worth spending time on, no one has looked for him there."

"And you just…dig? This is how you find the tomb? How do you know where to dig? It could be anywhere, *non*? You could miss by—" Georgette snapped her fingers.

Anna smiled wryly. "Isn't all archaeology just digging in the dirt and hoping for the best?" She turned more serious. "It's true that a tomb entrance may be missed by mere inches. It's happened time and again in the valley. Luckily, Dra' Abu el-Naga' is a relatively small area."

She stepped back and put her hands on her hips. Clara was entranced by her vivacity. "An American named Clarence Fisher has been excavating there for the last two years. Looking at where he's dug, I can see he's missed a few areas it would have made sense for the workers to build a tomb for Ahmose. Fisher's concession to dig is up this year, and I've already secured the concession for the next season. If I can sink exploratory shafts into those areas, I'll have a good idea whether any of the limestone has been carved out beneath or around it. If it has, I may just find Ahmose's tomb."

"A woman can run her own excavation?" Georgette asked.

Anna raised her eyebrows. "Of course! Gertie Bell's done it in Iraq for years. And Gertie Thompson is launching an excavation to find prehistoric settlements in Hemamieh on the east bank of the Nile next year. I'm hardly the only woman poking around in the sand out there." She snorted. "Why shouldn't a woman run her own excavation?"

"Lord, it won't just be you out there digging, will it?" Eliza asked, concerned.

Clara had a vision of Anna all alone on a dusty hill, a pickaxe in her hand, sweat pouring down her brow and soaking her stylish shirt. Anna had said the heat could reach fifty-four degrees Celsius in the summer in Egypt, which was a hundred and thirty degrees Fahrenheit. Surely she wouldn't dig then, would she? That was just about hot enough to fry bacon.

Anna shook her head. "No, it won't be just me. Excavations like this require dozens of laborers to dig and carry away rock. Depending on what we find, it can be a ton or more of dust and rock to move. Luckily, there are plenty of men and boys around Dra' Abu el-Naga' who have participated in other excavations in the area. There's no shortage of workers."

She gave a thoughtful smile. "In one way or another, the families around Luxor have been part of the lives of the pharaohs for millennia. Three thousand years ago, their ancestors buried the kings. Now they're helping to dig them up. It's a bit ironic, isn't it?"

The door to the Trophy Room swung open unexpectedly, and the receptionist from downstairs entered. He gave a short yet respectful bow. "Madams, if you would excuse me, I must ask you to leave. The club is closing for the evening."

"Oh my." Anna peered out the window at the dimming light of afternoon. "Is it so late already? I hadn't realized." She turned back to her guests. "Well, I thank you all for coming. It has been a pleasurable afternoon for me. I hope it was for you as well."

It was a tight fit in the elevator, the four of them plus the receptionist. Clara clutched her umbrella to her chest and pressed herself into a corner, making herself as small as possible. Anna faced her, their bodies so close their feet touched, while Georgette's shoulder pressed hard into her arm. Clara kept her eyes on the floor, embarrassed to meet Anna's eyes, which she could feel watching her. The archaeologist was rich and worldly and impressive and brilliant. She had attended Oxford University and traveled throughout the Middle East. Clara, on the other hand, was the daughter of corn farmers and had never even gone to high school. To share the same space felt almost like a transgression.

"It's a pity to have had such a short time together," Anna said as they unpacked themselves into the foyer. The sound of rain pattering against the glass windows echoed in the small space. "I should have liked to have got to know each of you better. I hardly ever meet new people. I've always got my nose in the sand."

"We could do dinner," Eliza suggested. "I got a few more days in the city and nothing much else to do."

Georgette looked pensive. "I would not mind hearing more about how *les momies* were made…"

Anna clapped, thrilled. "It's a wonderful idea! What do you say, ladies? Tomorrow, shall we? The Hotel Pennsylvania on 33rd Street and 7th Avenue, seven o'clock. It would be my deepest pleasure to host you."

Clara had ridden enough wild horses to know the feeling of something running away beneath her. The situation around her was like that now. She fidgeted with the hem of her jacket, feeling the frayed edge on the right side, and considered how to decline the invitation. It was surely not a place for someone like her.

Anna's eyes caught hers, the color of balsam fir. "I do hope you'll come. It would mean so much to me to know I have friends far from home."

Clara felt the same paralysis she'd felt when introducing herself. "I—I—" She swallowed, the words that would set her free caught in her throat.

"Come on, it's just a few hours." Anna flashed a broad, winning smile. "It will be lovely. I promise you won't regret it. If you come, I'll even tell you about Giovanni Belzoni, the circus strongman who became one of the greatest archaeologists in Egypt."

Clara bit her lip. She couldn't refuse now, not with Anna so determined. And she had to admit, she *was* curious about a strongman turned archaeologist.

"I suppose I could come," she mumbled.

"Perfect. Tomorrow at seven then."

Just when she thought things couldn't get worse, Anna winked at her.

CHAPTER THREE

Georgette

May 14, 1923

Georgette's mind was unique. It was like the Bibliothèque Mazarine at 23 quai de Conti in the 6th arrondissement of Paris: organized, orderly, and packed floor to ceiling with seemingly endless knowledge. Georgette collected knowledge the way magpies collected bric-a-brac: indiscriminately and with unrelenting curiosity. Like Leonardo da Vinci, she had only to read or hear something once and she never again forgot it.

Unfortunately, her fascination with knowledge was not widely matched by the rest of society, and it had gotten her in trouble at times. Most people, particularly strangers, were not keen to hear about the history of rail transportation in Europe or the reindeer herding practices of the Nenets people of Siberia. And so, Georgette had lived much of her life alone, with no friends and certainly no confidantes. This solitude, which would have weighed heavily on anyone else, hadn't particularly bothered her, however. It left her free to pursue her own interests, including a fellowship in mathematics at New York University, far from her home in Paris.

When she had arrived in the city a few days ago, the first thing she'd done was memorize a map of Manhattan. It had been easy, given the island had been set up on a grid system. Now as she walked the 3.2 kilometers north from her room at the university to the Hotel Pennsylvania, she knew exactly where the hotel would be without having to look at the map a second time. It was located just south of the Garment District, next to Pennsylvania Station.

"*Vingt-huitième rue. Vingt-neuvième rue. Trentième rue.*"

Georgette whispered the names of the streets as she passed them without needing to read the signs. They were not pretty names, as they would have been in Paris. There was no Avenue Victor Hugo or Avenue Montaigne, for example, but they were solidly practical, and Georgette appreciated that. It would be impossible, she thought, to become lost in New York City.

She was stopped in front of the station, waiting to cross the road, when all of the sudden the world around her exploded. A tide of people streamed out of the station, a smothering, endless human wave. The men and women jostled her in their haste, elbowing her in the ribs and stepping on her feet. She unleashed a strangled gargle of dismay and hugged her arms to her body, trying to avoid being touched by these strangers, but it was impossible. Ducking and dodging, she tried to make her way to the street and away from them, but to her dismay, it was impossible. Where she went, the horde went.

"*Non!*" she shrieked, battering energetically with her purse at the next man who shoved rudely against her. "*Va-t'en!*"

He gave her a dirty look and kept going. Luckily, Georgette's salvation lay just across the wide street. Swerving around honking motorcars, she crossed, flinging herself into the lobby of the Pennsylvania Hotel on the other side for dear life.

A bellhop in a solid blue costume approached her, his round hat slipping too far back on his head despite the black patent leather chinstrap meant to hold it in place. "Welcome to the Pennsylvania Hotel, the world's largest hotel. May I help you?"

Georgette took a moment to compose herself, peering around the lobby as she did. She was impressed despite herself. It wasn't often one ended up in the largest *anything* in the world. She gave a small, curt nod. "*Oui*, I am looking for the dining room."

The boy—he was far too young to be a man—pointed to the opposite end of the lobby. "The Café Rouge is that way. Take a right and the entrance will be on your left."

Contrary to its name, the Café Rouge was designed to look like an Italian villa, not a French café, and there were enough chairs and tables in it to seat hundreds of people. The murmur of voices was like the rushing in and out of an ocean tide. Georgette scowled. This was not a dining room, it was *une foule*—a mob—like the one she'd just escaped. She disliked it immensely, and wished the British archaeologist had chosen a different location—someplace quieter and less overwhelming. But at least she was able to spy the three other women from the Explorers Club. They were sitting at a table against the far wall, beneath one of the large, arched windows that ran the length of the room.

When she reached them, she unbuttoned her blue wool coat and sat down heavily in the open chair, exhausted by the indignity of the last few minutes. "You are all so early!" She hadn't expected to be the last to arrive.

Anna pulled a round, gold pocket watch from her tan vest and popped it open. She gave it a quick glance. "It's almost eight, Georgette."

Georgette shrugged. "*Et alors?* No one eats before eight."

The words had no sooner left her mouth than she noticed the mostly empty bowls of clam broth in front of the other women. She frowned, confused. The corner of Anna's mouth twitched into an amused smile. "The Americans do." She shut the watch with a snap and returned it to her pocket. "It's all right. I made the same mistake once too."

"Oh." Georgette was disconcerted by this new information. She looked around, suddenly thirsty. "Well, where is the wine? The Americans do not hate wine, do they?"

Eliza made a choking sound. She set down her water glass and dabbed at her mouth with a white napkin. "You don't know? Alcohol's been banned in America for the last three years."

"Haven't you heard of Prohibition?" Clara asked. Her brown eyes were wide.

"Prohibition?" Georgette cocked her head, puzzled. "But I thought it was a joke. How could anyone not drink wine for three years?"

"How not indeed?" Anna mused. She caught the attention of a passing server and motioned him to the table. "Another for our guest, please. Skip the appetizer."

When she turned back to the table, she addressed the two Americans as though continuing a previous conversation. "Anyway, as I was saying, there are around one hundred pyramids in Egypt, of which the oldest is over forty-five hundred years old. But the 'pyramid' has been a common religious structure the world over for millennia. They're found throughout Central America, for one thing. In all cases, regardless of who built them, we see a striving to reach the heavens, a lifting of man to the gods. The question is not *why* mankind built pyramids, but why he *stopped*. Aren't skyscrapers just a modern pyramid, of sorts?"

Clara leaned forward. She was wearing the same brown skirt suit as yesterday, Georgette noticed. "But you said the pyramids in Egypt were all robbed. Isn't that why they stopped building them?"

Anna nodded. "Yes. Unfortunately, it turns out burying someone under five billion kilograms of limestone still isn't enough to keep grave robbers out." She smiled wryly. "Not that burial in the Valley of the Kings was any more effective. You know, many of the pharaohs' tombs were robbed not by common thieves, but by later pharaohs, who wanted the gold for themselves. Why mine more gold when you know exactly where a cache of ready-made jewelry is buried?"

She made a face. "Some things never change. Looting"— she said the word as though it was a bitter poison—"is one of them. For centuries, Egypt's remaining antiquities have all but sprouted legs and sprinted out of the country. If someone could have put the pyramids on a boat and sailed them away, even they would have been taken. It's a wonder there's a single statue left in the country at all."

Georgette adjusted her glasses. The Louvre held more than a few Egyptian artifacts the French had carried back from Egypt, but she had never considered the question of how they'd been acquired before. She supposed it was only fair to call it looting. After all, thinking about it now, she doubted the scholars who had taken them had asked permission. Invading armies never did.

"But not King Tut's tomb," Eliza said. "The robbers didn't get to that. Someone put some kind of a spell on it to keep it safe? Some voodoo?"

"No." Anna spoke so abruptly, her face so closed, that conversation was temporarily halted. Even Georgette felt the chill that settled over the table. Anna winced. "Sorry. I didn't mean to come off so harshly. It's…a difficult subject." She forced a smile. "Eliza, before the others came you were saying you traveled across Morocco on horseback. Whatever were you doing there?"

All eyes shifted to Eliza. Georgette cocked her head. She couldn't imagine Eliza in anything other than the dark green velvet evening gown and black turban she was presently wearing, and that wouldn't do at all on horseback.

Eliza shrugged and took a sip of her water. "Toward the end of the war, the YMCA sent me to France to watch over our boys there. We had almost quarter of a million, you know. When it was all over, I thought I might as well go to Morocco. Spent a month riding around, getting sand in every place imaginable. That's all."

"And how was Morocco?" Anna asked.

"Did you know Morocco still has slaves?" Even though she herself was the source of the information, Eliza nevertheless sounded incredulous, and Georgette didn't blame her. Georgette had no idea slavery still existed anywhere in the world. "Even if most of the Black folks there are free now, it still exists, and I got more than my fair share of looks everywhere I went." She shook her head and smoothed the tablecloth beside her, although it hadn't been wrinkled.

Anna tutted. "I can't imagine. How terrible. How absolutely awful."

"But then why go *au Maroc*? Why not go to somewhere safer?" Georgette asked, perplexed by the obvious contradiction. There were much nicer, safer places in the world, many of which were easily accessible by train from France.

Eliza scoffed. "My parents moved from Natchez to Chicago after the war ended—that's our war, not the Great one—and never saw any other place in the world but that. All those years, they worked hard to build a better life for us. They didn't raise me to be safe. They raised me to look and see what's on the other side of the mountain; see all the things they ain't ever had the opportunity to. See the whole world even. Just because something is hard doesn't mean it ain't worth doing. Makes it all the more important *to* do, for all the people who couldn't."

She looked around at the other diners in the room, chin high as though challenging them. "Besides, ain't nothing they can do to me there worse than what's been said or done to me here, and that's the truth. Ain't let nobody scare me yet, and I don't intend to start."

She sat back and adjusted her black gloves regally. "Besides, my guide, Anouar, told them I was a princess from Timbuktu and if they touched a hair on my head the sultan's wrath would fall upon them."

"Timbuktu has a sultan?" Georgette asked.

Eliza gave a broad smile. "No, but they don't know that."

Waiters appeared from nowhere with plates of food, interrupting the conversation. Georgette identified potatoes a la Hollandaise, asparagus tips au gratin, lamb medallions, and walnut bread. She frowned. This was neither French nor Italian food; it was American. She poked it with her fork. The lamb was tough and overcooked.

"Wonderful. Just wonderful." Anna slapped a hand down on the table, making the silverware rattle. "What do you think, Georgette? Would you like to go to Morocco? It's just a jump away from France. The steamer can't take more than a few days."

She blinked, startled by the unexpected question. "*Bien, oui,* why not?"

But what was there to see in Morocco other than camels and sand dunes? Eliza hadn't said. Until she knew, Georgette couldn't provide a definite answer. At best, she could only give a theoretical answer. She recognized, however, that the conversation was about travel, and she endeavored to find a way to contribute. Of the European capitals, she had visited Paris, Rome, Amsterdam, and Vienna. But at less than eight percent of the total, this was not particularly notable. On the other hand, counting this present trip, she had visited six countries on three continents, which was almost forty-three percent of the world's continents. That was, perhaps, more impressive and worthy of mention.

"I have been to India," she blurted out. Somehow, the graceless words had circumvented her brain, and this was the outcome. She immediately pressed her lips together, stopping any further rebellion on their part.

Clara cocked her head. "Why India? They don't speak French there, do they?"

Georgette raised her chin. The reason was a distasteful one. "I could not go for *un doctorat* in *mathématiques.* A woman in France, it is not allowed." She looked out the window, stung to the quick by the continuing injustice of it. "I saw in the newspaper an advertisement to teach *mathématiques* at a college in Kolkata. A women's college, *oui,* but a college. So I went."

She looked down at her long, carefully manicured fingernails. "I hoped after a few years, France will change and I can go for *un doctorat.* I can teach. I left India and came back to France, but *non.* It is the same. Still there is nothing to be done."

In the last ten years, she had done nothing more than teach elementary math at girls' high schools in Paris. All her hopes of higher advancement, of contributing to the field of abstract algebra, were stymied. Even the few papers she'd managed to get published, she'd had to submit using a male pseudonym. It was difficult not to be bitter, but resentment had gotten her nowhere.

She shook her head. "Marie Curie, she received *un doctorat*, won *le prix Nobel* in both physics and chemistry and has a full professorship at the Sorbonne, but women still are not allowed to research or teach higher math in France." She shrugged helplessly. "Even I cannot explain this."

Anna leaned back in her chair, making the wood creak in protest, and crossed her arms. The combination of a white blouse under her fitted tan vest reminded Georgette of the colors of a fallow deer. It was hardly acceptable dinner attire for a lady, but she forgave the archaeologist. After all, she had lived in a desert for so many years she must have forgotten what was proper. Although those pants...

"'Liberty, equality, fraternity.'" Anna's bladed hand punctuated the air sharply with every word she spoke. The words crackled with anger. "That's what the French say, right? Where's the equality? Where's the justice? Why should those things apply only to men? What could possibly be wrong with allowing a woman to get a degree in mathematics or teach at a university?"

Georgette sighed. "What can we do? This is how things are."

Anna shook her head. "I don't accept that. We have to fight! How will things change if no one fights for it?"

"Hey now," Eliza interjected. "Let the poor woman be. She can't fight it all herself."

"You're right." She turned to Georgette, her face contrite. "I'm sorry. It just rankles me that things like this happen in this day and age. We're supposed to be *enlightened*. How can we pretend to have fair and just societies when there's so much injustice all around us? And always it's we women who are taken advantage of."

"You're an idealist," Eliza said, raising her eyebrows.

"A humanist, more like." She ran her hand through her hair, perturbed. "But enough about me. Clara, you've been awfully quiet this evening. Have you traveled at all?"

Clara blushed, her face turning a soft pink that rose from her collar to the roots of her blond hair. She shook her head so vigorously that a few strands fell out of her bun. "Oh, no, not like you all have. Just around the States." She checked herself. "Well, I've been to Canada heaps of times, but that's…well, it's just Canada. It's not like India or Morocco."

"I've heard parts of America are stunning," Anna said.

"They are. The Grand Canyon, for example, or Niagara Falls." She brightened. "One summer I went to a place called Maligne Lake, all the way out in Alberta. It's like nothing you've ever seen. The water is blue like I can't even describe, and you can see glaciers and mountains around it. It might as well be its own world, out in the middle of nowhere. Have you heard of it?"

"No, but it sounds lovely."

"Sounds like something worth exploring," Eliza agreed.

Anna snapped her fingers, suddenly full of excitement. She leaned forward, drawing the women's attention to her. "Kismet, ladies. Kismet has brought us together. Don't you see? What is the one thing we all have in common?"

She looked at the other women, challenging them to see the linkage, but so far as Georgette could see, they had nothing in common. They came from different countries, different backgrounds. When no one spoke, Anna cried, "We are explorers, all of us!"

She grinned triumphantly, as though she had made a monumental discovery, but Georgette only frowned. She was a mathematician, not an explorer. Anna was mistaken. She began to explain, *"Mais non—"*

Simultaneously, Clara exclaimed, "Oh no, not—"

Ignoring their protests, Anna cut both of them off. "Just think of it: yesterday we were guests at a club that we, as women, are excluded from joining. Why? Because of our sex and nothing else. Women can be every bit as qualified as men. But everywhere, even in the hallowed halls of exploration, there are walls put up before us."

"Ain't news women don't get a fair shake at life," Eliza grunted.

"But we don't have to stand for it! If they won't let us in, we'll form our own club."

Eliza's head jerked in surprise. "What now?"

"Why not? There are plenty of women's organizations. Why not create our own?"

"Our own what?" Clara asked.

"Our own exploration club."

Georgette was dumbfounded. It was such an odd and unexpected statement she didn't know how to make heads or tails of it. The women hardly even knew each other. And while they had traveled some, none of them were skiing to the South Pole or dogsledding across Greenland. Georgette didn't even know how to ski, and frankly, she was certain she wouldn't like dogsledding, the primary problem being all the dogs.

Clara must have felt similarly. "But we're not explorers. Not really." She looked sheepishly around the table, then amended, "Well, *I'm* not..."

"Aren't you?" Anna challenged. "You've been somewhere I wager almost no one else has. Why can't you be an explorer? Who's to say what an explorer is or isn't? All you need is the same chance to get out in the world that the men have."

Eliza nodded. "Ain't that the truth. Nobody's throwing money at *me* to go sailing down the Amazon."

"Exactly! We'll call our club..." Anna tapped her finger against the table as she thought. "The Lady Explorers Club."

Eliza shook her head. "Naw, that sounds like we're imitating the men. If we're gonna do this, we gotta find our own name." She, too, thought for a moment. Then she nodded. "Adventurers. The Lady Adventurers Club."

Georgette was baffled by the entire conversation, which seemed to be running full steam ahead without either her or Clara. In a few days, Anna would be setting sail on a steamer back to Egypt, and a few months later, Georgette herself would be returning to France to teach the girls of the Lycée Molière elementary mathematics. Who knew where in the United States Clara and Eliza would be? She asked the obvious question. "Why we would create this club? What would be the point?"

Anna looked at Clara even though Clara hadn't spoken and, in fact, looked white as a sheet. "Because we are brave, adventurous, extraordinary women. Why shouldn't we have our own club?"

Georgette wasn't convinced. The only adventuring she wanted to do was into a library. But as she took a moment to think about it, she realized the idea of being part of a "Lady Adventurers Club" was not entirely unwelcome. Since she was barred by her gender from joining France's mathematical societies, why shouldn't she find a group that wouldn't exclude her? It was a silly group, to be sure, but then, there were sillier things in life. And it wasn't as though this Lady Adventurers Club would demand anything of her. There was no danger in it.

"Okay, I agree to join," she said. Perhaps she wasn't a traditional explorer, but hadn't she probed the frontiers of mathematics? Shouldn't that count for something?

Clara shook her head, face stricken. Seeing this, Anna leaned close to her and began to whisper in her ear. After a moment, Clara nodded, although she still looked pale. Smiling victoriously, Anna held up her water glass. It sparkled in the yellow glow of the restaurant's chandeliers, refracting light like a golden chalice. Georgette couldn't help but mourn that there was no champagne. Only the Americans would do something as foolish as banning all alcohol when a little wine or champagne never hurt anyone.

"A toast," Anna said. "To the inaugural meeting of the Lady Adventurers Club."

"What happens now?" Eliza asked after taking a sip of her water.

"We'll stay in touch by post," Anna said, setting down her glass. "We'll keep each other appraised of our latest adventures, and if we're ever all in the same city again, we can hold another meeting. Or if someone does something notable, perhaps we could all meet for it, to celebrate—like Georgette being allowed to get her doctorate."

Georgette snorted. That would not happen. She took a sip and then pondered the dwindling water in her glass. It was a metaphor for their situation. Everything was temporary. This moment of sisterhood and solidarity, too, would be gone soon.

Still, even if it was fleeting, it was nice to feel part of a group. It had never happened before in her life. And it was not likely to happen again, not so long as la Société Mathématique de France refused to allow women.

She gazed curiously at the other women. Anna had leaned closer to Clara once more and was saying something to her, perhaps more encouragement. Eliza was scraping potatoes from her plate. The women were not unpleasant to be around. What a pity the club would never meet a second time. After all, when would all four of them ever be in the same city again? Or that one of them would do something so astounding they would all come to see? The odds against their ever meeting again were astronomical.

CHAPTER FOUR

Eliza

November 11, 1923
Wichita Falls, America

"Ready?" Eliza shouted. The buzzing of the two Curtiss JN-4 "Jenny" propellers was so loud it was questionable whether Billy would hear her, so she thumped on the wood frame of the fuselage to catch his attention.

The Jenny above them had dropped its rope ladder and the two planes were flying horizontally together at matching speeds, the ladder swinging freely in the space between them. In answer to Eliza's question, Billy turned and gave her a thumbs-up, then clambered from the bucket seat in front of her onto the biplane's dun fuselage. For a moment, his white-clothed body blocked her view of the horizon as he stood to pull himself onto the thin upper wing, then it disappeared. Eliza kept the plane level as he grasped two pegs that had been drilled into the wing and pulled himself into a headstand. His legs swayed slightly as he fought against the wind to stay vertical.

This was the most dangerous part of the maneuver. The Jenny was a light aircraft. If it hit an air pocket and the wings suddenly dipped, he might not be able to hold on and could go tumbling off. If he fell, he would die.

She waited, her hands absorbing the feedback from the stick, her eyes watching the swinging rope. The key to showmanship was to deliver the impossible right before people's eyes. Billy had only seconds to feel for the ladder and wrap his legs around the rungs; after that, the two planes would have passed the spectators. If that happened, they would have to double back and try again, at which point the spectators would be less excited about the maneuver. The trick would be ruined.

But Billy never missed. When the Jenny above banked right at the end of the row of onlookers, he was dangling upside down from the ladder by his knees, waving wildly with both hands. The crowd roared its awe and approval. Billy always said people paid the price of admission to barnstorming shows to see if people like him would live or die during the show. It wasn't always the former.

Eliza pulled backward on the stick, sending her plane climbing steeply as he scaled the ladder up to the other plane's lower wing. She continued climbing as he hooked a foot into one of the incidence wires that connected the biplane's upper and lower wings and dangled recklessly, hands still waving. When she reached a high enough altitude, she drove the stick forward, plunging her aircraft into a vertical dive. As it plummeted toward the ground, her body hung from the lap belt, a terrifically thin scrap of material to separate life and death. She clenched her teeth as the wind whipped at her face. At the last minute, before the plane reached the point at which it would have been too late to stop it from smashing into the ground and disintegrating, she pulled back on the stick.

The Jenny slowly responded, coming out of the dive just in time to swoop low over the hundreds of spectators. It was so close, in fact, that the tallest man could almost have touched the wheels. As it was meant to, the strong draft from its passage pulled off some of the spectator's hats, whipping them into the air like dandelion seeds. Rather than becoming angry, their owners laughed and clapped. It was all part of the experience.

This maneuver marked the end of her portion of the flying circus. Eliza aimed for an open space on the field and reduced the throttle. The wheels gently brushed the ground as the plane landed soft as a feather. After a hundred yards or so, it rolled to a smooth stop. She unbuckled her belt and jumped out.

She doffed her aviator cap, freeing her short, frizzy hair, then marched the hundred yards to the barn the pilots had made their temporary headquarters for the day. A white, hand-painted sign had been nailed to its side:

GATES FLYING CIRCUS,
GREATEST AVIATORS IN THE WORLD.

She slapped it for luck as she walked inside. There was only one person there: the flying circus's founder Ivan Gates. He was sitting on a hay bale counting money, a thick, unlit cigar clamped between his teeth. Like Eliza, he wore baggy khaki pants and black jackboots, the costume of an aviator. The black goggles pushed up onto his brown leather cap watched her enter, even as his eyes remained fixed on the green paper in front of him.

Eliza tossed her cap onto the ground, then fell onto a bale of hay, stretching out along it on her back as though it were the most comfortable couch in the world. "How'd we do today?"

Most times, they made enough from the show to stay in hotels, but sometimes they had to sleep in barns. And in the South, Eliza and a few wing walkers regularly ended up lodging with the pigs and chickens no matter how much money they made. This barn, with its high roof and soft piles of hay, was nice as barns went, but Eliza was happier not to wake up with straw in her hair.

Ivan grunted, his trim mustache twitching. "Letter came for you." He didn't look up.

"What now? A letter?" She scrambled to sit. "How'd it do that?"

Being part of a flying circus meant that for half the year or more she didn't have a steady address. The pilots and wing walkers stayed in different cities almost every night during the barnstorming season. In the last year, the Gates Flying Circus had flown 273 shows in 75 cities. Eliza couldn't imagine how, under the circumstances, she could possibly have received a letter.

Ivan raised his head. While he wasn't exactly a handsome man, he had a sort of timeless, swashbuckling quality that Eliza had always appreciated. With his heavy brow and cleft chin, she could picture him as the captain of a pirate ship. "Looks like it's been following us since Memphis." The words came out muffled around his cigar.

He reached for a tan envelope beside his left hand and tossed it to her. He raised his eyebrows at her as she caught it. "You got friends in Egypt?"

She frowned at him, confused. "Egypt? How would I—"

The rest of the words died in her throat as she saw the writing on the envelope. There, in beautiful calligraphy, was her name: Eliza Law, Care of the Gates Flying Circus. And in the corner was a stamp proclaiming the letter had arrived from Luxor, Egypt. She only knew one person in all of Egypt, someone she hadn't expected to ever hear from ever again. She was dumbfounded. How had Anna found her from a quarter of the way around the world?

She opened the envelope and pulled out the card inside. It read:

Luxor, Egypt
29 September, 1923

My dear Eliza,
I hope this letter finds you well. I am writing to inform you that I have found him. It is intact, and I believe it will be wonderful once opened. I want the Lady Adventurers Club present at the opening to celebrate this momentous event. I truly believe it will one day be known as one of the great wonders of the world. If you are able to come, I have reserved a first-class ticket in your name on the RMS Olympic, leaving from New York on November 17 and arriving in Southampton on the 24th. Mr. George Heye of the Explorers Club is holding the ticket for you and will provide you the

remainder of the itinerary should you be able to come. I pray you shall.

Ever yours affectionately,
Anna

The letter was written so cryptically that for a moment Eliza didn't know what Anna was talking about. Whom had she found? What was going to be opened? Then she remembered Anna had been searching for the tomb of a pharaoh, an Amos or Moses or something. She must have found it, and "intact" meant grave robbers hadn't gotten to it.

Eliza set the letter down, thinking. She barely knew Anna. One dinner together months ago didn't make them anything more than passing acquaintances. But she couldn't just dismiss the invitation, either. It wasn't every day one got to be present at the opening of a pharaoh's tomb. She definitely would never get that opportunity again. And she did want to see Egypt.

The harvest was over everywhere, and that meant soon there would be no more fields for them to land in. The cold weather had already come to parts of the Midwest, and as it spread people wouldn't want to be standing outside, no matter how exciting the air show was. At best, the Gates Flying Circus had only a few more weeks to fly before it was time to wrap up the season. If she left now, she would only miss a few shows. Surely Ivan wouldn't begrudge her that. They'd already flown the major cities. What was left were a few towns sprinkled throughout the South, where she wasn't welcome anyway.

Eliza wasn't one for acting rashly, but when she made a decision, she was decisive. If Anna wanted to convey her to Egypt first class, she wasn't going to say no. She knit her brow as she double-checked the date in the letter; it had taken a while to reach her. Now she only had six days to make it to New York before the boat left. She glanced at Ivan. His dark eyes were staring at her expectantly.

He took the cigar out of his mouth and laid it on the hay bale, narrowing his eyes. "Well, Blackbird?"

"It's an invitation to go to Egypt."

He shook his head, incredulous. "Why? What's in Egypt?"

Ivan may have been a daredevil, but he was no adventurer. As far as she knew, he'd never been anywhere outside the United States. During the Great War, he'd joined the Army Air Service, but peace broke out before he made it Europe. Eliza knew he would never understand the spell travel could cast over a person. Or what it was like to be freer halfway around the world than at home. To be seen as an ordinary person for once and not a second-class citizen.

"You wouldn't understand," she told him.

When she didn't show any sign of changing her mind, he sighed and started counting out some of the bills in front of him, which he handed to her. It was her share of the day's admissions take—plus maybe a little extra. She took the money and folded it into her pocket. Then she retrieved her cap from the floor, smacking it to get the straw off. She started for the door, already thinking about what it would take to reach New York City in time.

"Hey, Blackbird!" Ivan called at the last minute.

She stopped at the door and looked back at him.

"Take care of yourself, you hear?"

She snorted. "I always do."

* * *

November 17, 1923
New York City, America

"*Quelle mastodonte,*" Georgette said, crossing her arms and looking up at the massive steamship in front of them. In her bulky brown coat, she might have been a bear about to go into hibernation.

Eliza wrinkled her forehead, confused. Although she'd spent a few years in France after the war and even obtained her pilot's license there—they wouldn't teach a Black woman in America—there were still words whose meaning caught her off guard. "*Mastodonte?*"

A seagull screamed as it flew over them. It was just one more discordant instrument in the raucous orchestra of noise around them: honking horns and squealing brakes as cars threaded in and out of the dock area, dropping passengers; hammers striking steel as workers repaired ship parts; the shouts and whistles of sailors moving cargo. Still, it was more orderly than Eliza's last transatlantic trip, when the United States was in its final months of war and every ship was full of young men shipping off to Europe.

Georgette motioned toward the ship in front of them, the *RMS Olympic.* "It is meaning the ship, it is so big. It is the biggest in the world, did you know that?" Her cheeks were dyed pink from the sharp November wind, which was fluttering the red White Star Line pennant on the ship's foremast wildly.

When she had received Anna's letter, Eliza had made no assumption about whether she would see Georgette or Clara again. After all, it had been her understanding when they parted ways at the Café Rouge that Georgette would be returning to Paris at the end of the summer to teach the fall session, and as to Clara, she supposed there was every possibility the woman was deep in backwoods of Iowa, doing whatever it was she did there. At Eliza's meeting with Mr. Heye, however, she had been informed that Georgette had extended her time at New York University and that both she and Clara would be accompanying Eliza on the *Olympic.* It was, as Anna had said, kismet.

Eliza stamped her feet and rubbed her hands together, scowling at the cold. Although she had been raised in Chicago, the heat of the South was in her blood. She never could acclimatize to wind or snow. It always seemed to find a way to nip in through fabric and beneath hems.

Georgette scrutinized the area around them. "If Clara does not arrive soon, she will miss the ship."

Eliza shrugged, not particularly bothered whether the other woman came or not. What mattered was that she, herself, had made it in time, and in two weeks, she would be in Egypt.

"Oh! She is there!" Georgette exclaimed, pointing. She waved with unexpected emotion, catching Clara's attention.

Clara approached, her suitcase clutched in front of her. "Good morning."

Georgette smiled broadly. "Now we are all here! We can begin this *aventure*."

Clara licked her lips, her face pale, and said nothing. As excited as Georgette was for their long voyage, Clara was obviously equally nervous. Her eyes flickered to the ship and then quickly away.

"Guess you ain't ever been on something like this," Eliza said.

Clara grimaced. "No, I've only seen ships like this in pictures."

"Ain't anything to worry about. I've been on these plenty of times. You'll enjoy it. Besides, we're gonna be up in the fancy part. You're never gonna wanna leave."

"It is true, ships like this do not sink or catch on fire often," Georgette offered. "And if it does, maybe most people will live. Sometimes not everyone dies."

Eliza stared at her, horrified. What had possessed her to say such a thing?

Georgette shrugged. "*Et bien?* It is true."

Eliza pointed to the gangway, trying to redirect Clara's focus. If the skittish woman found out that both of the *Olympic*'s sister ships, the *Titanic* and the *Britannic* had sunk, she might turn tail and flee completely. "Come on, let's get a move on. We got a pharaoh to unbury."

Georgette set off obediently toward the ship, but Clara lingered. Eliza surveyed her. "You thinking about running?"

"I—" Clara stammered, face pained. "I don't know what I'm doing here. I don't belong on that ship. When Anna's letter came, I—I put it under my mattress for a week. I couldn't sleep. Of course I wouldn't go. How could I? But then in her other letters, she was so convincing…"

Eliza tilted her chin toward the *Olympic*. "What do you mean you don't belong on that ship?"

"On the ship, in Egypt, any of it. It's not—I'm not an adventurer. I'm not like Anna, like…any of you."

Eliza felt a flash of compassion for her. Here was a grown woman who was worried she wasn't as good as the mud on some people's shoes. Well, Eliza knew about being treated that way. She put her arm around Clara's shoulder. "*Anna* ain't the Anna you think she is. Now come on. You belong on that ship just as much as anyone else."

Clara nodded. She picked up her rectangular suitcase, and together the women walked to the wooden gangway, joining the rest of the passengers. When Eliza had arrived in New York, she'd wondered where, exactly, she would be housed on the boat. Anna's promise of a first-class ticket aside, she had slept in her fair share of sheds and been through enough side doors to keep her expectations low. But Mr. Heye had assured her that Jim Crow had no place on the ship. This was a British steamer, and British rules applied. On the *Olympic*, the only distinctions were those of cabin class, not race. She would believe it when she saw it. At least if she ended up in third class, she would still be Egypt bound.

The gangway brought them to the A Deck promenade. From there, they entered a sumptuous, large, wood-paneled room with cream-colored linoleum floors. Armchairs and couches with dark turquoise upholstery lined the walls, while an ornate, polished oak staircase done in neoclassical style unfurled majestically to the B Deck below. Above it, taking up much of the ceiling, was a large glass-and-iron dome, through which soft sunlight filtered from the open deck overhead. It was nicer than any place Eliza had ever been. Undoubtedly Clara, too, based on how she stopped to gape at it.

Inside their cabin were two beds, a dressing table, two thin wardrobes, a small chair, and a washstand. All the furniture was made of heavy oak. When the ship rocked, it wouldn't move far. She stepped inside, followed by the other two women. It was a luxurious room, but small. They had to crowd to all fit.

"*Hum*, I think there is some mistake," said Georgette, breathing down her neck. "There are only two beds here. We are missing one, *non?*"

Eliza set her suitcase on the carpet and yanked hard on the long wooden frame flush against the wall above the inside bed.

Reluctantly, with a sharp metallic gasp, it folded down, revealing a third bed. Now instead of only two beds, the room had a single bed and a bunk bed.

"Oh."

Eliza picked up her suitcase and threw it onto the single bed set against the outside wall. It bounced slightly as it landed on the thin mattress. She immediately followed, lying back with her feet propped up on her luggage and her hands behind her head. "You all better sort out who's sleeping on top and who's on the bottom. This one's mine."

Yes, this was the way to travel.

CHAPTER FIVE

Clara

November 21, 1923
Somewhere in the Atlantic Ocean

If ever a poem could describe a person, for Clara it was Dr. Brewster Higley's "My Western Home." Although most people were only familiar with the first verse, which began "Oh give me a home where the buffalo roam and the deer and the antelope play," Clara found herself drawn to the second-to-last verse:

I love the wild flowers in this bright land of ours,
I love the wild curlew's shrill scream;
The bluffs and white rocks, and antelope flocks
That graze on the mountains so green.

Just because she loved the rolling plains and thick forests of her home, however, didn't mean she wasn't swept up in the grandeur of the *Olympic*. To the contrary, once she got over her initial sense of unease, everything about the ship was exciting and marvelous. On land, she didn't belong in the world of the rich and well-to-do, but on the ship she was surprised by how quickly she became accustomed to moving through their spaces.

Clara kept one of Anna's letters in her pocket, the one that had finally convinced her to leave her home in Wellsburgh, Grundy County, Iowa and travel halfway around the world to Egypt. It said: The world belongs to those who have the courage to see it. Let yourself see. Well, she had seen the ship from bow to stern and as Eliza had promised, she wasn't sure she wanted to leave, at least for a while.

"How long do you think it will take to reach the Valley of the Kings once we arrive in Southampton?" Clara asked.

It was evening of the fifth day, and they were relaxing in the lounge in the hour before dinner. An ostentatious, grand room, it had been designed to mimic the style of the Palace of Versailles—the walls were paneled floor to ceiling in ornately carved oak and hung with bronze sconces and large mirrors. It was worth more than some towns she'd been in. A gentle melody, played by a violinist accompanied by a pianist, filled the air between snatches of conversation around them.

"To go from Southampton to Port Said it will be ten days. We will be stopping in Gibraltar, Algiers, Marseilles, and Malta first," Georgette said, rattling off the locations with the precision of a typewriter. Although her navy sweater and matching blue skirt were modest, she had managed to make the outfit glamorous by throwing a scarf over her shoulders almost like a cape. Clara envied how the Frenchwoman always managed to appear fashionable and put together. Her own drop-waist dress, by comparison, looked like a limp sack.

Georgette continued, "From Port Said to Cairo is four and a half hours by train, and then Cairo to Luxor is overnight also by train unless we go by steamer, *euhhhh*, in which case it is maybe a week." She made a tsking sound. "It is not fast to *go en Égypte*."

Clara picked at the long green necktie on her dress. "What do you think we'll see?"

She had thought a lot about what might await them in Luxor. Based on what Anna had written in her letters, Clara envisioned mountains of gold—glittering statues, jewelry, coins, cups, and platters stacked high in a room covered floor to ceiling in hieroglyphics. Georgette shrugged her thin shoulders. "Probably *une momie*, some gold, some jewelry. I think it could be anything."

"It'll be something worth seeing, that's for sure," Eliza said. "Maybe even be better than what they found in Tut's tomb." She leaned back and crossed her arms over her long pendant necklace. "And we'll be the first to see it. Ain't that something?"

They were sitting in front of the fireplace, with Clara and Eliza sharing a settee and Georgette seated in the armchair facing them. Unexpectedly, the man in the armchair behind the settee spoke up. "Forgive me, ladies, I could not help but overhear parts of your conversation. Have I understood correctly that you are going to Egypt?" He spoke in an extremely refined British accent, enunciating each word carefully.

As Clara and Eliza turned to face him, Georgette replied primly, "*Oui*, we are."

He smiled, a wistful expression crossing his narrow face. "I have been to Egypt countless times. It's almost like a second home to me now. I can assure you that you will not regret your travel there. Egypt is like nowhere else in the world. Even the Romans said so." He turned his body to face them more directly. "Arthur Pearce. It's a pleasure to meet you."

After the women introduced themselves, he continued, "If you're going to Luxor, you must be going to see the Valley of the Kings. Got a spot of the old Tut fever, have you?"

Eliza explained, "Our friend's an archaeologist. She's been digging near there in a place called Dra' Abu el-Naga' looking for the next Tut. We're going to visit her."

A frown flickered across his face, then he shrugged. "Dra' Abu el-Naga'? I haven't heard of it." He gave a rueful smile. "I suppose someone is always digging somewhere in Egypt. There's so much history you can find a *shabti* or scarab ornament under every rock."

He put down the newspaper he'd been holding and moved to the ladies' side of the settee. He was wearing a snug-fitting charcoal-gray suit that spoke of expensive tastes, and his black hair was slicked with so much Brilliantine it reflected the yellow of the electric ceiling lights like a halo. He put his finger to his mouth thoughtfully. "I will tell you what I would do if I were you: spend time in Cairo first. See the pyramids, go to the bazaars, visit the museum. Cairo is lovely if you know the right places to go.

"Then take the train down to Luxor and spend a few days at the Valley of the Kings, Karnak, and Luxor. Come back to Cairo by a leisurely trip down the Nile. You'll see the entire Egyptian countryside that way. It's like traveling back to the time of Moses. I would give anything to do it again myself, but alas, business keeps me from anywhere but Alexandria." He gave a dramatic, melancholy sigh.

"What do you do?" Clara asked, curious. She couldn't imagine what business someone like him would have in Egypt.

His morose expression immediately turned into a broad, proud smile. "Cotton, madam. I am a cotton exporter. In the last few years, Egypt has exported three hundred thousand tons of the stuff. Egypt has the finest cotton in the world. Its long fibers allow for both strength and pliability. It is the fuel that powers England's textile industry. It has, if you'll pardon me, quite eclipsed the American export industry."

He reached into his pocket and pulled out a long white cigarette, which he placed in his mouth. He evidently decided against lighting it, however, because a moment later he took it out and put it back in his pocket. "Where are you staying in Cairo? I know every restaurant and shop in the whole city. I can give you a recommendation near your hotel if you like."

"We're staying with our friend, Anna Baring," Clara replied.

His deep brown eyes widened. "What? Not that redheaded daughter of the old Consul-General Lord Cromer?" He shook his head. "I hope she's more interesting than her father was. He may have been a capital administrator for the Empire, but hardly the man to thrill dinner guests."

He crossed his arms and rocked on his black leather shoes. "I suppose with her as your guide you're in good hands. She was born in Egypt, I think. I'd all but forgotten she'd gone into the business of archaeology. Did you say she'd found something?"

"That's what we're going to see. It's a pharaoh's tomb," Clara replied. She was proud to share this news. The whole world should know what Anna had achieved. And soon it would.

Arthur raised his eyebrows, incredulous. "Has another tomb really been found, so soon? I cannot believe I would not have heard about it. It would have been the talk of Egypt. I would have heard about it even in London. Are you sure that's what she found?"

Clara shrugged. "I guess it will be announced after it's opened."

He rubbed his chin, pensive. "Dra' Abu el-Naga', eh? I suppose it has managed to avoid notice because it's not in the valley. No one would be looking there for a pharaoh's tomb."

"Are you going to Alexandria now?" she asked.

"London, I'm afraid. No, it will be a long time until I'm in the way of Egypt again. Will you be arriving to Port Said or Alexandria?"

"Port Said." Clara remembered what Mr. Heye had told them: a man would meet them at the dock carrying a white sign with their names on it.

He nodded. "You know what Kipling said about Port Said: 'If you truly wish to find someone you have known and who travels, there are two points on the globe you have but to sit and wait; sooner or later your man will come there: the docks of London and Port Said.' In my life, I have found that to be the case." He paused for a moment. Then he gave Clara an uncomfortably appraising look. "Perhaps we will meet again. There's no telling what fate has in store."

She squirmed and dropped her eyes. She didn't like this kind of attention from men. It was too intrusive and presumptuous, as though she were a horse they were considering buying. And a few times, they had done more than just look.

"I can give you my address, in case you're ever in London," Arthur continued, not seeming to notice Clara's discomfort. Although his comment was presented to all three women, it was clear it was directed at only her. "I would be glad to escort you through the city."

"Arthur, darling!" A woman's shrill voice cut through the low murmur of the room.

He looked up, following the sound, and Clara exhaled a sigh of relief that his attention had been redirected away from her. The speaker, a woman in a heavy purple evening gown draped with a black mink stole, was making her way toward them with determined strides. Arthur smiled at the three women before him ruefully, his gaze lingering on Clara for just a little too long. "Forgive me. The lady waits for no one."

He took a step forward, then paused as though considering something. "I hope Lady Baring's discovery was worth the trip. But if the tomb is empty, as so often is the case these days, I hope you enjoy your time in Egypt."

When he was out of earshot, Georgette sniffed. "The English, they are almost as bad as the Americans to talk when they are not asked."

Eliza chuckled. "I think he wanted to talk to Clara. Took a shining to her, seems to me."

Clara's cheeks burned red hot. She looked down at her hands, which were folded in her lap. "I wish he wouldn't." Already, she was thinking how she would have to avoid him for the remainder of the trip.

Eliza watched him disappear among the other passengers. "Why not? Rich men like that don't come along every day. Plenty of girls would be throwing themselves at him right now. Did you see that ruby on his finger? I bet it could buy half this boat."

Clara wrapped her arms around herself, shrinking into as small a space as she could, and said nothing. She didn't care how expensive his jewelry was. Eliza shrugged. "All right, plenty of other fish in the sea. This one time, I met a man in Charleston…"

Clara didn't listen as Eliza continued her story. She didn't want to think about men or fish or anything else. At thirty-eight years old, she was well past marrying age. Once upon a time, she had thought she would meet a man and settle down. But she had never found one with whom she had fallen in love. She guessed that by now, it wasn't part of God's plan for her. She didn't know why, but she did know that if she *were* going to fall in love, it wouldn't be with a stranger on a boat. And definitely not a man like Arthur Pearce.

* * *

December 3, 1923
Port Said, Egypt

Port Said was a sliver of a thing, a tiny town small as a fingernail, perched precariously on the mouth of the Suez Canal. Clara barely noticed its size, however. This was *Egypt*, and she was thrilled to be seeing it. She stood on the promenade deck, watching the white dinghies plying the waters around them like graceful swans as they ferried passengers and cargo to and from the other ships around them. She could have watched the scene around her for hours without getting bored.

"Come on," Eliza said, tugging at her arm. "You stay on this boat any longer and it's gonna keep on going to India with you still on it."

Clara adjusted her long khaki jacket and then her striped tie. She had dipped heavily into her savings to buy the outfit, but she knew she couldn't wear her usual clothing. She couldn't bear the thought of what Anna would think to see her dressed like she was still in the American wilderness. She thought a lot about Anna, in fact, and how she would feel seeing her again. More than anything, she didn't want Anna to regret having invited her. She couldn't bear the thought of disappointing her.

"Where's Georgette?" she asked.

"*Ici!*" Georgette chirruped, materializing from seemingly nowhere. In each hand she held a long suitcase. "Now we go?"

Clara and Eliza's eyes met and they shook their heads in silent communion. They each had packed only one small suitcase for the long voyage. Georgette, however, had brought everything but the kitchen sink, and even then Eliza had suggested under her breath that Georgette might have brought that too.

They joined the line of disembarking passengers, filing off the ship and onto the dock. They were immediately engulfed by a chaotic explosion of sound and movement. Porters swarmed everywhere, calling out their services and trying to identify passengers to take to hotels and onward to tours. Clara kept a keen lookout for the man who was supposed to meet them, but it wasn't until they'd reached the shore that Eliza spotted him, his red fez standing out between the blur of brown robes, white jackets, and white turbans. She pointed. "There! That must be him."

The man was wearing a European-style green jacket over a white shirt and gray slacks. In his hands, he held a white sign that read *"Mss. Martin, Pickering, Law"* in a loose black scrawl. When he spotted the ladies, he approached them immediately, tucking the sign under his arm. *"Ahlan wa sahlan.* Welcome to Egypt. I am Muhammad. Please, I take your baggage?"

Georgette happily handed him her suitcases, filling his hands. He whistled, catching the attention of another porter. Muhammad motioned him over. *"Ta'al,* Youssef. *Yalla, yalla. Saadni."*

The man scuttled over and bowed to Clara, then gently took her suitcase. Eliza passed hers next.

"Now we go to the station," Muhammad said. "It is a short walk. Very short." He paused. "But watch your pockets. Many thieves in Egypt." He shook his head.

Unlike the port at New York, there was no chaotic flock of taxis disgorging passengers for outbound travel and picking up those who were inbound. In fact, there were only a few cars on the road around the quay, although there were plenty of wooden carts drawn by thin horses and donkeys. Even so, Clara was amazed by how much the city was exploding with energy and life. Egyptians and Europeans alike moved everywhere around the women, popping into and out of the short buildings that lined the street. The ambiance reminded her of the American West. She could almost imagine cowboys stumbling out of a saloon next to one of the tobacco shops. In that sense, it felt a little like home.

But at the same time, Port Said wasn't like America at all. The design of the buildings was European belle epoque with a splash of Oriental. And rather than cowboy hats and denim pants, the

Egyptian men wore every type of clothing imaginable, from full three-piece suits to baggy, wide-legged pants, to long robes. Half wore suit jackets, while the other half wore long overcoats of some kind she'd never seen before. Some wore fezzes, others wore turbans, and still others wore European-style hats. Clara thought she could have spent the entire day just watching the city's denizens walk past.

Muhammad led them down a broad dirt road filled with large signs advertising things like tours, a ship chandler, and a general store—everything sailors passing through the Suez Canal might want or need. But after less than a quarter of a mile, the buildings petered out into empty fields, as though the town had run into an invisible wall and stopped. A long, low wooden building came into view, around which loitered a few suspicious looking men, who stared hard at them as they approached. Clara remembered Muhammad's warning and covered her pockets with her hands.

"Here we go, Port Said Station!" Muhammad announced cheerfully. "You will take the morning train and arrive in Cairo in the early afternoon. Then you can take a rest, maybe afternoon tea, and have a nice walk." He set down Georgette's suitcases and reached into the pocket of his jacket. When he withdrew his hand, he was holding three tickets.

"What happens when we arrive in Cairo?" Clara asked as she took hers.

"Lady Baring will meet you herself at Misr Station. She sends her best regards you will enjoy this train ride, and looks forward to seeing you when you come." He bowed. "*Ma'a salaama*, ladies. You are welcome to Egypt."

CHAPTER SIX

Eliza

Cairo, Egypt

"Do you see it?" Clara pressed her face against the glass, heedless of the forehead and nose prints it left, trying to spy the station ahead of them. "It's almost one thirty. We must be close now." She was as excited as a child waiting to open her birthday presents and had been for what felt like hours.

Her nose buried in a book, Georgette didn't look up, nor give any sign she'd heard. Eliza obliged Clara by peering over her shoulder. They were entering a city, that much was clear. The huts along the side of the track were clustering increasingly tightly together, and dirt trails had turned to roads. But she didn't know if that city was Cairo, and if it was, how far into the heart of the city the station lay. They could still be miles away.

"Maybe." She shrugged. They would get there when they got there. She was just glad to be on land after weeks at sea. She sat down next to Georgette and leaned back, closing her eyes.

A few minutes later, Clara cried, "There! I see it now. It's definitely the station." She pointed, the tip of her finger smashing against the window.

This time, there was no denying she was right. What started as little more than a tan dot on the horizon quickly grew into a large building. Misr Station was as large as any train station in the United States, but designed with what Eliza had come to recognize as a uniquely Arab flair. It had tall, arched windows, a flat roof, and walls the color of desert sand. There would have been no mistaking that they weren't in America, even if it hadn't been possible to see camels, donkeys, and palm trees out the windows.

The conductor hauled hard on the brake lever, causing the train to squeal loudly in protest. Although the metal wheels groaned, fighting against the inertia carrying them onward, the cars slowed quickly. Eliza's body pitched forward. She righted herself with a sniff of annoyance. She'd had more comfortable train rides.

Their car came to a halt beneath the station's awning, settling on the metal rails as the locomotive hissed in front of it like an angry snake. There was a moment of suspension, as though the train itself were taking a deep breath, then movement. Jackets were brandished and jewelry adjusted as the passengers gathered themselves, chattering enthusiastically. Eliza blotted perspiration from her forehead with a handkerchief.

"How we will find Anna?" Georgette asked, for the first time looking out the window over the black rims of her glasses.

The platform outside was as busy as any street in New York City. Dozens of passengers disembarked as dozens more waited to board. An even larger number of Egyptian men in flowing white robes and white turbans milled around with seemingly no purpose other than to add to the confusion. Eliza adjusted her skirt as though it were a suit of armor, preparing for the battle they would confront as soon as they left the train.

"I have a feeling it won't be hard," she said, thinking of the archaeologist and her flame-red hair.

When the women stepped off the train onto the platform, they were besieged by a barrage of sound: the clatter of leather-soled shoes, the rumble of luggage carts, and the shrill cries and whistles of runners waiting to pick up guests for hotels. The noise was almost deafening. Eliza worried that if the three travelers became separated, there would be little way to find each other again in the crowd until it thinned out some. *If it ever thinned out.* Perhaps it was this way at all hours, a merry-go-round of people and luggage. In any case, they could never call to each other. No one would ever hear it.

She grasped hold of each of her companions' hands, determined to keep the group together. Luckily, they didn't have to wait for long before a blaze of red hair appeared among the white turbans, a torch in a field of mushroom caps. It was followed shortly thereafter by the rest of Anna.

"Ladies, welcome to Cairo!" She threw her arms open as though she possessed all of the city—and barely avoided clocking a porter next to her. Eliza was astonished at how intimate Anna managed to sound, as though she were reuniting with old friends and not acquaintances of only a few hours and half a world away. Almost immediately, however, her broad smile quirked into a frown. She cocked her head, staring at Clara's waist. "Clara, darling, is that a gun?"

Eliza glanced down, automatically following the other woman's gaze. Clara's khaki jacket had flapped open a little, revealing the unmistakable shape of a leather pistol holster. Clara's right hand went to it, closing around it as though to hide it. Her cheeks reddened in a remarkable impersonation of a tomato.

Eliza snorted, amused. "Oh, it's a revolver all right—a Colt Bisley. She brought it all the way from Iowa. Turns out Clara's a real, honest-to-God Annie Oakley. She was in a Wild West show and everything."

Eliza's initial impression of Clara had been wrong. She had assumed Clara was a mouse. But Clara wasn't a mouse, she was just a fish out of water. Put her in the right water and she swam just fine. The only problem was, her natural habitat was rodeos and spectacles, and there was none of that in Egypt. Eliza had argued she didn't need to carry her gun here, but Clara had insisted. Old habits died hard.

Anna looked uncertain, as though she couldn't decide whether to pursue the matter further or let it drop, but a beat later, she said, "Well, it if makes you feel comfortable." She looked at the suitcases in their hands. "Is that all?"

When they nodded, she motioned to a short man dressed like the other porters on the platform. "Karim, would you please?"

He pushed a wooden luggage cart forward, then took the women's suitcases and carefully laid them on it. As he worked, Anna strode forward and kissed Georgette first on the right cheek, then the left. For her American guests, she shook hands instead. "Well then, how was your journey? I want to hear *everything*."

"Oh no," Eliza warned. "Don't get Georgette started." It wasn't only Clara's secrets she had learned during the long journey to Egypt. Georgette's included the fact that when she got to talking, often there was no stopping her. It was like a train run off its track. If Georgette began to recount their travel now, there was a good chance she would still be talking when it was time to go to bed.

To prevent that from happening, Eliza said, "Tell us instead about this tomb you found."

Anna's entire face lit up. "It's—well, you can imagine how exciting this is. I can't begin to guess what sorts of treasure might be inside. All I can say with confidence is that whatever is inside, it hasn't been touched in millennia. The seals are intact."

Clara raised her pale eyebrows, her brown eyes wide. "You haven't looked at all into the tomb? Not even a peek?"

Anna gave her a jaunty, almost flirtatious smile. "Did you used to open your Christmas presents early?"

Eliza was impressed at the self-restraint the archaeologist had exercised. *She* wouldn't have waited for months for total strangers to arrive before opening the tomb. She asked, "When will we see it?"

"Soon. I want you to see some of Egypt first. I've waited this long to open the tomb; I can wait a few more days."

She led their small group out of the station and into the bright Cairo sunlight. They were immediately surrounded by a quaint Egyptian scene. A flea-bitten gray horse pulling a wagon stacked high with burlap sacks of seeds passed them, trundled past them on the wide dirt road. Following it was a bridle-less donkey laden with bunches of green clover, its young owner riding with one leg hooked lazily over its withers. Eliza was so busy taking it all in that she barely avoided running into a man selling pistachio nuts and palm oil from a pushcart on the side of the road. A European man in a light linen suit leaning against the wall of the station watched the near miss from beneath a hat pulled low over his forehead.

Anna breathed in deeply and smiled ear to ear. "Welcome to Cairo," she said again. The pride in her voice was tangible. Eliza could hear how much she loved the city. She pointed to a black Fiat 501 parked under the weak shade of a tree, claiming it as her own. "It will be a bit tight between us all. Clara, you'll have to sit on my lap."

Eliza didn't understand why they wouldn't all fit until the man she had assumed was a porter climbed behind the wheel after securing their luggage to the back of the car. Apparently he was a driver as well. While she and Georgette slid onto the bench seat in the back, Clara wriggled onto Anna's lap. Anna wrapped an arm around her waist to anchor her, then looked over her shoulder, her eyes sparkling.

"Into the city we go!"

Eliza could never have guessed how vibrant and diverse Cairo was. More than anywhere else in the world but for perhaps Jerusalem or Rome, it was a city where antiquity and modernity coexisted harmoniously in the same space. Fashionable new cars, stylish black carriages, and roughly made, hand-pushed wooden carts all shared the same streets. Camels ambled down unpaved streets carrying bales of cotton, timber, and wheat, just as they had during the time of Abraham. Donkeys with big stone water jars stood idly swatting at flies. Yet only a few miles later, they passed trolley cars and stores with ambitious signs like "Brasserie Internationale."

"There are around eight hundred thousand people living in Cairo. It's the largest city in all of Africa, although that's nothing compared to New York or London. The city is divided into sections. We'll be staying in the European section," Anna explained.

Eliza was surprised to find herself a little nostalgic. She murmured, "I feel like I'm back in France."

Anna nodded. "This part of the city was designed by French architects. Khedive Ismail Pasha fell in love with Paris when he visited it. He was determined to build an even more beautiful version when he came back to Cairo."

"It is not more beautiful than Paris." Georgette sniffed, insulted. "Nothing can be more beautiful than Paris."

"No," Anna agreed. "And what's worse, he bankrupted the country in the process. There's no money to maintain these buildings. It will all go quite quickly to ruin. In some places, it already has."

The car turned down a narrow lane off the broad avenue. It was a quiet street, empty of both pedestrians and cars. They came to a halt in front of a long, white, belle epoque-style building.

"Well, ladies, we've arrived," Anna announced. "Welcome— this time properly—to Cairo."

Clara opened the door and carefully extricated herself from Anna's lap. Meanwhile, the driver helped Georgette and Eliza out, then began to untie the suitcases. As Anna led the women inside, she explained, "I haven't spent much time in Cairo lately. I've been so busy excavating down south. It's nice to finally have a moment here, even if it's only for a few days."

Eliza knew the feeling.

Anna's apartment was taller than it was wide, with the kitchen and servants' quarters on the first floor, the sitting and dining rooms on the second, and the bedrooms on the third. When they reached the landing in front of the bedrooms in the course of the grand tour, Anna grimaced ruefully. "I'm afraid this is quite a small apartment. I live alone and hardly ever entertain guests. There are only two bedrooms and three beds. One of you will have to sleep either on a cot or with me."

Her guests exchanged looks, but no one said anything. After a moment, she shrugged. "Anyway, you certainly don't have to decide who will sleep where right now. You must be peckish after your journey. I'll have Fatimah make sandwiches."

On cue, Eliza's stomach rumbled.

* * *

After lunch, Anna took her guests to Khan el-Khalili, which she explained was the city's largest and most vibrant bazaar. It was made up of dozens of big shops in stone caravanserais interspersed with a hundred or more smaller shops that merchants had set up on the streets between them. Eliza was overwhelmed by the magnitude of it all. Brass ewers, lamps, and bronze plates lined the streets as far as the eye could see. Silk scarves cascaded out of windows. Alabaster chess sets, vases, and inlaid wood boxes reached toward the sky in freestanding pillars higher than she was tall. Her ears rang with the ceaseless calls of merchants coaxing them to visit their stores, modern sirens.

While Eliza would have been happy to leave it all behind and go someplace quieter, Georgette seemed to want to visit every stall. They were stopped beneath a stone arch, Georgette admiring a mummified cat and the other women inspecting enormous white bags piled high with dried dates and spices, when something struck the bag next to Anna, causing the thyme inside it to kick up into the air in a small puff. It was only because Eliza had been contemplating the spices at that exact moment that she noticed it at all.

"What was that?" she asked loudly enough to draw the others' attention.

The second shot came a moment later, whizzing into a bag of red dates several feet from them and leaving a perfectly round hole. This time, she heard the unmistakable report of the gun that fired it echoing clearly down the alley. Anna froze, surprised and confused, but Clara's gun was in her hand in an instant. She was already drawing it level, trying to sight the shooter, by the time Eliza recognized what she was doing. Instinctively, Eliza lashed out at the barrel, pushing it aside before Clara could pull the trigger.

"What are you doing?" Eliza's body was screaming for them to run. They were in danger. They needed to flee, to get away, not fight.

"Someone's shooting at us!" There was indignation in Clara's voice, as though the attack were a personal affront.

She had the barrel up again and was looking down the alley, trying to find the gunman, but lane was totally empty. On hearing the shots, the shopkeepers had all disappeared into their stores like gophers ducking back into their holes. Whoever had taken the shots was either hiding too or hadn't stuck around.

"That doesn't mean you gotta shoot back!"

A flash of motion at the end of the alley revealed where the gunman had temporarily taken refuge. Before Eliza could grasp what was happening, Clara took off after him. Her arms and legs pumped as she dashed down the alley, her boots smacking against the hard paving stones. Eliza was too surprised to move. What in the world was she thinking going off after someone who had just tried to kill them?

A fraction of a second later, Anna followed, her unbound hair streaming behind her like a flag. Eliza watched them go, astounded. Were they crazy? Then she realized with a shock that without Anna, she and Georgette would never make it home. They didn't know where Anna lived, nor did they have any means of transportation even if they did. They couldn't afford to be separated from her.

She grabbed Georgette's hand and started to drag her after the others. "Come on, we gotta go with them!" Hopefully by the time they caught up, the shooter would be long gone.

Eliza wasn't a fast runner—her body was built for strength, not speed—but she didn't have to be. The street was so crowded by stands of knickknacks and rugs that it was impossible for anyone to run quickly. The bazaar was like a giant obstacle course, full of things to dodge, jump over, or duck under. Thus, despite Clara and Anna's head start, Eliza and Georgette were only about fifty yards behind them—close enough to see them, but too far away to stop them. And somewhere even farther ahead of them, out of Eliza's vision, was the shooter. She had no desire to catch up to him.

Clara crashed through a display of metal lampshades that had sprawled too far across the alley. Several went clattering to the ground, ringing like cymbals. A few moments later, Anna kicked them aside as she passed. The shopkeeper squawked in protest, shaking an angry fist.

"Sorry!" Eliza called over her shoulder as she and Georgette jumped over them and dashed past.

"They are very beautiful!" Georgette added, as though that would mollify him.

"Clara, stop! Why are you chasing him?" Anna appeared to be gaining on her, but Eliza couldn't be sure.

"We have to catch him!" The words drifted behind Clara like steam from the locomotive that had brought them to Cairo.

"Why?" Anna sounded mystified as she juked nimbly around a tourist who had just emerged from a shop, a large wooden camel in her hands. The woman gasped and almost dropped her purchase as Eliza nearly barreled into her.

"For the police! Come on, I think he went this way!"

Clara cut sharply right, and abruptly the women found themselves surrounded by dozens of stalls of gold jewelry. The metal was so bright it seemed to shine with its own light. Eliza's stride was momentarily broken as her eye caught on all the sparkling ornaments. If El Dorado existed, it was here, on this street. The Spaniards had sailed in the wrong direction. But now it was even harder to run; the way ahead was full of tourists, a thick scrum through which it was all but impossible to pass. Eliza just barely avoided colliding with a man and his wife, who gave her horrified looks as she careened past. She called out another apology.

"Stop! *Stop!*" Anna yelled, finally catching hold of Clara. She dug her heels into the ground, dragging her to a standstill even as Clara fought to keep going.

The pause enabled Eliza and Georgette to catch up. Eliza put her hands on her knees and took deep, labored breaths. She couldn't remember when she'd last run like that. She was too old to be running around anywhere. At least Georgette, too, was winded. Her glasses were askew on her face and her cheeks had bright pink spots.

Clara looked desperately in the direction she'd been running, like a foxhound watching the fox escape. "He's going to get away!"

"Let him, for God's sake!" Anna exclaimed.

"Why?"

Anna looked around, taking in the tourists staring at them. Her face was flushed red with exertion. Her hair was absolutely wild. "Let's go home. I'll explain there."

Back at the apartment, Anna's servant Fatimah poured them tea while they settled around the dining table. They had collected themselves a little, patting fabric and stray hairs back into place, but Eliza could still feel cold sweat on her back.

"Why did you let him get away?" Clara asked, petulant. Eliza thought if Anna hadn't stopped her, she would probably still be out there running like a hound. At least *she* was wearing pants, unlike Eliza and Georgette, who'd suffered the indignity of running in dresses.

It was Eliza, not Anna who responded. "Why'd you go and chase him anyway? Ain't you got any common sense at all? He could have shot you!"

"Why was someone shooting at us?" Georgette asked.

It was a good question. Eliza looked at Anna hard, waiting for an answer. Their host sighed. "He wasn't shooting at you, he was shooting at me."

Her guests stared at her. It was an answer that begged more explanation.

"Three and a half years ago, the Egyptians revolted against the British Protectorate, demanding self-rule. For months, there were almost daily protests. The whole country was in flames. A year and a half ago, they got independence, but..." She grimaced. "Not enough has changed. King Fuad is a British puppet and the nationalists and everyone else know it."

She paused to take a swig of her tea. "Elections are next month. All of Cairo is on edge. If Zaghlul doesn't win, it's certain there will be blood in the streets. Everyone will know democracy in Egypt is a sham. The country will explode."

Eliza frowned and crossed her arms, trying to understand how that led to someone shooting at them. "What's that got to do with you?"

Anna sighed again and gave a wry, almost tired smile. "It's no secret I'm the daughter of the Briton who ruled Egypt for thirty years—Overbearing Khedive Baring, they call him. Under the circumstances, it's not entirely unexpected that a nationalist might try to take a potshot at me just to say he'd done it. Down with the imperialists and all that. Really, it's a wonder no one has tried before now. Just look at what they did to Ghali."

Clara was appalled. "But you're an archaeologist, not a politician! You have nothing to do with any of it!"

She shrugged. "No, but I am his daughter, and while he's dead and buried in England, I'm here, within reach."

"Are you not scared they will try again?" Georgette asked, blinking owlishly behind her glasses.

"I suppose they could. Although there are better targets, if they wanted..."

Eliza was immediately uneasy. A few feet to the left and the assassin would have killed Anna. A few feet more and he would have killed *her*. If Anna was in danger, they were *all* in danger so long as they were with her. "Maybe you should leave Egypt."

"No." Anna shook her head. "Egypt is my home. I won't be chased out of it. Besides, we won't be in Cairo long. I want you to see the pyramids and the Egyptian Museum tomorrow—no trip to Cairo is complete without it. Then we can go. We'll be safe outside the city."

Eliza wondered if she hadn't made a mistake after all in coming to Egypt. Between Anna dismissing the risk posed by half of Egypt wanting to shoot her and Clara running straight toward the man with the gun, she couldn't decide who was more reckless.

"What if the man comes back?" she asked. If he had found them among the labyrinthine alleys of the bazaar, he could just as easily find them at the pyramids or the museum.

Anna polished off her tea and set the cup down on the table with a clink. "My father always said, 'Cowards never try twice.'

By now that man is probably halfway across the city. But you're right. I'll have Karim borrow another pistol and accompany us tomorrow. Between him and Clara"—she smiled winningly at the other American—"we'll be more than safe."

Eliza hoped she was right.

CHAPTER SEVEN

Anna

After finishing her tea, Georgette disappeared into the spare bedroom, claiming one of the beds as her own. Eliza, asserting a headache from running through the bazaar, retired to the sitting room with a book. The fragmentation of the group suited Anna just fine. She touched Clara's shoulder lightly. "Come, I want to show you something."

With no further explanation, she led her to the third floor. At the end of the landing was a narrow wood door, painted white to camouflage it against the wall. On the other side was a dark closet, in the middle of which a rickety metal staircase seemed to spiral directly into the ceiling. Ignoring the pronounced wobble beneath her boots, Anna climbed the stairs. When her head struck something solid, she pushed. It was a wooden hatch, and when she swung it open with some effort, the hinges not having been oiled recently, it revealed a brilliant, cloudless blue sky.

"Come on," she called down after crawling up onto the flat roof.

Clara peered up at her from the base of the staircase. "Are you sure it's safe?"

"Positive. I've been coming up here for years."

Clara grasped the metal railing and climbed after her slowly. When she was near the top, Anna reached down to help steady her.

Once she had made it through, Clara looked around in awe, then dashed to the edge of the roof, leaning as far as she could over the wall. "Oh, it's beautiful!"

Anna followed, smiling. From their vantage point, it was possible to see most of Cairo. Hundreds of mosque domes broke the endless landscape of square and rectangular buildings. Tall, thin minarets—Cairo was nicknamed the City of a Thousand Minarets for good reason—stabbed into the sky at odd intervals like the tips of spears. And in the distance, sitting on the summit of the citadel overlooking the city, was the imposing mosque of Muhammad Ali.

Khedive Ismail had tried to make Cairo a European city, but it never could be. It was a city where the East met the West and the East ultimately prevailed, regardless of how many foreign conquerors came. Egypt had outlasted the Greeks, Romans, Persians, French, Turks, and now the English. It would always be Egyptian.

"It's my favorite view in the whole city," Anna said, lounging against the wall and enjoying the sight of Clara marveling at the panorama. What was it that drew one person to another if not the view? "It's why I bought this apartment."

"I can see why."

Anna sauntered around Clara, giving her time to enjoy the city, then quietly slipped up behind her. She leaned her body against her back, pressing her hips into Clara's and moving her right hand along her waist. Clara stiffened instantly. "What—?"

Anna deftly pulled the revolver from the holster at Clara's hip and stepped back, holding it up to show her that's what she'd been after. It was a small gun, with a mother-of-pearl grip and plantlike whorls engraved in the metal. It was an unusual, fancy weapon that clearly wasn't meant for ordinary tasks. How odd that Clara had never mentioned this part of her life in her letters. It was intriguing.

She cocked her head and examined Clara's face. She found many things about the American intriguing. Anna hadn't found many women like that. "You surprise me, Miss Pickering. You chased a gunman through Egypt's biggest bazaar with only this little pistol. For me."

Clara looked at the top button of Anna's shirt, pink creeping up her neck on its way to her cheeks. "I didn't think about it at the time, I guess. I just thought he shouldn't be able to get away with it. It wasn't right."

Anna smiled, charmed by the innocence of the response. "Weren't you afraid?"

Clara looked surprised. "Afraid? Why would I be?"

"He could have shot you."

She shrugged. "If he got close enough to shoot again, I'd shoot him first." It was that simple to her.

"You're very brave."

Clara rubbed the back of her neck, dropping her eyes again. "Not really. Anyone would have done it."

"I don't think they would have. *I* would not have."

The blush had made it to Clara's cheeks and was now headed to her hairline. "Well, he got away anyway."

Anna watched her keenly. Like a lake whose topography it's impossible to discern from the surface, it was clear Clara had hidden depths to her. "I'm glad you came to Egypt. I had feared you might refuse." In fact, until Muhammad had sent the message from Port Said confirming he had seen all three women off on the train to Cairo, she had wondered whether her cajoling letters had been enough to persuade the shy woman to come. She didn't take for granted the presence of the members of the Lady Adventurers Club in Cairo. Especially Clara.

"I almost didn't come," Clara admitted.

"What convinced you?"

Clara stared at Anna's boots as though the answer were written there. "I guess I felt like I should. Like I would always regret it if I didn't. And you were so nice and I just thought that I didn't want to disappoint you by saying no…"

"Mm. I *would* have been sad not to see you again." She said it gently, trying to catch her attention, but when Clara didn't respond, she waved the gun a little. "So, my brave defender, what *do* you normally do with this?"

Clara's head bounced up and at last she met Anna's eyes. This was a subject about which she clearly felt more confident. "I shoot things."

"You don't say." Anna tried and failed to suppress a laugh.

Clara blinked, then realized the need for more explanation. "In the show, I used to shoot things like playing cards thrown into the air, stamps on an envelope, buttons off of coats, that type of thing. Now it's just for squirrels, I guess. I just…couldn't stop wearing it. I'd feel naked without it."

Anna understood better why Clara had the confidence to go running after a would-be assassin. Perhaps it was he who should have been scared. Turning, she leveled the gun at the city around them and closed one eye, sighting over the barrel as though looking for a target to shoot. Then she looked back to Clara with a playful smile. "You are a most pleasant surprise, Miss Pickering. Tell me about these shows of yours."

Clara brightened immediately. It was like a cloud had been in front of the sun and then passed. "Oh, well, I joined the Cummings and Mulhall show for the St. Louis World's Fair. That was my first show. Then after that I was with L. O. Hillman's for fifteen years. We traveled all over the country putting on shows. It was a swell time."

Unexpectedly, her face fell and the light in her eyes dimmed, shadowed by some deep sadness. "The show shut down a few years ago. People don't care about the Old West anymore."

There was such heartbreaking sadness in her voice that it made Anna's heart ache in sympathy. Trying to salvage the mood, she held up the gun again. "Could you teach me to shoot? You never know when I might run into another maniac in a bazaar."

The light returned to Clara's face, as quickly as it had gone. "Of course! It's easy. Anyone can shoot a gun. What you do is, first you put your feet shoulder width apart." She demonstrated, planting her feet wide and bending her knees just a little. "Then you cock the hammer back with your thumb and hold the gun level with your eye. You use the sight on the end of the barrel—that's the little metal blade there—to aim. Then you point at the target and gently pull the trigger."

She shook her head reprovingly. "You can't jerk the trigger. That's the key to it all. If you pull it too hard, you'll miss every time. You have to be gentle. You have to squeeze it until the gun fires."

Anna nodded sagely. "Squeeze like you're holding a lover. Caress the trigger." She used the simile intentionally, intending to provoke a reaction, and it worked. Clara boggled at her, astonished.

She bit back a chuckle and pressed on. "Like this?" She purposely stood wrong, keeping her feet too far together and holding the gun too high. As she had anticipated, Clara couldn't resist correcting her.

Clara moved beside her, lowering the barrel so the gun was at Anna's eye level and gently touching her right hip. "Wider. You want to be stable, especially for guns with a big recoil. You can't shoot a shotgun with a stance like that or you'll blow over like a tumbleweed."

Anna watched her out of the corner of her eye. "Will you show me how to draw and aim like you do?" She loved the earnestness on Clara's face, the way her entire body filled with confidence and authority when she talked about shooting. And she loved that it made the other woman so easy to manipulate.

"Okay. What you do is—"

"No, don't tell me. *Show* me."

"Oh. Well, I guess…" Clara moved to stand behind her, pressing lightly against her like her shadow. Her breath tickled the nape of Anna's neck. It made the hairs rise and her skin tingle. Her heart beat faster. It had been some time since she had been this close to another woman. She had missed it. Oh, how she had missed it. But she had to move carefully with Clara. She couldn't startle her.

Clara reached around her so that her hand was over Anna's on the weapon. Her grip was strong, but not crushing. Gently, she guided the revolver to Anna's side, as though Anna were wearing a holster. Anna bit her lower lip and held her breath, trying to calm herself. "They" drew the weapon. When Anna's arm was fully extended, Clara tapped on Anna's index finger. "Click," she said, breathing out a long breath.

Even though she had asked for it, Anna was having trouble focusing on the guidance Clara was giving her. She was too distracted by the feeling of Clara's chest against her back, her chin on her shoulder. Everywhere their bodies met, Anna's skin prickled. Her body was filled with yearning. It took all of her willpower not to turn around and…

Clara guided the weapon back down to Anna's hip. "That's how you do it. That's all there is. Move smooth and steady and you'll hit your target every time."

Even Cupid wasn't that accurate.

Although they were no longer pretending to shoot, Clara's arm was still wrapped around her, her hand on Anna's. It must have been comfortable for Clara. For Anna, it was almost agonizing.

"How many times have you held a woman like this?" she asked. She couldn't resist.

Her question shattered the moment. Clara let go of her and took a step back. "What?"

Anna instantly missed the contact, and wished she hadn't spoken. How much longer might she have enjoyed the intimacy of the moment? But the damage was done. She turned to face Clara with wide, innocent eyes. "I mean, how many women have you taught to shoot?"

"Oh." Clara snatched the gun back from her and holstered it. "None, I guess. Where I come from, the women grow up shooting. For some folks, it's the only way to put meat on the table. Grundy is a poor county."

Anna tilted her head, watching her. "You have a beautiful smile."

"What?" Clara's eyes widened.

"When you were talking about the show. It goes all the way to your eyes."

She wanted to trace that smile with her finger, to run her fingertips over the smooth skin of Clara's cheeks. She stepped forward so they were almost nose to nose. It was uncomfortably close, the type of close that sets off alarm bells. At that range, two people either had to kiss or fight. She didn't think Clara would do either, at least not so soon, but she wanted Clara to feel that crackle of electricity that could occur between two women. To be as aware of Anna's body as she was of Clara's.

She put her left hand on the gun's grip, as if to grab it backward. "What if someone tries to take your gun from you? What then?" Her voice was a low purr, as seductive as Anna could make it.

Clara was frozen, eyes wide, lips half-parted. Anna could almost see the pulse throbbing in her neck. It was clear no woman had ever come this close or spoken like this to her before. Clara instinctively knew it meant something, even if she didn't know what or how she felt about it. Anna licked her lips, drawing Clara's attention there, and waited. Several seconds passed before she felt Clara's right hand come down on hers and press.

"Well—" Clara's voice was slightly choked. "F—First I would push down so you couldn't draw it."

Anna raised her right eyebrow. This was getting more interesting. She hadn't anticipated that. "And then?"

Clara's throat bobbed as she swallowed. Her eyes never blinked. "I—I guess I would...punch you."

So it was fight, not kiss. Anna wasn't ready to give up yet, though. She inched even closer, until she could feel Clara's breath against her lips. Her body thrilled with excitement. "Punch me? That seems a little unfair. What if we weren't strangers? And you *wanted* me to have the gun?" She gently laid her right hand on Clara's left hip, resting it on the wide leather belt.

It took all her self-control not to pull the other woman into her. For her part, Clara seemed to be mesmerized. The only thing that moved was her shoulders as she breathed. Anna wondered what would happen if she dared take things further. If she touched Clara's shirt, for example. Clara hadn't pushed her away or expressed horror at Anna's overture. Anna was certain she wasn't reading her wrong, but Clara could still run at any time.

Before Anna could do anything else, however, Eliza's voice cut through Cairo's dry, hot air. "Anna! Your man Karim is looking for you. Says he needs to know what you want packed for the trip."

Anna and Clara automatically looked toward the staircase, where Eliza's disembodied head was poking out of the hole in the roof like a magician's trick. The moment between them was broken. Clara took a step back, reclaiming control over her gun and body. Then she took off for the staircase as though she had spotted the shooter from the bazaar and intended to resume the chase. She didn't wait for Anna, nor did she look back. Anna sighed. The problem with having multiple guests was you could never predict when one might interrupt.

When she reached the landing, Eliza was waiting for her. Eliza planted her feet and crossed her thick arms over her white lace dress, blocking her way like a palace guard. "I know what you're doing."

Her voice was firm but not accusatory. Even so, Anna narrowed her eyes warily. "What is it, exactly, you think I'm doing?"

Eliza tilted her head toward the stairs. "I don't care what you do or who you do it with, but *her*? Where she's from, they ain't ever heard a woman can love another woman. They're still living in the Stone Age with Adam and Eve and burning bushes. What you want from her, she can't ever give you."

Anna gave her a disapproving look. "She's a grown woman, not a child."

"Mm-hmm, but you don't know the world she's from. She ain't…worldly. She ain't seen the things you and I have."

Anna raised her chin defiantly. She didn't like how Eliza was characterizing Clara. Clara may not have traveled to Morocco, but that didn't mean she couldn't learn—and try—new things. Here she was in Egypt, after all. Wasn't that proof enough that she had courage and adventurousness? Furthermore, Eliza had no right to speak for her. Clara could speak for herself perfectly well.

Anna crossed her arms, mirroring Eliza's stance. "She's perfectly capable of making her own decisions."

Eliza threw up her hands. "All right then, see what happens. But I told you."

Anna smiled graciously. She would see what happened.

* * *

After dinner, they retired to the sitting room. As Anna handed out tumblers of gin with honey and lemon juice, Georgette and Eliza made themselves comfortable on the red, Georgian-style couch while Clara settled in one of the armchairs. Anna leaned against the fireplace's ornate mantel. She held up her glass. "Cheers, ladies. To the start of an exciting adventure, to the opening of the tomb of the pharaoh Ahmose I, and to the discovery of a lifetime."

After she took a sip, she set her tumbler down and clapped her hands together. "Come on, let's play a game. It's still early and we hardly know each other. Any ideas? How about 'For or Against'?"

Georgette cocked her head. "How do we play this game? I have not heard of it."

"It couldn't be easier. I'll name a subject, and you have to say if you're for or against it. Let's try something easy. Paris: for or against?"

Georgette scoffed. "Of course for. How anyone can say they are against Paris? This is a ridiculous question."

"For," Eliza agreed. "I'd go back just for some of that red wine, a slice of brie, and a baguette."

"Wonderful. Independence for all the European colonies: for or against?"

"For," Eliza declared. "It's 1923. Ain't any sense having colonies anymore. Everyone has a right to self-determination. President Wilson said it himself."

"And yet even the United States still has them," Anna commented wryly. Out of the corner of her eye, she watched Clara, who hadn't spoken yet. In fact, the other woman had been quiet all evening, refusing to make any eye contact with her. She was starting to worry she had pushed too far on the roof…or Eliza was right. She decided to probe a little. "All right then, something less controversial. Love: for or against?"

Georgette made a face and looked away. "I prefer *la science, merci*."

"What's wrong with love, Georgette? Got your heart broken a few times?"

Georgette looked simultaneously horrified and insulted. "*Non*, I have not 'had my heart broken,' as you say. But I am not going around everywhere writing hearts like a girl. I have better things to do."

Anna suppressed a chuckle. "I suppose that's one way to look at it. Eliza? Clara?"

Eliza looked at her suspiciously and said nothing. Anna wasn't bothered. She turned her gaze to Clara. "Go on, Clara, what do you think?"

Clara stared into the untouched tumbler in her lap. "Oh, I don't know. It's such a big question."

Anna could barely control the grin spreading across her face. She couldn't have planned things better. "Then I'll make it more difficult. Love between two women: for or against?"

Clara looked up immediately. "But that's not…It's not possible." Her confusion was genuine. Eliza was right: she really hadn't heard of it before.

Anna didn't miss a beat. "Nonsense. Love between two women is as old as time. Women in Egypt used to marry each other, even. Go to Paris right now and half the women you see walking together on the streets are in love with each other."

Bewildered, Clara looked to Georgette for confirmation. The Frenchwoman shrugged, unbothered by the topic. "*Je suppose, oui*. It is neither common nor uncommon. It happens."

Clara looked back at Anna, the slackness in her face and the white around her eyes indicating just how lost she was. "But I've never heard of such a thing."

Anna took a casual sip of her gin, relishing the role of serpent in the Garden of Eden. "Just because you haven't heard of a thing doesn't mean it doesn't happen, and with great regularity. Why *shouldn't* women love each other? That's the question you should be asking."

Clara licked her lips. Her fingers played unconsciously with the tie knot at her throat. Anna knew it was a lot for her to learn at once—a full paradigm shift, in fact.

"But how do two women..." Clara didn't finish the sentence. It could have been almost anything. For someone who was just learning there were other possible permutations of love, there were any number of unresolved questions she might have.

Anna was willing to answer any and all of them. In detail. She grinned wolfishly. "Would you like to know?"

"Anna." Eliza's voice was a low warning growl. It hit Anna like a splash of cold water. She frowned at Eliza, irritated both by the interruption and the caution.

Clara didn't seem to hear Eliza, however. Her eyes were locked with luminous intensity on Anna. She dropped her voice to almost a whisper. "Have *you*...?"

Anna redirected her attention to Clara and gave Clara her best, most alluring smile. "Yes. Many times. Do you—"

Eliza slapped her hands on her thighs. The sound made everyone jump. "You know what? I'll sleep in Anna's bed tonight. Georgette and Clara, you two take the other room. Now who wants some more of that gin?"

CHAPTER EIGHT

Georgette

December 5, 1923

Georgette regretted they were leaving Cairo after only two days. She could have stayed in the Egyptian Museum, with its endless glass cases full of relics and antiques, for days. She had appreciated the grandeur of the pyramids, too, particularly the impossible precision of their masonry and their majestic, incomparable antiquity, but the experience had been marred by the loud, smelly camels Anna had insisted they ride to get there. With their awkward, swaying gait, it had been like clinging to a drunken giraffe, and no more pleasant. She would be quite happy never to ride one again in all her life.

Now it was time to begin their journey up the Nile, and then from there to open the tomb they had come so far to see. By coincidence, Egypt's most famous river bisected Cairo only a short drive from Anna's apartment. They left in the morning after breakfast, Georgette perched uncomfortably on Anna's lap, and arrived at a small dock a few hours after sunrise. The Nile was one of those rare rivers that flowed north rather than south, which meant they would be traveling against the current to reach Luxor and the Valley of the Kings. Luckily, they would be traveling with the wind, which was stronger than the current and more than compensated for it.

"There are no *crocodiles* here, *hein?*" Georgette scanned the opaque water from the car, looking for dark, oblong shapes that might indicate the presence of the dread reptiles in the deep blue water. She had read that the adult male Nile crocodile could be between three and five meters long and weigh up to 750 kilograms. Nile crocodiles killed hundreds and perhaps thousands of people each year in Africa. Having seen drawings of their crooked mouths and irregularly sized white teeth, she had no desire to meet one in person.

Anna chuckled, her shoulders rubbing against Georgette's back. "Why of course there are. You'll doubtless see them sunning themselves on the banks as we sail. Not to worry; so long as you don't go for a swim there's no risk at all. They're not going to climb onboard the boat at night and into bed with you."

Georgette eyed the bank in front of them suspiciously. If they sunned themselves on banks, one could be there now, hidden in the reeds. Anna tapped her lightly on the shoulder. "Come on, I promise you won't get within twenty meters of a crocodile."

The women spilled out of the car—Georgette more reluctantly than the others—while Karim untied their luggage. A small steamship bobbed gently in the water. It was a beautiful boat, with a bright white hull, staterooms along the deck, and a canopy on top to shield passengers from the glare of the sun. Anna had rented the *Nitocris* just for them for the trip; they would be the only passengers.

"*Oh, que c'est joli,*" Georgette exclaimed, pleased by the ship's appearance. She could imagine it making a day trip up the Seine, gliding effortlessly over the calm water.

"Not bad. Not bad at all," Eliza said, impressed.

"How long we will be sailing?"

Anna peered down the river, hands on her hips. "It should be just under four and a half days. We'll reach Luxor after breakfast on the ninth."

Three men with skin dark as coal wearing sweaters and black skirts jogged down the wooden gangway from the ship and past the women to the car. They grabbed the suitcases and carried them weightlessly back onto the boat. Nubians, Georgette recognized, likely from the southern part of the country. As the other women followed them, she noticed a black car slowly roll past, its tires crunching quietly on the sandy, unpaved road. It was out of place along the sleepy bank, where Anna's Fiat was the only other car. It seemed to catch Georgette watching it and sped away.

For a moment, her mind flashed back to the man in the bazaar, but then she dismissed the idea as ridiculous. The car was likely out on an errand, nothing nefarious about it. She shouldn't let her imagination run wild. She hitched up her khaki skirt so she wouldn't risk tripping on the gangway and falling into the crocodile-infested waters, then followed the others onto the boat. They were leaving Cairo now, and with it anyone who wanted their host dead.

* * *

December 6, 1923
Tahna al-Gabal, Egypt

The next morning, she sat on the top deck of the ship as the sun rose, drinking tea and watching the feluccas that plied the river in both directions carrying passengers and cargo. When they were face on, the rudimentary sailboats looked like butterflies whose wings were pulled together, gliding peacefully over the dark water. When the *Nitocris* passed them, however, their wings became a single dramatic blade that caught the wind and drove the simple boats forward. The feluccas could have been built yesterday or two thousand years ago. Their design hadn't changed in all that time.

The landscape they passed, too, was ageless. Sometimes Georgette saw mud villages, with goats and cattle grazing on the horizon and young boys splashing in the water. Other times, she could see nothing but orange and yellow stone bluffs as the river carved through kilometer after kilometer of cliffs.

"The barges, what do they carry?" she asked Anna after a second one passed. The wide boats were only a little larger than the feluccas and powered by steam engines.

Anna looked up from the paper she was reading and watched the barge's slowly retreating outline. "Most likely it's sugarcane. There are farms and factories all up and down the Nile. Although it could be anything, really. Most things here in Egypt are still shipped by boat rather than by rail. It could just as well be papyrus or alabaster."

Georgette squinted after the boat. It was impossible to see what it was carrying because the deck was covered by a dark tarpaulin. She cocked her head, watching the small figures of the men walking back and forth along the bow. "But why the men are carrying guns?"

"What?" Anna frowned, setting the paper down. She leaned forward, trying to see the barge better, but already it was too far away. "Are you sure? There's hardly anything in Egypt worth protecting with guns. It's not like they're shipping gold."

Georgette nodded vigorously. "*Oui, oui,* they were carrying…" She mimed the appearance of a long gun with her hands. She didn't know the exact word for that type of weapon in English.

Anna leaned back, considering the problem. Then her eyes widened. She was out of her chair and on her feet in a flash, leaning far over the water as though she could somehow bring the barge back into sight. She turned to Georgette. "How many barges like that have you seen?"

Georgette shrugged. "Three. Two today, one yesterday." At the time, it hadn't seemed worth mentioning. For all she knew, what she was seeing was quite normal.

Anna ran her hand through her hair, then rubbed her lips with her index finger. "It could be weapons stockpiling. The nationalists could be preparing another revolt if they lose the election, bringing guns into Cairo from the south."

Georgette considered the hypothesis.

"*Non*, I do not think so." Although she was only a visitor and didn't know much about Egypt's politics, she was relatively confident in her assertion. "The men, they were, *euh*, I think they were not *Égyptiens*." In her mind, she saw the white faces and European-style shirts and trousers of the armed men. Definitely not Egyptian, and therefore unlikely to be part of a nationalist insurrection.

Anna's mouth twitched down at the corners, a wrinkle forming between her eyebrows, but her burst of frenetic energy ebbed a little. "Hmm. I hope King Fuad hasn't hired mercenaries to protect himself. Forty years ago, Khedive Ismail tried using some Americans to lead an Egyptian army into Ethiopia and look how well that turned out."

Georgette knew a great many things, but she did not know how well "that" turned out. She didn't even know Egypt had fought Ethiopia or why. She looked at Anna blankly. "*Non*, I don't know."

Anna grunted. "Well, it went badly. If Fuad's trying something similar to keep down the nationalists, it's likely to go just as poorly."

Georgette remembered what Anna had said about Cairo being a powder keg. If she was right and the barges carried mercenaries, it sounded like matches were being placed around that keg. "Are we *en danger*?"

Anna shook her head vigorously. "No, not at all. This is a fight between the nationalists and the royalists."

Georgette didn't bother to point out that Anna was neither and someone had tried to kill *her* only a few days ago. Anna must have realized the contradiction herself, however, because she added, "Luxor is very different from Cairo. It will be safe there, I promise. I would never put you in danger."

At that moment, Clara climbed the staircase at the front of the ship. One of the boat's two servants, Ahmad, jumped forward to meet her, kettle in one hand, teacup in the other. "Tea, madam?"

Georgette liked Ahmad's white costume and red fez. Tall and thin as he was, he looked like a matchstick. Clara waved him away with a polite smile. "No, thank you. Maybe later."

He retreated to the back of the boat, crestfallen. Clara leaned against the railing, staring out at the passing riverbank. Anna moved to join her, standing so close that her arm lightly brushed against Clara's. "Did you sleep well?"

Clara yawned and rubbed her eyes. "I don't know how you're awake. We stayed up way too late watching the stars. I can't imagine what time it was when we finally went to bed."

"Quite a few cups of tea." Anna nudged her with her elbow. "It was worth it, though, wasn't it? Isn't it invigorating to know you're seeing the same stars that Cleopatra and Ramses the Great watched, sailing along the Nile as they once did?"

Clara smiled. Georgette had noticed that since arriving in Egypt, Clara was smiling and talking more. "I never thought I'd see Egypt, much less sail up the Nile."

Anna nodded. "Life has a funny way of working out, doesn't it? You never know what adventure awaits. And now you know all about Seret the sheep; Wia the boat; Anu, the falcon-headed god; Meskhetyu, the foreleg—"

"About that," Clara interrupted. "Why would the Egyptians create a constellation that's just the foreleg of a bull? Why not call it something else, like a snake? Doesn't that make more sense?"

Anna shook her head, her red mane undulating in waves past her shoulders. "Who looks at stars and sees *anything* but pinpricks of light? There's no guessing what figure someone might imagine. You and I could create our own constellations and who would say we're wrong?" She raised her eyebrows. "In fact, maybe we should. I think the Snake is a wonderful constellation, don't you?"

She squinted at Clara's neck. "Hang on, you've made a mistake. Let me fix it." Before Clara could move, she unknotted the blue tie at Clara's throat, adjusting the length of the two ends and smoothing them out against Clara's chest. Then she stepped a half step closer, her hands moving carefully under Clara's chin as she tied a knot. She snugged it to Clara's collar and tucked the tail back inside her brown cable-knit sweater. She kept her hands on Clara's shoulders for a moment, still standing close. "There. You look very handsome."

Clara ducked her head to the side, her chin almost touching her chest. "Oh, no..."

Anna pulled her face back, thumb pressed against her chin, and smiled. Anna had a way of looking at someone as though they were the only person in the world, and she was doing it to Clara now. "No one's ever called you that before, have they? Has anyone told you you're beautiful? I mean, really told you that?"

"No. I'm not really—People don't tend to—"

Georgette leaned forward, curious about the conversation, but just then Eliza dropped heavily into the chair next to her. Georgette had been so absorbed by watching the other two women that she hadn't noticed Eliza's arrival onto the deck. She jumped in surprise, her knees slamming into the table, making the cups rattle against their saucers. She grimaced and rubbed them under the table.

"What is that woman doing?" Eliza asked.

Since she was looking at both Anna and Clara, Georgette didn't know which of the two women she meant.

"Clara has made a mistake with her *cravate*. Anna is fixing it for her."

"Mm-hmm, did she now? Clara seemed to have done just fine with ties every other day." Eliza leaned back against the bench seat and crossed her arms. In her khaki pants and blue sweater, she matched the colors of the landscape around them.

"Perhaps it is because she is tired she has made a mistake. You were also watching the stars last night and that is why you wake up late today?"

Eliza snorted. "Watching the stars, were they? No, I was sleeping. We don't all have to be up here with the birds every morning. Some of us could use a little beauty sleep every now and then."

"Ah, but there is so much to see, and our journey is so short." Georgette gestured at the river around them. A felucca sailed past, its lateen sail stretched taut by the wind. Its deck was stacked high with green stalks of sugarcane. She waved at the sailors on deck, and the men waved back.

Then she looked back at Anna and Clara. A warm sense of contentment suffused her. "Anna is being nice to Clara. She is making her feel good about herself by telling her she is beautiful. This is a nice thing, *non*?"

"Georgette!" Eliza's voice crackled with exasperation.

She blinked, surprised by the emotion in Eliza's voice. "What?"

Eliza glared at her. "Open your eyes, woman! Don't you remember us talking in Cairo about women loving other women? Don't you know what it looks like when someone is trying to woo someone else?"

Georgette turned over the idea in her head slowly. "You are thinking Anna is trying to be more than friends with Clara?"

"Yes!"

She peered more carefully at the two women. Clara was shrinking away from Anna, turning to watch the water. Anna's hand, meanwhile, was still resting on Clara's elbow. Georgette supposed Eliza could be right that they were engaged in a flirtation, but perhaps not. Who knew what went on between two people? Love, friendship, an affair, a night together…these things were all part of life in Paris. Why not here in Egypt too?

She shrugged. It was not her business, nor Eliza's either. "It may be. I do not know."

Eliza boggled at her. "Ain't you ever been wooed before?" There was no small amount of incredulity in her voice.

Georgette furrowed her eyebrows, insulted. "*Non.*" As she had already said in Cairo, she had neither time nor interest in romance. There was more to life than the pursuit of a mate. She crossed her arms, still scowling, and flicked an imaginary crumb from her floral print dress.

The moment between Anna and Clara, whether amicable or romantic, passed, and they joined Georgette and Eliza at the table. The tips of Clara's ears, Georgette noticed, were still pink. Ahmad stepped forward once more and poured tea carefully into the cups in front of Eliza and Clara. With his left hand, he set down a tray of rolls.

"Get that tie fixed?" Eliza asked.

Anna smiled at her. "Of course."

Eliza rolled her eyes. "What's your plan once we reach Luxor?"

Anna picked up one of the rolls and began to slather it with date preserves. "First, we'll check in at the Winter Palace Hotel and have lunch. They do the most wonderful marquise à la fraise. Then, in the afternoon, you'll visit the Luxor Temple while I meet with Ibrahim Effendi, the Luxor inspector for the Department of Antiquities. No tomb can be opened without a Department representative present, so he'll have to be informed of our plans. If Chief Inspector Engelbach is in Luxor, I'll discuss with him the transport of the tomb's contents back to Cairo, to the Museum."

A flicker of emotion crossed her face. "Carter's taken months so far to clear out even a fraction of Tutankhamun's tomb, but Dra' Abu el-Naga' is too exposed to leave anything in place. Once word gets out there's been a tomb found full of gold, the hills will be swarming with looters. We'll have to move fast."

Clara gasped, her right hand flying to the base of her throat. "No. Would someone really try to rob it? How could they?"

Anna, who had taken a bite of the roll, wiped her mouth with a napkin. "The list of who *wouldn't* try to rob it is shorter than the list of people who would. For starters, there are the local workers. I try my best to select good men, but Egypt is a poor country. Once the tomb is opened and they see exactly what's inside, it will be an exceedingly difficult temptation for them to resist." She frowned. "I can't say I blame them. I don't know what *I* would do if my family was on the brink of starvation and I found a tomb full of gold."

"But it's meant to go to a museum!"

Anna sighed heavily. "Of course, but that's never stopped anyone. What's worse, in the last century, more than a few archaeologists and scholars themselves have looted tombs and temples in order to sell what's inside to European collectors. When there wasn't anything they could carry away by hand, they even chiseled out parts of tomb walls and sold that. Of course, the Department has tried to stop this black market, but

things always get through. There's too much money to be made."
She shook her head and made a face. "In the end, *anyone* who
steps into Ahmose's tomb, from a reporter to an Egyptologist, is
liable to snatch the nearest statue lying around and stuff it down
his pants."

Georgette leaned forward, taking care to not knock over her
half-full teacup. This was an interesting conundrum, like trying
to fill a hole in a dam while water was already pouring through.
"What you will do to stop these thieves from stealing from your
tombeau?"

The archaeologist crossed her arms. "Try to outrun them.
Document as much as I can as quickly as I can and then try to
keep it all out of reach of their grasping fingers. With any luck,
people will be too distracted by the elections to take notice of
new activity in dusty Dra' Abu el-Naga'. And at least I won't
have to worry about tourists mucking things up. As soon as
can be arranged, we'll load it onto barges and sail it back down
the river. The press can take as many photos as they like once
everything is safely in Cairo, but until then, the tomb and its
contents must be closely guarded."

She took a deep breath and smiled at her guests. "But that's
all for me to work out. You, in the meantime, have only to see
and enjoy it all." She indicated the ship and its surroundings.
"And could anything be lovelier than this moment right here,
sailing along the Nile?"

Georgette wasn't ready to move on from this troubling
subject, however. "But nothing was stolen from *le tombeau* of
Tutankhamun, *non*? Maybe the robbers will not come."

"I hope so, but the valley is well guarded and has limited
access, while currently Dra' Abu el-Naga' is protected by an old
but kind gentleman and his equally hoary donkey. Anyone could
walk up and steal anything, and there's little the Department or
I can do about it. At least, not until the tomb is officially opened
and recognized." She gave a helpless shrug. "It's a shame, but
that's how it is. Although it would be better to examine the
contents of the tomb in place, I simply can't risk it."

Georgette fell silent, pondering this problem. She supposed
Anna must be right. It was a pity that the contents of the tomb

would have to be boxed up so quickly, but at least they would get to see it before that happened. The Lady Adventurers Club and no one else would have that signal honor.

CHAPTER NINE

Anna

December 9, 1923
Luxor, Egypt

Anna was waiting for the women when they returned from their visit to Luxor Temple. Her meeting with Inspector Ibrahim had gone flawlessly, and the matter of opening the tomb was all settled. He would accompany them to Dra' Abu el-Naga' the next morning and then, should the tomb prove to be all that Anna believed, the director general of the Department of Antiquities himself, Pierre Lacau, would come from Cairo and be there the next day to help arrange the transfer of its contents back to the capital. By this time in a few days, the first barges could be making their way back down the Nile to Cairo. Everything was running as smoothly as she could have possibly hoped.

She rose from her armchair and set down the paper she'd been reading when she saw her guests enter the lobby. "Well? How was it?"

"*Extraordinaire*," Georgette said. "The temple is so big. But so much sand. It is as though *le désert* has swallowed it." She was fanning herself with a blue fan she must have brought from Paris. It was hotter today than it had been all week. The cool mornings on the Nile had given way to the dry heat of Luxor. It would be even worse at Dra' Abu el-Naga'.

Eliza nodded. "I liked all the sphinxes."

She was referring to the Avenue of Sphinxes that once stretched three kilometers between the temples of Karnak and Luxor, the two holiest sites in all of ancient Egypt. Of the original thousand ram-headed sphinx statues, only a fraction remained. Now, to the chagrin of the archaeologists working to unearth the site, the local children liked to climb on them and ride them like ponies.

Anna clapped her hands together, pleased. "It's in ruins, I know, but you have to imagine what it would have looked like during the New Kingdom. *This* was where the pharaohs were crowned. It's the Westminster Abbey of old Egypt. Even Alexander the Great claimed to have been anointed there." Not that it had actually happened, of course. Alexander never went south of Cairo.

Eliza wiped the perspiration from her brow with the back of her hand. Sweat had beaded near her hairline next to her ears and soaked through her tan linen shirt a little at the stomach and arms. "Phew, it sure is hot today. I'm going to the room to change. You got a key?"

"I do." Anna produced it from the pocket of her brown trousers and held it out. "You and Georgette will be sharing suite 102. Clara will be with me in suite 103. You'll find your room on the second floor. I've already had your suitcases brought up. Take all the time you need. Dinner will be at eight."

Eliza's eyes traveled to Clara, and for a moment Anna thought she would object. But she only shrugged, then reached for the key.

"By the way, your room has two beds, so you and Georgette won't have to share. Unfortunately, it was the only suite for which that arrangement was possible."

Eliza fixed her with a stern stare, and the two faced each other down in a silent battle of wills. Then the other woman shook her head, her face puckering in disgust. "Awful coincidental isn't it, all these single beds? I don't know why you invited any of the rest of us here if all you were trying to do was get to that girl."

Anna was instantly on the defensive. Eliza couldn't have been more wrong about her motives. "It is my pleasure to have you *all* here. I want the Lady Adventurers Club to have meaning. How else can we be taken seriously as an association of distinguished women?"

Besides, since the rooftop in Cairo she'd been a total gentlewoman to Clara. Even Eliza couldn't accuse her of making overly aggressive advances. She had been a kind and caring friend. That was all.

Eliza grunted. "We'll see about that." She tucked the key into her pocket and marched the few steps to the stairs. The heels of her shoes clicked sharply against the lobby tile, which was decorated with row after row of dizzying green circles.

Georgette followed, giving the other two women a small wave as she departed. *"À tout à l'heure!"* The eternally optimistic woman hadn't even noticed the tension between her traveling companions.

The staircase to the rooms on the second floor wound, unusually, around the wall of the lobby like the inside of a nautilus shell. Anna watched her guests ascend, then turned back to Clara and smiled graciously. "Would you like to take tea on the veranda overlooking the Nile, or retire to our room?"

Clara took off her white hat and fanned herself with it. Her blond hair was damp; stray strands clung to her forehead. "I think I'd like to go upstairs, if that's all right. The sun was something fierce in the temple."

Anna tipped her head in polite assent. "Of course. I think you'll find the room quite comfortable." Comfortable and intimate. Anna thought it was time to be a *better* friend to her dear American guest.

Inside the suite, as Clara threw her hat on the bed, Anna sat down on the pale blue settee and poured herself a drink from the bottle she'd ordered brought to the room just for Clara. She took a sip, swallowing down the burning liquor and fighting the reflex to cough, then poured a second glass and held it up so her companion could see the caramel liquid inside. It was

Glenfiddich single malt. "I hope you like it. The hotel doesn't have anything else." Her voice had a slight rasp to it from the fire still lingering in her throat.

Clara crossed the room and took the glass from her. She tossed back the liquor inside with a single, smooth gesture. Anna stared, surprised. Whiskey neat in a single gulp? The blaze in her throat and stomach must have been fierce.

Clara saw her expression and winced. "Sorry. What with Prohibition, I haven't had much more than moonshine for years—other than that gin at your apartment, that is. It'll take paint off, so you have to drink it fast. I guess it's habit now."

Anna had forgotten about America's unusual experiment, which was now in its third year. She held her hand out and Clara returned to her the empty glass. She poured another splash of the whiskey. This time Clara took a small sip, then cradled the glass in her hands. Anna leaned back, propping her boots on the table and draping her arms over the back of the settee comfortably.

"You weren't too hot today, were you?" she asked. It was an unseasonably warm winter, even by Egyptian standards.

"No, it's not so bad here. I don't mind it, really."

"Good. Tomorrow it will be even warmer. But don't worry, if you feel overheated, you can come back here to the hotel. We'll have a car and driver."

"I suppose you'll be busy for a long time once the tomb is opened, what with all the work to be done." It was both a statement and a question.

Anna made a dismissive gesture. "I won't be doing it all on my own. Finds like this quickly belong to the world, not a single archaeologist. Besides, my expertise is in the excavation and preservation of artifacts. Once everything is back in Cairo, it will be mostly out of my hands."

Clara looked into the bottom of her glass. "Must be nice to have so much to do. I mean, to be that important and all."

Anna cocked her head. "I suppose so. I hadn't thought of it like that." What was important was what was inside the tomb. But yes, she supposed she would suddenly become key to its exploitation. God knows she might even have to host a luncheon or two. She took a sip. "What about you? What will you do when you go back to America?"

It was a return to the subject they had discussed on the rooftop of her apartment in Cairo and intermittently during the trip up the Nile: what does a trick shooter from a Wild West show do once there are no more Wild West shows? Since L. O. Hillman's had shut down in 1920, Clara had worked odd jobs without having settled on a permanent new direction. She was a cowgirl in a world that no longer wanted cowgirls; a modern world of flappers, jazz, and speakeasies.

Clara's lips pressed together into a thin line. The sadness that came sometimes when she discussed her life returned, dying her soft brown eyes a darker shade. "I don't know. I'll find something." Her listless tone suggested she wasn't confident of her claim.

After a moment's silent reflection, she sighed heavily and ran her finger along the rim of the glass. "You live your life one way for so many years, it's hard to think about doing things any other way. I feel like an old dog who's too old to learn new tricks. I've been doing things here and there but…I feel like I've just been waiting for someone to tell me what to do next." She walked to the window and set her glass down on the wide ledge of the windowsill. She leaned against the wood, staring out the window at the Nile flowing past the hotel as though she could see beyond it and into the future.

Anna admired her profile. Beauty wasn't only the symmetry of a person's face or the shape of their lips. It was the quiet resolve that powered them, the strength they didn't know they carried. Anna had recognized it in Clara the day they'd met. All it would take was for her to realize it too.

Anna rose and joined her, shadowing behind her body the same way she had in Cairo. But this time, she wasn't reaching for Clara's gun. "You could stay here with me in Egypt." Her mouth was close to Clara's ear, close enough she could feel Clara's blond hair tickling her lips. She put her hands gently on top of Clara's where they rested on the sill. With her chest lightly pressing against Clara's back, she could feel the sharp breath Clara took and the way her body stiffened.

"What are you doing?"

"You know what I'm doing. We're not children, Clara."

She wanted to nuzzle Clara's neck, to nibble her earlobe, but she couldn't yet. She had to know it was what Clara wanted first. Although unlikely, there was always the possibility she had misread Clara. She took a single step back to allow Clara to turn and face her. It didn't leave much space, only a few handbreadths.

Clara swallowed hard. Her eyes, wide and anxious, darted over Anna's face and around the room, as though trying to find somewhere to look that wasn't Anna's eyes. Eyes, after all, were the window to the soul, but in this case, they were a mirror too.

"No, I don't…"

Anna would never do what she was doing if she wasn't certain that, whether Clara could immediately admit it to herself or not, there was a chemistry between them. She had felt it ever since Cairo, and on their nights stargazing. Even listening to Georgette prattle on about Paris, when their eyes met across the table. It was just a question of bringing Clara to see it too. And of Clara allowing herself to embrace the feeling.

She reached out to cup Clara's cheek with her right hand, pulling Clara's eyes back to her. "Do you remember what I said in Cairo? How it's possible for two women to fall in love?"

"Yes." The word came out breathlessly. Clara's face had turned pale. But she didn't move away, and she didn't ask Anna to move.

"Do you think *you* could love another woman?"

Anna traced the line of Clara's jaw to her chin, stopping with her thumb just under Clara's lower lip. Her lips were what were called a Cupid's bow: full on the bottom and curved like a bow on top. Clara's body responded automatically to this intimacy. Her breathing turned labored, her chest rising and falling too fast. She licked her lips. "I—I don't know—"

If she hadn't thought about it before, she was thinking about it now. Anna moved her left hand to Clara's right hip, pulling just enough to catch Clara's attention. "If you tell me, I'll stop."

And she would. All Clara had to say was no. But she hoped Clara wouldn't. The air between them crackled with electricity.

It danced along her skin, making every nerve fire. She couldn't imagine Clara didn't feel it too.

"I—I've never—"

Kissed another woman? Certainly. Kissed another person? Possibly. Anna didn't mind, in any case. This was a dance she could easily lead. She was experienced, confident. She brushed her right hand behind Clara's ear, her fingers gently wrapping around the back of Clara's head. "I won't hurt you."

Her body was a meteor shower of sensation. The quickening of her pulse was causing her head to ring. Her breath was short and shallow. She slowly leaned forward, giving Clara time to react.

Clara drew her hands up, putting them against Anna's chest, stopping her. "Why *me*?" she asked, panicked. "Why would you want *me*? I'm…not like you."

Anna raised an eyebrow. "Like me?"

"You're so elegant and intelligent and accomplished. I'm… well, I'm just *me*."

"And?" She took Clara's left hand and kissed the knuckles. "You're brave and gentle and beautiful, isn't that enough?"

Clara didn't answer, but she didn't pull away.

"You're a very attractive woman, Clara, in all senses of the word. I wouldn't say it if I didn't believe it." Anna leaned forward to place a gentle kiss below her ear on her neck, moving slowly so that Clara could stop her if she didn't want it. Their bodies were lightly touching now, and Anna felt the slight buck into her as Clara's body responded to the kiss. Clara breathed in sharply, perhaps an involuntary gasp. Anna's own body shivered in response.

Still, a reaction was just that. Clara had not yet confirmed this was what she wanted. Anna leaned back. "Do you want me to stop?"

Clara's eyes were still wide, but now slightly dazed and unfocused. She swallowed. "No." It was a small, short word, said so quietly it was barely a whisper, but she'd said it.

A pulse of excitement and anticipation raced through Anna, although she knew she still had to tread carefully. She closed her hand more firmly around the back of Clara's head and pulled her into a gentle kiss. Clara absorbed it willingly, although her body was still tense. Anna drew her closer with her left hand, nesting their bodies together from their hips to their chests. Any closer and they would be able to feel each other's hearts beat.

After what could have been seconds or minutes, Clara's hands came to rest on her hips and her body slackened slightly. The contact set Anna's body on fire. She had to force herself to slow her breathing. It had been years since she'd held a woman like this. Like the first rain after a long drought, her body was coming back to life, remembering all the things it had missed. Still, she had to take care of Clara. This was new for her.

She leaned back slightly once more, dropping her hand to Clara's collar, and watched Clara's face intently. "Do you want me to continue?"

Clara's fingers twitched against her hips. A wave of worry crossed her flushed face. "You're sure it's not wrong?" Despite her trepidation, there was a breathless shine to her eyes.

"Not if it's what you want. Do you want me to go on?"

Clara hesitated. Her eyes dropped, fearful. "I don't know how—"

Anna understood. She had felt that way once too. But the only way to learn how to swim was to get in the water. "You're doing just fine."

She kissed Clara again, this time moving her left hand up Clara's side and to her chest. She passed it over Clara's right breast and felt the immediate arching of Clara's body into her hand. She gave a gentle squeeze, feeling Clara's mouth still as her focus was redirected. Then she moved her right hand to Clara's hip, opening space for her to drop her head to Clara's jawline and run a series of kisses down her neck. Clara lifted her chin and tilted her head backward, lengthening her neck. She gave a small shudder as Anna reached her collarbone.

Anna had to remind herself at every moment to not move too quickly or forcefully, no matter how hard it was not to. Clara was not someone who knew exactly how to touch and be touched by another woman. Still, arousal was like an opium addiction, and it was hard to keep control of herself. She wanted to play her hands over Clara's body the way a potter does clay on a wheel. She wanted to see what places would make her sigh and writhe. She wanted Clara's hands all over her just as much as she wanted to be touching Clara. Most of all, she wanted to throw Clara on the bed, to lose herself in the exploration of Clara's sensitive skin.

She ran her fingertips over the fabric of Clara's shirt, excited by the promise of what lay beneath it. She returned to kissing Clara's lips, saving that particular delight for later. Clara moved her hands to Anna's shoulders, then interlaced her fingers behind Anna's neck. Kissing, Anna thought, was like riding a bicycle. It didn't matter what kind of bicycle it was; the mechanics were the same. And Clara was doing just fine without ever having kissed a woman before.

Just then, a knock came at the door. The two women froze. When it came again, Anna pulled away, frowning. She wasn't expecting room service. She just had time to turn around before the door swung open without invitation, revealing Georgette.

"Georgette!" Anna barked, irritated.

Although it was universally inexcusable to open a door without express permission, Georgette showed no sign she knew what she'd done was wrong. At least she hadn't noticed what she'd walked in on. "I came to tell you Eliza and I will be having tea outside, if you would like to join us. *Aussi*, there is this *carte* at your door." She held up a small, perfectly square white envelope.

Anna bit back an angry growl. "Put it down and I'll read it later."

Georgette walked into the room and put the letter on the coffee table. "There. Will you be coming to tea?"

"No," Anna said.

At the same time, Clara exclaimed, "Yes!"

Anna looked at her, surprised and dismayed by the response. She had hoped they could continue once Georgette was gone. She smiled weakly at their companion. "Maybe."

Georgette shrugged, unconcerned. "Okay, if we do not see you, *à ce soir*." She breezed out of the suite as quickly as she'd come, closing the door behind her as she left.

Anna spun back to Clara. No, no, no, this wasn't fair—they'd only just started! She didn't want to stop now, not when they were alone for the first time and had hours yet until dinner. There was no telling when they might have an opportunity like this again.

"We should join them," Clara said. She didn't meet Anna's eyes. In fact, her entire body was shrinking away from her, trying to collapse into itself.

Anna's stomach lurched. Was Clara having second thoughts? She tried to smile encouragingly. "We don't have to. We can stay here. They'll be fine by themselves. We can just talk if you like…"

But it was too late. The intimacy of only a minute before had been broken, replaced by ungainly awkwardness that settled between them like a fat, ugly toad. Anna curled the fingers of her left hand into her palm, feeling the bite of her nails digging in. If Clara was spooked enough, she might not let Anna get close again. Damn Georgette for coming at just the wrong moment. Next time she would lock the door.

Clara shook her head. "No, I think it's better we go."

Anna stepped back, giving Clara space. "Is it all right? Have I done something I shouldn't?"

"No, of course not." But Clara didn't seem entirely convinced. Her weak smile was little more than a reflexive flicker of empty politeness. "I'm going to go." Stepping around Anna, she darted for the door. She disappeared through it without a glance back and was gone, leaving Anna alone in the room. It was Cairo all over again.

Anna sat down on the settee and poured herself another drink. This was not how she'd hoped the afternoon would go. But it was progress. Clara would come around. She had been unnerved by Georgette's appearance, but she would recover. She just needed time. Perhaps after dinner they could discuss things.

When she raised her head, she noticed the letter Georgette had left, lying on the coffee table. She stood and retrieved it, turning it over in her hand. Her name was written in black ink on its face. She didn't recognize the handwriting. She pulled out the card inside. It read simply:

Miss Anna Cromer
You should talk to Sharif at the docks about the shipments from the tomb.

She threw the card back down on the table. It was an inelegant and hastily scrawled message from Inspector Ibrahim. He must have had someone else write it, given he, himself, had beautiful writing and always called her Lady Baring. But if this Sharif was the fellow to talk to about shipping the contents of Ahmose's tomb to Cairo, Inspector Ibrahim might as well speak to the man himself, since she would be busy all the next day at Dra' Abu el-Naga' and wouldn't have time.

She stood and caught sight of herself in the mirror above the mantel. Her hair was just tousled enough to be noticeable, but she decided not to fix it. Let it look unkempt. She adjusted the collar of her loose white shirt, opening it a little further at the chest and letting her hair cascade down around it. It was an invitation. She hoped Clara would choose to take her up on it later.

When she joined them, Eliza, Georgette, and Clara were watching the feluccas and barges sail past the veranda. Clara didn't look at her as she sat down. Anna hated to admit it stung a little. She had hoped for at least a glance.

She squinted at a small gaggle of tourists gathered near the bank of the river across from the hotel. Based on the sharp, dramatic movements of the men, they appeared to be arguing with a local in a brown gallabiyah and a white turban. She pointed to them. "What's going on there?"

Eliza indicated the Egyptian. "He was trying to sell antiques up here on the veranda 'til the waiters chased him off. Said he had pottery and gold from some new tomb. After he left, the Swedish family staying here went to see what he was selling."

Anna scoffed. "If it's not selling mummies, it's 'gold' from some secret tomb no one else knows about. The Egyptians have been running the same con against visitors since the Greeks, and just as successfully. It's only gotten worse since Tutankhamun's tomb was opened last year. If there were that many 'secret tombs,' there'd be no gold left in all of Egypt. Not to mention this absurd business of selling curses."

As soon as the words were out of her mouth, she frowned to herself. Actually, there *wasn't* much gold left; only what remained in Tutankhamun's tomb and whatever they would find tomorrow in Ahmose's tomb. The rest of it really had been stolen or sold off to foreigners over the centuries. It was no wonder Egypt was now such a poor country.

Eliza looked at the scene with renewed curiosity. "What's he got then?"

She shrugged. "It could be anything. At best, it's low-karat gold he's scraped together from something else. And as to the pottery, anyone can make a vase and pretend it comes from the New Kingdom. Tourists aren't archaeologists. They'll never know the difference. You can make anything *look* old, really."

The Swedes crossed the street back to the hotel, chattering excitedly to each other and smiling in satisfaction. She groaned. "I hope they haven't paid much for whatever they've bought."

"If it's fake, why don't the police stop it?" Clara asked.

Anna was relieved Clara was at least speaking to her. She sighed, watching the Egyptian head off to another hotel and more tourists to swindle. "There's no use. For one thing, it's almost never reported by the tourists. They think they've got the real stuff in their hands. If they do realize what's happened, they're too ashamed to tell anyone. But even if they do tell the police, the swindlers can almost always bribe them to look the other way."

She poured herself a cup of tea and added two sugars. "The legal system won't do anything to them anyway, not for a few pounds swindled here and there from people who have more money than the average Egyptian would make in ten lifetimes. So it becomes a sort of donation to the local economy. If tourists are rich enough to come here, they're rich enough to lose some money on a piece of colored glass masquerading as a gemstone." A European would be appalled by that logic, but she, herself, had come to embrace it. It was only fair, in its own way.

She smiled so broadly her cheeks pinched. "But enough about counterfeits. Tomorrow you'll see the real thing. I absolutely cannot wait." Finally, she would be the first to see a pharaoh's treasure. No Carter monopolizing the view, this time, *she* would be the one peering through the hole in the wall. No one could take that away from her.

CHAPTER TEN

Clara

December 10, 1923

Clara had folded herself into the settee to sleep, a thin yellow blanket wrapped tightly around her. She was wearing all of her clothing, even her boots, as though it were a suit of armor. Even though the night—technically morning, since it was well past midnight—was hot and the settee was so short it made her legs cramp, she refused to even consider sharing the bed with Anna. Now, wide awake, she watched the dark lump on the bed where the archaeologist lay motionless. And worried.

What had happened the day before had been... Clara was still trying to process it. She hadn't expected it, although now she realized she should have. The moment on the rooftop in Cairo, Anna's quick touches and flirtations on the *Nitocris*—they formed a trail of breadcrumbs to this very moment. Had she known, consciously or subconsciously, where things had been headed? Had she allowed it...or even encouraged it?

"Do you think you could love another woman?"

It was a question she'd never asked herself. Hadn't thought she would ever be in the position to ask. Yet suddenly the answer was vitally important, and she didn't know it. There had been a girl once, with long hair like wheat and freckles splashed across her nose. With cheeks like sesame seeds, whose laugh turned the world four shades brighter and made the days longer. And then a woman with twinkling eyes whose charming smile made time stand still. As the minute hand of the clock marched on interminably, the line between admiration and longing seemed much fuzzier than it ever had before. What had she really felt for those others?

Perhaps, she realized with nervous trepidation, over the years she *had* felt emotions for some women that might be interpreted as romantic. Perhaps she had even…been in love with them. The discovery of this alternate version of events was overwhelming, but as it was in the past, she could ignore it if she wanted. What she could not ignore was the woman in the bed in front of her. Without wanting to, she remembered the feeling of Anna's soft lips against hers, Anna's hands against her body. A jolt of electricity ran beneath her skin. This was not the past. This was here and now.

She rolled toward the back of the settee, burrowing her face into the blue velvet. Her past, her future, her identity—all these things were in question. What kind of a woman fell in love with other women? It might be fine for a Parisian woman or for Anna, who seemed to live by her own rules here in Egypt, but not someone from Grundy County. If she was the kind of woman who kissed other women, there was no place for her in Grundy County. Maybe not even in all of America.

She squeezed her eyes together tighter, anguished. But were her feelings for Anna love? Was this what love was? Breathless anticipation and debilitating dread? Waiting to be seen and at the same time fearing it?

Restless and overwhelmed, she tossed the blanket to the floor and rose from the settee, tiptoeing across the room to the window. She opened it as quietly as she could and took a deep breath of the cool night air. Above her, the moon was bright and full. After a moment's searching, she found Meskhetyu, the bull leg constellation. In a flash, she was lying next to Anna on the

Nitocris, the canvas shade rolled back so they could stare at the thousands of stars above.

She saw it all in a new light now. Even if she hadn't admitted it to herself, from the moment Anna had asked her to teach her how to shoot, she had felt a pull toward her—a strange and unfamiliar gravity from which she couldn't escape. Anna was like no one she had ever met. She was passionate but refined, educated, and ambitious. She was everything Clara wasn't. It had made sense that Clara would be spellbound by her. Only, she hadn't anticipated that her admiration would turn to… something else.

She turned back to face the room. Her eyes were drawn to Anna's sleeping figure, and she stared, terrified. She had never been so frightened of anyone in her life. Giving in to Anna's magnetism, allowing what happened yesterday to happen again would mean opening a box whose contents she wasn't sure she wanted to see, contents that would surely lead to misery. The only solution was to keep away from the beautiful archaeologist. And as for the breathlessness she felt around her, the helpless pull of attraction, well, she would just have to stuff that all down and ignore it. She might be a woman who loved other women, but that didn't mean she had to *act* on it.

* * *

When dawn finally broke, the sun peeking over the horizon, Clara rose and changed modestly in the bathroom. When she emerged, Anna was rolled over to face the door to the hall. Clara's stride caught and she found herself staring. There was something unique about Anna. It was as though the sun was always shining on her, or as though *she* were the sun and everyone else was a planet in her orbit. Or perhaps it was just her, Clara, trapped in that orbit. The worst part was that deep down, she wasn't sure she wanted to escape it.

It took all the strength she had to keep walking, to not kneel beside Anna's sleeping figure and caress the beautiful lines of her cheek. Clara couldn't explain it. It was as though she'd been bewitched. Three weeks ago, she would never have thought twice about caressing another woman. Now she had to fight the urge.

Taking a breath, she compelled her feet to carry her first out of the room and then out of the hotel entirely. She had intended to take a walk along the Nile, but as she crossed the street in front of the hotel, she was surprised to see Georgette sitting on the bank, her knees to her chest and her arms wrapped around them. A small green hat that matched her dress was angled above her bun, too small to provide actual protection from the sun but perfectly stylish.

"I didn't expect to find anyone out here so early," Clara said, making the decision to abandon her walk and join her.

"Ah, *oui*. I have been watching the ships." Georgette indicated the river. Three passenger steamers were tied to the bank to the right of where the women were sitting. To their left, a felucca bobbed at the end of a long, frayed rope.

"Does it remind you of home?"

She nodded. "A little. Sometimes I walk along *la Seine* when I am going home from the school. It is very nice." She looked over her shoulder at a camel ambling past them, two women draped in black and a child on its back, and made a face. "There are no camels there." Her words dripped with disdain.

Clara experienced an unexpected pang of nostalgia. The land around the Nile was nothing like home for her. She missed the miles of forests and the quiet chirping of insects at night. She missed babbling brooks and fields of corn. She even missed the rowdy celebrations with hooch in barns after rodeos. But then, all those things were disappearing. The cities were starting to carve deep hollows into the beauty of the land, filling it with cars and concrete and buildings and restaurants. The things she knew and loved wouldn't be there forever.

She asked, "Do you miss home?"

Clara realized there was much she didn't know about Georgette. She didn't talk about herself much, although she talked enough about other things.

Georgette looked wistful. "*Oui*. Always when I am not at home I miss home. And I have been away for many months." She brightened. "But it is worth it to be here, *non*? Today we will see *le tombeau* of *le Pharaon* Ahmose. Who would have thought when we met in New York that we would one day be here to see such a thing?"

She looked down and wound her fingers together uncomfortably, seeming to struggle with what she wanted to say next. After a moment, she said, "And also...it has been nice to spend time with you all. I did not think it would be so nice." She gave a small, uncertain smile. "We are...friends...*non?*"

Clara hadn't thought about it, but she supposed they must be. After weeks together on various boats, she knew more about Eliza and, to a much lesser extent, Georgette than she knew about some people she'd been around almost her whole life. She knew, for example, that Eliza had once been a journalist for *The Chicago Conservator* and that her mother had been a maid while her father had been a railcar porter. And she knew that Georgette hated any kind of disorder and could count cards. The idea of friendship seemed important to Georgette, so she smiled back. "Sure we are."

Georgette nodded, more to herself than to Clara. "*Oui*, I thought so." She relaxed her fingers so that her palms rested on her knees. "It is not *la Société Mathématique de France*, but it is still nice to be part of this *club*. Maybe, I don't know, one day we can go someplace else. We must have more than one adventure to be 'lady adventurers,' *non?*"

Clara took a sharp breath. Go someplace else with Anna? How could she spend any more time with her? She bit a fingernail and worried it between her teeth, trying to calm the racing of her heart. Seeing Georgette scrutinizing her closely, however, she gave a weak, noncommittal nod. "Perhaps."

Georgette bobbed her head "I would like that."

They fell into easy silence, Clara thinking about *not* thinking about Anna, and Georgette thinking about who knew what. Half an hour later, having watched a dozen or more boats sail past, they made their way back to the hotel and into the dining room for breakfast. Eliza arrived just as the tea did, and Anna followed a few minutes later, sweeping into the room with the chaotic energy of a summer storm. Clara dropped her eyes, ashamed at how seeing her immediately reminded her of the feeling of

Anna's body pressed to hers and Anna's hot breath on her neck. With a stirring of despair, she wondered how she would ever *not* think of that when she looked at her.

But if Anna, too, was thinking about what had happened between them, she gave no sign of it. Instead, she was energized by what lay ahead of them, her face glowing with excitement.

"It's impossible to know exactly what Ahmose's tomb will look like once we've broken through the door," she said, buttering a slice of toast with gusto. "But the tomb of Thutmose III, who ruled soon after him, has multiple corridors and chambers, so I expect Ahmose's tomb will have a similar design." She set the bread down and rubbed her hands together gleefully. "It could be a hundred meters long and filled absolutely floor to ceiling with gold and jewels." She waved the knife. "Well, and the usual funerary items."

Eliza raised an eyebrow. "You sound like one of those treasure hunters you hate."

Georgette nodded in agreement, mouth full.

Anna snorted, dismissing the comparison. "Nonsense. What's in that tomb belongs to the Egyptian people. I wouldn't dream of taking a pound."

"You sure history is all it's about?"

She grinned. "All right, I shan't deny I'd love to see Carter's face when he hears what I've found. You know, he dug for a few years in Dra' Abu el-Naga'. He'll be sick with jealousy to have missed the tomb."

A tall man wearing a black three-piece suit and a fez walked into the half-empty dining room and looked around. His mustache had been twisted and curled up at the ends in what Clara had learned was the Ottoman style, giving him a refined but distinctly Turkish look. He spotted the women and cut across the room to reach them.

Anna smiled brightly at him. "Good morning, Inspector Ibrahim. Won't you join us?" She motioned to the table, although there wasn't actually room for a fifth guest.

The inspector gave a polite half-bow. "*Sabah el-khayr*, Lady Baring. I have brought two cars to take us to Dra' Abu el-Naga'. They are waiting outside."

She nodded. "Wonderful. I've sent word to Ali to meet us at the tomb with a mallet and chisels."

He bowed again. "*Inshallah*, the tomb will not be flooded. Please, enjoy your breakfast. I will be waiting with the cars when you are finished."

At the last minute, she put out her hand to stay him. "Oh, Inspector, one more thing: I won't have time to speak to this Sharif fellow today. Couldn't you speak to him yourself about the shipments? After all, as you well know, everything in that tomb will belong to the Department once we've opened it."

The inspector's black eyebrows pulled together into a thick, single line. "Sharif?"

"In your note from last night, you said I should speak to a Sharif at the docks about shipping the artifacts from the tomb down to Cairo."

He shook his head, making the black tassel on the fez dance. "I'm afraid I do not know to what note you are referring, Lady Baring. Perhaps it was sent by someone else?"

Anna frowned. "Well, I had assumed it came from you, but I suppose not. Perhaps a friend of Ali, seeking to be helpful." She shrugged. "No matter." She tipped her teacup toward him in acknowledgement. "We'll be down shortly. Then onwards to the tomb!"

* * *

Dra' Abu el-Naga', Egypt

Clara had vastly mis-imagined what Dra' Abu el-Naga' would look like. She had envisioned soaring cliffs overlooking a deep crevasse in which Ahmose's tomb was carefully camouflaged from would-be thieves by limestone walls. She had anticipated a hauntingly beautiful landscape fit to be the final resting place of a great pharaoh. Instead, the necropolis of Dra' Abu el-Naga' was an unremarkable outcropping of rough brown rocks and beige sand. It was clear how the tomb had survived this long:

no one would look twice at the low cliff and its underwhelming landscape.

The car in which she, Anna, and Eliza were riding pulled to a halt at the edge of the dirt road. Eliza pressed her nose to the window, staring out at the bleak, unappealing landscape. "It sure ain't much to look at, is it?"

"No," Anna agreed, voice tight with excitement. "And yet it was hallowed ground for the ancient Egyptians. If you look across the Nile there, you can see Karnak Temple, the holiest site in all of Egypt." She craned her neck, searching for something. "Where is Hussein? It's unlike him not to come meet me."

"Hussein?" Eliza echoed.

"He's my guard. Well, of a kind. He's older than Methuselah, but he keeps an eye on the site when I'm away. He must be napping on his donkey somewhere." She chuckled. "It's a good thing all he has to chase away are goats. He's hardly a Yeoman of the Guard. And that donkey may be older than he is."

She stepped out of the car and looked around, her green eyes sparkling. Her pride in this site, in the discovery she had made and was about to reveal, was palpable. Clara, in turn, was proud for her. Anna had done the almost impossible, and she had done it all on her own, through hard work and determination. Now she was about to reap the fruits of that effort, and Clara was honored to be part of that…regardless of everything else she felt about her.

As if from thin air, a man materialized at Anna's side, a large wooden mallet balanced over his shoulder and a frayed brown bag slung under his other arm. Anna clapped him heartily on the shoulder. "Ali, it's good to see you. How is your family?"

"*Alhamdulillah*, they are well, Miss Anna." His white robe hung from his tall, thin frame like a sheet draped over a scarecrow. When he smiled, it revealed a missing left incisor. "They thank you for your generosity, and wish you health for the new year."

Anna explained to her companions, "This is my foreman, Ali. There's not a better man in all of Egypt. Nor one who knows more about the tombs here on the west bank."

He bowed, accepting the compliment. "How was Cairo?"

She made a face. "The usual mess. I'll be glad to be well away from it come election time. That reminds me: have you heard anything about weapons being shipped down the Nile?"

Ali's eyebrows rose. "Weapons? No. Do you want Ali to ask the workers? It is possible someone may have heard of this."

She shook her head. "No. If there's going to be trouble, there's no use getting into the crosshairs. We had trouble enough in Cairo. We've got to keep our heads low and keep working." She reached for the mallet and took it from him, hefting it easily over her own shoulder although it must have been heavy. The shaft left a streak of ecru dust against her white linen shirt. She thrust her chin in the direction of the sloping cliff face. "Come on, let's go make history, shall we?"

Clara had won many shooting contests in her life. She knew the thrill of achievement and the roar of a crowd. But she couldn't imagine what Anna was feeling as they prepared to open the tomb. Anyone could shoot a gun, with practice. What Anna had done, almost no one else had. Clara had made national news as a sharpshooter; Anna's name would be splashed across the front page of newspapers around the world. Her discovery would rewrite history. There was no comparison.

The six of them marched up a narrow path that was little more than a goat trail, Anna in the lead with Eliza, Clara, and Georgette behind her. Inspector Ibrahim and Ali brought up the rear. The ground was rough and devoid of vegetation, not unlike the deserts of the southwestern United States. Clara wondered how Anna could have found *anything* here other than rocks. To her eyes, it looked like a regular old mountain.

They hadn't gone more than a few hundred yards before Anna stopped dead in her tracks.

"It is here?" Georgette asked, looking around curiously.

Clara peered ahead, trying to see what Anna was seeing. Just visible over a natural rise in the landscape above them was the top of a limestone doorframe. Inside was darkness too black to see through.

"Ali..." Anna's pinched voice was full of dread. It made the hair on Clara's arms stand up. Something was wrong. "Did you open the tomb while I was away?"

"No, Miss Anna, of course not. Ali has been in Qena with family for one month. This is the first day Ali is here in Luxor." His voice was indignant. Still several steps behind the women, he hadn't yet seen what Anna had.

She proceeded slowly toward the hole in the cliff. Her steps, so confident and eager a moment ago, were jerky and unwilling, as though she were walking to the gallows. Clara and Eliza exchanged glances as they followed, sensing the pall. The pit of Clara's stomach gurgled unhappily.

Clara remembered Anna had said they would have to break down a wall in order to access the interior of the tomb. This wall was what had protected the tomb from thieves for millennia, and how she had known the tomb was still intact. But when they reached the tomb, there was no wall. Instead, a gaping void awaited them, the rock face around it chiseled away savagely. Footprints were imprinted into the dust in front of the entry, too many to count, and there was an unmistakable impression of wagon wheels. Clara's hands went to her mouth, her jaw slack behind them. Oh no.

Anna stopped in front of the open tomb and dropped the mallet as though it weighed a thousand pounds. Her knees buckling, she sagged against the tomb's frame. Her shoulders hiccupped as she swallowed a sob.

"*Euuuh*, the door is supposed to be open like this?" Georgette asked, looking confused.

Eliza glared at her. "Quiet," she hissed.

Clara felt lightheaded. She couldn't believe what was happening. Poor Anna.

"How?" Anna asked, looking to Ali, who was now seeing the damage. Her eyes were vacant with loss. "How could someone have found out?"

Ali had no answer. His own face was full of horror. Beside him, Inspector Ibrahim looked green. Anna stumbled like a sleepwalker through the open tomb mouth, at the last minute detaching the flashlight she'd hung at her waist so she could see what lay before her. The pale light swept over bare, perfectly straight limestone walls that angled into the heart of the cliff.

Clara exchanged another glance with Eliza, full of pity for the archaeologist. It wasn't supposed to be like this. Their entry into the tomb was supposed to be a celebratory moment. Instead, it felt like a funeral.

Eliza grudgingly brandished her flashlight. "Come on, let's see what they left."

The group advanced slowly in the tomb, their flashlights casting the only light in the dark cavern. The tall, wide corridor sloped for approximately twenty yards until it met a short flight of stairs. At its base was a second, shorter corridor. Every step deeper into the tomb filled Clara with dread. By the time they reached the end of the second corridor, their footsteps muffled against the sandy floor, the weight on her shoulders was as heavy as the rock above them. The way Anna was staggering in front of her, she clearly felt the same. And still, all they could do was press forward toward heartbreak.

Clara followed Anna closely, endeavoring to stay near her. The darkness in the tomb was blacker than any night. It felt like they were walking into the underworld. The tomb turned sharply to the left, and the beam of Anna's flashlight seemed to flicker for a moment, searching for a focal point.

What it found was a room in anarchic disarray.

Anna froze, the light jumping as her hand shook. Anna had promised Ahmose's tomb would be full of gold, jewelry, and the full wealth of Egypt's god-kings. If any of it was still here, it was buried under waist-high piles of shattered clay pots and smashed wooden chests. The room looked like a tornado had ripped through it. Trampled baskets of barley and shriveled fruits littered the ground. Bundles of dried wheat had been kicked open and spread over decaying cloth. The scale of the ruin was breathtaking, and that was even with most of the room hidden by the darkness.

"Oh no." Inspector Ibrahim moaned behind them. The beam of his flashlight traveled over a cluster of stone jars and settled on a scattered collection of white figurines that had spilled out of a chest. "The devastation! This is terrible. Terrible!"

Seconds passed like hours as six narrow yellow lights flickered around the room, taking in the full extent of the destruction. Then Anna's light found a hole in the floor. Immediately, she pushed toward it, stepping nimbly over a collection of oars and all but running through a minefield of potsherds. Her movement was frantic, desperate.

The hole contained a second flight of stairs steeper than the first. She disappeared into it. Clara was right behind her.

Clara may have known nothing about Egyptian tombs, but she knew a coffin when she saw one. In the middle of the room at the base of the stairs—the only thing in it, in fact—was a massive stone sarcophagus. Beside it lay the lid, broken in half. It would have taken an unimaginable amount of leverage to move the heavy red granite. Someone had desperately wanted what had been inside.

Anna walked to the sarcophagus with stiff legs and looked in. Her shoulders heaved, and for a moment Clara thought she might vomit. Clara hastened to join her, knowing what she would see but dreading it nonetheless. The sarcophagus was empty. The thieves had been so thorough they'd even taken the mummy of the king himself.

Anna's legs buckled and she collapsed. Clara caught her just in time, holding her up by the shoulder and taking the brunt of her weight so she didn't crumple to the floor. She guided Anna to sit on the edge of the sarcophagus.

"It's all gone," Anna whispered. Her voice was so small, so frail. "All of it."

"It's not *all* gone. There was so much upstairs." Clara didn't know what else to say. It was hard to find anything positive in such a devastating situation.

Anna's fingers gripped her arms with desperate emotion. She was breathing heavily. "This is the burial chamber. This is where all the gold should be. There should be canopic jars here…and shabti boxes…There should be—" She squeezed her eyes closed. Her head dropped in defeat. "They've taken *everything*."

"Didn't you say there should be several rooms here? We could look. Maybe the thieves didn't know…" Clara shone her flashlight around, trying to find *something* to give Anna hope, but the light showed a space so bare it might as well have been swept clean.

"It's all gone," Anna repeated. Her voice was flat and lifeless.

The burial chamber had been picked clean as the carcass of a cow in a field. All hope for claiming the find of the millennium was gone. Clara's heart ached for the archaeologist. It was a terrible, unfair catastrophe.

Eliza, who had followed them into the burial chamber, put her hands on her hips. In the dim light, shadows made her look twice as large as she was, a giant from the netherworld. "Then we gotta go get it back."

"What?"

Although it was Anna who had spoken, Clara was just as confused. The two of them gaped at Eliza. She stared back unblinkingly. "Thieves took your gold. So we go get it back from them."

CHAPTER ELEVEN

Georgette

A beat passed as the women in the room grappled with Eliza's pronouncement. Georgette, who had been descending the stairs, was so surprised she paused midway.

"It's no use. It could have been taken any time. It could be halfway around the world by now." Georgette only knew Anna was shaking her head because of how her flashlight's beam danced against the wall. "There's no way to get it back. We're too late."

As she reached the ground, Georgette's mind set into motion like the gears of a clock, ticking with methodical, inexorable precision. The robbery was a puzzle, and without being consciously aware of it, she had been collecting pieces of that puzzle ever since they entered the tomb. Now she laid them out to examine them. The smudged but still evident footprints in the sand at the entry. Anna's short absence from Luxor. The completely empty burial chamber and opened sarcophagus. The fact that no one had caught the theft before today. Together, it meant there was only a narrow window of time in which the tomb could have been robbed. And that the crime had been conducted by an efficient, organized group rather than a single individual.

Into the miserable, heavy silence of the room, she said, "I agree with Eliza. I think it is possible to find the gold."

"How?" Clara asked.

"The robbers, they were here not so long ago. Of course, they could not have come while you were here, so they must have watched for you to leave. And you have not been gone for long. Also, the sand outside with the footprints, it has not been covered by wind. So maybe it has only been a few days, *non?*"

She allowed the idea to develop as she spoke, confident that she was right. "But where does it go? It cannot go by car. *Impossible*, it is too much. And it cannot go by train because someone will see. So it must go by boat."

"It's true someone would have seen it at Luxor Station," Anna agreed. "You couldn't load a gold coffin without everyone in town knowing about it, much less entire train cars full of treasure. And what about all the people who would see it in Cairo? I'd have heard about it within hours. Everyone would have. There's no way they could have got away with it."

"But you *could* pull a boat up anywhere on the west bank in the middle of the night. Who would see? Only locals live here, and they would be asleep. Or if not, they could be bribed. Then you could cast off in the morning and look like any other boat making your way down the Nile. So long as you had the gold covered, of course."

She threw up her hand, agitated. "But where was Hussein? Even if he couldn't stop them, he would have told me about the thieves! He would have called the police. He wouldn't have let them just make off with it all."

That part mattered less to Georgette. It was moot now what had transpired between Anna's watchman and the thieves. What mattered was that although they had loaded the treasure and sailed off with it, they were still within reach. "The boat, it will not go fast. Maybe, we calculate, it goes eight *kilomètres* each hour. It is six hundred and seventy-six *kilomètres* from Luxor to Cairo, which means it will take the robbers ten days to go to Cairo. Is this correct?"

Anna nodded. With Eliza's flashlight now illuminating her face, it was possible to see that her expression was thoughtful. "Approximately, although the boat could go much faster. It could take as few as five days to make it to Cairo. I suppose it would depend on what type of boat it was and how heavy its load."

"And after Cairo, where would *le trésor* go?"

"Alexandria, most likely. The Nile flows all the way to the Mediterranean. Then the thieves would sail it west. From there, they could put the treasure on steamers bound for Europe."

"How long would that take, to go from Cairo to Alexandria?" Clara asked.

"Seven days? It's only a hundred and thirty nautical miles from Cairo to Rosetta, but it's hardly an easy sail. In many places, a boat—especially a heavily laden one—would risk running aground on sandbanks. The captain would have to go very slowly."

Georgette nodded to herself, still calculating. "Then *oui*, we can stop them. Definitely."

"How? If they are still in Egypt, we haven't a clue where they are. They could have reached Alexandria days ago. The treasure could be steaming its way to Venice at this very moment."

Georgette smiled. The answer was clear as day to her. The key was something Anna had said: *So long as you had the gold covered*. "*Mais oui*. The boats are approximately two days from Alexandria."

"What?"

Anna's disbelief echoed off the tomb walls like a peal of thunder, but Georgette was unperturbed. She was right and she knew it. "The barges that I saw when we began to sail up *le Nil*—they did not carry weapons for *une révolution*, I think. It was *le trésor*. You said there was nothing *en Égypte* that was worth protecting with guns, but gold, jewels, *oui*. They would certainly protect these things with guns."

She paused to allow this fact to sink in, wishing there was a little more light in the burial chamber. "The barges would have arrived to Cairo on December five and six. Today is ten December, so they are two and three days from Alexandria."

A long, thick silence followed. Whether the other women believed her or not, Georgette was confident that she was correct. Anna had left Luxor on 12 November to meet her guests in the capital. Under the timeline Georgette had laid out, the tomb would have been robbed sometime in late November and its contents loaded onto the three barges she'd seen sailing for Cairo. She wrinkled her nose with disapproval. Shame on the thieves. The things they'd stolen belonged in a museum, where everyone could see them. And it was a particularly rude thing to do to Anna, who had worked so hard and did not deserve such terrible treatment.

Eliza whistled. The sound echoed in the cavernous space. "She might just be right about that. What do you think, Anna? Could she be?"

"Perhaps. It would explain the tarps on the barges and the armed men on the deck. If it's not got anything to do with the nationalists, it could only be something extremely valuable that someone wanted to be kept hidden. A looted pharaoh's tomb would certainly make sense."

"But how do we stop them? We can't sail fast enough to catch up to them. They have too far of a head start," Clara said.

Anna stood and stepped away from the sarcophagus. Her voice vibrated with tense excitement when she spoke. "The Luxor Express runs tonight. We could be in Cairo by tomorrow morning. Then if we take the express train to Alexandria, we could be there just after noon. We'll beat the thieves by a day and be waiting for them when they arrive."

"What about all the things still in the tomb? We can't just leave them."

Georgette had been so focused on determining whether it would be possible to catch the thieves that she had all but forgotten the ransacked room above them. Clara was right. The tomb held far more than just the gold that had been taken from it. It may have been looted of its most valuable treasures, but it was still a pharaoh's tomb, and even the smallest, meanest artifacts were surely still of scientific interest. They couldn't simply run off and abandon it.

"The Department of Antiquities can take care of it," Anna said. "Inspector Ibrahim can call in the Antiquities guard from the valley. They'll seal off the tomb until we can get things sorted." She waved at the chamber around them. "Although there's nothing more thieves would want to take." Her voice was bitter.

"Couldn't the police stop the thieves themselves?" Clara asked. "Then you could stay here and take care of things yourself. Don't you want to see what's upstairs?"

Anna marched toward the stairs with quick, determined strides. The other women had to scramble to follow or be left behind in the cool, black burial chamber. "I won't risk the Alexandria police making a mess of things. If that treasure makes it onto a steamer, we'll never find so much as an amulet. It will all be lost in the wind. It's *my* gold. I'm going to get it back. If you want something done right, you have to do it yourself."

Back in the upper room, they found Ali and Inspector Ibrahim examining a pair of larger-than-life wooden statues that flanked the stairs to the burial chamber. Georgette suspected the gold paint that covered them top to bottom must have been paper thin or else the robbers would have tried to steal them, too. One of the statues carried a lamp and wore the dramatic, cobra-like headdress of a pharaoh. The other held a mace and wore what Georgette had learned was called a bag-wig. The faces of both were so finely carved they looked lifelike.

They were tomb guardians, she remembered. The archaeologist Howard Carter had found similar statues in the antechamber of King Tutankhamun's tomb, protecting the entrance to the burial chamber. Well, these ones hadn't done much to guard this tomb. They had watched the robbers with unseeing eyes, never raising a finger. So much for superstition over science. The king should have used booby traps instead.

"Come on, Ali," Anna said, her voice shattering the silence of the room. "We're going after them."

Ali immediately snapped to attention, his flashlight beam cutting across the room. Contrasted against the darkness, his white gallabiyah floated in the air like a ghost. "Who, Miss Anna?"

"The thieves. If the women and I take the overnight train to Cairo, we can catch them in Alexandria. Inspector, I'll need you to secure the tomb in my absence. Once word gets out about it, more would-be thieves will come sniffing around. I don't want them getting so much as a toe over the threshold. The damage is bad enough without someone chiseling out chunks of the wall too." Her voice was stern and commanding.

"How do you know where they are, Lady Baring? Do you know who's behind this?" Inspector Ibrahim asked. His flashlight momentarily blinded the women as he raised it to see them. He lowered it immediately when he realized his mistake.

"No, but Georgette worked out their itinerary and I'm certain she's right. Now come, there's work to be done before the Express leaves. Once we have the treasure back in our possession, we'll have to immediately send it to Cairo. We need to warn Chief Inspector Engelbach both of the theft and of the need to prepare an emergency space to receive the items. And for God's sake, none of this can leak to the press. The last thing we need are reporters crawling about."

Ali bowed. "Yes, Miss Anna."

Georgette experienced a pang of regret as she carefully picked her way out of the tomb. With every step, her flashlight revealed a new scene on the wall or an interesting trinket on the floor. She could only imagine how glorious the tomb must have looked before the thieves broke in. Now she would never know. Even if they recovered the treasure, the once-in-a-lifetime experience of walking into a pristine, untouched tomb had been ruined.

The journey back to the tomb mouth was as silent and somber as the walk in. When they reached it, they paused for a moment under the shade of the lintel to let their eyes adjust to the light. The sky was bright and cloudless, an endless dome of blue. The heat, which had been kept at bay in the tomb, hit like a furnace. After bracing herself to face it, Georgette hitched up her pale green dress and set out toward the cars.

She had only gone four meters when a sharp crack echoed through the air like a thick branch snapping. Something whizzed near enough to her that she could hear the buzzing in her ear like a horsefly. Whatever it was hit the ground a few meters in front of her, sending up a small puff of dust. She stopped, confused.

A breath later, she was bowled forward. Dra' Abu el-Naga' tilted wildly in front of her. She crashed into the ground heavily, all the air crushed out of her by someone landing on her. Her chin struck the dirt; sand found its way between her lips and into her mouth. Her mind went blank with surprise. *"Qu'est-ce qui—?"*

"Georgette, *move!*" Clara's mouth was right next to Georgette's ear when she bellowed. It made Georgette's ear hurt.

Clara rolled off her, then half-pulled, half-dragged her back into the tomb. Georgette was so dazed it was all she could do to keep her feet under her and stumble behind the American. The other four members of their party, who were watching with shocked expressions, made room for them as they toppled back into the tomb.

"What is it? What has happened?" Georgette asked, still bewildered. When she reached up to right her glasses, which had been knocked slightly askew, her palms were gritty with sand.

"That's a rifle," Clara said. "Someone shot at you."

Georgette gasped. *"Moi? Mais pourquoi?"* She remembered at the last minute to translate. "Why?" And then, a beat later, recalling their wild scramble through Khan el-Khalili, *"Again?* Is this the same man from Cairo?"

"It can't be. No one would come all the way from Cairo to Luxor just for that!" Anna exclaimed.

"Seems more likely the robbers don't want us to come after them and left us a little surprise," Eliza suggested darkly.

Clara looked out the tomb mouth, scanning the land around them. She had drawn her revolver, which she now held level to her chest, cocked and ready. Georgette had become so used to seeing the weapon holstered at Clara's side she had forgotten the other woman was even carrying it. Now she was grateful for Clara's peculiar quirk.

Clara said, "The shooter is somewhere above the tomb. There was an outcropping of rocks on top of the cliff, wasn't there?" The question was directed at Anna. "Maybe three hundred or so yards up?"

Anna looked bemused. "Yes, I suppose so."

Clara nodded. "That'll be where he is. It would give him a view of the entire area while also providing some cover. That's why we didn't see him when we came. He probably hid behind a rock."

"What do we do now?" Eliza asked.

Clara lowered her gun. "While he's got us pinned down, we've got two options. Option one is we wait until nightfall, when he can't see to shoot, then leave."

Georgette didn't like that option, although it was certainly better than being shot. What would they do for ten hours in the tomb with no food and no water, constantly worrying the shooter would come after them? "What is option two?"

"Based on the slope of the cliff above us, I bet he can only see us once we get a few yards out from the tomb, where he took a shot at you. If I crawl to the right for a hundred yards, keeping close to the cliff, most likely he won't be able to see me. He'll think we're all hiding in the tomb. Once I know he hasn't seen me, I can climb up the side of the cliff and ambush him."

"Out of the question! You will do no such thing!" Anna said, aghast. "How could you even suggest it? You could be killed!"

Clara shrugged. "He won't be looking for someone to come from the side. He'll be too busy watching the tomb. Besides, if we're stuck here until night, we'll miss the train to Cairo."

Anna shook her head forcefully. "Then we'll miss it. I won't have you chasing after a madman with a gun. Again." She dropped her voice and touched Clara's forearm. "It's not worth it, Clara."

"But I can do it," Clara protested. "I'm not scared."

Anna looked to Eliza for support.

"I say we wait him out," the other woman said. "Ain't any sense going after him, not if there's another option."

Anna turned to the men, who had so far been silent. "Inspector Ibrahim, will someone come looking for us if we're here long enough? Have you told anyone where we've gone? What about the drivers? Surely they'll come investigate in a few hours. They'll notice something is amiss."

"If the drivers come, they'll get shot at too," Clara pointed out.

"Ali will go," Ali said. "If Ali runs, he can get the police—"

Anna's foreman never got the chance to finish describing how he would evade the shooter. While he was still midsentence, Clara disappeared out the door. When Georgette, who was closest to the tomb mouth, stuck her head out to peer after her, she was crawling along the ground just as she'd said she would, her gun still held tightly in her right hand.

"Clara! Get back inside!" Anna hissed through clenched teeth, looking around Georgette.

"It's the only way," Clara whispered back. She kept her eyes forward, watching the path ahead of her. "It will be all right. I'll be careful. He won't see me coming."

"You're being ridiculous. Come back!"

Georgette saw two options: she could stay in the tomb, defenseless, and hope the gunman didn't come down the hill after them, or she could follow the only weapon they had. Clara was a professional shooter. She doubted whoever was above them was half as good a shot. Even though it meant getting closer to him, she was safer with Clara than she was staying in the cave. The choice was clear. She got down onto her hands and knees, ignoring the uncomfortable bite of tiny stones into her skin.

"I am going too," she announced.

"Georgette!" Anna exclaimed, horrified. She grabbed Georgette's ankle, trying to hold her back.

"It will be safer with Clara. Besides, if this man is one of the thieves, he can tell us where they are sending your *trésor*." That way, if for some reason they weren't able to stop it at Alexandria, they could still recover it when it reached its next destination.

Her argument must have stirred something in Anna. "I'm coming too, then."

By the time Clara was several meters away from the tomb, what had started as one woman setting off to surprise the gunman had turned into a train of four: Clara at the head, followed by Georgette, Anna, and a grumbling, none-too-happy Eliza, who had announced they were likely all going to die from lack of common sense but that she refused to be seen as a coward if everyone else was going. Ali and Inspector Ibrahim, meanwhile, remained in the cave with the promise that they would occasionally create movement to keep the gunman focused on the tomb mouth. The women inched around the side of the cliff, moving as slowly as caterpillars. Georgette concentrated with all her might on where she placed her hands and knees. She barely breathed. A single mistake and the gunman would know where they were. Sweat poured down her brow and collected at her armpits and chest.

At Clara's signal, they began to climb the rough slope, keeping their bodies pressed as flat to the ground as they could. This was the most dangerous part—they were no longer hidden by the natural overhang of the cliff. They would be exposed to anyone above it who looked in their direction. If they had been discovered, they would only know when they heard the first rapport of the long gun. But it never came.

At the top of the slope, Clara stopped them. Her white shirt was dyed a patchwork of brown. She pointed with her revolver at the tall boulders that overlooked the tomb. "You stay here. I'll go find him." Her voice was a whisper.

"We came this far. Might as well keep going," Eliza said, hoisting her beige linen pants up. Her white shirt was completely soaked through with sweat, exposing the brassiere beneath. "Besides, you may need help."

Clara pressed her lips together as she considered the argument, then nodded. "But stay behind me. And walk quietly."

She began to creep toward the boulders, holding her pistol out in front of her. Each step was agonizingly slow and cautious. Georgette began to doubt their decision to go after the shooter. Perhaps they should have waited until night after all.

Moving in a single-file line, they navigated among the boulders, checking behind and around every rock with meticulous care. But no one was there. At the edge of the outcropping, they stopped beside a tall boulder shaped like a thumb. The women's faces reflected their befuddlement.

Eliza crossed her arms. "Well, where is he?"

Clara shook her head, perplexed. "He must have been here. It's the only place he could have been. Look, you can see exactly how he would have taken the shot at Georgette." She pointed down the cliff face. Although the tomb mouth itself was hidden, the view of where Georgette had been standing was clear.

"Maybe he has gone away," Georgette suggested. Perhaps having missed, he had run from the scene.

The next person to speak, however, wasn't one of the four women.

"Put the gun down and step away from it."

CHAPTER TWELVE

Eliza

A cold shiver ran down Eliza's body all the way to her toes.

"That's right," the man said as the women slowly turned to face him. "That's a good lass. Set it down now. You wouldn't want to hurt yourself."

He motioned toward the ground with his rifle, his finger not moving from the trigger. Eliza couldn't look away from the weapon. This was not the first time she'd found herself on the wrong end of a gun. In her forty-one years, she had lived enough to have had it happen a few times. Farmers who hadn't wanted their fields taken over by barnstormers, for example, and walking into the wrong place at the wrong time in Chicago. But it never lost its heart-stopping effect. Her muscles were locked tight with fear. She couldn't have run even if she'd tried.

The man's flat hat slouched low over eyes so dark they were almost black. Eliza had seen his sort all over America: rough-and-tumble criminals with wolflike faces who would sell their own mothers for half a pack of cigarettes. She watched Clara from the corner of her eye. Clara could outshoot him, but would she try or would she obey his instructions? Clara didn't seem to know either. Her eyes flickered between the man and her companions uncertainly.

"Are you one of the thieves?" Georgette asked unexpectedly. "Where they are taking *le trésor*?"

He was taken aback, his round face bunching into a collection of lines and wrinkles like an English bulldog. "That's none of your business. All you need to know is it's gone. If you want gold of your own, you'll have to find another tomb. This is ours now."

Anna glared at him, eyes smoldering. "You bloody bastards. You'd steal that too if you could. How dare you? That gold belongs to the Egyptian people. You have no right to take it."

Eliza wished her companions would shut up. It wasn't a good idea to scold a man holding them at gunpoint. He snarled. "I'll do whatever I damn well please. You'll do well to shut your mouth. It's too late now anyway."

Georgette cocked her head. "But if it is too late, why you are here?"

If she was afraid of him, she didn't show it, and her quiet curiosity was enough to break through some of Eliza's paralysis. Why *was* he at Dra' Abu el-Naga'? To keep an eye on the tomb? To deter anyone from going after the thieves? But if he was telling the truth and the treasure was too far gone to be stopped, it wouldn't matter either way. Could it be he was lying?

The man opened his wide, frog-like mouth to answer. But before he could speak, something unexpected happened: the world tumbled into darkness.

The extinguishing of the sun was so sudden and astonishing that at first Eliza thought she had gone blind. She could barely see her own hands in front of her, much less the thief. Then she realized the darkness wasn't limited to her—the whole world really had gone dark. As the women had ascended the cliff, the sky had been a bright, cloudless, cornflower blue. Now, as though someone had flipped a switch, it had turned black as coal.

Silence fell over the group as everyone stared up at the white corona of the sun framing the ebony circle of the moon. Eliza had never seen a full solar eclipse. She had never imagined the day could become so astonishingly dark—and so quickly. Her companions were transformed into mere outlines, shadows against shadows.

Eliza had learned by experience never to waste a good opportunity. Life wasn't about waiting for something to happen. You had to *make* it happen. And she had no intention of finding out what the thief would do once—or if—Clara surrendered her gun. She lunged toward him, figuring that while he was distracted she could yank the gun out of his hand. If that failed, she would knock him over and pin him to the ground. She was not a small woman; he wouldn't have an easy time grappling with her.

In the darkness, however, she miscalculated the distance. Her bulk smashed into his right shoulder like a frigate onto partially submerged rocks. Her swinging arms missed as she tried to grab the barrel of the rifle, leaving her hands grasping nothing but air.

The gun went off with a deafening boom.

Instantly, she froze. Her ribcage rattled. Her ears rang. Her heart leapt into her throat. The explosion was as galvanizing as the roar of a lion. Something primitive and primal in her mind screamed in fear and terror. She had to get away from the danger. But her body had turned to ice, freezing her in place.

A woman screamed, a long, high wail of fear that punctuated the air like an exclamation mark. Georgette. The raw emotion in her voice was like a dagger plunged into Eliza's chest, so visceral it hurt. Had someone been shot? She couldn't see well enough to know.

"Run!"

Anna's voice was fire. It melted away the ice in Eliza's limbs. She threw herself to the ground and started to crawl as quickly as she could in the direction she thought led back to the tomb, focused with single-minded determination on getting away from the deadly weapon. The instinct for self-preservation had taken over, overriding everything else. Gone was any thought of wrestling for the gun. She didn't even think about Georgette or Anna or Clara. All that mattered was getting to safety.

Clara's revolver fired once, then a second time.

She didn't look back. Her heart pounded, filled with dread. The fingers of her left hand scraped against a massive boulder, and she rushed to hide behind it. All she could hear was the sound of her heavy breathing. All she could think of was staying away from the terrible roar of the gun. They shouldn't have climbed the cliff. It had been foolhardy to go after the shooter, four women and a small pistol. And it had been even more reckless to try to take his gun from him. Now they were paying for their mistakes in the worst possible way.

She didn't have long to stew over their decisions and their consequences, however. As quickly as it had started, the eclipse finished. Immediately, the sky was as clear and cerulean as it had been before. Eliza peered cautiously around the side of the boulder, heart racing, terrified of what she would see. And indeed, what she saw alarmed her.

Clara was standing where she had been before the eclipse, revolver in hand. Her head swiveled back and forth as though she were searching for something. Anna was slowly standing up from where she'd been crouching next to her, looking shell-shocked. Neither of them appeared injured. But Georgette, who had made it approximately halfway between Eliza and the other two women, was lying motionless on her stomach.

Eliza's heart skipped a beat. Had she been shot? Was she dead?

"Georgette! Georgette, are you okay?" she called.

Georgette slowly unwrapped her arms from the cradle she'd formed around her head and looked up. Half her hair had come out of its bun and was hanging limply around her face. *"Oui."*

"Where is he?" Eliza asked no one in particular. "Where'd he go?"

She had accounted for all four women, but the man was missing. Every nerve in her body fired, on high alert. She imagined him hiding among the rocks around them or over the swell of the cliff. He could be anywhere, sighting them with his rifle. They were in the same position they'd been in when they climbed the cliff: vulnerable and at a disadvantage.

"He's gone," Clara called back.

"What?"

She pointed to the ground. Lying several yards from her, abandoned, was the rifle. In her worry over locating the thief, Eliza hadn't noticed it. Now Clara was the only one with a gun. If the man was still skulking around, he'd be foolish to confront them again. Still wary, Eliza tiptoed back to Clara and Anna, stopping to help Georgette to her feet as she went. In the meantime, Clara knelt down and emptied the bullets out of the rifle.

"Did the man run away?" Georgette asked, trying to smooth the front of her green dress, which had taken on a few new wrinkles.

Even though she was seeing it with her own eyes, Eliza could hardly believe he was gone. Her ears still echoed with the bellow of his gun. The electric spark of fear still coursed through her veins. At any moment, she expected him to turn up behind them again.

Clara nodded, staring down the side of the cliff as though she might catch a glimpse of his fleeing figure. "Must have. Maybe the eclipse scared him. That sure was lucky, wasn't it?"

"Or maybe because you shot at him and he became afraid," Georgette suggested.

Clara looked momentarily confused. "Shot at *him*? No, I didn't. Something hit me from behind, so I turned and shot at *it*. I thought he had a friend who was trying to ambush us." She looked at Anna. "Did you feel it? He must have crept up behind us."

Anna was leaning heavily against her, clutching her arm for support. Concern and worry had deepened the fine lines around her eyes. She was not the confident woman who had promised them a pharaoh's riches that morning. She replied, "I heard wings. I thought his shot must have scared a vulture roosting behind us. They can often be found around here. I certainly didn't hear a person."

Clara squinted at the unblemished sky, perhaps looking for a sign that a bird had been there, then shrugged. "I guess it could have been that. Well, whatever it was, it's gone."

Georgette crossed her arms uneasily and looked over her shoulder. "What do we do now?"

In the aftermath of their encounter with the gunman, their location on the top of the cliff felt excruciatingly exposed. Anyone could have come after them, especially if Clara was right and the man wasn't alone.

"I guess we go to the cars and then back to the hotel. We can't stay around here, that's for sure," Clara said.

"Is it safe there? How do we know the man will not follow us?"

A thrill ran through Eliza's body. They still didn't know why he had been waiting for them at Dra' Abu el-Naga'. Although he had dropped his gun and run, he might not be finished with them yet. It would be easy enough for him to find out where they were staying in Luxor. Perhaps, in fact, he already knew. They stuck out from the rest of the European tourist crowd like an ostrich in a henhouse, Eliza herself most of all.

"You're right. I'll have Ali collect your suitcases from the hotel. We can wait for the train at Inspector Ibrahim's office," Anna said. "Once we've made it to Cairo, you'll be safe at my apartment. I can go on to Alexandria alone."

"You still wanna go chasing after the thieves after what just happened?" Eliza asked, incredulous. "Seems like you better let the police handle it."

The color was slowly returning to Anna's face, and with it some of her fire. "The police can't even stop a peddler in Luxor from conning tourists. You don't really believe they can stop something bigger than that, do you?" She huffed emotionally. "I admit, I didn't expect the thieves to leave a man behind to try to cover their tracks, but now I know to be more careful. I won't be ambushed again." She shook her head. "I'm not letting them get away with it."

Eliza didn't know how the archaeologist planned to evade an ambush. This being the second time in less than a week that someone had shot at them, the odds suggested otherwise.

"You can't go alone," Clara protested. "It's too dangerous."

Anna's face shone with righteous passion. "We're talking about what could be the greatest theft in the history of the world. I have to at least try to stop them."

Clara squared her shoulders. "Then I'll come with you. You need someone to protect you."

"No, Clara, I couldn't allow it..."

As the two began to argue, the sunlight illuminated something white at Eliza's feet, catching her attention. She did a double take. It was the largest feather she'd ever seen. She leaned down to pick it up, holding it between her two fingers. It was longer than her entire hand. The bird to which it belonged must have been absolutely immense. This must have been the vulture Anna heard. No wonder Clara had thought it was a person.

* * *

Luxor, Egypt

Luxor Station was smaller than Port Said Station, but it was much busier. Men in robes, on foot and on small white donkeys, massed around the low building to gossip and share news. Chattering groups of tourists stood by miniature pyramids of luggage stacked on carts pushed by porters. Small black carriages queued in a line to ferry new arrivals to hotels throughout the city. Eliza observed it all keenly as their car pulled up, searching through the deepening dusk for any sign that the man from the cliff had somehow guessed they would come and was waiting for them.

"Thank you, Inspector," Anna said as the car shifted to park. "I'll send word when we reach Alexandria."

He nodded to her over his shoulder. "Good luck, Lady Baring. May *Allah* watch over you."

She sighed. "Horus might be the better choice for this one."

It had been a long, difficult day for the two of them as they'd huddled in his office, rallying guards from the Valley of the Kings to discreetly protect what remained in the tomb. According to Anna, it would soon be clear whether they had managed to hide the tomb's existence or not, although Eliza didn't know what was left of value to steal. The inspector got out of the car, then opened the back door to help first Eliza out, then Anna.

"*Inshallah* all will go well," he said. "In the meantime, you must be careful. They are very bad men. I wish you would not go after them yourself." Anna opened her mouth, and he held up his hand. "I know you do not believe in *Allah*, but though you do not believe in him, he believes in you. He has protected you today."

Anna raised her eyebrows. "With respect, Inspector, I think we can give that one to the moon."

"Ah, but who has brought the moon at just such a time? Science can tell you *how* the moon can hide the sun, but can it tell you *why* it happened at that moment? Do you not wonder at the coincidence of the timing?"

"I'll think about it," Anna replied in a tone that suggested she would do the opposite.

Georgette and Clara approached from the second car. Eliza took Georgette's hand to avoid the smaller woman becoming separated in the press of bodies. On Eliza's other side, a man walking past barely missed stepping on her foot, clipping her toe instead. His gray donkey brayed in her ear. She jutted out her elbow, trying to push it away. Raising her voice to be heard over the commotion, she asked Georgette, "You sure you wanna go on to Alexandria?"

To her surprise, it hadn't been just Clara who had voiced support for continuing on to the port city. Just before they had departed the inspector's office, Georgette had announced that she, too, intended to accompany Anna to Alexandria. Eliza still had hope she would do the sensible thing and stay in Cairo, however. Anna and Clara might be hell-bent on charging after the thieves, but the mathematician should be more amenable to reason. They didn't all have to throw themselves into harm's way.

But Georgette nodded without hesitation. "*Oui*, of course. Anna, she needs help."

"You ain't worried about the thieves?" Eliza was thinking about the missing man from Dra' Abu el-Naga'. They still didn't know why he'd run away. All they knew was that he could still be in Luxor somewhere. And there were other unanswered questions too. It was no coincidence that he had been waiting for them on the cliff that morning, so when exactly had they come under surveillance? Had it been when they arrived in Luxor, or could it have been even earlier? Just how many thieves were in the ring?

"*Oui. Mais…*" Georgette waggled her head in a sort of dismissal. "It is like Anna has said: we will be careful. It is only a few hours until we will reach Alexandria. That is not so long."

Eliza shook her head and said nothing. She didn't understand Georgette's inexplicable courage—or foolhardiness, in her opinion—but she didn't have time to think about it now. She continued to scan the station grounds, looking for any sign the man from the cliff or one of his associates had followed them. At the right end of the short station building, a man in a red fez and white robe squatted behind a tan cloth upon which he'd piled dates for sale. A European man in a gray three-piece suit, his red hair slicked to a glistening shine, leaned against one of the thin pillars next to him. He stared at the women with an unblinking intensity. When Eliza caught him, he looked away, a furtive, suspicious movement.

Her senses tingled, instantly on alert. She tugged on Georgette's arm to catch her attention and then pointed. "I think that man's watching us."

Georgette squinted at him. "Him? I do not know, maybe he is waiting for *le train*, like us. He does not look *dangereux* to me."

It was true that he *did* look like many of the other well-dressed men milling around the station. Still, Eliza narrowed her eyes, unconvinced. He didn't have any suitcases with him. Nor was he with the other tourists, who were clustered at the left end of the station near the sign that read "First Class Booking Office." Before she could scrutinize him any further, however, he turned and disappeared around the side of the building. The next moment, Georgette was pulling her forward and into the station, and Eliza had to place all her attention and energy into trying not to lose the other women in the throng of passengers.

A cream-colored train awaited them on the tracks, only a few cars longer than the one they'd taken from Port Said to Cairo. Anna led the way into the first car.

"It's a bit tight, but it will do for the night," she said, squeezing her suitcases through the narrow wooden corridor between the windows and the sleeping cabins. She stopped in front of one of the doors and checked the number written on it against the ticket in her hand. Her eyes flickered to Clara, then away. "Well, it's two people per cabin. I'll let you decide who wants to sleep in mine." Her words were soft with quiet defeat.

Eliza didn't know if she would have volunteered, but the point was moot. Before either she or Georgette could speak, Clara rested her hand on Anna's shoulder. "I'll stay with you. Georgette and Eliza can have the other cabin."

The train whistled, calling any passengers still lingering on the platform to board. Eliza glanced out, unconsciously scanning the station one last time. She caught sight of the man in the gray suit. She threw herself against the window and pressed her face to the glass, watching to see what he would do. As she suspected, he looked around in both directions as though checking to see no one was surveilling him, then boarded the last first-class sleeper car.

"I knew it!" she said.

"What?" Georgette asked, leaning over her shoulder to look.

"We've been followed."

CHAPTER THIRTEEN

Clara

Clara pressed her left hand to the glass, her right already reaching for her gun. Her stomach dropped. She couldn't believe they'd been followed. It was just what they'd been afraid of. It was a nightmare. The train whistled one final time, announcing its imminent departure, but the platform was already empty. A chill ran up her arms like the feet of a dozen frantic spiders.

"What did you see? What did he look like?" The current of stress in Anna's voice was like the vibration of a plucked bass string.

"It was a white man with red hair in a gray suit. Didn't seem to have any business being here. I saw him watching us outside the station too. He got on the train after us in one of the last cars."

Anna stepped back. Her eyebrows were drawn down over the bridge of her nose. "Red hair. Was he about your height and good-looking?"

Eliza bobbed her head. "Yeah, that would describe him."

Anna's face broke into a smile. Her shoulders dropped with relief. "That's Fernand. I thought I caught a glimpse of him around the station. Fernand wouldn't hurt a fly. He's been excavating at Abu Rawash, north of Cairo, the last few years, but he's been trying to get a permit to excavate the Temple of Montu, several kilometers outside of Luxor. I imagine he visited the site and now is headed back to Cairo." She chuckled. "Carnarvon used to say you couldn't throw a stone in Egypt without hitting an archaeologist and sometimes I think he's right."

Instantly, the tension was broken. Clara released her revolver, her heartbeat slowing to a more reasonable tempo. Georgette stepped back from the window she'd been pressed to and adjusted her hat.

"It's all right. It's been a challenging day and we're all on edge. Perhaps a nap before dinner and we'll be a bit more relaxed," Anna said.

Clara couldn't have agreed more. She was exhausted from the long day. The excitement of the morning had given way to interminably long hours squeezed into Inspector Ibrahim's small office. At least they hadn't had to fit Ali in as well, who had stayed at the tomb to organize its protection.

She opened the door to the cabin she would be sharing with Anna and stepped inside. While clean and neat, it was every bit as small as Anna had promised. The two women could barely stand in the small space between the wood-paneled wall and the narrow bed without their elbows touching. They stacked their suitcases on the rack against the wall, then Anna pulled the second bed down to form a bunk bed. She patted its thin mattress. "Top or bottom?"

"Whichever you prefer. I don't mind." Clara kept her eyes on the threadbare pillow of the bottom bunk. She had volunteered to share the cabin impulsively, without thinking. Anna had seemed so dispirited. She couldn't bear for Anna to think any of the women wouldn't want to stay with her, especially after all that had happened that morning. But now this proximity evoked uncomfortably vivid memories of the night before and her vows to stay away from Anna.

Anna clearly didn't feel the same. She lowered the ladder and clambered to the top bed, ducking to avoid cracking her head against the low ceiling. "I'll take the top in that case."

Clara untied her boots and set them neatly against the foot of the lower bed, then lay down, her hands crossed on her chest. She had only intended to rest a little, not fall asleep, but once the train trundled into motion, the rocking of the cabin and the steady rattle of the wheels against the track lulled her into a deep sleep. She must have slept for hours, because when she woke, it was full night. Anna was standing next to the small, square window, staring into the blackness beyond. She turned when she heard Clara moving and smiled. "Sleep well?"

Clara patted her hair, trying to discern how disheveled it had become. It seemed passable enough. She yawned. "How long have I been asleep?"

"A few hours." Anna motioned to the tiny table beneath the window, which couldn't have been more than three feet square. "I brought you food from the dining car in case you're hungry."

"Oh." It was such a very thoughtful thing to do that Clara almost felt guilty. "Did you sleep?"

Anna's mouth quirked unhappily. "No." The word was abrupt, like a door closing. Her face was pinched, and Clara realized it was pain. Clara wondered how long she'd been standing at the window.

"I'm sorry. I'm sorry thieves took your gold." In all that had happened since the morning, she hadn't had the chance to say it before now. But she meant it. She could hardly imagine what Anna was going through. The months of digging, of fighting tooth and nail against unyielding rock and shifting sand—and then her euphoric dreams had all been shattered in an instant. She'd been left holding a puff of smoke. "I'm sorry" wasn't hardly enough to convey Clara's sympathy, but they were the only words she could find.

Anna winced, the expression pulling her face together like the drawstrings of a purse. She sat down on the end of Clara's bed and stared blankly at the suitcases in front of her. "It's my fault, isn't it? I was reckless and arrogant and stupid. I thought I could do it all myself without needing anyone's help. If I was careful enough, if I was sneaky enough, the robbers wouldn't find out about the tomb."

"You did what you could," Clara protested

She shook her head. "If I'd taken on a patron, someone like Carnarvon…But after what happened with Carter, I wanted to prove I could do it on my own. I didn't want anyone else to be able to claim any of the credit. And now…" She smiled bitterly, a terrible rictus of a grin. "I'll be famous for something else, won't I? Not the person who found a New Kingdom pharaoh's intact tomb, but rather the pathetic archaeologist whose fantastic recklessness lost it all."

Clara was startled to hear Anna speak so disparagingly of herself. It didn't seem like her at all. "No, no one will think that!"

"Won't they? Who else has lost the entire treasure of an Egyptian pharaoh? It's like losing the Crown Jewels. I'll never be granted another excavation permit in Egypt. I may have to leave the field of archaeology entirely."

"You can't be so hard on yourself. You didn't know what would happen."

Anna ran her thumb over her lower lip. Red spots had appeared on her cheeks below her eyes. "Why shouldn't I be? My father would be. He would say this is all proof I've no business mucking about in the desert, that he was right all along, and I've wasted my time and that of everyone who's worked with me on this 'ridiculous archaeology business.'"

She ran her hand through her hair. Her cheeks flexed as she clenched and then unclenched her jaw. "Then he'd have said I was English not Egyptian, and it was silly of me to ever have thought any differently. I should get on a steamer right away and sail home to Norfolk." She snorted. "He'd have some other choice words about my life as well."

Clara gaped at her, appalled. "But you haven't made a mess at all! You found Ahmose's tomb when no one else could, not in more than three thousand years! He—*you*—should be proud of that. You've done an amazing, wonderful thing, and people will know that once they find out about it."

Anna grunted. "I don't think my father would quite agree. He'd have said if I couldn't secure a tomb properly, I deserved to have it robbed. He'd have all but cheered on the thieves. If he was feeling sentimental, he might even have bought a trinket or two from them to put on the mantel at home—if they were willing to discount the price."

Clara couldn't believe what she was hearing. "That's just awful! Why do you think he would say such a terrible thing?"

"Because that's exactly the type of man my father was. There were two people he could never stand seeing succeed: nationalists and women. He did everything he could to tear them down. For him, this would have been a vindication—proof that every choice I'd made was just as catastrophic as he predicted."

Clara opened her mouth to protest that it couldn't possibly be true, that no one could be so cruel, but Anna wasn't finished. "If my father had his way, I would have never gone to university. I'd have been married with five children by now. That was the only kind of woman he could stand: the kind who stayed home and minded the house and never put a foot out of line. Bastard."

Clara scooted closer on the bed and put her hand on Anna's, trying to comfort her. Anna gave a small, rueful smile. "I've made a right mess of everything, haven't I? Between Cairo and the tomb...I don't know what I would have done if you—if anyone—had been hurt."

Clara didn't think. She reached out and traced her palm along Anna's cheek. "You're a beautiful, successful woman. You found the tomb of an Egyptian pharaoh. Anyone would be lucky to have a daughter who's half as amazing as you are. And that's the truth."

Anna's eyes met hers. Normally sparkling with lively energy, now they were subdued and flat. The passionate, confident archaeologist who had lectured at the Explorers Club and led the women up the Nile had been replaced by someone much more vulnerable. Someone much more human. Clara guessed this was a side of Anna she rarely showed. Perhaps, in fact, there was no one in her life to whom she could show it. After all, like Clara, she had lived much of her life surrounded by others and yet alone.

But she shouldn't believe the bad things she was saying about herself. They weren't true at all. She was... She was...

Impulsively, Clara cupped Anna's chin in her hands and kissed her. It was a soft, gentle kiss. Clara couldn't have said why she'd done it. Perhaps it had been meant to show compassion or to comfort Anna. All she knew was that it had felt right in the moment.

She pulled back when she realized what she was doing, stunned by herself. Only the night before, she had spent hours worrying about the consequences of kissing Anna, and now she had done it again not even twenty-four hours later. But the desire to keep her distance was much weaker than the urge to get closer again. The feeling of kissing Anna was exhilarating. It made her scalp tingle and her heart beat faster. After a moment's hesitation, she leaned in a second time.

Anna hadn't moved during the first kiss. This time, her left arm moved to curl around the small of Clara's back, her hand hooking against Clara's hip. Her right hand rested on Clara's knee. Until yesterday, Clara hadn't known the explosions of sensations that could be created by touching and being touched by another person. Everywhere Anna's hands made contact with her, her skin prickled beneath her clothing and blossomed with heat.

Euphoria filled her chest like air into a balloon. The sensation was intoxicating. She was breathless. She wanted more. She wanted to feel the softness of Anna's skin beneath her fingertips and on her palms. To know what it was like to kiss those places on Anna where she, herself, had been kissed in Luxor. She wanted… She didn't even know the things she wanted, only that an urgent desire was driving her, pushing her forward into Anna. Clara's fingers tangled in Anna's hair, white birch branches in a sea of red leaves.

Instinct took over. Electricity coursing through her body, she unbuttoned Anna's double-breasted, fitted brown vest. It was simultaneously debonair and beautiful, feminine and masculine, and in a moment, it was a shapeless pile on the floor as Anna helpfully threw it away. Two breathless seconds later, Anna's red tie landed on top of it, catching at her hair as it passed over her head.

If Clara had taken a moment to think about what she was doing, she might have stopped. But there was no time to think. There was only desire and sensation and nameless hunger. Anna's hands went to the small buttons of Clara's white shirt, her fingers swift, agile, and impatient. When she finished unhooking them, Clara's shirt was open at the center, revealing the peach satin bandeau beneath. She yanked the bottom of the shirt free of Clara's skirt and ran her hand around Clara's stomach. Clara shivered at the contact, her fingers tightening in response.

Anna ducked her head and kissed the point of Clara's chest just above her bandeau. It was both too much and not enough. A quiet whimper slipped out of Clara's lips. With overwhelming urgency, she drew Anna's head back to her to kiss her. The force of the contact made Clara's lips tingle. A tide swept through her body, settling below her stomach. Matching what Anna had done, Clara unbuttoned Anna's shirt, then ran a tentative hand from Anna's neck to the waist of her brown jodhpurs. Clara had never touched anyone like this; she could barely believe she was doing it now. But it felt right, and she didn't want to stop.

Clara had never been particularly curious about her own body, but Anna's was different. She kissed Anna below her jaw, running her lips down to her left collarbone. At the same time, she slid her hands down Anna's sides. Anna trembled, and the feeling was both exquisite and exciting. It sent shivers from Clara's chest to her hips.

Anna pulled the pin from Clara's hair, sending it cascading past her shoulders. Her fingers wrapped around the back of Clara's head, her thumb just in front of Clara's left ear. Such a small gesture and she took control. Gently but firmly, she pressed on Clara's shoulders, pushing her backward onto the bed. Clara automatically brought both feet off the ground; Anna expertly maneuvered herself to allow Clara's right leg to sweep under her and onto the bed. When she reset her body, her left leg was between Clara's legs.

Clara's heartbeat filled her ears with a sound like crashing ocean waves. Electricity sparked through her veins. She had never been in such an intimate position. She could feel every breath Anna took; her stomach pressed against Clara's and retreated. Clara's own breath was quick and shallow, nervous yet exhilarated. The cabin around them disappeared. All that was left was Anna.

Every cell in Clara's body was alive, aching, clamoring for more contact, straining to close even the small distance that separated her from Anna. Hungrily, she grasped Anna behind the neck and pulled her closer. Firecrackers of sensation set off everywhere Anna's body pressed along the length of her. For all the things she didn't know from experience, her body knew by reflex. Her hips tilted to meet Anna's. Her hands scrambled wildly, desperate to touch every square inch of Anna's back and chest and find the places that made her shiver.

Anna's mouth moved against hers, bold and confident as Anna herself. Her hair fell around them like a red curtain. A minute might have passed, or it could have been ten. When her left leg inadvertently—or not—pressed against Clara, Clara experienced an entirely new sensation. Had her eyes been open, they would have crossed. Instead, she gasped and shuddered, her toes reflexively curling. All her attention was immediately redirected to that leg and where it was touching.

Anna's lips smiled against hers. She shifted her weight so that her right arm was free and ran her hand along Clara's bandeau, eliciting a quiet squeak and then a full-body shudder. Clara's body arched into the contact. Clara hadn't known until that moment how much her body could truly yearn for something. What it was to want with every fiber of her being. Her breath turned heavy, husky with a need and desire whose intensity she never could have anticipated. Anna kissed her neck at the same time her fist balled in the tan cotton of Clara's skirt and began to hike it toward her knee.

Clara's senses abandoned her. All of her attention was absorbed by the hand moving along her leg. She barely even noticed when Anna kissed her chest. Her fingers curled into Anna's sides, dimpling the skin.

Anna released the skirt and ran her fingertips up the inside of Clara's thigh, rounding her knee and beginning to travel higher.

Clara made an involuntary, undignified, half-strangled sound. Acting outside her control, her body wriggled, trying to move closer to Anna's hand. Clara's skin rippled, painfully sensitive to every place Anna touched.

Clara anchored her hands against Anna's hips, her fingers hooked into the brown waistband. She tried to keep still, but her body bucked, alive with feeling. She tilted her head back, eyes squeezed shut.

The door to the cabin flew open, smacking against the wall with a crack.

Clara turned her head automatically to look, devoid for the moment of any feeling but surprise. Eliza stood in the doorway, startled eyes fixed on the two women she'd caught in an intimate embrace. Fast as lightning, Anna removed her hand, but of course, there was no hiding what Eliza was seeing. A beat passed.

Then Eliza spoke. "Georgette is missing."

The concern in her voice was like an alarm bell. It suggested she suspected something much worse than that the Frenchwoman had wandered off somewhere and gotten lost, if such a thing was even possible on the short train. Had it not been pressed against the mattress, the hair on the back of Clara's neck would have risen.

"What do you mean she's missing?" Anna still hadn't moved. She was still on top of Clara, still caught in a delicate moment.

"We were having dinner in the dining car, then I went to use the bathroom. When I came back, she was gone. I looked for her, but..." Eliza shook her head. "She'd vanished."

"You're certain she didn't go back to your cabin?"

The look Eliza gave Anna said more than any words could. Spry as a gymnast, Anna launched herself off the bed, her fingers buttoning her shirt almost before her feet touched the ground. As Eliza looked away politely, Clara sat up and pushed her skirt back down, then began to button her own shirt. From the prickling feeling on her face, she knew she must be turning red as a rose. She didn't know how she would ever look Eliza in the eyes again.

If Anna felt similarly self-conscious, she didn't show it. "Where have you looked?" Her tone and posture suggested she would be taking control of the situation now.

"Outside of the sleeper cabins, there's nowhere else but the dining and baggage cars."

And there was no reason for Georgette to go there.

Anna ran her hand through her hair, which was noticeably tousled. "Well, we know she's still on the train. We haven't slowed since we left Luxor."

That wasn't necessarily true, but Clara didn't want to be the one to mention it. When Anna looked at her, she winced, as though remembering what they had been doing before they had been interrupted. She said to Eliza, "Would you give us a moment, please?"

Eliza's eyes cut to Clara and then away. "I'll be just outside." She stepped back into the corridor and closed the door, leaving the two women alone.

Anna knelt in front of Clara and ran her hands tenderly along the sides of Clara's face. "It will be all right. Eliza won't— she won't say anything. And I'm sure Georgette isn't lost. It won't take but a moment to find her."

Clara nodded, but she barely absorbed the words. Of course she cared what Eliza thought, but right now she was more worried about Georgette. She could have gotten confused and walked into the wrong cabin, then stayed to talk with its occupants. That would have been very like Georgette. But what if she'd made a mistake—opened the wrong door and stumbled off the train into the dark night? Such accidents happened from time to time. If that was the case, how would they ever find her?

Anna kissed Clara's forehead, her lips lingering for a minute. Then she snatched her vest from the ground and shrugged it on, not bothering to button it. Clara put on her boots and stood to join her. Anna opened the door, then, with a nod to Eliza, took off toward the back of the train.

The train had four sleeper cars. As the three women walked through them, Clara could just make out the low murmur of voices inside their cabins. Most of the Luxor Express's passengers had retired to their rooms for the evening. She strained her ears, listening for a French accent, but if Georgette was in one of them, she couldn't tell.

The dining car was the last car of the train. It was lusciously decorated, with inviting, warm electric sconces, upholstered wood chairs, and tables covered with perfectly white tablecloths and gold-edged china plates. A handful of the eight tables were still occupied by passengers drinking liqueurs or coffee, but it was immediately evident Georgette was not among them. Clara's stomach dropped. Despite Eliza's claim that Georgette wasn't in the dining car, she had nevertheless hoped to find their missing companion there.

Anna pushed through to the end of the car without pausing. On the left side, just before the final vestibule, was a small bathroom. She tried the handle. It was unlocked. When she pushed it, the door swung open easily. The bathroom was empty. She pulled the door shut forcefully. Her face had turned grim.

"You're certain there's no way she could have gone back to your cabin?" she asked Eliza.

Eliza nodded.

"Then we'll just have to try the baggage car."

Clara's chest tightened with every step as they made their way back to the front of the train. Anna moved much slower now, her confidence shaken. Although it was the last place they could look, surely Georgette wouldn't be there. But if she wasn't... The night rolled past them black as tar outside the train's windows. A passenger could disappear into that endless void without anyone ever seeing or knowing. Clara shivered.

As they passed the cabin she shared with Anna, she noticed a white piece of paper sticking out from under the door. She stooped to pick it up, frowning. She was certain it hadn't been there when they'd left a minute ago. A message was written on it in cramped, barely legible letters.

If you want to see your friend again, come to the baggage car. No guns if you want her to live.

Clara's heart leapt into her throat and stuck there, a thick, quivering obstruction that stopped her from swallowing.

Someone had kidnapped Georgette. It could only be the thieves. They *were* on the train. She laid a heavy hand on Anna's shoulder to catch her attention. When the other woman stopped, she handed her the note. Anna quickly read it, then passed it to Eliza, her face ashen. Eliza scanned it and looked at Clara.

"Well? What do we do?" Eliza asked.

Clara's hand went to her revolver, her thumb brushing over the hammer. "We have to save Georgette." She couldn't imagine leaving the gun and walking into whatever awaited them without any sort of protection, but she didn't see an alternative. She couldn't put Georgette into any more danger than she was likely already in. Reluctantly, she unbuckled her belt and gathered the holster in her hands. Then she opened the cabin door and left her most prized possession—and their only defense—on the bed.

CHAPTER FOURTEEN

Anna

Somewhere north of Luxor, Egypt

Anna was furious at herself. Red-hot anger clawed at her throat and up her cheeks, choking her. For a moment, it crowded out the other emotions she had about the situation, such as fear and worry. She had managed to not only put her guests in danger *again*, but Georgette was being held hostage and in mortal peril. If anything happened to her, Anna would never forgive herself. It was Dra' Abu el-Naga' all over again. She had vastly underestimated the tomb robbers; at every turn, they were two steps ahead of her. She didn't know how they managed to do it, and worse yet, she didn't know what to do to get Georgette back and keep the other women safe.

Clara stepped back out from their cabin. She looked toward the baggage car, then swallowed, her hands smoothing the sides of her skirt at her hips, unconsciously feeling for the revolver that should have been there. Eliza, too, looked worried. Their fear was palpable.

Anna realized she couldn't allow them to put themselves in harm's way. If they barricaded themselves in the cabin, they would be safe. No one else could come snatch them. It was only right that she face the consequences of her pride alone. Everything that had happened in the last twenty-four hours, one catastrophe followed by another, was directly her fault. Eliza and Clara had nothing to do with any of it.

"No, you two stay here and lock the door. I'll go after Georgette myself," she said. She tried to sound confident, but it was impossible, under the circumstances.

Eliza shook her head. "I think the note meant we all gotta go." The twist to her mouth suggested she didn't want to.

Anna bit her lip. She wasn't sure. The note hadn't been explicit about who had to come. There was room for interpretation.

"I agree. You don't know what they'll do if only you show up," Clara said.

Anna wanted to refuse. She wanted to order them into the cabin for their own good. But there was the possibility they were right. And if that was the case, leaving them behind might guarantee that Georgette would be harmed. "All right. But…be careful." She didn't know what else to say. She hoped she was making the right choice.

Anna didn't know what they would find in the baggage car when she opened the door, but she didn't expect almost total darkness. The few small windows admitted all but no moonlight, nor were there electric lights like in the passenger cars. Only a small lamp, balanced precariously on a stack of suitcases, provided a hint of illumination. It was just enough to see that two people were already in the car, clustered beside each other at the far end.

"Put your hands up and shut the door behind you," one of the figures, a man, said.

"We're here now. You can let her go." Eliza spoke in a low, cautious voice. Perhaps she had already seen what Anna spotted a moment later: the glint of metal in the lamplight. The gun barrel was short and thick, and it was pointing at Georgette's head.

Anna froze, fearful of endangering their companion any more than she already was. As Anna's eyes slowly adjusted to the faint light, she saw that Georgette was sitting on a pile of suitcases. Her hands were held behind her back in a way that indicated they were bound. A gag was wrapped around her head, covering her mouth. Her captor was standing to her right, directly beside the lamp.

Anna's heart lurched, sickened. He was wearing a light-colored suit that could have been gray or tan, and although his hair was slicked back, she could just make out that it was red. The French archaeologist Fernand Bisson de la Roque had not boarded the train with them at Luxor. Eliza had been right—they had been followed. And Anna had done nothing to stop him or protect them.

"Let her go?" the man repeated. "I don't think so. In fact, now that I have you, I think I'll keep *all* of you."

His words sent a shiver down Anna's arms.

"What do you want from us?" she asked. Although she tried to sound stern, her voice was small and worried.

Georgette's captor turned his pistol so that the barrel now pointed at the three new arrivals. "Listen to me very carefully. What's going to happen next is I'm going to tie you up just like I've tied your friend. So long as you behave, when we reach Cairo I will release you. Then you will go directly to Port Said and board the next steamer to Europe and forget you ever heard of Luxor." His voice dropped menacingly. "If you do not behave, I will shoot all of you and push your bodies out of this train, where no one will ever find them."

Anna's mouth went dry. From the cold emotionlessness of his voice, it was clear he wasn't bluffing. He grabbed a length of pale rope from Georgette's lap and tossed it at Eliza's feet. It landed with a dull thud. He pointed to Anna. "Tie her first, then the other one. Don't bother trying to be clever. I'll test the rope myself, and if I find it a centimeter loose, I will shoot one of you. Do I make myself clear?"

"Yeah, I hear you." Slowly, unwillingly, Eliza bent to pick up the rope. She held it awkwardly in her hands, as though it were a dead snake. She looked between Anna and their captor, her face full of misgiving, but the instructions had been clear. Anna nodded to her, giving her permission to do what she must. At least he hadn't killed them outright.

"On the ground. Lie down on the ground," the man ordered, impatient.

Reluctantly, Anna got to her knees, then lay on her stomach. The warm metal floor vibrated beneath her as the train clattered over meter after meter of track, hurtling endlessly onward in the night. No one else on the train knew what was happening. No one would come to their rescue. They were at his mercy.

Eliza knelt beside her and gently moved Anna's left hand onto the small of her back, then her right. The thin cord bit into her wrists as Eliza cinched it tightly. Eliza wasn't taking any chances the man would find it too loose. In her shoes, Anna wouldn't have either.

She had no sooner finished than a second rope landed beside her. "And the blonde."

Clara joined Anna on the floor. Anna's stomach churned with so much dread and regret it was almost nauseating. She had gambled wrong in leading the other women to this. And if he killed them, it would be entirely on her. Powerless, all she could do now was hope the man would keep his word and let them go in Cairo. Then she would do exactly as he ordered and put the women on the first ship home.

Eliza made quick work of tying Clara's hands. When she was done, their captor stepped forward, carrying the lamp with him. "Now you."

She sank obediently to the ground, stretching her wide body alongside Anna's and placing her hands behind her back. The man crossed the distance between them and took a knee beside her, setting the lamp down next to him. Tucking his pistol into the waistband of his pants, he whipped out a third piece of cord from his pocket and bound Eliza so tightly she grunted. Then he stood and walked somewhere Anna couldn't see.

A moment later, she felt unyielding rope snake around her ankles like a noose and pull. Her boots knocked together, held fast. When he checked the rope at her wrists, it didn't move a centimeter. Still one more indignity awaited her. Straddling her waist, the man looped a folded bandana around her face so that it seated across her mouth. The fabric pulled so tightly against her cheeks it felt like she was smiling. She could whimper around the gag, but she would never be able to call for help. She was so anxious she could barely breathe. He could do *anything* to them, including toss them from the train like bundles of sugarcane, and there would be nothing they could do to stop him.

He moved on to Eliza and Clara, repeating the process. When he was done, all four women were as still and silent as mummies. He looked over his work with satisfaction, then picked up his lamp. "That'll do. Be good girls now and when the train stops, I'll let you out."

It was a thirteen-and-a-half-hour trip from Luxor to Cairo, and they were barely more than a few hours into it. Anna couldn't imagine how she would be able to walk by the time the train arrived. Already, the rope was cutting off some circulation in her legs, making them tingle. Her arms were in even worse shape. But it was better than the alternative.

The man began to whistle, a light, almost happy tune. He walked jauntily to the door and thrust it open. The light from the first sleeper car backlit him, bathing him in yellow light. "Try to get some sleep now. Cheerio."

The door locked behind him with a definitive click.

With the lamp gone, the car was plunged into darkness black as Ahmose's tomb. Deprived of her sight, Anna's other senses heightened. She could hear the suitcases rattling on their racks. She could feel the rumbling of the train's wheels as they passed over uneven iron tracks. She could smell hot oil, leather, and steam. Anna thought if she had to endure this barrage of sensations for the next ten hours, with nothing to do but think about their situation and how it was all down to her mistakes, she might go mad.

But she didn't end up having long to dwell on it. A few minutes after he left, Clara rolled into her. Their bodies jostled against each other like mints in a tin. Reflexively, Anna started to ask what she was doing, but she'd forgotten the gag in her mouth. The question came out a muffled, unintelligible gargle instead.

Clara continued to wriggle against her, a shimmying, inelegant yet intentional motion. What was she doing? Anna couldn't tell by feel alone. The American pushed against her for an uncomfortably long time, then Clara's weight landed heavily against her as she rolled halfway onto Anna's back. Anna was still baffled as to her motive until Clara's hands groped over hers, feeling for the rope binding her wrists.

No! she thought, panicked. If the man returned and discovered what Clara was up to, he would shoot one or all of them. It wasn't worth the risk. Better to wait out the night until they reached Cairo, no matter how long and difficult it would be.

She grunted and twisted, trying to buck Clara off, but it was almost impossible with Clara's weight pinning her down and her hands and feet tied. Meanwhile, seemingly not understanding what Anna was doing, Clara kept working the rope with dogged determination.

Eventually, she succeeded at loosening it. Benumbed, Anna's arms separated automatically, her right hand smacking with dead weight against the floor. Clara rolled off.

Anna ripped her gag down. Her dry tongue tasted of grease. "What are you doing? He could come back at any moment!" She hissed the words, looking nervously at the door as though even referencing their captor might cause him to materialize there.

When Clara didn't respond, she remembered Clara was still gagged. Turning on her side, she felt for the cloth knot at the back of Clara's head. When she found it, she released it, letting the gag fall to the floor.

"Hurry up and untie me," Clara said.

Anna was aghast. "He'll kill us if he finds out!"

"Who says he won't do that anyway? Or that we won't be met in Cairo by more of the robbers and taken somewhere else? I don't want to risk it, do you? We have to have a fighting chance. Now come on, we need to untie the others."

Anna hesitated. She wanted to believe the man would honor his word and let them go unhurt, but now she realized Clara was right: there was every chance worse things awaited them, either on the train or in Cairo. They had no reason to trust him and every reason to mistrust him. Stay or try to escape—either choice could lead to death. She made a snap decision. Quickly, feeling with trembling fingers where her eyes couldn't see, she finished releasing the bindings at Clara's hands.

They each untied their own feet, then Clara stood. "Georgette! Where are you?"

A stifled burble answered from the front of the car.

"I'll go get her. You help Eliza," she told Anna.

Without waiting, she disappeared. Anna fumbled in the dark for Eliza's bindings, her hands catching in Eliza's skirt. The knots were tighter than Clara's had been, and she had to dig her fingernails into them to force them to release. A minute later, all four women reunited on the left side of the car next to one of its windows. A shard of moonlight shone through it, the light fainter than a lit match. It was enough to illuminate the women's outlines, but nothing else.

"What do we do now?" Eliza asked, grimacing and rubbing her wrists.

"We cannot stay here. What if he comes back? It is certain he will shoot us," Georgette said.

"But we can't leave. The door is locked, remember?"

There was only one door into and out of the car, and the man had made sure it was locked. Climbing out the window was out of the question. For one thing, it was too narrow for anyone to pass through but Georgette. For another, even if she did get through, there was no place to go.

"Oh, that is not a problem!" Georgette exclaimed. She reached behind her head and pulled a bobby pin from her bun. Anna only knew that's what it was because she could see the sliver of thin, dark metal between her pinched fingers. Georgette worked the brittle metal with her hands until it snapped in two. Putting one half in her mouth, she bent the other half into an L shape.

She took the first half back out of her mouth and held up the two pieces. "This will open it. Most locks, they are very easy to open."

Anna couldn't help but gawk at her. Could she really pick locks? Where had she learned it? And why? Pulling herself together, Anna asked, "What do we do once we get the door open? How do we know he's not sitting or standing on the other side of it to make sure we don't escape?"

"He cannot be," Georgette said with her usual certainty. "For so many hours? How he could explain to someone why he is there? And also, there is no chair, and he will not sit on the ground. He must have gone to a cabin or to the dining car. He will not know we have left."

Anna had to admit, Georgette had a point. But getting out of the car was only their first challenge.

"When he realizes we've escaped, he'll come after us," she said. "What do we do then?"

"If we all stay in one room, he cannot make us come out. He is one and we are four. And Clara has her *revolver*. When we arrive to Cairo, he cannot stop us from leaving."

Anna wasn't so sure. She imagined him reappearing on the platform, gun pressed into one of the women's backs with a snarl of vindictiveness. Even if they shouted for help, there was no telling whether anyone would dare help them. She supposed all she could do was handle that situation if or when it came. For now, they had to get out of the baggage car.

She took Georgette by the hand. "Come on, let's see if you can open the lock, first." If she couldn't, they would have to come up with a new plan, such as trying to jump the man when he entered the car or calling for help out the window when the train rolled into the station.

She tiptoed toward where she knew the door must be, holding her free hand in front of her to feel for any obstacles in her path. After a few meters, her fingers brushed against metal. She laid her palms against it, feeling for the seams and confirming there was a knob at the proper height. She guided Georgette's hand to it. "The door is here. Can you feel it?"

"*Oui.*"

"Can you pick it?"

Georgette groped at the knob for a moment, feeling it. "I believe I can."

Anna moved to the side as Georgette hovered over the lock, her arms working, her hands invisible in the dark. Nervously, she listened for any sounds coming from the other side of the door that would indicate they had been wrong about the man waiting there. All she heard, however, was silence.

After what felt like only seconds, the lock clicked.

"It is done," Georgette announced.

She spoke loudly enough that the other women heard her. They hastened forward, gathering around the door. Anna took the knob in her hand. It was still warm from Georgette's touch. Her heart was beating wildly. Just because she hadn't heard anything on the other side didn't mean it was safe.

Holding her breath, she turned the knob and opened the door just enough to press her eye to the crack. For a moment, the bright yellow light of the sleeper car blinded her. She blinked, squinting against the glare. The first thing she noticed as her eyes adjusted was that their captor was nowhere to be seen. She let out a breath of relief. That was one danger passed.

The second thing she noticed was a small crowd of passengers huddled around the sleeping cabin at the far end of the car. She realized with a spark of hope that this throng provided the perfect cover. Wherever the man was, he wouldn't be able to see his captives escaping the baggage car through the mass of bodies. The timing couldn't be more perfect. She cracked the door open just enough for them to squeeze out. "Let's go."

They crept quickly toward Anna and Clara's cabin. As they moved closer to the crowd, however, it became clear that something was wrong. The pitch of the murmuring suggested fear, and the passengers' faces were full of concern and apprehension. Georgette, who was in the lead, slowed, her attention caught by it.

"Ignore it," Eliza growled. "Just get in the cabin and shut the door."

"But what is wrong?"

"It doesn't matter. All that matters is getting safe."

Eliza might as well have saved her breath. Instead of taking refuge in the safety of the cabin, Georgette walked past it and onward until she was standing at the periphery of the crowd.

She leaned over a short woman in a kaftan and a silk turban to see inside.

"What has happened?" she asked.

The woman turned to her, watery blue eyes wide with shock. "A man was killed."

Anna, who had followed Georgette with the intention of wrangling her back into the cabin, felt her knees go weak. The thief had killed someone. Who? And why? Had someone seen him and confronted him? Where was he now? Had he been caught?

The woman, an American, continued, "It was a cobra, they say. Someone saw it slither out of the room. Apparently it was enormous. A full nine feet long and gold colored."

Georgette gasped and stepped back, looking around frantically. "Then why everyone is here? The snake, it could still be here!"

"Oh, it's all right now. The porters looked everywhere and couldn't find it. They put down naphthalene to make sure it wouldn't come back, but they think it went through a hole and fell out of the train. We're safe, thank God."

Driven by morbid curiosity, Anna pushed her way into the crowd, trying to get a better look. Although the Egyptian cobra was the most dangerous snake in Egypt, she'd never actually heard of someone being killed by one. They were shy creatures, more apt to flee than to fight. The dead man must have startled one and it attacked out of fear. Bad luck for him.

Her eyes alighted on a pair of black shoes, their soles pointing to the ceiling. The porters hadn't moved the body, leaving it for the police to handle instead. So she could see that the man had died in his suit, face down on the floor. The light of the cabin dyed his hair a sort of strawberry blond, but that wasn't its true color. It was red.

Anna's body drained of every emotion but shock. The thief was dead.

CHAPTER FIFTEEN

Georgette

Georgette locked the cabin door behind her with a weak click. Although she had just demonstrated how easily the lock could be picked, a three-meter-long snake had killed a man and disappeared. For all they knew, it could still be on the train. She turned to her companions and shook her head, bewildered. "Killed by *un serpent. Incroyable.*"

Clara shivered and rubbed her arms. At her hip once more was her revolver. Georgette was glad of it, although she wasn't sure even Clara could shoot a rapidly slithering snake, should it come to it. "I can't believe he's dead. Just minutes ago he was—"

"Tying us up and threatening to kill us," Anna grumbled, face stormy.

"What do we do now?" Clara asked.

Eliza crossed her arms and leaned back against the window. Behind her, flashes of light indicated the train was passing through a lightning storm. A mixture of anger and sourness animated her face. "We stay right here and don't leave until we reach Cairo. He could have an accomplice on the train. We ain't getting tied up in the baggage car again."

There were many unresolved questions about their current situation, but to that, at least, Georgette had an answer. She perked up, sensing the opportunity to be useful. "Oh! He does not."

"How do you know?" Eliza asked.

The inexorable machine of Georgette's mind was in motion, showing her everything that had happened from when the dead man had approached her in the dining car until now. He had been a cruel, villainous man. And he had had a bad habit of talking aloud to himself, something that was useful to them now. While tying her up, he had complained that his associate in Luxor had disappeared without a word, leaving him to follow the women by himself although it wasn't his job to babysit them. Georgette summarized all this with a shrug. "This is what he said. I am certain that there are no other thieves on the train. It was only him."

Eliza grunted, unconvinced. "Well, even if that's true, we ain't totally out of the woods yet. We don't know who's gonna show up in Cairo. It could be a whole gang of them."

Anna put her head in her hands. "This is all terrible. I can't believe I've put you in so much danger. I feel awful."

"I guess we got lucky," Clara said. "First that solar eclipse, then the snake. What are the odds?"

Georgette cocked her head, confused. She had assumed the other women knew. "But it was not *une éclipse solaire*."

Eliza's eyebrows drew together into an uneven line. "What do you mean it wasn't a solar eclipse?"

"*Une éclipse solaire* happens not even once in three hundred and sixty-five days. This year it has already happened, *en septembre au Mexique*. The next one will not be until January 1925, in America." She was quite certain of this information, having once seen a chart of total solar eclipses for the entire twentieth century. Egypt would only have one in one hundred years, and it had already happened in 1905. It was therefore utterly and scientifically impossible for what had happened at Dra' Abu el-Naga' to have been a solar eclipse. Not to mention a solar eclipse could never occur so suddenly and produce such enveloping darkness.

"But then what did we see?" Clara asked, quizzical.

Georgette shrugged. This was a question she had been pondering for some time without settling on a satisfying answer. Her primary hypothesis was that they had experienced a freak meteorological event—her best guess was a small wall cloud. If she was right, the women hadn't noticed the arrival of the thick clouds above them because they had been so focused on climbing to reach the shooter. And once the clouds' shadow had passed, they had been too busy looking for him to see the storm rushing away. It was not a perfect hypothesis—for one thing, the clouds should have been visible for long after they returned to the cars—but it was certainly more plausible than a rogue solar eclipse. Egypt's weather, as indicated by the lightning outside, was unpredictable. And frankly, she hadn't been able to think of a second hypothesis.

Eliza rubbed her temples, squeezing her eyes together. "In any case, we gotta decide what we're gonna do once we reach Cairo. What if the thieves are waiting for us there?"

Anna stood up abruptly from where she had been sitting beside Clara on the lower bunk, holding Clara's hand in hers. "You're getting on the next train to Port Said, that's what you'll do. This has gone far enough. You're going back home on the next steamer."

Georgette put her hand to her heart, dismayed by the suggestion. "Leave *Égypte*? We cannot! We must keep going. It is only a little farther to Alexandria, then everything will be finished. We cannot stop now."

"Georgette!" Anna could have been angry, exasperated, scared, or all three. "How could you possibly say that? We could have been killed just now, not to mention how close things came at Dra' Abu el-Naga'. I can't put you into more danger." She stomped her foot dramatically. "You going any further is out of the question."

"But what about *le trésor*?" Even now, it was sailing toward Alexandria.

Anna rubbed her forehead with the heel of her palm so hard her skin flushed pink, then put her hands on her hips. "I don't know. I'll find a way to get it. I'll work with the Alexandria police or the Department of Antiquities. Something. It doesn't matter. What matters is you'll be safe, all of you."

Georgette pouted. It was true that both situations had been terrifying and that they had come quite close to death, but she wasn't willing to give up so easily. Not with what she knew.

"But it will not be *dangereux*."

"How could it not be?" Anna exclaimed, hands flying into the air. "Look at what's happened already."

Georgette presented her key piece of information, their ace in the hole—the reason her friends did not need to worry what would happen once they reached Cairo. "The thieves, they do not know we are coming after them, and so they will not try to stop us."

It was the perfect opportunity. They couldn't be in danger if the thieves thought they were still in Luxor. The room was silent for a moment, then Clara spoke up. "Why wouldn't they?" She pointed in the direction of the dead man. "*He* knew."

Georgette waggled her head. "*Oui*, but only him. When we left for the station from the office of *Inspecteur* Ibrahim, he could not have stopped to give a phone call to anyone. He had to follow us and always be watching. And he did not see anyone because the other man, he did not come back to Luxor from Dra' Abu el-Naga'. So only the dead man knew we are on the train."

Anna looked thoughtful. "He wouldn't have found a telephone or telegraph office if he'd wanted to, not between the Inspector's office and the station."

Georgette smiled, pleased that Anna agreed with her. "So now he is dead, the thieves will think we are still in Luxor. They do not know we are on the train to Cairo to catch them. We will surprise them."

She crossed her arms and smiled smugly. Everything came together neatly, like a package tied with string. It was her favorite kind of outcome. "We will still see *le trésor*. We do not have to leave *Égypte*. It will be safe for us." She had come to Egypt to see the treasure of a pharaoh, and despite all that had happened and the danger they had faced, she still could.

Clara looked to Anna questioningly. "Is she right?"

Anna drummed the long fingers of her right hand against her hip. "I suppose she could be, if he really was the only member of the gang who saw us get on the train. But we don't know how many men they have in Luxor. All it would take was for one to ask the stationmaster whether we'd boarded a train and they'd know we'd left for Cairo."

Georgette shook her head. "*Non*, there were only the two."

"Well then what about that man from the cliff? He could call ahead from Luxor, couldn't he?" Eliza challenged.

Georgette had already considered this. "He will assume his friend is following us, so he will not call. You see? This is why no one knows we are going to Alexandria. The one man who knew, he is *mort*."

Anna rubbed her mouth, agitated. "Even if you're right, I can't ask you to continue on to Alexandria with me. If anything—"

Georgette flapped her hand, dismissing everything Anna was about to say about the danger of going on. She had just proven there was no danger. There was nothing more to discuss. "*Fin de discussion*. We are going."

"Why are you so determined to go running after those thieves after everything they've done?" Eliza demanded.

"Because I know what it is like to have a heart that cries for something. I know what it is like to want and to want, but to get nothing. In New York, Anna said we must fight, always. You cannot convince the men of France to allow me to go for *un doctorat*, but we can help Anna. We can still find *le trésor*. Why do I want to go after the thieves? Because I believe this story has not ended. The end, it can still be happy."

Her impassioned speech was followed by a long silence. Eliza stared hard at her, but when she spoke, her question was for Anna. "Once we get to Alexandria, we won't run into the thieves again, right? You'll talk to the police and make sure they catch them, but that's all?"

Anna gave her a look that was half insulted, half horrified. "Well, I'm certainly not boarding their barges with a cutlass between my teeth, if that's what you're asking. My intention is to see the thieves arrested and the treasure from the tomb sent back to Cairo under appropriate guard. I won't be apprehending them myself."

Eliza's eyes moved between Anna and Georgette, calculating. At last, she nodded. "All right, I'll come." She fixed Georgette with a hard look. "But if there's even a whiff of danger, I'm leaving on the next steamer home."

Georgette scoffed. That wouldn't be necessary. She looked to Clara. She felt optimistic. For the first time since the incident at the tomb, the women seemed to be pulling together. "You will come too, Clara, *non*?"

Clara nodded. "When you put it that way, how could anyone say no?"

* * *

December 11, 1923
Somewhere south of Cairo, Egypt

When she woke up many hours later, feeling light and refreshed and only a little cramped by the short, narrow bunk that had originally been claimed by Anna, the light was still on in the cabin. Eliza was staring out the small window at the pink dawn above the horizon. Anna had fallen asleep on the tiny stool across from her, her head tilted backward against the wall and her arms hanging loosely at her sides. On the bottom bunk, Clara was snoring softly. Georgette climbed down the ladder from the top bunk as quietly as she could, planning to go to the dining car to have tea and read her book.

When she reached the ground, Eliza said softly, "I hope you're right."

Georgette cocked her head, confused by the missing antecedent. "About what?"

"The thieves thinking we're still in Luxor."

Georgette furrowed her brow. This topic again. She had thought it had been completely settled the night before when she went to bed. She shook her head. "They cannot know we are not there. It is *impossible*."

"What if you're wrong?"

Georgette remembered how it had felt when the world had gone dark at Dra' Abu el-Naga' and gunshots had rung out around her. She remembered the fear that had raced through every nerve of her body as she collapsed to the ground and tried to crawl away, the choking dread. Being abducted by the dead man and threatened with murder had been only slightly less shocking. But she had learned something about herself in the aftermath of these terrifying events: for all the fear she'd felt, she did not feel regret. Of course she did not want to die, but she was willing to face danger to do what was right, and stopping the thieves was right. And besides, perhaps of all the ways to die, at least this carried with it intrigue and adventure. What other mathematician could claim that?

But it was a moot question anyway. "I am not wrong. But maybe for some things, we must take a small risk, *non*? It is not so different from you and your *avion*. Each time you fly, it is *dangereux*, but you fly anyway."

Eliza leaned back against the wood-paneled wall and looked at her appraisingly. "Georgette, you may just be the bravest of any of us."

She considered the idea. "What is *la bravoure*? You fly your *avion*, Clara, she chased the men in Khan el-Khalili and Dra' Abu el-Naga'. Who decides what thing is braver than something else? We can all be *courageuses*." Her eyes fell on Anna and she felt a warm flush of compassion. "Even if there is *danger*, we cannot allow Anna to face it alone. She would not let us."

Eliza looked unconvinced. "Maybe. But we ain't known her long. Ain't any of us known each other more than a few days, when it comes down to it. It's a lot to ask someone to keep risking their life for that."

"A few days, *oui*, but even so we are friends."

The Georgette who had lived almost her entire life in France did not have friends. She did not have obligations or strong ties of affection. She understood the concept of friendship only in the abstract. But the Georgette who had chased an assassin in a bazaar, sailed up the Nile, and picked the lock of a baggage car to escape a kidnapper was not the same woman. After having spent so many hours with her companions and undergone these experiences, it felt only right to call them "friends." And for the first time in her life, she had come to understand that friendship meant both affection *and* obligation. She finished her argument. "And friends, they help."

Eliza grunted. "You ain't had many friends, have you?"

Georgette affixed her hat to her head, preparing to head to the dining car. *"Non."*

As she closed the door to the cabin behind her, she smiled. Friends. She could say now, and with certainty, that for the first time, she had friends. And it was a good feeling.

* * *

Alexandria, Egypt

By the time their train rolled into the station at Alexandria just after noon, the women's spirits had lifted immensely. For one thing, they had spotted no trace of the thieves since disembarking from the Luxor Express in Cairo. As far as they could tell, they were traveling undetected and unobserved, just as Georgette had predicted. For another, it was impossible to feel anything but awe for the beauty of the city beyond the train's windows.

"It's a pity we shan't be staying longer," Anna said as they gathered their suitcases from the racks above their seats. "Alexandria is one of the most beautiful cities in Egypt, full of history. Alexander the Great himself founded it. It was Egypt's capital, you know, until the Muslim conquest in 641."

"How far is it to the police station?" Clara asked, peering through the window at the cream-colored station outside.

"We're not going to the police, at least not immediately." Anna had to raise her voice to be heard over the chatter of the other passengers as she led the women to the car's exit. "We're going to the harbor."

"The harbor? Why there?" Eliza asked from behind Georgette.

"In order to ship the treasure out of Egypt, the thieves must have it booked as cargo on one of the steamers currently at anchor. The harbormaster will be able to tell us which boats are bound for Europe and when they're leaving. And since it's his job to know everything that's happening in the harbor, we can have him keep an eye out for the gold. If the police don't stop it, he'll be able to give us a heads-up in time to do something."

"But if the police do not do anything, how we will stop the thieves?" Georgette asked. Given Anna had promised they wouldn't be boarding any ships, she didn't know what options remained.

"We'll find out who owns the ship and call the company directly. That cargo is contraband. Anything found in an ancient Egyptian tomb is the property of the Egyptian Government. If the ship leaves the harbor with the treasure, it will be breaking Egyptian law. And knowingly transporting the stolen contents of a pharaoh's tomb would be a major international scandal once word got out. The shipping company won't risk being banned from Egypt's ports. It could ruin the firm."

They filed off the train and out the station, Anna in the lead. Outside was a broad, unpaved lane where half a dozen black horse-drawn carriages were parked waiting for passengers. Anna put her fingers in her mouth and gave a loud, shrill whistle, attracting the attention of the drivers. She held up four fingers, and in response, the driver of the biggest carriage mounted his seat and wheeled the horses to meet the women.

"*Hayyat al-mina', low samaht,*" Anna told him as the four women climbed in.

The driver nodded and cracked the whip as soon as they were settled, sending his two bay horses prancing forward. As they rolled away from the station, Georgette made careful note of the fact that no carriages followed them. It was one more confirmation, the best yet, that the thieves did not know the women were after them.

Alexandria was even more like home than Georgette could have imagined. There were patisseries and terraces, tram tracks, and motorcycles with sidecars. She recognized the dresses in the shop windows at the Au Printemps store as identical to those in Paris itself. And unlike in Cairo, there were no camels marring the beauty of the paved streets. It made Georgette a little homesick. Alexandria was beautiful, but there was no place in the world as beautiful and wonderful as Paris.

After a few kilometers, the rows of stores and apartments in the heart of the city gave way to the usual warehouses, low buildings, and shanties that surrounded every large port in the world. The driver pulled the carriage to a halt in front of a plain, square building. Anna leapt spryly to the ground and addressed the driver. *"Estanna, low samaht."* To her companions, she said, "I've told the driver to wait. This shouldn't take long. Leave your suitcases in the carriage. They'll be safe."

She barely waited for them to descend from the carriage before she pushed open the door to the harbormaster's office. Inside were three desks, belonging, Georgette assumed, to the harbormaster and his two assistants. The men sitting at them looked up as the four women entered, surprised by the unexpected intrusion.

Anna put her hands on her hips and announced, "I'm here to report the greatest theft in the history of Egypt. At this very moment, the thieves are sailing the contents of a pharaoh's tomb to this port with the intention of transshipping it onward to Europe. Under Egyptian law, that cargo belongs to Egypt and the Department of Antiquities. It must be seized and returned to the Department immediately."

If she had expected shock and incredulity, she didn't get it. The assistant on the right pushed his thin, gold glasses onto his balding forehead and peered at her, almost weary. "Ah yes, the police rang us yesterday about it. Said we're to check all cargo before loading, no exceptions. There's a port-wide notice out about it."

Georgette blinked. Was it really that easy?

The assistant across from him, a middle-aged man with thick brown hair and a mustache like a comb, grabbed a stack of papers from his desk. "Hang on, didn't someone just now cancel freight on one of the steamers bound for Venice tomorrow?"

He began to paw through the papers. He paused, reading one, then held it up. "Yes, here it is. Five tons of cargo, freight unspecified. It was a last-minute addition, now withdrawn. You don't suppose it's got anything to do with this, do you?"

Georgette and Clara exchanged glances. Georgette didn't know.

"Doesn't cargo have to be declared?" Anna asked.

"Yes, for customs' purposes. It's odd this wasn't…"

Anna took a step toward him. "It must be the treasure then. If the ship sails tomorrow, the cargo must be here already, at the port. Where is it?"

Georgette raised her eyebrows. So they had done it. They really had found the treasure. How easy this part had been after all.

The man scanned the paper again. "It's gone."

CHAPTER SIXTEEN

Eliza

"*What?*" Anna bellowed.

Eliza felt like she'd crashed her Jenny nose-first into the ground. The air was pushed out of her lungs with a forceful shove.

"No." Anna shook her head violently. "No, then it can't be the right cargo. The treasure must not have arrived in Alexandria yet. The barges aren't supposed to come until tomorrow anyway. It's a coincidence. Is there any other recently booked cargo scheduled to be shipped in the next few days?"

"No. It's—"

Simultaneously, Georgette said, "It could be *le trésor*. The boats could have sailed fast up *le Nil*. It is only two days' difference."

Eliza wanted to shush her. Georgette was too caught up in the mathematics of windspeed and velocity to realize the awful implications of what she was saying. It wasn't that she was wrong—Eliza was sure she was right—but rather the situation required tact. After all she'd gone though, Anna deserved to be let down gently.

Anna waved her arms wildly, face flushed. "But then where did they take it? It's got to be somewhere. It can't be *gone*."

The man made a small, helpless gesture, grimacing. "The paperwork says it's been loaded onto lorries and sent overland, miss."

Anna's arms fell motionless. "Lorries?"

Eliza was just as confused as Anna. Where had the thieves found trucks on such short notice, and how had they loaded them so quickly? Then again, what wouldn't criminals do to save the fortune of a lifetime? Her mind spun, trying to process this new information. The assistant had said the bill of lading had been for five tons of cargo. "How many would it take to carry the treasure?" She imagined a short caravan of trucks slipping out of the city, packed full of gold and jewels.

It was Georgette who answered. "Only two."

"That can't be right. Shouldn't it be more?" It didn't seem possible that the loot they'd chased across half of Egypt would fit in a mere two vehicles.

"The trucks, they are likely to be either the *FWD Modèle B* or the *Berliet CBA*. These are common. Both trucks can carry up to five thousand *kilogrammes* each, but most likely the thieves cannot put all the gold in one truck. *Alors deux.* Two trucks. Really, it is not so *difficile* for them." She adjusted her glasses, everything in her world satisfyingly predictable and calculable.

Eliza nibbled on the bottom of her lip. She was familiar with both vehicles. She had seen plenty of them in France during the war and she had even driven in a Model B once, that strange, snub-nosed combination of a car and a tractor. But she hadn't expected to encounter them here in Egypt.

Anna's hands balled into angry fists. "Where? Where are they going?"

The first assistant answered. "The next port to which they could send cargo would be Tripoli."

Horror extinguished the blaze of Anna's passion. Her body shrank a little into the void it created. "They wouldn't. They'd have to drive across all of Italian North Africa to get there. That's what, two thousand kilometers from Alexandria? Even if they drove ten hours a day, I can't imagine how long it would take them to reach the city. There are no roads in the east, are there? Driving would be a nightmare."

"Ten days." Georgette somehow managed to brandish the answer like a weapon. "I think maybe the Berliet, it can go at most twenty *kilomètres par heure* with this cargo. So it will take ten days if the thieves drive ten hours each day." She tilted her head, thinking. "The *Modèle B*, it is faster. Maybe it will take only nine days."

Georgette was an endless fountain of knowledge, but Eliza wasn't sure this information helped them. They were standing in Alexandria while the treasure rolled farther away with every passing minute. Anna shook her head again, then ran her hands through her hair. "What about Bengasi? The Italians have been building up the port there, haven't they? And it's half the distance. Could the thieves try to ship the treasure out of there?"

The first assistant snorted so hard his glasses fell down his forehead and almost to the tip of his small nose. He hastily pushed them back into position. "No European ship will go there unless it wants to be scuttled by the rebels. The Italians have been fighting the Senussis all year. No, if your thieves want their cargo out of Africa by sea, it will have to be from Tripoli."

He leaned back and crossed his thin arms. "If it were me, I'd load at night onto a small, two-masted gaff-rigged schooner, then sail it into one of the smaller European ports where nobody would be looking for it." His white eyebrows jumped. "Then again, if it were me, and if it's the sort of treasure you say it is, I wouldn't let it out of my sight. I'd sleep next to it at night and sail with it all the way to Europe."

Anna ran her hands over her face, her palms coming together in front of her mouth as though folded in prayer. When she glanced back at the other women, her distress was palpable. "We can't monitor every small port in southern Europe. There must be hundreds of them."

She looked so lost that Eliza's heart ached for her. They had been so close, and now this. It was rotten luck.

"Why can't we call ahead? Get the police there to stop them," Eliza asked. Anna hadn't trusted the Alexandria police, but perhaps the police in Italian North Africa were different.

The assistant shook his head. "They've got a rebellion on their hands. They've hardly got the resources to dedicate to something like this. Not to mention they might just help themselves to the cargo in Tripoli instead." He gave a superior sniff, as though Englishmen like himself would never even consider it.

"What about the Egyptian police? Can't they do anything while it's still in Egypt?" Clara asked.

"The telegraph line to the border has been down for days. There's no way to reach the border post at el-Salloum, and nothing but desert between it and Alexandria."

As a wave of helplessness threatened to drown them all, Eliza remembered what Georgette had said on the train. *We must have something of our own because the world does not give it to us. We must fight always.* They had just crossed hundreds of miles to get from Luxor to Alexandria. She'd come to Egypt to see the sights, not to go chasing after grave robbers and criminals. But they were in it now. They'd come too far to give up. She drew herself up straighter. "Then we tell the police ourselves."

Anna blinked. "What?"

"We go after the thieves. We race around them to the border and get the police there to stop them before they cross."

"But they're a day ahead of us!"

Eliza shrugged. She was making it up as she went along. "The trucks will be slow and heavy. We can drive faster than them. How far is it to the border?"

"A little over five hundred kilometers, if you stick to the coast," the assistant offered.

About the distance from Atlanta, Georgia to Memphis, Tennessee. In her Jenny, they could have flown it in five hours, stopping twice to refuel, but her Jenny was thousands of miles away. She calculated in her head, not bothering to include Georgette in the analysis. If they set off by car immediately and traveled twice as fast as the trucks they were chasing, they might be able to just reach the border in time. But it would be a nail-biting race to the finish. She couldn't guarantee it would work. Trying to project confidence anyway, she nodded. "We can do it."

She looked to Anna to gauge her reaction. It was all moot if she didn't want to go. "Well? Do you want to try?" If not, their journey was at an end. They might as well catch the next steamer home.

Before Anna could answer, Clara asked, "But we don't have a car. How will we drive to catch them?"

Eliza frowned. Clara was right: there was no hope at all if they couldn't somehow gain access to a car. By the time Anna's Fiat arrived from Cairo, the thieves and their treasure would be long gone. Anna thought for a long moment, then snapped her fingers. "Prince Omar." The energy returned to her body, breathing life back into her. "Why didn't I think of him before? He's part of the Egyptian royal family, but he's nothing like the others—he's a scholar. He's been doing archaeological work for years around Alexandria. He all but rules the city, really. If someone can lend us a car on short notice, it will certainly be him."

She addressed the men in the room, who had been watching with interest. "Where can we find him? Is he here, or is he at one of his estates outside the city?"

Unexpectedly, it was the harbormaster—a burly man with small, dark eyes and a wild gray beard like a bird's nest—who answered. Leaning over his desk, he rumbled in a gruff voice, "He's been staying at his palace on Mahmoudieh Canal."

"Thank you." She spun and headed for the door. Eliza didn't have to wonder if she wanted to keep going after the treasure.

"Good luck," the harbormaster called at her retreating figure. "I hope you find what you're looking for. But be careful—the desert's been known to swallow up unwary travelers."

* * *

Eliza, who had visited Versailles and the Château de Chambord while living in France, had expected the prince's palace to be ostentatious and lavish. Instead, it was relatively modest. Its simple gray face was modern and unadorned, and although the home was larger than the residences around it, she had seen much grander mansions even in Chicago.

As their carriage rolled into the driveway, a man in a navy pinstripe suit hastened down the front steps, his head down. Eliza narrowed her eyes as he patted his breast pocket, searching for something. There was something familiar about him.

Georgette grabbed her hand enthusiastically. "Oh! *C'est Monsieur* Pearce." With her other hand, she pointed him out to the other women. Now that Eliza remembered him, Arthur Pearce's black, slicked-down hair and aquiline nose were unmistakable. His suit, she couldn't fail to notice, was just as impeccable as the one he'd worn on the steamship.

"You're right, it is him," Clara said.

Anna looked, curious. "Who is he?"

"We met him on the *Olympic*. He sells cotton," Clara answered. Her face suggested she wasn't as excited as Georgette to be seeing him again.

Eliza asked, "Wasn't he supposed to be in London?"

She remembered he had said he did business in Alexandria. She supposed he must have been unexpectedly called to the city for an emergency—a problem with a shipment, for example, or a dispute over prices. Now, by one of those coincidences that seemed to keep happening to them in Egypt, their paths had crossed again. Quoting Kipling, Arthur had said Port Said and London were serendipitous places of meeting. Apparently, Alexandria was too.

The cotton exporter looked up as he reached the bottom of the stairs, and as he did, he saw the women for the first time, watching him from their carriage. His eyes widened and his head jerked back, incredulous. "You? What are you doing here in Alexandria? Why are you not in Luxor?" If they were surprised to see him, it was obvious he was even more surprised to see them.

Georgette waved gaily. "*Bonjour, Monsieur* Pearce! *Quelle surprise* to see you here."

Her light, happy tone did little to disperse the shock on his face. He smoothed the front of his suit jacket as he tried to regain his composure. "What are you doing here? When did you arrive?"

"We arrived today. Now, as you can see, we are here to see the prince, if he is at home."

Arthur looked back at the building he'd just left as though mystified by its existence. "Home, yes, he is." He patted his pockets again, looking, presumably, for the cigarettes he carried there. "Is that all? You're here merely to visit Prince Omar? There's no other reason? What happened in Luxor?"

Eliza didn't know what other reason there could be for visiting the prince's house. But Luxor was a long answer, and they didn't have time to give it. They had to get the car from the prince before the thieves got any farther ahead of them.

"We have a favor to ask him," she replied.

"Ah, well, that makes sense. There are always people asking the prince for favors. May I ask…? No, no." He shook his head. "It's none of my business, is it? Still, if there's anything I can do, I'm happy to be of service." He glanced anxiously at the shiny black motorcar sitting in the driveway in front of the carriage. It was long and new and fantastically expensive, with four white-edged tires and a spare attached to the passenger-side door. Eliza had assumed it belonged to the prince, but now she understood that it was waiting for him.

Looking back at the women, he flashed them a hasty smile. "I beg your pardon, but I must be off. There's been a hitch in one of our shipments. I've been running about the city all day trying to work it out. I think it's sorted now, but I'll have to see to it personally. I hope you enjoy your time in Alexandria and the prince grants your favor." He gave them a half-bow, then ducked into the back seat of the car. The engine immediately roared to life, and the sedan rolled away down the road, as impatient to be off as its occupant.

Eliza shook her head as she watched him go. She might not make a fortune as a barnstormer, but at least she didn't have all the stress that businessmen seemed to carry. Arthur looked like he might just give himself a heart attack.

The servant who answered the door led the women through the palace to a small oasis that had been constructed behind it. Swans and ducks floated on a quaint, man-made lake ringed with lush plants and date palms dozens of feet tall. In a country where water was in short supply, Eliza recognized it as a subtle display of wealth and power. A lanky man in a brown suit and fez sat at a wicker table reading a newspaper and smoking a hookah. He looked up when he heard footsteps, revealing unexpectedly pale eyes over a curled black mustache.

"Bonsoir. Comment puis-je vous aider?" He was asking how he could help them.

Eliza hadn't expected the prince to speak French. To her ear, his deep, rich voice carried no trace of anything but a Parisian accent, as though he had been born there. She knew Georgette would be pleased by the touch of home.

Anna bowed, low and submissive. "Anna Baring, Your Highness. I...have a favor to ask."

The prince's eyes sharpened, piercing as a hawk's. They bore through her mercilessly. "Cromer's daughter." The words, spoken now in English, had an undefined accent, something neither Egyptian nor French. They carried with them a tang of venom.

Anna had warned the women during the ride from the harbor to the palace that the prince was no friend of the British. In fact, King Fuad had all but exiled him to Alexandria to keep him from making trouble in the capital with his demands for Egyptian self-rule. Eliza glanced at Anna out of the corner of her eye, concerned. Of all the people to come asking the prince for a favor, the daughter of the former British consul-general was the very least likely to be positively received. Still, they had to try.

Anna, to her credit, didn't so much as flinch at the mention of her father. "Yes. But this isn't about him. This is about stopping a tomb robbery."

The prince set down his newspaper, eyes still locked on her, and folded his hands together. "I hear you were part of the team that discovered the tomb of the pharaoh Tutankhamun, a most exceptional, historic find. I hope this is not in regard to that."

"No, it's—"

"But you know, I did not see your photograph in any of the papers, nor your name mentioned. It is as though you were not, in fact, at the site. As though you do not exist. Unusual, is it not?" It was a wicked, hurtful barb. Eliza, who, like the rest of the group, knew the full story, grimaced on Anna's behalf. He leaned back and tented his fingers. Eliza had to admit that although his palace was unlike those of Europe, he carried himself with the same inimitable grandeur of royalty—someone for whom work is recreation and money a toy. That, at least, was universal.

Anna's throat bobbed and the muscles of her cheeks jumped as she failed to suppress a wince. "The politics of archaeology, Your Highness."

"Mmm," he grunted. His expression was inscrutable. Eliza couldn't guess what he would do next. Would he throw them out? Would he continue to insult Anna? Would he play with them and give them hope, only to cruelly yank it away at the last minute?

He reached for the mouthpiece of his hookah, stretching the hose toward him, and took a puff. "This is what happens when you make the mistake of trusting the British. The politics of the English are, by nature, rooted in oppression. For one to gain, another must lose."

A long moment passed, during which none of the women seemed to know what to say. All possibility of asking for help hung in a precarious limbo. The smallest mistake now might tip the balance irrevocably against them.

He took another puff, the smoke streaming from the corners of his mouth as though he were a dragon. "I read your monograph on burial chambers during the New Kingdom, Lady Baring. It has informed my own work on the finances of Egypt under the pharaohs."

Eliza raised her eyebrows. She hadn't expected this shift in direction.

He looked levelly at Anna. "Several years ago, I heard you speak at a meeting of the Archaeological Society of Alexandria. You are a first-rate archaeologist. You deserve better than your countrymen have treated you." He laid the mouthpiece down. "Your father did not care for Egypt, and he did not respect its people. In your writing, your love for this country is clear. You may be English, but I am glad you have not repeated his errors. Now, what is this favor you have come all the way to Alexandria to ask of me?"

For a moment, Anna was too flustered to speak. No doubt, she hadn't expected this praise from the prince after the way their conversation had started. Finally, she said, "We need to borrow a motorcar."

The prince's mustache twitched. "How odd that you should ask for this. Mr. Pearce asked the same just now. Surely you have met him? He has been exporting alabaster from Luxor for years."

Alabaster? Eliza cocked her head, catching the discrepancy between what Mr. Pearce had told them and what he'd told the prince.

Prince Omar continued, "He has had a problem with a shipment in the last day. He has had to send it overland to Italian North Africa. It's lucky that all he required was two trucks. They are not easily come by in Alexandria."

Eliza didn't hear anything else he said. She was too thunderstruck. In the last two days, she had never stopped to wonder how the thieves had found out about Ahmose's tomb. She had assumed they had been watching Dra' Abu el-Naga' or that one of Anna's workers had tipped them off. It would have made sense. But now she knew the true source.

She, Clara, and Georgette had inadvertently told one of them midway across the Atlantic Ocean. *They* were the reason Anna's tomb had been looted.

CHAPTER SEVENTEEN

Anna

Anna had never met Arthur Pearce before a few minutes ago, nor, despite his evident profession as an alabaster exporter, had she ever heard of him. The well-dressed man they'd encountered on Prince Omar's steps was a stranger to her, just one more rich Englishman making a fortune off Egypt's resources in a country swarming with them. But the way Eliza's face went slack, her chest rising as she sucked in a sharp breath, told her Mr. Pearce was in some way important. The hair rose on the back of her neck.

"What? What is it?"

"He's one of them. He's one of the thieves." Eliza pressed her hand to her ample chest as though covering her heart. She looked like she'd seen a ghost.

Clara and Georgette, too, had shell-shocked expressions. Anna looked between the three, confused. They had seen the man only a few minutes ago. Obviously he couldn't be one of the thieves, who at this moment were doubtless kilometers deep into the Western Desert. "What do you mean?"

"On the boat going to England we were talking about the tomb. He overheard us, and that's when he came to talk to us. He wanted to know what we were gonna do in Egypt. We told him where you were digging. We said you'd found the tomb of a pharaoh. He must have telegraphed ahead and told someone about it. That's how the thieves knew about the tomb—we told them!"

Although Eliza was aghast, Anna was unconvinced. "It's a bit far-fetched."

She and Ali had agreed the culprits had likely been men who lived and worked around Luxor. They would have spotted evidence of the discovery of a new tomb and taken advantage. Although now that she thought about it, there was a problem with that theory: local men wouldn't have had the means to ship the treasure down river by barge under armed guard. Instead, they would have hidden the contents out of the tomb somewhere nearby. In order to avoid being caught, they would have sent small shipments of the treasure by felucca up the Nile over the course of a few years, to be sold to visiting European tourists or carefully exported to Europe. Whoever had orchestrated this heist, on the other hand, had significant resources at their disposal and enough familiarity with the shipping lines to know how to get it booked as cargo—with exceptional haste.

And it was more than unusual that Mr. Peace would have redirected a disrupted alabaster shipment overland to Italian North Africa instead of the much closer and accessible harbor at Port Said. It made no business sense to send a shipment over the thousands of kilometers of the two Italian colonies, where there was active war between the Italian military and the Senussis. And the fact that he'd required two trucks to do it seemed far too specific to be mere coincidence.

A chill passed through her. Without knowing it, they had been mere meters away from the man who had helped steal Ahmose's treasure. More than that, he had masterminded it. And they had let him go.

The prince raised an eyebrow, looking between her and Eliza calmly. "Is there a problem?"

Her face must have shown her horror and dismay. Eliza pointed in the direction by which they'd come, agitated. "That man, Mr. Pearce, is a thief!"

The prince's eyes became narrow, suspicious slits. "What do you allege he stole?"

With all that had happened since their arrival at Prince Omar's palace, Anna had forgotten that they had yet to tell him about the discovery of Pharaoh Ahmose I's tomb and the details of its subsequent robbery. Succinctly, she summarized the tale, emphasizing the participation of armed foreigners and the news they'd just received at the harbormaster's office that the shipment had likely been redirected to Tripoli. As she spoke, the prince's face darkened. His hookah and newspaper lay untouched on the table, forgotten.

When she finished, he stood, towering over even Eliza like a telegraph pole. His voice quivered with outraged anger. "I'll have the Alexandria police arrest Mr. Pearce at once. This is an outrage. An unimaginable crime against the Egyptian people. That he would include *me* as his accomplice in this larceny is unconscionable. It will not go unpunished."

"What about the treasure on the trucks?" Eliza asked. "If Mr. Pearce is in Alexandria, is there any chance the trucks are too?"

"No, they left the city yesterday. He was tying up loose ends here before driving out to meet them. I lent him my Duesenberg. I'll have the border guard put on alert. The trucks won't leave Egypt." The prince motioned to the servant who had escorted the women to him and issued orders in rapid-fire Arabic. When he finished, the servant spun and dashed away on silent feet, his robe flying behind him like a white flag.

"Does that mean we don't need the car?" Clara asked, looking at Anna.

"There is no need. The criminals will be stopped," the prince informed her.

Anna rubbed her forehead, thinking. The prince had significant influence throughout Egypt, particularly in the north and west of the country, but that didn't guarantee his name alone could stop the thieves. The border guards were paid all but nothing. Just as she'd worried the thieves might bribe corrupt members of the Alexandria police to look the other way as the treasure was loaded onto a steamship, she feared they could slip past the guards just by throwing them a few lapis lazuli necklaces and gold broaches from their haul. It would be more money than any of the guards could otherwise hope to make in their entire lives, and they could deflect the prince's wrath by claiming they never received the message or that the thieves hadn't crossed at the border point.

Although they now knew who had stolen the treasure, she was in the same situation she'd been in when they arrived at the palace. The only way to be certain the thieves wouldn't succeed was to go to the border herself, no matter how long and arduous the drive. Besides, someone had to accompany the treasure back to Alexandria and then onward to Cairo. God forbid someone steal it a *second* time.

She cleared her throat. "Your Highness, if you'll lend me a car, I'll drive to the border myself and make sure the trucks are stopped before they can cross into Cyrenaica. I'll take charge of the treasure on behalf of the Department of Antiquities and see that it's returned safely to the museum in Cairo."

The prince sighed and looked wistfully out across his oasis as though he could see beyond it all the way to the border. "I understand. I would go myself if business did not keep me here. I will have my Napier readied for your use. It is the fastest car in Alexandria. You will certainly be able to reach the border in time with it."

She bowed, truly and deeply grateful. "Thank you, Your Highness. I am in your debt."

The prince inclined his head in regal acknowledgment, the tassel of his fez sliding forward. A second servant appeared, and the prince rattled off a much more complex sequence of orders to him. When he, too, departed, the prince gestured to the palace. "Please, come with me."

The internal machinery of the palace was fully in motion as they walked through it. Servants ran past, arms full of papers, baskets, and food. It didn't surprise Anna that by the time they reached the front door, the Napier was waiting for them where the carriage had been. It was long and blue and built for speed, a gorgeous piece of British engineering that must have cost the prince dearly to buy and have shipped all the way to Egypt. Anna recognized the sacrifice he was making sending it with them. The desert sand would wreak absolute havoc on the machine. It was meant for paved roads, not sand dunes.

One servant polished the driver's side door while another placed bags of dates and oranges in the back seat. There were enough to last a week when Anna anticipated she would only be gone three days. Eliza trotted down the stairs and thumped the car's steel body with her palm. She whistled. "Well I'll be. It looks like a racecar. How fast can it go?"

"One hundred kilometers per hour." The prince's voice was factual, without a hint of the overweening pride Anna might have expected. "It should not, however, exceed sixty-five kilometers per hour over an extended distance or the engine will likely overheat." Then it would no longer be a car but a car-shaped metal statue.

Although the prince had assumed the other women would accompany Anna, she was already making plans to leave them in Alexandria. The drive to el-Salloum would be grueling and uncomfortable. Better they stay in Alexandria where they could take shelter in the shade and rest in a comfortable bed. They could see the treasure when it was back in Cairo.

"It's beautiful. Can you drive it?" Clara asked her.

"Yes, of course." Despite her best effort, however, she couldn't hide the slight hesitation in her voice. The truth was, she had only driven a few times. In Cairo, she had relied on Karim to handle the Fiat. Then again, to retrieve the treasure, she would drive a tank if she had to.

Eliza looked up from her examination of the car's dashboard. "You don't sound so sure."

"Well, I understand the fundamentals. Surely it can't be so different from—"

"The fundamentals? That's all? That's it, I'm driving. We ain't wrecking in the desert because you don't know how to drive."

"I didn't say that. I said—Wait!" She flew down the stairs to the car. "Not 'we.' You're to stay in Alexandria. All of you. I'm going on alone."

"*Ah mais non*, we must all go," Georgette protested.

"We've come this far. What's a few more days?" Eliza agreed.

"You could need us," Clara chimed in.

Anna looked between the women, stunned by this unanticipated solidarity. And yet she shouldn't have been surprised. Each of them had, in her own way, made clear her commitment to see things through to the end. Tears of gratitude pricked the corners of her eyes. She had invited them to Egypt to see the opening of a pharaoh's tomb, but when that had proven a disaster, they had stayed for *her*. If they wanted to come now on one last dash through the desert, she would no longer say no.

Prince Omar took a map from the young servant beside him and unfurled it over the hood of the car. It looked old and hand-drawn, with yellowing, curling edges. Using his index finger, he traced a path along the northern coast. He tapped an almost invisible spot, marking the location. "If you can reach it, I would recommend you spend tonight at Mersa Matruh. It is two hundred and forty kilometers west from here."

Anna winced, knowing what awaited them. The road on the western side of Alexandria was tattered and rough at best. Even the Khedival Motor Road, along which Mersa Matruh lay, was only a cleared track. And while Mersa Matruh had been a key garrison for the British when the Great War had spilled into North Africa, in the time since, the small port town had fallen back into the sleepy desert outpost it had been before the war. Who knew where they might find lodging there?

She squinted at the sky, tracking the path of the sun. By her guess, it must have been sometime after two in the afternoon. The sun would set around five, meaning that by the time they reached Mersa Matruh, they would be driving in full darkness. And that was assuming they encountered no trouble on the road. If they blew a tire, as was common on Egypt's roads, they would be trying to change it in total darkness. She plastered a confident smile across her face for the other women. If the

Bedouin had spent millennia crossing the Western Desert using only the light of the moon to guide them, they could follow the Khedival Motor Road to Mersa Matruh with only two headlights.

* * *

Mersa Matruh, Egypt

By the time the Napier rattled into Mersa Matruh, long hours after the sun had set, the women were more than ready to call it a night. They were covered head to toe in thick brown dust, and even when Eliza pulled the car to a stop, it still felt like they were rumbling over the uneven, rocky dunes of the Western Desert. She let the engine idle as they peered into the total blackness around them. "Well? What now?"

It was almost impossible to see anything beyond their headlights other than the large wooden sign announcing they'd arrived in Mersa Matruh. Anna climbed out of the car, her legs screaming their resistance to moving after so many hours of cramped sitting. The sand crunched beneath her boots, as she took a few steps to get the blood flowing again. She looked around. "Right. We need shelter for the night."

She had expected to find a village. Instead, they seemed to have found the remnants of the former garrison. The village itself must have been farther north. Her eyes landed on the wall of a building. She knew it must be empty, because otherwise the occupant would have come out to investigate upon hearing the Napier. She pointed at it. "There. We'll sleep there tonight."

She could just make out the unhappy face Georgette made in the passenger seat by the light of the moon. "I guess that is why the prince, he gave us these blankets." She picked at the brown coverlet on her lap. The women had laid the blankets over themselves during the drive to protect against the dust, but the effort had been mostly futile. The tiny particles of sand and earth had gotten into every crevice of their skin and clothes. Anna could even feel them on her eyelashes every time she blinked.

Georgette pulled out a picnic basket that had ridden the whole way under her feet and held it up. "At least he has also given us dinner. I am certain there is *une bouteille de vin* inside."

Anna reached back into the car and brought out a lantern, which she lit with a match from her pocket. "There must be a well around here we can use to wash up. I'll be back in a minute. In the meantime, Clara, can you check to see that someone hasn't turned the building into a goat pen?"

"Goats?" Georgette yelped, dismayed.

"Why not? The Egyptians will turn anything into a goat pen. It's quite efficient, actually," Anna said before setting off into the abandoned camp. For the British to have maintained an outpost of thousands of soldiers here during the war, they must have established a good water supply. It was only a matter of finding it.

She walked blindly for a minute or two until she all but walked into the metal handle of a hand pump. Thank God. Setting the lantern down, she pumped the handle a few times. It squeaked, reluctant to move after what might have been years of disuse. She waited, confident it would still work. After a pause, water gushed out. She cupped her hands beneath the spout to catch the tepid water, splashing it over her face and bare forearms. She relished the feeling of dirt and grime being carried away. Working in the Valley of the Kings for years meant she was used to shaking sand from her boots and hair every night, but the dust kicked up by the road was worse than anything she'd experienced digging, and there had been much more of it.

When she felt more human, she lifted the lantern and waved it over her head so the other women could see. "Here it is! The water is over here!"

A moment later, Georgette and Eliza came stumbling over to her, lurching as their shoes stuck in the deep sand. Heedless of dirtying her skirt, Georgette dropped to her knees and thrust her hands under the water, then took her glasses off and scrubbed her face with her palms. When she was finished, Eliza rinsed her hands, then used a handkerchief from the pocket in her shirt as a washcloth to wipe her forehead.

"Lord but it feels good to be clean again," Eliza said.

"I think I am wearing half of *le désert*," Georgette moaned, batting at her clothing with wet hands. "How there can be any sand left? It is all on me."

"It's even in my teeth," Eliza said, swishing water in her mouth and then spitting it out.

"You might as well get used to it. There will be more tomorrow, and then on the return," Anna said.

"When we are back in Alexandria, I will take a bath so long that my skin will be like *un pruneau*," Georgette said.

A few minutes later, Clara joined them, splashing water from the top of her forehead to the nape of her neck.

"Is the building empty?" Anna asked.

Clara looked up, water dripping from her chin. "Yes. It looks like it was an office. There's a desk still in there."

Anna nodded. It would do for the night. And, if things went well at el-Salloum, the next as well as they retraced their steps to Alexandria with the treasure. She tried not to think about what would happen if they somehow missed the treasure. They had a single moment of opportunity; everything hinged on the trucks traveling on the road and not trying to evade the border post. Otherwise, finding them in the desert would be like finding a needle in a field of haystacks.

Once the women were well washed, they made their way back to the old office, where they huddled together in the small circle of light cast by Anna's lantern. Clara and Eliza laid out the blankets while Georgette unpacked the picnic basket. She held up a chunk of white cheese triumphantly. "*Ah!* There is *fromage!*"

Eliza crawled over the blankets on her hands and knees and dug out some of roasted pistachios from the basket, which she tossed into her mouth. "How many more miles we got left?"

"Approximately two hundred and twenty-five kilometers," Anna replied, peeling an orange. The citrus juice was sweet when it hit her tongue, like a fine delicacy. She closed her eyes for a moment, savoring the taste. "We're halfway there. If we leave at dawn, we can reach el-Salloum around noon."

Clara wrapped her arms around her knees and pulled them close to her chin. Her face was mostly hidden in shadow. "I can't believe that this time tomorrow it could all be over."

Anna thought she heard an echo of sadness in Clara's voice, or else perhaps it was a projection of her own regret. Her guests had come to Egypt to see the opening of Ahmose's tomb. Instead, their first glimpse of the treasure that should have been there would be in crates in the back of lorries.

"Don't jinx it," Eliza said. "Seems like every time we think we're getting close, it's just out of reach. What's next? Rowing across the ocean after it?" She snorted and leaned back on her elbows. "I'm just glad it's almost over and we can go back to Alexandria and relax."

The wine bottle made a loud and startling pop as Georgette pulled the cork out. The other women jumped. They might be safe from the thieves now, but it was only yesterday they had almost gotten into a shootout at Dra' Abu el-Naga'. The sound still brought back unpleasant memories. Since they had no glasses to pour the wine into, Georgette put her lips to the bottle mouth and drank directly. When she set it down, she said, "We see le *trésor*, then we go to Alexandria. It is a beautiful ending to this *aventure*."

"Enough," Anna said. It felt like bad luck even talking about recovering the treasure. "Let's talk about something else. Eliza, what will you do when you return home? You said it was the end of the flying season, didn't you?"

Eliza shrugged and took the bottle from Georgette. "Yeah. We won't be flying again until the spring. I've been thinking: since I got some time before I gotta get back to the flying circus, I could take a steamer to Constantinople and look around some. Don't know when I'll have the chance to again."

Surprised by the answer, Anna contemplated the idea. Only two months before, British and Italian forces had left Constantinople after years of fighting the Turkish nationalists. Who knew what Eliza would find there now? Or, more importantly, what reception she would receive as an English-speaking—but Black—foreigner? The tide of the British

Empire was ebbing all over the Mediterranean, but whether that made the region safer or more dangerous for a woman like Eliza, she didn't know. The world itself didn't seem to know what the future held.

"And you, Georgette? When do you return to France?"

The mathematician was visible only as a white face floating in the darkness, the reflection of the lamp's light two embers of white at the bottom edge of her glasses. "March. This is when classes will begin again after the break for winter." She gazed in Eliza's direction. "I also would like to see Constantinople. There would be time. It is only *décembre*..."

Anna turned to include Clara in the conversation, but before she could speak, Clara turned her back to the women and pulled a blanket over her shoulders. "I'm going to sleep." Her tone was sharp and unhappy. "I'm tired."

Anna remembered too late their discussion at the Winter Palace and Clara's melancholy about her future. This was the exact subject that pained her. She pressed her lips together and vowed to make it up to Clara tomorrow. There was nothing she could do now.

For the next hour, she, Eliza, and Georgette traded stories, until at last the kerosene in the lantern was exhausted. Then she wrapped herself in a blanket and passed out on the floor, spent. It had been a long two days, and tomorrow would be just as long. Not even the excitement and anticipation of at last—if all went well—reclaiming Ahmose's treasure could keep her awake a second longer.

* * *

December 12, 1923

When Anna woke, it was to the same total darkness as when she'd fallen asleep. She guessed it was long past midnight, in that still and silent time between twilight and dawn when nothing moves but the wind and the scavengers of the desert. Although she didn't know what had awakened her, she had the distinct impression she was being watched. Holding as still as she could, she strained to see what was around her, but all she could make out was the presence of a dark mass in front of her.

There weren't many predators in the desert. If one had gotten in somehow, it was likely a fox or a weasel. The desert was too inhospitable for animals to grow large enough to be a threat to humans, so she wasn't scared, just alert.

Unexpectedly, a hand touched her face, soft and tender. Fingertips traced across the ridge of her eyebrows, feeling for her cheek. The touch was so light it was like being kissed by a butterfly. Anna knew neither Georgette nor Eliza would ever touch her like that. As she slept, she must have rolled closer to Clara. Did Clara realize she had awakened? She stayed motionless, waiting to see what Clara would do.

The fingers continued their exploration, careful yet persistent. Anna wondered what Clara was thinking. If she wanted something from Anna, she had only to ask. Clara reached her lips, running her fingers lightly across them. Anna's lips tingled. She was at a crossroads: she could remain still as a statue and allow Clara to continue her clandestine examination, or she could move and tip Clara off to the fact that she was awake.

She chose the latter. She opened her mouth and moved to capture one of the investigating fingers. For a brief moment, she sucked lightly on it. A faint intake of breath told her she'd surprised Clara. When she let go, Clara hastily withdrew her fingers.

Anna wriggled closer. Unable to see, she could only feel for Clara—the jut of her right shoulder under the blanket, the feathering of her blond hair at her neck, the cotton of her tan dress. Anna put her hand around the back of Clara's head and guided her forehead to Clara's, using it as an index for where their faces were in the dark. Clara neither stiffened nor resisted.

It was only last night that Clara had kissed her on the train, opening a door Anna had feared had been closed in Luxor. Although she had been distracted all day by the hunt for the treasure, Clara's fingers on her skin reminded her of exactly what they had been doing and how it had felt before Eliza had burst in to tell them about Georgette's capture. She ran her left hand over the curve of Clara's neck and to her shoulder as Clara's hand came to rest on her chest, directly over her heart. Anna shifted her hand to Clara's hip, moving her body even closer. They were centimeters apart, separated only by thin fabric. There were no thieves to interrupt them, no danger threatening to rip them apart.

Clara's hand traveled up her neck to her jaw, making every nerve in its path fire. When Clara leaned forward and kissed her, her lips were as timid as they'd been the first time on the train. The kiss went all the way to Anna's knees, sending waves of desire pulsing through her so strong she couldn't stop a small groan from escaping her lips. To avoid becoming lost in them, she focused on finding the curves of Clara's body—the dip between her hip and her ribs, the flat of her stomach. The bone and muscle of Clara's body were anchors that tethered her focus, the hard ground beneath her the rope tying her to the present.

As Clara continued to kiss her—or was *she* kissing *Clara?*—she felt Clara's hands at her waist, pulling her loose white shirt free from where it was tucked into her pants. Warm shivers raced down her legs. She sucked in a shaky breath, surprised but pleased at the direction things were going. Her body was buzzing, desperate to be touched. She swallowed, feeling the ache developing between her legs.

An abandoned office in the middle of the desert was hardly an ideal location for what they were doing. The floor was dusty and hard, nothing like the bed at the Winter Palace, or even the thin mattress of the sleeping cabin on the train. But Anna didn't notice any of it. She was too absorbed in the feeling of Clara's lips against hers, Clara's hands at her waist. She wrapped her hand around Clara's bottom and pulled her tight to her body, sliding her left leg between Clara's legs. The husky, shuddering breath and soft groan the movement evoked made Anna's eyelids flutter with a shudder of arousal and her heart race. She dropped her head to Clara's neck and kissed her there while she moved her hand over Clara's hip and across the front of her dress.

Clara's body was coming alive, pushing into her with an eagerness matched by Anna's own. When Anna squeezed her breast, her back arched and she whimpered more loudly. Lightning scored through Anna's veins. The ache was so strong it hurt, a smoldering burn that demanded her attention.

Clara's hands tangled in Anna's hair at her ears. Her breath came fast and ragged. When Clara huffed in Anna's ear, Anna had to bite down on her lower lip to stifle the small moan the sound provoked. Clara's hips started to rock as her body instinctively looked for more from Anna.

Someone on the other side of the room coughed.

Both women froze.

CHAPTER EIGHTEEN

Clara

Whoever else was awake in the small office—Clara couldn't tell—was shifting under the blankets, her shoes scraping against the concrete as she moved. Clara held her breath, a chill settling over her so cold it could have stopped her heart. What had the other woman heard? *Had* she heard? Did she know?

Clara's face flushed, mortified. The prickling feeling spread over her cheeks and down her neck. What she and Anna had been doing had been reckless and irresponsible. It wasn't like her at all. What had she been thinking? They were on the floor of an abandoned building, the other two women almost within arm's reach, not in a private train cabin or hotel room.

She started to wriggle away from Anna, wanting to burrow under the blanket and down into the ground beneath, but Anna grasped her wrist firmly, stopping her. In a moment, Anna was on her feet, pulling Clara with her and looping her blanket over her arm. Clara stumbled as she followed, her boots catching clumsily in her own blanket. Anna tugged gently, pulling her insistently toward the door. Although she didn't know what Anna was doing, Clara didn't resist.

Anna reached the door in only a few strides and pulled it open. They spilled out into the night, dark shadows against an even darker landscape as a small cloud briefly passed in front of the moon. Above them, the sky was full of dozens of constellations and thousands upon thousands of stars, but Clara couldn't appreciate the beauty of it. Her mind was preoccupied by the fear that they had been overheard and worry about how she would face whoever had heard them.

Anna pulled a small flashlight from her pocket and turned it on, shining it around them.

"Where did you get that?" Clara asked, surprised.

"It was in the picnic basket. Prince Omar's people really did think of everything. Come on, there's another building here—with a lock, I hope. I saw it when I was looking for the water pump. It's close."

The narrow beam of the flashlight swept the ground before them like a silver searchlight as Anna led Clara away from the office. The building Anna had been seeking turned out to be much closer than Clara expected, only a dozen steps in the opposite direction from the car. In the thin light, she couldn't tell anything about it other than that it looked small. Anna found the door and pushed it open. The hinges squealed like a dying sea monster. It had likely been years since the door had last been opened.

As they stepped inside, Anna shone the flashlight into each corner. The light was met by nothing but dust. The room was smaller than the office, but it was bare and relatively clean except for piles of sand that had collected near the door, carried in by the wind. Anna closed the door behind them, then turned the flashlight off. She unfurled the blanket she'd been carrying and laid it on the ground, spreading it to cover as much of the floor as she could. Then she took Clara's hands. "It's all right, we're alone here."

Clara was self-conscious. The organicness from the office was lost, replaced by an ungainly, uncomfortable expectation. Anna stepped closer and put her hands on Clara's hips. It was like electricity being applied to a magnet. Instantly, her doubts and fears were swept aside, her focus entirely on Anna.

Anna kissed her, and the electricity crackled everywhere along her body. Anna was warm as a campfire on a cool summer night. Clara leaned into it, slipping her hand beneath Anna's loosened shirt and running it up Anna's side. In response, Anna kissed harder, leaving a burning trail of lip prints down Clara's neck. She stepped back and knelt on the blanket, inviting Clara to join her. Clara did.

What happened next was a blur for Clara, but somehow Anna was above her, and conscious thought gave way to an overwhelming rush of feelings and sensations. The weight of Anna's body pressing into hers. The warmth of Anna's mouth as it covered hers and moved to kiss the line of her jaw, her neck, the skin just below her ears. The whisper of Anna's breath against her nose. The brush of linen against her wrists.

Warmth spread over Clara's body like summer sun despite the cold of the desert night. She was agonizingly conscious of every part of herself...and how much all those parts yearned to be touched. The dress she was wearing was a barrier between Anna's hands and her skin, but Anna's own clothing was not so restrictive. Clara undid the buttons of Anna's shirt and let her hands roam unreservedly over what lay beneath, feeling everything from the ribs beneath Anna's soft skin to the small breasts held gently by her bandeau. A month ago, she would never have considered touching another woman in this way. She would have been horrified by even the idea. Now it was an irresistible urge.

Anna's body twitched and pushed into her. Anna's breath came more rapidly, responding to Clara's touch. Clara was drunk with the feeling, Anna's arousal resonating and amplifying within her own body. Anna's right hand reached along the outside of Clara's leg, grabbing a handful of her dress and drawing it up. A flurry of tingles exploded from the pit of Clara's stomach that ran all the way to her toes. In its wake, it left the feeling of building pressure.

Clara breathed heavily, as though her lungs were struggling to find air. Her body squirmed, trying to get closer to Anna. She was drowning in the desire to be touched. It was overwhelming; it was all she could think about.

The same hand pivoted and ran along the inside of her thigh, featherlight. A high moan, full of raw desire, escaped Clara's lips. Her hips jerked toward Anna, seeking the hand. Her shoulders scraped against the ground. She didn't even notice the gasping, panting sounds she was making or the way her fingers clenched against Anna's hips. Her attention was fixed entirely on that hand and what it was doing.

Anna gently eased Clara's underwear off, encouraging her to raise her lower half to ease the process. All Clara could do was whimper, her legs quivering. She was helpless, caught under Anna's spell. She couldn't have stopped herself now if she'd wanted to, and she did not want to. Anna kissed her neck, her hands firm as they swept over Clara's body, and Clara could feel that Anna was taking care of her. Anna was with her. Anna would keep her safe.

Anna shifted her position to straddle Clara's right leg. Her left hand moved to cup against Clara's head. Clara had clamped her left leg against Anna's body after her underwear had been removed, but now Anna gently pushed it down as she kissed Clara on the lips again.

What Anna did next, Clara didn't know completely. All she knew was that her body arced up as though she had been struck by lightning, her shoulders pressing into the ground while her hips bucked upward. It was as though Anna had found the place where her soul met her body and touched it. Waves of pleasure washed over her. It was like nothing Clara had ever felt before. It was like finding water after having wandered the desert for days. It was thrilling and wonderful all at once. She moaned, thick and full-throated.

Anna's fingers, strong from years of manual labor, were agile and sensitive. They sent ripples of unbearable sensation dancing through Clara's hips. Outside of her control, her body responded to this new feeling. Her hips twitched. Her legs shook. She tilted her head back, swallowing back another moan. She'd never felt anything like this in her life. It didn't seem possible that one person could create these feelings in another.

Her hands fell to the floor, forgotten, as she whimpered. The feeling of pressure inside her built. She wanted more. Without being able to articulate the need, she felt an emptiness begging to be filled. Then Anna…

Clara's body arched again, and a new sound came out of her mouth. It was guttural and ecstatic all at once. This was the fulfillment she had needed. She shuddered. Her breath was loud in the small, empty room. It filled her ears, drowning everything else out. The building feeling was so much stronger now. Anna was the only thing tethering her to the earth, otherwise she might have floated away.

What started as a vibration became a hum and then a pulsing. With each move Anna made, Clara's body filled with electricity, until Clara thought there couldn't possibly be room for any more. Any more and she would blow apart. It was a crescendo building within her, starting at her extremities: the backs of her knees, the balls of her feet. She wanted to grasp Anna and clutch her to her chest. She wanted Anna to engulf her, to weigh her down. But more than anything, she wanted the crescendo to reach its peak. She didn't know what lay on the other side, all she knew was she had to get there.

Her legs began to shake in earnest, wild and out of her control. Her breath turned thin and reedy. Without realizing it, she began to whine.

The sensation reached its impossible, heady apex. Her entire body spasmed and lifted, straining toward the ceiling, curved like a bow. She gasped out a loud moan, her fingers scraping against the blanket. Every muscle in her body seemed to contract as a firework of pure pleasure exploded inside her, racing through every nerve of her body. Her head spun. Her hips rocked jerkily.

The feeling lasted forever and for no time at all. When her muscles relaxed, she fell back to earth. Her body went limp. Gently, carefully, Anna stopped what she was doing. Clara took deep breaths, trying to recover as her heartbeat slowed. So much blood had rushed to her head she felt as though she'd gone deaf.

Anna crawled next to her and pushed the hair away from her forehead. Then she kissed it, her lips resting against Clara's skin for just a moment. Clara felt she should say something, but there were no words to describe what she was feeling, and besides, the silence around them was too warm and comfortable to break. When Anna lay back, Clara nestled into the space between her chin and shoulder and wrapped her arm around her chest. Her breathing slowed as Anna stroked her cheek. She felt a profound peace.

For the first time in a long time, Clara didn't feel the quiet ache of being alone. She was not adrift in the world. Someone, Anna, had seen her for who she was and had loved her for it. She had carved a space for the two of them in the world to exist together, despite all the other chaos around them.

After a few minutes of enjoying this feeling, Clara remembered they couldn't lie there forever. If they fell asleep, there was the risk Georgette and Eliza would wake up the next morning, wonder where they were, and come looking for them. Clara had no desire to explain why they'd gone and what they had been doing. But nor could they leave now to go back to the office. The moment wasn't over yet. Clara wanted to give Anna the same pleasure she had given Clara. She just didn't know how.

She lifted her head and felt for Anna's face in the dark. Her exploring fingers found the familiar eyebrows and high cheekbones. Using them as landmarks, she kissed Anna, and when the kiss was too chaste to convey her intentions, kissed her more urgently. That caught Anna's attention. She rolled a little toward Clara, her breath warming Clara's cheeks as her hand came to rest on Clara's arm. Her right leg slipped over Clara's left.

Clara ran her hand lightly over Anna's chest. The sharp intake of Anna's breath was loud in her ear. It unleashed wild butterflies in her stomach. She glided her hand beneath Anna's bandeau. Anna's body shifted against hers, her leg pulling them closer together. Her hands settled at Clara's hips.

As Anna leaned forward to capture her lips in a deep, passionate kiss, Clara ran her hand down Anna's stomach. She found the button of Anna's pants and undid it. Her heart beat faster, fear swirling with excitement. Although she couldn't see Anna's eyes well in the dark, she looked toward them anyway out of habit. "I...don't know what to do."

Anna's right hand caressed her face. Her voice was gentle and understanding. "It's all right. I'll show you."

Her hand left Clara's face, and when Clara next felt it, it was on top of hers, guiding it past the waist of her pants and her underwear. "Here." She pressed firmly against Clara's hand, and Clara's fingertips found what they were meant to. Then she began moving Clara's fingers in a circle. She continued for several seconds, then she removed her hand.

Clara carried on the motion, at the same time trying to remember what Anna had done to her that had felt so incredible. It was difficult. She had been so lost in sensation that it was hard to know exactly how Anna had touched her. Anna sighed, and Clara thought she could just barely make out her eyes fluttering shut. It made Clara's heart flutter in her chest. She swallowed, the air thicker than it had been a moment before. Anna's hand returned to her neck, pulling their faces together into a deep kiss that Clara felt to her core.

After a few moments, during which time Clara worried she wasn't doing things well enough, she became conscious of Anna's hips working against her hand, pressing rhythmically against it. At the same time, Anna's breath became higher and sharper, like barely suppressed hiccups. Clara's body flushed with heat, remembering the feeling of being touched and thrilling at the reaction she was causing in Anna. She clenched her teeth together to stop herself from whimpering.

Anna grasped her shoulder, insistent but without hurting her. "Just…a little…lower." Her voice was rough and shaky.

Clara complied. Anna immediately grunted and twisted harder into her. The leg she had rested on Clara started to tremble, squeezing against her. Clara had never felt anything like this before. Being able to elicit reactions like these from another person was enthralling. It made her feel… There was no word to describe it.

Anna's breath rasped against her ear, making Clara's scalp tingle. Without realizing it, her fingers moved faster, trying to match the rhythm of Anna's breath. She pressed her own legs together, trying to staunch the ache building in herself again.

She sensed when Anna began to crescendo. Anna huffed, a primal sound that sent a thrill down Clara's spine. Her body stiffened and twitched and her arms shook, her fingers tapping out an uneven, unconscious rhythm against Clara's arm. The tension in her body seemed to fill the air all around them. Then the dam broke. Anna gurgled, a strangled cry. Her arms wrapped around Clara and clutched her tightly. Her body convulsed once, twice, a third time, then was finished.

She lay still, breathing heavily. Clara withdrew her hand, which was slightly cramped. Her heart was still pounding, and she had to push back against her body's request to be touched again. But she felt exhilarated. Flushed with elation and joy.

Anna wrapped her arms around Clara, pulling her close to her chest, and kissed her between her eyebrows. Clara could feel from the pull of her lips that she was smiling.

"We should go," Clara said, anxiously thinking of Eliza and Georgette once more. Lying with Anna in the quiet night was nice, but she couldn't forget they weren't alone.

Anna didn't move. "Stay a little while longer. There's no hurry."

But as they lay in silence once more, doubt and melancholy began to creep into Clara's mind. In a few hours, they would set off for el-Salloum. If all went well after that, Anna would be preoccupied with the treasure. She wouldn't have time to spend with Clara. Clara had exposed herself to Anna in a way she never would have imagined. She had dared to open Pandora's box, to ignore her fears, and to let raw emotion and feeling direct her. She had gone from promising to stay away from Anna to lying in her arms. This experience with Anna had fundamentally changed everything she knew about herself. She could never look at her life the same way.

But it didn't, couldn't mean the same to Anna. As she had said in Cairo, she had done this many times. Her world had not been turned upside down as Clara's had. And soon, Clara would be sailing back to America, six thousand miles away. What then?

* * *

The next morning brought with it more than just worry for Clara. It brought an unpleasant surprise: the Napier wouldn't start. Eliza rapped on the hood with her knuckles, then looked back at the women, squinting in the bright light of the sun, which had recently crept above the horizon. "It's not out of gas. But no way to tell what's wrong without a mechanic."

Clara, who was standing at the door to the office with the blankets the prince had lent them folded and stacked in her arms, felt her stomach drop. The car had worked perfectly the day before. It hadn't so much as coughed once. She couldn't understand how it could have broken overnight. Nor, evidently, could Anna. She crawled into the driver's seat and turned the key over and over again, as though hoping Eliza hadn't tried hard enough. But the car didn't so much as wheeze. She slammed her palms against the driving wheel, letting loose a growl of frustration. "No! This can't be happening. Not now!"

Georgette, who was standing next to Clara, crossed her arms and scowled at the car. "This is *un désastre*. Cars, they are beautiful, but they are not reliable."

Clara wished there was something—anything—she could do. Yet again, everything was coming crashing down around their heads. Every minute the car didn't start, the thieves moved closer to the border and farther out of their reach. She asked, "What do we do now?"

"*Bon alors, qu'est-ce qu'on peut faire?*" Georgette shrugged. "If the car will not start, we will be stuck here. After a few days, the prince, he will know there has been a problem. He will send help."

Clara ran her hand along the top blanket, contemplating Georgette's assumption. It was true the prince would want his car back, but how long would it take before he sent someone to find it? Anna stalked back to the office, face stormy. She didn't have to say anything for Clara to know what she was thinking. If the thieves slipped between their fingers, this time it would be for good. She would never see Ahmose's treasure.

Clara reached out, trying to catch her attention. She wished there was a way she could comfort her. "Maybe someone will come by…"

Anna's eyes were dull as she turned her face to Clara. "We're in the middle of the desert. No one will come, Clara. It's all over." And like that, the intimacy between them from the night before was snuffed out, replaced by the inaccessible, insurmountable solitude of loss and defeat.

* * *

Despite her sullen pronouncement, Anna and Eliza continued to try to coax the car into starting well into the morning, although without any hope of success. Neither was a mechanic, nor did they have any tools. All they could do was turn pieces of metal and clean them with the fine cloth napkins the prince had sent. Finally, at noon they admitted defeat, retreating back to the office sweat-soaked, stained by streaks of grease, and exhausted. Georgette offered them the wine bottle, which she had helpfully filled with water. Eliza took long, loud gulps, then handed it to Anna, wiping her mouth as Anna drank thirstily.

"Alors c'est fini?" Georgette asked. "It is finished? The car is *morte?*"

Eliza sighed gustily. Dust sprinkled her hair like beige dew. There was a streak of oil beneath her left eye. "Whatever's gone wrong, we ain't gonna figure it out ourselves." She collapsed with a grunt next to Georgette, resting her back against the office wall and kicking her legs out in front of her. "Least we got water and some shade here. If this had happened down the road, we would have boiled like lobsters."

It would have been a truly dangerous situation then. A person could die of dehydration in the desert in under two days. Anna shaded her eyes and looked out over the flat land in front of them. "There should be a small village within a kilometer or so north, along the sea. There won't be a telephone or another car, but there may be something to help us."

"Should be?" Eliza challenged.

"I…think so."

It was a weak answer. And even if there was a village, was it directly north, northeast, or northwest? If Anna didn't know exactly, she could spend hours or more wandering around trying to find it, if she ever did at all. And becoming lost in the desert would be fatal.

Just then, a dark spot appeared on the knife-edge where the tan sand met the bright blue sky. At first, Clara thought it was a mirage, but over the course of a minute, it resolved itself into a man on a camel. A train of five more camels ranged behind him. Despite their circumstances, she couldn't help finding the sight a little exotic. A camel caravan in the desert was exactly the type of thing one heard about but never expected to see in person. She pointed, indicating him to the other women. "Look!"

"It's a Berber." Anna sounded surprised. "He's far from home. He must be returning from Italian North Africa to the Siwa Oasis, three hundred kilometers south of here. He's come here for water, I suppose. The Berbers have traveled the trade routes across North Africa for centuries. They know every place for water." She narrowed her eyes. "Looks like he hasn't brought anything back with him or the camels would be loaded down."

They lapsed into silence as they watched the camels move closer with their long, ungainly steps. More of the Berber's details resolved themselves in time. He wore a long, deep blue tunic and black trousers. His large black turban became a thick scarf at his neck that he had pulled up to cover his nose and mouth. In his right hand, he held a long black whip. When he was only a dozen yards away, Anna stepped out to meet him.

"He'll know if there's a town and in which direction to find it," she told her companions.

She waved her arms with big, flailing motions, trying to catch his attention. When he was a few feet away from her, he pulled the train to a stop. She trotted forward, and while the other women looked on, engaged him in an animated conversation. When she returned a few minutes later, her face was flushed. An excited smile stretched from one ear to the other. Clara expected good news, but she never would have anticipated what came next.

"He found the thieves!"

"What?" Clara gasped.

Anna was so giddy she was almost bouncing on the balls of her feet. Her eyes sparkled like sunlight over water. "He found abandoned vehicles along the motor road up ahead. It can't be anything else."

"Abandoned? What happened to them?" Eliza asked, suspicious.

Anna tossed her hair, which was shot through with sandy streaks. "They probably ran out of gas and set out to find shelter. Come on, let's go."

"Go?" Although it was Eliza who asked the question, Clara was just as perplexed. By the expression on her face, Georgette, too, felt the same way. "Go where?"

And how? Unless the Berber was also a mechanic, the Napier was still dishearteningly inoperable.

Anna pointed to the Berber. "Gwafa has agreed to let us ride his camels and lead us to the trucks. They're close, only a few hours away."

Clara was too surprised to speak, but not Georgette. "I *hate* camels."

CHAPTER NINETEEN

Eliza

"Hold on a minute now, just hold on." Eliza held up her hands, looking between Anna and the Berber and his camels. The world was spinning a little beneath her feet. Not too much for anyone else to notice, but just enough to make her dizzy. "What exactly do you think we're gonna do, riding out there into the desert with nothing but those camels?"

Anna's plan had about as many holes as a fishing net. Still, Anna cocked her head, puzzled, as though she genuinely couldn't see them. "Find the trucks, of course."

"Mm-hmm." Eliza crossed her arms. Her palms were simultaneously gritty and greasy as she closed her fingers into fists. "And then what? What if those thieves are there with guns? You got a plan for that?"

The Berber might have said the trucks were abandoned, but Eliza didn't imagine they would leave millions of dollars' worth of treasure just lying around the desert without anyone to guard it. Nor would they happily hand it over to Anna. If the women went after the trucks, they would be walking into an ambush for sure, and Clara's tiny revolver wasn't enough to help them this time.

Anna wrinkled her forehead. It was no small point of frustration for Eliza that even covered with grease and dirt, Anna still managed to look elegant and graceful, unlike herself, who looked like a horse who had just finished a race. "Gwafa is positive they're gone. Flat as the desert is, he'd have seen them if they were anywhere nearby. They've probably set off north toward the ocean to find water and a way to get the trucks moving again."

Eliza snorted, skeptical. "Or else Gwafa didn't take a good look in the trucks. Who's to say they're not holed up in the back?"

Anna pressed her lips together and tapped her foot impatiently. "He's not an imbecile. I'm sure he looked."

Eliza wasn't fool enough to assume anything. If he'd looked, why didn't he load up his camels with free loot? But she let it go. "Okay, let's say he's right and the thieves are gone. How'd you think we're gonna move the trucks if they couldn't?"

They already couldn't fire up the Napier. If one of the trucks had broken down, they certainly didn't have the mechanical abilities to get it started again. Anna opened her mouth. Her shoulders rose as she took a breath to speak. But no words came out. As Eliza had known, she hadn't thought that part through. Like a bull seeing red, she had wanted to charge, but that outcome would be just as useless for them as it was for a bull. Unless they could somehow load five tons of treasure onto the camels, that treasure would still be stranded after they found it. They might as well wait until help came, then go after it.

"We'll figure it out when we get there," Anna said a beat later, refusing to be dissuaded.

Eliza surveyed the other two women for their reactions. Georgette, distracted, was making a face at the camels as though they had left dung in her shoe. Clara was chewing her lower lip nervously. Eliza shook her head. It wasn't fair of Anna to ask them to go loping off to God knew where in the middle of the desert, under the circumstances. Aside from the fact that it would be hot and sweaty, with no shade to protect them from the sun and only the water they could carry, at best, they would arrive to find two deserted trucks as useless as a bag of rocks. At worst, they might run straight into a bunch of gun-toting criminals willing to kill to keep their loot.

She had taken the train to Alexandria and then kept on in the Napier because she thought they weren't going to see the criminals face-to-face again. Georgette had made a convincing enough argument that it was safe. But this was different. This was Dra' Abu el-Naga' again, and she wasn't making that mistake a second time. She had learned her lesson.

Unexpectedly Clara spoke. "We could bring gasoline with us. Then, if they were just out of gas, we could drive the trucks back here."

Eliza followed her gaze to the blue car in front of them. When they left Alexandria, the prince's servants had tied cans of gasoline to it, enough to get the car to el-Salloum and back again. Now that it was dead, they had gasoline to spare. But even *if* the thieves were well and truly gone, and *if* the trucks' problem was fuel related and not mechanical, how much gas would it take to get two trucks loaded down with gold back to Mersa Matruh, much less Alexandria? It would do them no good to become as stranded in the desert as the thieves had been.

And it was a lot of *ifs*.

Anna didn't share her concerns, however. "That's right! Brilliant idea, Clara!"

She was full of energy, the sizzling wire in a light bulb. Success and victory danced in her eyes, clear as day. But Eliza wasn't having it. They needed to be realistic about what was happening and admit they had finally reached the end of the road. No amount of hoping or wishing would change their situation.

"No." She planted her feet in the earth, unyielding as a mountain. She could no more be moved than the Rockies. "Since we got here we've been shot at, tied up, and scared half to death a few times over again. We've near about traveled the whole country by steamship, train, and automobile. We tried as hard as any person could be expected to trying to get that treasure back, but no more. I ain't riding a camel to the middle of the desert on the *hope* the thieves are gone. And none of you should either."

Anna's face fell. "But…it's only a little farther."

Eliza drew herself up to her full height, which was several inches taller than Anna and much broader. "It's always just a little farther. That treasure's always over the next hill. But we've been like a cat with nine lives, and we ain't got many more left to spare. If we go after those trucks, ain't no telling what we'll find. You can go on if you like, but not me. I'm through. I'm staying here 'til someone comes and rescues me."

Anna's mouth twisted into an unhappy tangle. Behind her, the sand of the desert stretched endlessly, older even than Adam. She was just a temporary speck on it. It would swallow her whole or spit her back out, but either way, it would go on as it had for millennia. Eliza didn't want any part of it anymore. She wanted to go back to the cornfields and cities of her home. She was done with Egypt.

"But the trucks…" Anna protested weakly.

Eliza shook her head forcefully, unswayed. "They ain't going anywhere. Let the police or the prince or someone else go get them. Doesn't gotta be us who does it. We can wait here for them, where there's water and shelter and it's safe."

"But what if the thieves come back and take the trucks first?" Clara asked.

"I don't care anymore! The desert can swallow them up for all I care. You go on if you want, but I'm staying."

Anna looked helplessly to Clara and Georgette, searching their faces to see if they agreed with her. Clara had set down the blankets; now her fingers tapped against the holster at her hip. Her forehead wrinkled as she thought. After a pause, she said, "We've come this far. We can go a little farther. It's only a few hours. Besides, we'll be able to see anyone lurking near the trucks from a distance. If it looks dangerous, we can turn back. Even if we can't move the trucks, at least we'll have seen if the treasure is all there."

Eliza was briefly disappointed in Clara, but she could have predicted it. Caught under the charismatic archaeologist's spell, Clara would do whatever Anna wanted, even if it meant running headlong into danger. But what about Georgette? Perhaps the Frenchwoman would be more reasonable. Perhaps her kidnapping on the train had finally put some sense into her.

Georgette held the wine bottle tightly, twisting it nervously in her hands. She glanced at Eliza, then away quickly. For once, she was not well-groomed and put together. Her hair was gathered into a messy bun, her glasses covered with a thin film of dust. Having slept in her navy skirt, it was creased and rumpled and splotched with beige and brown. This Georgette was a far cry from the prim and proper woman whom she'd met in New York. She grimaced, still not meeting Eliza's eyes. "I... agree with Clara."

Sweat rolled down Eliza's back between her shoulder blades, damp and salty. Her dress was already soaked from her neck to the top of her stomach, and it wasn't anywhere near midday yet. Her body was exhausted by the strain of days of running flat out, trying to catch what felt like ghosts, real or imagined danger lurking behind every rock. Was there even any gold to be found in the trucks? With their luck, they would be empty, or worse yet, full of alabaster vases, Ahmose's gold just one more Egyptian mirage. She had been the one in Luxor to encourage them to chase the thieves, then, in Alexandria, to drive hundreds of miles through the desert, but she had come far enough. She was hanging up her shoes, no matter what the others did.

"That's all right," Clara suggested. "We'll go on without you. You can see the treasure when we come back."

"*Mais non!*" Georgette protested. "She cannot stay here."

"Why not?" Clara asked, perplexed.

"Because she is the only other person who can drive. There are two trucks. If she does not come, who will drive the other one?"

Eliza hadn't thought about that. If she didn't go and it turned out all the trucks needed was a little gas, her companions could only bring back one at a time. Their efforts would take twice as long, and that meant twice the danger. She rubbed her knuckles so hard into her eyes it hurt. She hadn't signed up for this when she agreed to come to Egypt. She had come to sightsee like any other tourist, not dodge bullets. She didn't owe the other women anything, not even—maybe—driving a truck full of gold across the desert.

"I won't do it." She glared at the other women, challenging them to argue with her.

Georgette crossed her thin arms, hugging herself, and rocked slightly as though soothing herself. Her eyes were large and watery like a puppy's and full of hurt. "I thought we will do this together, all of us. How can you stop now?"

Clara put her hand on Georgette's shoulder, then removed it immediately when she shrugged it off uncomfortably. "It's all right, Georgette, she doesn't have to come if she doesn't want to. We'll find a way to do it without her. We could figure out how to drive, couldn't we? Come on."

Not meeting Eliza's eyes, she stepped past Eliza to the Napier and began to untie the gas cans from it. Although Anna joined her, Georgette didn't move. She continued to stare at Eliza mournfully.

"What?" Eliza asked, nonplussed.

"I thought we are friends. I do not understand why you will not come."

The way Georgette said "friends," as though it were a precious, cherished thing, cracked a small hole in Eliza's hard shell. The word meant so much more to Georgette than it ever had to Eliza, like a magical talisman that warded off evil in the world. She deflated a little, some of her righteous anger seeping out of her. "We are, Georgette, but…" She rubbed her temples.

"Mais quoi?"

But what? Eliza wanted to shake some sense into her. "It ain't safe! Why don't you see?"

Georgette had been close to having her head taken off at Dra' Abu el-Naga', and all four women had been trussed up and almost thrown off the Luxor Express. These thieves were willing to kill to keep what they'd stolen. Why was Eliza the only one with the sense to see that? Their plan had never been to confront the criminals directly; it was always going to be the port authorities or the border guard who apprehended them. But now the plan was to gallop up on some camels and hope their luck had finally turned in their favor. Well, it hadn't yet and she didn't see it happening now.

Georgette's eyes sharpened, her lips tightening. "*Oui*, I do see. Of course I see, I am not *stupide*. But always it has been *dangereux*. So why you do not come now?"

Eliza had always relied first and only on herself. It was hard to trust other people. But riding into the desert meant placing her life entirely in the hands of others: Anna, the Berber, even Clara and Georgette, if it came down to it. She couldn't run away if things got bad because if she ran the wrong way, she'd be lost in the desert forever. At least elsewhere in Egypt she'd always had the option to walk away, to board the next steamer home. But that wasn't possible once she got on a camel. Sink or swim, she would be all in.

Georgette stepped forward and put her hands on Eliza's shoulders. Light as she was, her arms were surprisingly heavy. "*Une table*, it can stand with only three legs, but it is not strong. It is broken. It needs all four legs. Together, you, me, Clara, Anna, we are *cette table métaphorique*."

It was perhaps a dramatic metaphor, but at its heart there was raw sincerity and truth. Eliza flinched and dropped her eyes.

"You are afraid, but what if there is no *danger*? Then you have not come and it is for nothing."

For the first time, Eliza's resolve flickered, just a little. Perhaps Clara and Anna were right and they would see any danger well in advance. Perhaps she was exhausted and overstating the danger of the situation.

Georgette continued, "We came all the way to *Égypte* to see this *trésor*—thousands of *kilomètres* and days on ships and trains. I think you will want to be there when we finally can touch it. That moment, it does not come a second time."

By now, Anna and Clara had finished untying the gas cans. Anna wiped her hair from her forehead with the back of her wrist and waved the camels over while Clara drank some water from one of the canteens the prince had sent with them. The graceless creatures, more like a child's immature attempt to draw horses than real, live animals, moseyed closer, their feet stepping like snowshoes on the sand. Watching them, Eliza couldn't help thinking: what if Georgette was right? If the trucks *were* abandoned like the Berber had said, how would she feel seeing the first one rolling back into Mersa Matruh, knowing she hadn't been there for that earth-shattering moment the other three women cracked open the lid of a box and confirmed the vast treasure inside?

Gwafa dismounted, then held his hand up in front of one of the other camels. Obediently, the creature lowered itself to the ground, folding its limbs beneath itself like origami until it was sitting comfortably upon them. When it was still, he nodded to Anna. Clara stepped forward and began tying a gas can to its back. This was the moment of decision for Eliza. Stay safe in Mersa Matruh and potentially miss the defining moment of the entire trip to Egypt, or go with the women and risk running into a deadly ambush.

What felt like several lifetimes ago, she had told the women at the Café Rouge that she hadn't let anyone scare her in her life. It was time to make that true. She pushed her sleeves up to her elbows. "Fine, I'll come. But any whiff of danger and we're flying out of there like the Devil's after us, treasure or not, you hear?"

One way or another, they would stop chasing this gold. A few more hours wouldn't kill her. Unless, of course, tomb robbers did.

* * *

Somewhere west of Mersa Matruh, Egypt

The sand around Mersa Matruh was pink and orange and endless. Eliza thought if she ever visited the moon, it would look exactly as lifeless and barren as the Egyptian desert. Although Gwafa kept promising that the trucks were just ahead, the land stretched interminably before them, with only occasional patches of scrub to break the monotony. There was nothing remotely mechanical in sight. At least they didn't have to ride all the way to el-Salloum. Georgette had calculated that at an average speed of five kilometers per hour by camelback, it would have taken them four and a half days to reach the border crossing instead of the four hours it would have taken in the Napier.

The knowledge brought Georgette little consolation.

"Are you sure we are going the right way?" she moaned, clutching the mound of fabric on the camel's back in front of her hips. The camels had been tied in a line behind Gwafa. Because they had been used to carry packs full of trade items, they had neither saddles nor bridles. At least there were thick cushions on their backs.

"Gwafa says we're almost there," Anna called over her shoulder from her position immediately behind him.

"He said that two hours ago," Clara said, immediately in front of Eliza. She, too, sounded miserable. There was a barely suppressed wail of despair in her voice.

"It will be true eventually."

"I would rather walk home than ride this camel again," Georgette pouted. "If the trucks do not start, leave me. I will walk."

Eliza laughed. They would feel much worse when the pain set in. She had spent a few days in Morocco on the uncomfortably wide back of a camel, at the tail end of her journey. If they thought things were bad now, they would be miserable later. She patted the shoulder of her camel affectionately, the wiry hair rough beneath her skin. It wasn't the camels' fault the Khedival Motor Road was long and tedious. If Georgette and Clara had wanted to be comfortable, they should have stayed at Mersa Matruh.

Luckily for the hot, uncomfortable women, this time Gwafa was right. After only half an hour more, an unnatural shape came into view on the horizon. It gradually separated into three distinct silhouettes which eventually turned into two trucks and a car. The other women whooped in excitement, chattering happily about the discovery, but Eliza didn't share in their joy. Instead, the hair on the back of her neck rose. There was something wrong about the way they were sitting out in the open like that.

"Hush!" she hissed in a low, tense voice. "If anyone's here, they'll hear you."

Georgette snorted. "*C'est absurde.* No one is here. You can see that."

With her hand, she indicated the landscape around them. It was true the earth was so flat and devoid of cover that they would easily have seen if anyone was moving around the trucks, but that didn't mean the thieves weren't there. They could be inside the vehicles, sitting in the cab too far away for the women to make out or lying in wait hidden in the bed. Even now, they could be readying their guns, preparing to attack. Georgette might be right, but she might not be. It was better safe than sorry.

"Even so, let's stop and watch for a minute," she said.

Obligingly, but with evident impatience, Anna asked Gwafa to stop. As the camels came to a halt, Eliza squinted at the trucks, watching for any sign of movement. Even a flutter of fabric and she would demand they leave. But there was nothing.

"Come on," Clara urged. "Georgette is right. The thieves are gone. No one is there." And yet Eliza noticed she'd drawn her revolver. It glinted dully in her right hand, held barrel down at her thigh. Like Eliza, she wasn't taking any chances.

Anna and Gwafa exchanged a short burst of dialogue. When they finished, Anna turned her upper body to address the women behind her. "I've asked Gwafa to go and confirm the trucks are empty."

Eliza opened her mouth to protest. In the first place, if there *was* danger, it wasn't fair to send him out looking for it. In the second place, if something were to happen to him, they'd have to figure out how to get the camel train to move without him or face the same fate. But before she could voice those concerns, he took off, having untied the rope that stretched from the back of his saddle to the head of Anna's camel.

If it had been her, Eliza would have advanced cautiously toward the trucks, moving slowly and taking care not to expose herself to any undue danger. Gwafa had a different idea. He kicked his camel forward with a loud cry, racing toward the vehicles like a tornado. He circled the trucks twice, then stopped and whistled, a piercing sound as loud as a foghorn.

Eliza had to grab tight to the cotton pads beneath her to avoid tipping off her camel as it lurched unexpectedly into motion, responding to the summoning call. With Anna's camel now in the lead, the train moved to rejoin its master. The women were committed now, no matter what happened next.

The two dark green trucks—Eliza recognized them immediately as Berliet CBAs—were parked bumper-to-bumper in the middle of the road. Even up close, she couldn't see what lay in their beds. The tall wooden sides and green canvas roofs were like wrapping paper, concealing everything inside. If any thieves were hiding there, they were well hidden. But if they hadn't exposed themselves yet, Eliza didn't know what they were waiting for.

Parked in front of the trucks was a surprise: the car from Prince Omar's palace. The Duesenberg's black sheen was now a splotchy brown, the white on the tires dyed buff. So much for the police arresting the criminal mastermind Arthur Pearce in Alexandria.

Gwafa dismounted and came to help Anna down. She was on her feet before her camel had even finished sinking to its knees. She dashed to the back of the nearest truck and disappeared around the corner without any evident pause to consider the danger. Eliza understood. This was the moment for which she'd been waiting, the moment she would know whether they had recovered the treasure or not. Seeing what cargo the trucks carried was her moment of triumph…or her nightmare.

Gwafa coaxed Georgette's camel down, then continued to Clara's. Georgette walked to the front of the first truck, staring intently at the doorless cab. "The key, it is still in the…" She pointed at the ignition.

Eliza furrowed her eyebrows. That was odd. And that wasn't the only thing. She could understand a vehicle running out of gas or having mechanical difficulties and being abandoned until such a time as it could be refueled or fixed, but there was no way two trucks and a car had all run out of gas or broken at the same time. So why hadn't they left the disabled vehicle and continued on without it?

Georgette walked around the front of the truck and then to the Duesenberg, staring at the sand. She seemed to have forgotten that the real focus, the source of all their excitement and disappointment, was only a few feet away in the bed. Gwafa tapped the knee of Eliza's camel, commanding it to kneel. Awkwardly, it did, pitching Eliza first forward, then backward. As she took her first step away from it, Georgette's head came up sharply. Her face was pulled together in a tight expression of concern. "Something is wrong."

Eliza stopped. The feeling of unease she had experienced as they'd approached the trucks returned full force. "What?"

"The thieves, they did not leave the trucks to find gas. Actually, they—"

At that moment, Anna reappeared from around the corner. Her face was radiant, full of joy, happiness, and triumph. All of the concern and stress from the last few days was gone. Interrupting Georgette, she held up a small, gold figurine of a pharaoh a foot tall. "The gold, it's here. All of it."

CHAPTER TWENTY

Georgette

Georgette didn't notice Anna or the small statue in her hands. She was too busy staring at the sand around the driver-side door of the black sedan. It had been violently disturbed, with deep troughs carved into some areas, the surface smoothed flat in others. There had been a struggle, and a dramatic one at that. From the marks, Georgette surmised that the driver had fought beside the car and then been dragged away. But to where? The drag marks stopped suddenly after several meters, with no clue to the fate of either the person who had been dragged or the person who had done the dragging.

Her eyes caught a round outline in the sand a few centimeters from her boot. She knelt down and fingered the object lightly, brushing the sand from its face. It was a small black button, most likely from a pair of pants. Undoubtedly, it had been torn off in the struggle; there was still frayed thread hanging from it. There were a few more small objects in the sand, which she picked up and put in her pocket without looking at, intending to examine them later.

She stood once more and squinted out over the land around them, so focused on her inner thoughts that she was deaf to the conversation and movement happening behind her. There were no camel tracks anywhere near the vehicles other than what Gwafa had left, and while she could see the marks the vehicles' tires had made as they'd traveled up the Khedival Motor Road, there was no evidence of any other vehicles having passed along it. What had happened here, and where had the three drivers— and however many passengers the trucks might have carried— gone?

"Georgette!" Eliza's large hand settled on the Frenchwoman's shoulder and shook it gently.

She snapped back to attention, blinking as she turned to look at Eliza. "*Oui?*"

"Don't you wanna see the treasure?"

Georgette boggled at her as though she were a stranger. Treasure? She'd momentarily forgotten that was what the trucks held. As she remembered, her thin eyebrows shot up. "Oh! It is here!" She glanced eagerly toward the back of the truck, seeing nothing but Anna and Clara's backs as they walked away from her.

Eliza rolled her eyes and pushed Georgette toward them. "Didn't you listen to *anything* Anna just said?"

As it was, Georgette wasn't completely listening *now*. Her mind was drifting back to the mystery of the missing thieves, generating various hypotheses to explain their absence. Had the telegraph line been fixed and the prince somehow gotten word to the border police, who had then intercepted the vehicles from the west? But if that was the case, why were there no tracks to show where they'd gone? And why had they left the vehicles, particularly the prince's expensive car? Had it been Berbers like Gwafa who had stopped the thieves? If so, what did they want from the men and why hadn't they scavenged the trucks' contents? And where were their footprints?

She turned the corner of the truck to find Anna standing on the lowered wooden gate of the bed. She had opened the lids of several of the boxes, revealing some of what lay inside. Georgette stopped dead in her tracks. All other thoughts evaporated as her eyes took in the sight before her. It was like peering into Aladdin's cave through a crack in the wall. Gold and jewels winked back at them, the barest hint of the vast treasure inside.

"*Waouh*," she whispered.

Eliza whistled. "It really is here. We finally found it."

Anna opened a small wooden box sitting on a stack of larger boxes and lifted a bracelet out. It was a thick gold cuff, decorated with a large beetle made of lapis lazuli. Semiprecious stones like turquoise and carnelian were embedded along the sides. She examined it, entranced.

"Under Ahmose, mines were reopened and trade routes expanded. Egypt was the richest it had ever been. Gold and silver were brought from Nubia. Lapis lazuli was imported from Central Asia. Turquoise was mined in the Sinai…"

She replaced the bracelet and pulled out a new object: a dagger with a hammered gold sheath and an ivory handle inlaid with more semiprecious stones. She smiled at it almost fondly. "There was a dagger like this in Tutankhamun's tomb. See how the iron hasn't rusted at all?" She ran her finger along the edge. "It's unbelievable. This metal is over three thousand years old and yet it looks like it was forged yesterday. Just as sharp, too."

She put it away and pulled out a small statue barely taller than the length of her hand. The standing figure wore a hat that looked like a jug of water flanked by two bird feathers. In its hands, it held a crook and flail. The bronze had developed patina with age; it was now more green than black. She explained, "Osiris, king of the underworld, god of death, resurrection, and the afterlife."

She squinted at the statue's rectangular base. "It says, 'Cursed be those who disturb the rest of a pharaoh. They that shall break the seal of this tomb shall meet death by—'" She stopped and shook her head. "No, I can't read the rest. Too much verdigris."

Eliza looked over her shoulder at Gwafa. He had retied Anna's camel to his own and was now waiting impatiently, paying no attention to the objects Anna was drawing from the larger-than-life treasure chest before them. She nodded toward him. "We should get that gasoline off those camels and see if we can head on back to Mersa Matruh before your man Gwafa decides he's had enough and takes off with them."

"Oh!" Georgette's quiet exclamation drew the other three women's attention. She grimaced at the bad news she was about to deliver. "I do not think we will need the gasoline, at least, not *immédiatement*." She paused, troubled by the mystery she was as yet unable to solve. "I believe the trucks did not run out of gasoline."

Clara cocked her head, her brown eyes quizzical. Her face was starting to shade red from exposure to the sun, even under her hat. If they didn't take cover soon, it would hurt later. "But they must have. Why else would the thieves have left all this?" She waved vaguely at the two trucks, implying the invaluable treasure within.

Georgette shook her head. "They did not leave it. They were…" She searched for the appropriate word. "Taken."

As close as the women were to the cab of the second truck, she could see that whatever had happened to the occupant of the car had happened to the occupant or occupants of that truck as well. There were the unmistakable scuffs in the sand where someone had been hauled unwillingly from the vehicle, the signs of failed resistance. But as with the car, these signs of conflict seemed to simply vanish after a few meters. The sight made Georgette uneasy. It was like stumbling upon the scene of a murder without finding the body. Not that she wanted to see dead bodies.

"Easy enough to figure out if they're out of gas," Eliza said. In a few strides, she was at the cab, swinging herself onto the bench seat to sit in front of the big black steering wheel. "The key's in the ignition in this one too." She grabbed the steering wheel and reached to turn the key, but her hand was only halfway there when she recoiled violently. "Ugh!" She held up the hand that had been on the wheel. It was glistening. "Blood."

Violence. Struggle. Blood. Something far more sinister than running out of gas had led to the three vehicles being abandoned in the desert. Out of habit, the women looked to

Anna for an answer, but the surprise on her face showed she was just as mystified as they were.

"Maybe they fought amongst themselves," she suggested. "A mutiny over whether to take the treasure to Tripoli or keep it for themselves. Someone could have double-crossed someone else, trying to get more of the treasure."

"But if it was a fight over the treasure, why abandon the trucks and not take any of it?" Clara asked. "And also, where did they go?"

It was true; Anna's snap hypothesis didn't make sense. There was another problem: where were the footprints? There were no bodies here. Mutiny or not, everyone was gone. Even if the thieves *had* voluntarily left the trucks and set off into the desert for some unknown reason, their footprints still would have been visible in the sand, just as Georgette could see the tracks Gwafa and the women had made. But there were no footprints leading away from the trucks. The men had simply vanished. Against their will.

Without warning, the truck roared to life, making Georgette jump. Eliza shouted over the loud rumble of the motor. "Georgette was right! It's got gas in it."

She cut the ignition and the desert was silent once more. Anna leaped down from the bed and closed the gate with a grating, metallic squeal. "It doesn't matter why they left the trucks, what matters is that we've recovered them now. We'll get the treasure back to Alexandria and the police can worry about where the thieves went." She glanced at the sedan. "Prince Omar will have to send someone else for his car, I'm afraid."

As she marched over to talk to Gwafa, Clara's thumb tapped the hammer of her revolver restlessly. Her eyes traveled over the trucks. "What do you think happened, Georgette? That blood…"

"I do not know." She crossed her arms, pouting. It wasn't often she couldn't produce even a single theory. It was unnerving and frustrating all at once. Especially because she wasn't entirely sure they weren't presently in danger.

"We should get that gasoline and bring it with us anyway," Eliza said, returning from the truck. "We don't know how much gas these trucks will go through or whether they're carrying any extra. Wouldn't want to run out halfway to Mersa Matruh."

As she, Eliza, and Anna got to work unloading the gasoline from the camels, Georgette circled around the second truck, looking for more clues. Whatever had happened to the driver, his wound likely hadn't been fatal. Although there was a sticky patch of blood on the wheel, the one Eliza had found, there was no pool beneath it. Nor were there any drops of blood in the sand beside the truck. Perhaps the driver had nicked himself on something at some point during the drive, enough of a cut to bleed a little but easily staunched. Although she doubted it, it could have been a simple accident, a coincidence unrelated to the thieves' disappearance.

A faint scent caught her attention, and she sniffed the air. Urine. She climbed back out of the truck and found the source next to the back tire. So the thieves had been stopped to take a break when…*whatever* happened. She ran her fingers over a deep line scored in the chassis of the truck. There was no way to tell what had made it or when.

Giving up, she walked back to the front of the truck. There were no more clues to be had. The desert would keep this secret, at least for now. And it was time to go.

Anna slid behind the wheel of the first truck. When Georgette joined her, she did a double take. "I…thought you would ride with Eliza. You two seem to get along well."

Georgette shrugged. She noticed a smudge on the left lens of her glasses, so she removed them and used her skirt to clean it. Anna didn't move.

"We are waiting?" Georgette looked around. "For what?"

"I suppose nothing." Anna turned the key and the engine growled like an angry lion. Grasping the stick shift, she yanked the truck into gear. The vehicle responded sluggishly, finally jerking into motion. She hauled on the wheel, pulling the left side down so that the truck turned in a slow, wide, half circle in front of the watching camels. Like that, they had finally recovered the treasure and were headed back to Cairo.

* * *

Even at its fastest speed—empty and on an ideal surface—the Berliet could only travel thirty kilometers per hour. But the Khedival Motor Road was hardly ideal, and the truck was loaded down with over two tons of cargo. As a result, they moved at half that speed, the engine whining unhappily. After an hour of staring at the sandy road in front of them, breathing in dust and oil fumes and rocking with every dip and bump in the road, Georgette fell asleep.

When she awoke, she thought at first she was still dreaming. She stared blearily at the figures beside them. Then she realized she was awake and what she had thought were dogs were not. She sat up immediately, her boots scrabbling over the floor.

"*Hum*, Anna, those are wolves, *non*?"

Traveling along the horizon, parallel to the truck, were two small, reddish-brown wolves. Even at a distance, their profiles—triangular heads and ears, short muzzles and bushy tails—were unmistakable. They were traveling at a speed exactly matching that of the Berliet, their long legs easily keeping up the pace.

Anna glanced over at them. "Golden jackals, actually. And there are several following us, not just those two."

Georgette was flummoxed and not a little perturbed by this information. "Why they are following us?"

She didn't know much about jackals other than that they were predators. If they were following the trucks, maybe they thought the women inside were prey. The creatures looked small, but that didn't mean they couldn't be man-eaters, especially if the entire pack attacked.

Anna shrugged, unconcerned, and returned her gaze to the road in front of them. "I don't know. It's possible they've never seen trucks before and think they're giant predators. Jackals are scavengers for the most part. Maybe they think we'll lead them to food."

Her indifference to the potential threat posed by the carnivores around them did little to assuage Georgette's concern. "You are certain? You are not worried even a little?"

"Why should I be? They're hardly going to attack us."

Georgette shifted uncomfortably, imagining them leaping through the open sides of the cab, sharp teeth bared. She eyed the distant animals sideways. "They could."

Anna snorted. "They're no bigger than a dog. But if you're that worried, there's a rifle under the seat. I noticed it while you were sleeping. Get it, if you like."

"*What?*" Georgette gaped at her. She groped under the seat and her fingers brushed against a long, cylindrical metal object. She grabbed it and pulled. It was the battered barrel of a gun. She held the rifle gingerly, avoiding the trigger. She had never touched a gun in her life. If the jackals did attack, her best bet would be to use it like a cudgel to beat them off since she had no idea how to properly fire it.

Something tickled at the back of her mind, a piano note misplayed. It called for her consideration. But before she could ponder it, a falcon flew into view from the south. It was a gorgeous brown creature, with darker, umber streaks that came down from its eyes like tears. It circled the truck as though examining it, then continued its path north. Georgette was distracted for a moment by the bird. It amazed her how such a desolate place as the Western Desert could have so many animals.

Then she returned to the problem at hand. "It is *bizarre*, *non*, that the thieves, they did not use the gun?" She put it back under the seat. She didn't want to risk it going off.

Anna frowned. "What do you mean?"

"There was a fight. The men were dragged from *les véhicules*. If they had this gun, why they did not use it? Maybe they would not have been taken. They could have saved themselves."

Anna sighed, a long exhalation of exasperation. "What does it matter what happened to them? They're gone; we don't have to worry about them anymore. Really, it's the best thing that could have happened to us."

Out of nowhere, a vulture landed on the short hood of the truck, immediately in front of them. The bird's appearance was so sudden and unexpected that Anna shrieked in surprise and jerked the steering wheel. The truck heaved to the left, its balance shifting to its outside wheels. The vulture, which had small, black eyes in its yellow face, extended its wings to keep its balance. The world turned cream edged with dark brown as the wings blocked the women's view of anything else. The vulture opened its fiercely hooked beak in a silent scream as the truck lurched off the road and into deeper sand.

"Bloody hell!" Anna tugged desperately on the wheel, trying to keep control of the truck as its thin wheels swerved and skidded.

Georgette gargled a yelp of her own, unable to look away from the creature's piercing, terrifying eyes. She grabbed anything she could to avoid being thrown from the bouncing cab. Against all reason, the bird held on, croaking, flapping its wings, and generally making the situation worse as the truck continued to careen blindly.

"*Pschtt! Ouste!*" Georgette hissed, trying ineffectively to shoo it away while at the same time clinging for dear life.

The bird ignored her, glaring at her with what felt like malignant intent. Anna jammed on the brake and steadied the wheel, but it was hard to overcome the inertia propelling the heavy truck forward. It took a several beats to respond. After a few more breathless moments, it ground to a halt.

As the truck rocked back on its chassis, the vulture issued a final, challenging, high-pitched mew. Then it flapped its wings and flew away, casting one last malicious look over its shoulder. Georgette's heart wasn't just racing, it felt as though they had left it several meters back on the road.

"Well." When Anna looked at her, Georgette could see the rise and fall of her shoulders as her chest heaved. "That was unexpected." She rubbed her chest. "My heart is still pounding." She tried to smile, but her lips were bloodless.

"What was that?" Georgette asked.

"An Egyptian vulture. Once upon a time, they were considered the protectors of the pharaohs—the vulture for Upper Egypt, the cobra for Lower Egypt. They were so common at the time they were called the 'pharaoh's chicken.' But one hardly sees them up close nowadays."

Georgette knew it was a vulture. She had meant to ask *why* it had done what it had. But before she could, the other truck pulled up on the right beside them. Clara leaned out. "What happened?"

Anna gesticulated in the direction the vulture had flown. "Didn't you see the bloody vulture? It landed right in front of us. I can't imagine what it was thinking."

Clara scanned the sky above them, but the vulture was already gone. Georgette noticed the group of jackals standing beyond the second truck, watching. Although they were far away enough that she couldn't see much more than their outline, she counted seven of them. She didn't like it. It felt as though they were waiting for something.

"Allons-y," she said. "Let's go. I hope maybe we are close to being finished driving." There couldn't possibly be that much farther to go.

Anna cranked the truck into gear and hit the gas pedal. The truck stalled. She growled and tried again. This time, it lunged forward. Georgette was momentarily pressed into the seat, then she once again had to scrabble to find something to hold on to as the Berliet bobbed over the small sand dunes back onto the road. When she looked once more toward where the jackals had been, she did a double take.

"The jackals, they are gone." The hair stood up on her arms. How? There was nowhere for them to go.

"What?" Anna asked.

Georgette couldn't keep the slight hint of hysteria from creeping into her voice. "There were seven just one moment ago and now they are gone. Where did they go?"

CHAPTER TWENTY-ONE

Clara

The truck in front of them rumbled away, kicking up a cloud of tan dust behind it that drifted into the open cab of their own truck like gritty mist. Clara squeezed her eyes shut and held her breath, but she could nevertheless feel it settle on her eyelashes and over the skin of her hands. She would never be truly clean again until they reached Alexandria. Eliza pushed the engine into gear and followed. As their truck trundled back onto the road, she remarked, "At least they didn't get stuck in the sand. No way to pull them loose if they did, not with this much weight in the trucks. We'd have to leave their truck and squeeze in this one."

It would have cost them time, which was now increasingly precious and in short supply. Clara, herself, needed more of it. Time to talk to Anna, time to think about what awaited her at the end of this frantic adventure. Eliza and Georgette were already thinking about Constantinople, but Clara couldn't help feeling there was so much that was still unresolved here in Egypt. Every minute that passed, every mile they drove, was bringing them closer to the end of their time together. And what then? Now that the gold had been reclaimed, the glue that had bound them would quickly dissolve. The comradery that had formed between them was finite and transient, and when they parted ways, it might never return.

She wished she could trap this moment and keep it in a specimen jar, or that she could slow time and draw it out like taffy to delay the inevitable fracturing of their group. At the same time, she felt guilty for wanting to hold the others back from their lives. They had professions to return to, things to do. *She* was the only one with nothing waiting for her back home. It was selfish of her to want to tether them here.

"How long do you think you'll stay in Constantinople?" she asked Eliza, trying to distract herself.

Eliza shrugged, a light, casual motion. "A week? Two weeks?" She snorted. A small smile tugged at the corner of her mouth. "If Georgette comes with me, maybe I'll let her decide. Can you imagine the two of us there? She's crazier than a loon, but she grows on you, that one."

Clara looked down at her lap. While they were in Constantinople, she would be sailing back to America alone. She couldn't imagine the weeks at sea without them, the long hours alone.

"You could come too, you know."

Clara looked up, surprised by the suggestion.

"Why not? We get along all right. And at least there no one will be shooting at us. We can have an actual vacation." She dropped her eyes pointedly to the revolver at Clara's side. "Although maybe you better not wear that around. We don't want to attract any more trouble than we've already been in."

Clara felt like brittle glass. Eliza's offer was kind. It offered a temporary reprieve until their final parting. But...no matter which direction she sailed, she would still be sailing away from Anna. Most likely, she would never see her again.

Thinking about it made her stomach roil. Setting out from America, she had never dreamed that she would embark on an affair with Anna. Now she couldn't bear the thought of it all ending so soon. Would it really be all over in a matter of days?

She couldn't imagine boarding a ship and never again feeling Anna's hands brush against her skin or her lips press hard against her neck. She couldn't envision what it would be like to not have Anna's sparkling, beautiful eyes catch hers from across a room.

But then, what was the alternative? Anna could never come to Wellsburgh. For one thing, that kind of relationship would never be accepted there. They would be run out of town or worse if it were discovered. For another, there would be nothing there for her, just as there was nothing for Clara herself. But Clara couldn't stay in Egypt either.

Maybe none of it mattered anyway. Anna hadn't said anything about what would happen once they returned the treasure to Cairo. Did she care that Clara would be leaving soon, or was Clara just a pleasant but temporary diversion to her? Would she be happy to see Clara off and return to her life of excavating in Luxor?

"Your face gets any longer it won't fit on that skinny neck of yours," Eliza said.

Clara wrinkled her nose and shook her head, pulling out of her maudlin thoughts with difficulty. "I don't know what you're talking about."

"Mm-hmm, sure. You're not thinking about someone in the truck in front of us?"

Clara's face blazed from more than just the Egyptian sun. She ducked her head and looked away, remembering the scene on the train. Apparently, Eliza hadn't forgotten what she'd seen. And possibly heard last night too. Her cheeks burned even hotter. "No, of course not."

"It's all right, I ain't judging you. Ain't the first time I've seen women with other women and won't be the last. Besides, you deserve a little happiness. Doesn't matter who it's with."

Her stomach wrenched. "I suppose it doesn't matter anyway." Plenty of women had fallen head over heels into the embrace of dashing, handsome men who were gone on the next train out of town. That Anna was a woman didn't make the situation any different. And at least she couldn't become pregnant from their liaison.

Eliza tilted her head, curious. "Why not?"

Clara brushed dust from her lap. The sand had dyed her tan dress an uneven, pale beige that water and soap might never be able to remove. In a way, Egypt itself had stained her. Or else it had revealed what had been there all along. She supposed it must be the latter. If not Anna, perhaps some other woman would eventually have turned her head and opened her eyes to all the things she'd been missing before.

She stared out into the landscape beyond them, so different from Iowa and everywhere else she'd been. "Everything will be over soon. After we set sail for home we'll probably never see each other again." Why would they? It's not like there were many other tombs to be found. And if Anna did find another one, what use inviting them to come to Egypt a second time? It was a once-in-a-lifetime trip, and now they'd done it.

Eliza looked at her appraisingly. "You could stay a little longer. No one says you gotta be on the first steamer out of Egypt. You got somewhere to be?"

"No, but I couldn't…" She shook her head firmly. How could she stay? Anna hadn't extended the invitation, and she could hardly invite herself. She didn't know how long she, Eliza, and Georgette would stay in Cairo, but she couldn't imagine it would be more than a few days. Just long enough to see the treasure taken out of its boxes.

"Mmm." The sound was ambiguous. "You're afraid to stay."

No. Yes. The answer was too complex for words. Clara didn't know how she could possibly articulate it. She said instead, "Anna will be busy with her work. I would just be in the way."

Eliza raised her eyebrows. "Ain't none of my business, but… are you sure Anna wants you to go?"

Clara hunched her shoulders, folding into herself like a letter into an envelope. "She hasn't said anything. Isn't that evidence enough that she does?"

Eliza stared at her, exasperated. "Woman, we've been up, down, and sideways across Egypt trying to hunt down these thieves and rescue this treasure. I guarantee you she ain't even thought about what's happening tomorrow, much less in a week's time. Give her a few days. Let her settle all this. Then you see what she feels. Until then, don't be putting thoughts into her head for her."

Clara grimaced. Anna could have said something last night as they'd lain in the office. Or in the morning, she could have pulled her aside… "But what future is there anyway, Eliza? Two women living together as…as husband and wife? Where would we live? What would we do? What if someone found out?"

She sank back into her misery. She didn't know if Anna even wanted the next week with her, much less anything more. But even if Anna did, in the long term, a relationship between women like them was impractical. Even Eliza had to admit it.

Eliza snorted. "How would you do it? You'd get by just like every other person on this earth. You think no other folks out there ever fell in love and made it work when the world said they couldn't? Happens every day. Besides, you ain't putting an ad out in the paper about your business. As far as anyone has to know, you and Anna are just good friends. Ain't nobody's business but your own what the truth is."

Eliza had made sound, thought-provoking points. Clara sat back, trying to absorb them, but before she could, the sky began to darken. In the space of a minute, the color changed from cerulean to buff. The temperature dropped by several degrees. The truck slowed as Eliza craned her neck to see what had caused the surprising transformation.

"Oh noooo." The tone in Eliza's voice spelled trouble.

Clara followed her gaze and emitted a gasp. To their right, a wall of dust bigger than anything she'd ever seen was barreling toward them, moving fast. Clara had heard of dust storms in some parts of America, but this was something else entirely. It was as tall as a New York skyscraper and so dense she couldn't see anything past its surface. And it was coming right at them.

She gripped the dash in front of her, her heart starting to race. "What do we do?"

"I don't know." Eliza's fingers flexed on the steering wheel. Stress pulled her mouth into a tight line. "No matter which direction we go, we can't outrun it. It's too big and moving too fast."

She slammed her foot down on the accelerator. The truck's gears briefly ground as she hastened to change them. Sluggishly, the vehicle responded, drawing level with the first truck. The wind was picking up around them, creating a soft but constant whistle. Eliza caught Anna's attention and jabbed her finger at the wall of destruction. "What is that and how do we get away from it?"

"Sandstorm," Anna yelled back over the combined roar of the engines. "Based on how quickly it appeared, I'd guess it's moving somewhere around a hundred kilometers per hour. It will be on us in minutes. We'd best hunker down and wait it out. It's too dangerous to try to drive through."

She braked, causing Eliza and Clara to shoot past for a few dozen yards before Eliza wrangled their truck to a stop in front of Anna's. She put it in park and pulled the key from the ignition. Anna jumped out of her truck. "Start unloading some of the boxes from the back. We'll get under the canvas and ride the storm out in there. It won't last longer than half an hour or an hour. The wind will make an atrocious noise, but at least we'll be protected from the worst of the dust. That's the real danger in a sandstorm. You can easily suffocate."

"You are certain we will not be *écrasées?*" Georgette made a crushing motion with her hands, intimating they might be flattened like a pancake by the force of the storm. Clara was relieved to see she wasn't the only one concerned it could roll the truck over and batter it like an angry giant.

"Yes. The wind would have to be double that at least to move the trucks, especially with all the weight we're carrying." Anna grabbed a canteen from under the seat and extended it to Georgette after taking a sip. "Pour this over any cloth you have and cover your nose and mouth. It will keep most of the sand out. And when the storm hits, shut your eyes."

"But I do not—"

Before Georgette could finish her protest, Eliza had already whipped her shirt off, exposing her broad shoulders and richly dark skin. Anna handed her the canteen instead. Eliza poured the water liberally over the fabric, then folded it over her knee into a long strip and tied it around the back of her head so that it covered her nose and mouth. She looked like a train robber from the Old West.

Clara looked down at her own clothing helplessly. As she was wearing a dress, she had nothing to remove. Seeing the problem, Anna reached into her pocket and withdrew a white handkerchief, which she handed to Clara. During the brief moment of contact, their eyes met. Even in such a desperate situation, Clara's heart thrilled. For all her fears and concerns and doubts, she was helplessly under Anna's spell.

Anna held her gaze a few seconds too long, then withdrew her hand and, with the same boldness Eliza had shown, unbuttoned her shirt. Clara looked away sharply, finding the action too intimate. Her lips knew that skin too well now and all the places she had kissed in the dark and all the many more she would have liked to. To distract herself, she took the canteen from Eliza and drenched the handkerchief. It was too short to tie around her head, so she would have to hold it against her nose and mouth when the time came.

Georgette looked over the partially clad Anna and Eliza with resignation. "I did not imagine this is how I would die: in a truck *en Égypte*, swallowed by *le désert*." She sighed. "I suppose it could be worse. At least we are not on the camels."

"Nonsense," Anna admonished. "No one is going to die. It's only a little wind and sand. Now come on, you need to cover your nose."

Reluctantly, the Frenchwoman undid the buttons down the front of her shirt, revealing the top of a white rayon chemise beneath. Her lips pressed together unhappily, she turned her back and removed the shirt. Putting it between her knees, she quickly slipped the chemise over her head. She put her shirt back on, and when she turned around again, no one would have ever known that she wore nothing beneath it. Clara handed her the canteen and she dumped the remainder of what was inside over the chemise, turning it almost translucent. Letting the empty canteen fall to the ground, she tied it around her face.

Had anyone been around to see them, the women would have presented a wild, almost Bacchanal picture. But there was no one to see. They were utterly alone in the desert. And if the storm swallowed them whole, no one would ever know what happened to them, either.

The grotesquely massive cloud of sand was so close by now that the wind had become a loud, alarming roar. It snatched at the women's clothing and hair, pulling loose anything it could reach. Anna climbed into the back of her truck and began to lift wooden boxes out. "Hurry. We don't have much time. Put these in the cab."

The three other women formed a line around the truck to pass the boxes down. In minutes, they had emptied enough of the bed that the four of them could just fit, surrounded by a cocoon of mostly crated treasure. Anna helped Georgette in first, followed by Eliza and then Clara. As she pressed her hand against Clara's back to keep her from falling backward, she whispered, "It will be all right. I won't let anything happen to you."

Clara didn't know what to say, so she kept her eyes forward and took a seat across from Georgette. The other woman had picked up a small statue carved from bone-white alabaster and was clutching it to her chest as though it were a child she needed to protect from the storm. Beside her, Eliza stared grimly ahead, her hands gripping the rough boxes beneath her. She muttered under her breath, "If we get buried with this damn treasure…"

Anna had no sooner sat down next to Clara than the wind began to assault them in earnest. It shook the truck from top to bottom, battering the canvas and trying to peel it back like a tin of sardines. The vehicle shuddered and creaked on its axles. Georgette's knuckles whitened as she clutched the statue tighter. Clara ground her teeth together. It sounded like the truck was being torn to pieces.

"It's all right," Anna said, loud enough to be heard through the shirt over her mouth and above the wind. "It's just a bit of noise."

It was more than that. The wind became a high-pitched scream. The world outside transformed into a uniform, impenetrable tan. The storm was fully upon them now. A constant barrage of sand pelted furiously against the canvas.

Something hit the cab of the truck so hard it rocked on its wheels. Georgette unleashed a burbled, muffled squeal.

Clara couldn't have said how it happened, but she found herself with her head cradled to Anna's chest, Anna's arms wrapped protectively around her. She shut her eyes, as if by doing so she could shut out the storm as well. Anna murmured, "I've got you. You're safe."

Clara wanted to believe her, but she wasn't sure. It seemed as though the truck might collapse around them at any moment. The wind swirled into the bed, tearing half her hair from its bun. It lashed like a whip against her face and her back in the eddying currents. It must have felt like a cat-o'-nine-tails to Anna, but she didn't complain. Sand particles carried by the wind scoured Clara's exposed face and hands like pumice stone. A few even made it through her handkerchief, and she felt the grit find purchase on her tongue and the insides of her cheeks.

The minutes trickled by like years, but Anna's embrace never slackened. All Clara could do was hope the truck would hold out. With every squeal and shriek of metal, she was convinced it would be split to pieces. It seemed impossible that nature could be so potent, so vicious. Eventually, she thought, a person could go mad trapped in a storm like this.

Had ten minutes passed or twenty? She lost track of time. The truck rocked as though being shaken by giants. Georgette moaned, and Clara waited tensely for the moment the wind would finally break through the canvas and tear them to shreds. But it never came.

Finally, the storm began to abate. The roar of the wind softened to a rush and the air no longer carried the scouring desert into the truck. Clara opened her eyes. Looking around, she saw Georgette was curled into a ball at their feet, wrapped around her figurine. Eliza had her head between her knees and was covering it with her arms. Everything in the truck was coated with a thick layer of orange-beige sand, including the women. They were filthy and disheveled, but they were alive, just as Anna had promised.

She looked up to find Anna watching her with soft eyes. Anna caressed her cheek. "See? It's all over now. The worst has passed." She pulled her shirt down from her nose and kissed Clara on the forehead. Clara could feel the sand press into her skin where Anna's lips met it.

Still holding Clara to her, Anna announced to the other women, "It's all right, you can open your eyes now. The storm has passed."

"You are certain we are not dead?" Georgette asked. Her round glasses were so totally covered by dust it was impossible to see her eyes. She must have been totally blind.

Clara wanted to stay where she was a while longer, to process what had happened, but Anna was shifting beneath her. Grudgingly, she sat up and brushed the sand off her. It sheeted away and pooled at her feet, the way snow might after a snowstorm. She moved the handkerchief from her mouth. It had collected so much dirt it was almost muddy. The white had turned tawny.

"When we leave *Égypte*, I will not come back," Georgette announced, removing her glasses and trying to clean them with her chemise. "Too much this country is trying to kill us."

Anna and Eliza both reclothed themselves with their damp, dirt-stained shirts, but Georgette didn't bother putting her chemise back on. Instead, she threw it in a pile on one of the boxes. "Why bother? It is *ruinée*," she said, shrugging when they looked at her.

The women crawled out of the truck and found that a new world awaited them. The landscape was unrecognizable from what it had been before the storm. Sand so completely covered the road it was all but invisible, only the faintest lines showing where the flat road ended and the sand dunes began. Clara was amazed by the transformation. There was no past, no future, only an endless desert and two filthy, sandy trucks.

Eliza spit, then rubbed her mouth. "Will the trucks still start with all this sand in them?"

Massive drifts of sand had piled up against the trucks' wheels, while smaller drifts had found their way into every crack and crevice of the hood. If sand was the culprit behind the death of the Napier, there was every chance it could have affected the Berliets as well.

"I hope so," Anna replied.

Clara looked into the cab. Sand lay inches deep over every surface. She grabbed one of the boxes and walked it back to the bed, not bothering to shake the sand off. They couldn't go anywhere until the cab was empty again; they might as well start clearing it. As she returned, Eliza crawled onto the seat and tried turning the key in the ignition. For a moment, the engine sputtered. Clara held her breath. If it didn't start...

It coughed back to life with a choking growl. Clara released the breath and grabbed a second box. As she passed Georgette, the Frenchwoman seized her arm. Her face—half white, half brown-orange—looked worried. The expression was enough to be alarming. "Clara, do you see those prints?"

Clara looked where she was pointing. Apart from noticing the small hillocks of sand, she hadn't paid attention to the area around the truck. Now she saw the truck was surrounded by dozens of indentations no larger than the palm of her hand.

"They are from dogs, *non*? Maybe wolf?"

Clara had spent much of her life tracking animals, so she recognized the canine prints for what they were. And yet there was more to them than that. "Yes, but these prints are enormous. We haven't seen any animal in Egypt that could have made them." She squinted at the landscape around them. "And how could they be here at all? The wind should have blown everything away."

Georgette's eyes bored into her, full of meaning. "I know."

CHAPTER TWENTY-TWO

Georgette

For Georgette, the existence of the pawprints was as great a mystery as the signs of struggle around the abandoned trucks. Like those other tracks, the prints appeared *only* around the vehicle. Everywhere else, the sand was blown smooth by the wind.

Clara knelt beside one of the prints and examined it. It was so clearly defined it was even possible to see the impression each claw had made in the sand. "Could the jackals that were following us have taken shelter around the truck, then fled when the storm passed? They didn't seem big from a distance, but maybe up close…" She was grasping for a justification, mulling the same hypothesis Georgette had already considered. She shook her head. "It's odd that the tracks only face the truck. Where are ones leading away?"

Georgette was glad to see she wasn't the only one who had spotted that anomaly. Clara stood and adjusted the leather belt from which her holster hung. "Maybe a gust of wind covered them. But…" She hesitated. "There's something wrong with the tracks anyway. It's crazy, but it almost looks like the animals were walking on two legs, not four. The spacing isn't right." She shrugged. "I don't know."

Georgette pondered this conundrum. Jackals walking on their hind legs in the middle of a sandstorm and then vanishing into thin air at its termination. It wasn't a logical theory. Clearly, they were missing something.

Eliza walked past with a box in her arms. Sand drained out of the bottom of it as though it had been buried for centuries beneath the desert. She tilted her head to indicate the cab. "Come on, we better get a move on. Anna says we got a long way to go still. Don't wanna be caught out in the dark again."

Georgette and Clara exchanged glances. Georgette didn't know whether they should tell anyone else about the tracks. There was nothing to be done about them; the jackals that had made them were gone now. Nevertheless, their existence sent a whisper of fear down her spine. The jackals had followed them for untold kilometers; now they had gotten within a few meters. What might they do next?

"We can ask Anna about it later, I guess," Clara said.

And like that, the mystery of the prints was set aside and ignored, just like the disappearance of the thieves. This lack of resolution chafed Georgette worse than the sand that had gotten into her boots during the storm, but there was nothing she could do about it. Perhaps later, when night had fallen and she was alone with her thoughts in Mersa Matruh, she might return to the issue and give it a more thorough consideration. For now, she would have to let it go.

She walked to the front of the truck and lifted the closest of the remaining boxes. Its lid had been staved in, perhaps crushed by the weight of the box that had been placed hastily above it as the women braced for the storm. Around the broken boards, she could see the statue inside. It was as long as her forearm, with a sharp, canine face and golden eyes that gave it a fierce expression. Its gilt-edged ears were so disproportionately long for its triangular head they reminded her of the sails of feluccas.

"That's a nice Anubis," Anna commented, peering over Georgette's shoulder as she passed by with a box of her own in her arms. "The Egyptians believed he guided dead souls to the afterlife. On its own, the statue isn't worth much—it's just some wood and black paint—but European collectors love this type of thing. It would fetch a high price on the black market."

Now it would go to a museum instead, along with everything else in the trucks. A flush of satisfaction warmed Georgette's chest. They may not have seen the antiques in the tomb, but they had nevertheless managed to recover them so that people around the world could see them. She followed Anna to the back of the truck and placed her box carefully between two others, making sure nothing could fall upon it and crush the statue inside. It would be disappointing for it to have survived intact for so many thousands of years, only to be chipped and damaged now. She started to walk back around the truck, ruminating on the delicacy required to take care of antiques such as the ones in the truck bed, when she saw something so shocking she was momentarily struck motionless.

The prints were gone.

She looked around frantically, misbelieving her own eyes. How was it possible? There had been no wind. Yet the only tracks visible in the sand now belonged to the women—pointed soles and square heels. It wasn't that the women's footprints were covering the animal tracks; it was that there was no trace they had ever been there at all. Not a single print remained.

"*Non.*" She said the word aloud, through trembling hands that had risen to cover her mouth. "*Non, c'est impossible.*"

She took off her glasses and rubbed her eyes, half-convinced that when she opened them again the tracks would be there once more, that this apparent paradox would be nothing more than a trick of the light and fatigue. But when she returned her glasses to their rightful place, the tracks were still missing. She stared dumbly at the sand. Perhaps she was going crazy. Objectively, there were few alternative hypotheses. But there had been a witness to the tracks, and although psychology was not a particular specialty of hers, she suspected the odds of them both having hallucinated the same thing at the same time were infinitesimally small. Which meant the tracks *had* been there, and now they were gone.

When Clara approached to pass her with another box, Georgette stepped in front, blocking the way. She pointed at the ground. "Look! The tracks, they are gone."

Obediently, Clara looked down. Her head jerked in surprise. "But...Where did they go?"

"I don't know!" Emotion lashed at Georgette like a whip. "What is happening, Clara?"

Everything in the world could be explained through science and reason. The earth was predictable and knowable. Georgette had always taken comfort in these things. But now all possibility of logical explanation had abandoned her. The void it left was bleak and terrible. She didn't know how to fill it. She started to hyperventilate.

"Georgette! Georgette, calm down." Eliza's hands landed on her shoulders. She was too overwhelmed to react. All her energy had left her, burned out in a hot, fast blaze of fear. Eliza released her. "What's going on?"

"Georgette found tracks by the truck. Big tracks. It must have been the jackals that have been following us. Now they're gone. I can't explain it." Clara hastened to add, "But I'm sure there's some explanation."

"But there is not!" Georgette challenged, some of the fire returning. "How could there be?"

Disappearing prints and unsolved mysteries. Something was deeply wrong. It was a tickling sensation in the back of Georgette's mind, a half-veiled intimation of danger. The desert was gobbling things whole. Would it try to consume them as well?

Eliza's eyes traveled from Georgette to Clara and back again, assessing. "Hmm." She didn't offer any opinion on the matter of the missing prints. "Let's get on back to Mersa Matruh. It won't matter once we're moving again. Whatever made those tracks ain't here now."

"But where did they go?" Georgette insisted. *Someone* had to see that the natural order of the world had been disrupted.

Having finished delivering another box to the back of the truck, Anna joined them. She touched Clara and Eliza each lightly on the shoulder as she came between them. She murmured, "Start your truck. I'll handle this."

Eliza looked at her with misgiving but nodded and walked away. Clara stayed a moment longer, then followed. Anna took Georgette gently by the elbow. "Come now, Georgette. It's all right."

Georgette went obediently, folding into the cab of the truck without protest when Anna deposited her there. She felt deflated and adrift. And scared. Anna walked around to the other side and slid behind the steering wheel. The engine sputtered, making a choking sound as she tried to start it, then died. She clenched her teeth and tried again. The same result.

"Come on," she muttered. "Start."

On the third try, it did. Behind them, the second truck came alive with even more difficulty. Anna put the truck in gear and gently pressed down on the pedal. As they inched forward, sand cascaded out of every opening it could find in the hood. Georgette realized how close they had come to the vehicles not starting at all. She couldn't imagine how long the walk to Mersa Matruh would have been.

Anna's mood was somber as she kept the truck on the barely visible road. Whereas before the storm she had chattered happily about the treasure they carried and what it meant for Egypt and the field of archaeology, now she was silent, her fingers clenched around the steering wheel. After they had been driving in silence for a few minutes, she finally voiced what was bothering her. "I saw the tracks too."

Georgette was so surprised by the admission that all she could do was stare at Anna. The archaeologist's face was closed and pinched, her mouth a flat line. She stared unwaveringly at the road ahead. At last, Georgette sputtered, "You did?"

"They were all around the truck after the storm—jackal prints, definitely. I…didn't want to say anything for fear of worrying everyone, not when we'd just been through the storm. I thought if jackals had come to escape the wind, they would certainly be gone when we got out of the truck. And they were." She hesitated, then swallowed. Falteringly, she continued, "I… saw something else too."

Georgette waited, curious what Anna would say next. When Anna fell silent instead however, her skin prickled with alarm. What had she seen?

Anna shuddered. When she spoke, her voice was full of horror. "In the middle of the storm, I risked a glance outside. Of course, it was impossible to see anything; it was an impenetrable wall of sand. But still, I saw—" She stopped abruptly and shook her head. "No, it was nothing. Just my own imagination running wild."

It was evident Anna didn't believe her own words. She had seen *something*, or else believed she had. Her face was too drawn, her expression too worried for it to have been nothing. But before Georgette could press her further on what it had been, the truck's tires hit a divot in the road, causing it to bounce and lurch. As Anna fought to keep control of the large steering wheel, something hard and metal rattled into Georgette's ankle. She winced, pain radiating up her calf. When the truck recovered its bearings, she reached down and picked the object up. It was the little bronze statue of Osiris that Anna had shown them. She held it up to examine more closely.

Seeing it, the muscles in Anna's face went slack. She demanded, "Did you bring that here?"

"*Non.* It was on the floor. I think it must have fallen out of one of the boxes."

"It couldn't have. We didn't move the box it was in. It's still in the back of the truck." Anna's eyes didn't leave the statuette. Her body shrank away from it.

Georgette was confused by Anna's reaction. What did it matter where it had come from? It hadn't walked into the cab on its own. "Then Eliza or Clara must have brought it."

"Why? Why would they have taken it?" Anna's voice was bordering on shrill.

Georgette shrugged. "I do not know. Perhaps they liked it and wanted to look at it more later." She angled it to see the hieroglyphics on the base, the ones Anna had tried to read. "It is nice."

Anna licked her lips. She was trying to divide her attention between the road and the statue, but it meant the truck kept swerving every time she looked toward Georgette. Georgette lowered the figure. "What?"

"Curses were very uncommon after the Old Kingdom. The presence of one on this statue is extremely unusual. Perhaps even unique. If my workers had found this effigy in the tomb and discovered it was inscribed with a curse, work would have stopped for the day, if not longer. The workers are very superstitious. The slightest thing will set them off."

Georgette waited, sensing Anna was trying to say something.

Anna continued, "Of course, there was talk of curses and all that when Carnarvon died. The press went absolutely wild with it. But it was all tommyrot. That was blood poisoning, pure and simple. Nothing supernatural about it at all. Bad luck for Carnarvon." There was a little too much emotion in her words. She tried to run her hand through her hair, but it was far too tangled by the storm winds and she had to give up.

"Okay..." Georgette offered, prodding for further detail.

"The idea of a 'mummy's curse' has been around for years. People love a good superstitious yarn. A few centuries ago, there was a story about a Polish traveler who bought two mummies in Alexandria. He was going to sell them in Europe. But things didn't go as planned. A priest on board the ship taking them there was haunted by two specters dressed as mummies. Then the ship was hit by a big storm. To save it, the Pole threw the mummies overboard. The storm abated, and the priest was left in peace."

Georgette narrowed her eyes, curious about what Anna seemed to be implying in a roundabout way. "*Alors* you think a curse, it can exist?"

Anna furrowed her eyebrows, dismissing the idea with a shake of her head. "Not at all! Thousands of mummies have been brought to Europe from Egypt over the centuries. If there was such a thing as a mummy's curse, no one would dare touch a mummy, much less try to remove one from Egypt."

Anna's efforts to project a light and carefree tone were undermined by the grim expression on her face, however. There was something she wasn't saying. "But in that case, why you are so"—she searched for an appropriate word—"*nerveuse?*"

Anna sucked part of her lower lip into her mouth, then let it go. She appeared to be debating with herself. "The jackals that were following us—I've lived my entire life in Egypt and have never seen one outside of the Giza Zoo. They hunt at twilight; they shouldn't have been out at this hour. And that sandstorm—the Khamsin, Egypt's season for sandstorms, is still months away. Where did it come from?"

"The jackals cannot *only* be out at night, *non*? Maybe they heard the trucks and came to see. And the sandstorm…I don't know. The weather has been unusual, has it not?" She was thinking of the wall cloud at Dra' Abu el-Naga' and the lightning storm during their return to Cairo. In that context, a sudden sandstorm didn't seem odd at all.

Anna shook her head. "There's something off."

Georgette held the statuette up and looked at it with new eyes. "You are thinking maybe the curse on this statue, it is real?"

Anna rubbed her forehead, leaving a streak of white where she rubbed the dirt off. "I don't know what to think." She indicated the statue with a tilt of her head. "Finding that here, in the truck…I can't deny it's unsettling, under the circumstances. I'll feel better once it's back in Cairo and in the hands of the museum."

Georgette cradled the piece in her lap and considered what Anna had said. Of course, as a woman of science she couldn't subscribe to curses, but if there *was* such a thing as a curse, how could one measure for it? What distinguished a bad storm from an accursed one, a priest's imagination from encounters with real spirits? But surely Anna wasn't spooked by only the jackals and the storm. There had to be something else.

"What did you see in the storm?"

Anna flinched, her face twisting into a grimace. Her jaw worked as she summoned the strength to answer. Then she said a single word. "Ammit."

"What?" Georgette wondered if it was an English word she didn't know.

"In ancient Egyptian mythology, after Anubis guided the dead to the underworld, he took them to the Hall of Two Truths, where he weighed their hearts against a feather from the goddess Ma'at. If their hearts were heavy, showing they were impure, their hearts were thrown to Ammit to devour."

So Ammit was a creature. A mythical one.

"But how you knew it was this Ammit?"

"Head of a crocodile, mane and forelegs of a lion, back legs of a hippopotamus—it was her." Anna licked her lips. "It was absolutely terrifying. For a moment I was afraid she would jump into the truck with us. Then I blinked and she was gone."

With great effort, she pulled herself together, shaking her body as though to rid herself of the memory of what she'd seen. "I must sound mad. An Egyptian demon goddess." She took a deep breath, then blew it out with an uncomfortable chuckle. "Between the stress of the last few days and the storm, my imagination certainly has run wild, hasn't it? Imagine, thinking I'd seen Ammit. It's ridiculous. I'm embarrassed to even tell you about it."

Georgette didn't know what to make of either Anna's story or her immediate recantation. Of course Anna could have been hallucinating. Maybe she'd seen a statue of Ammit in a box and her mind had turned it into a shadowy figure during the stress of the sandstorm. Or perhaps she had seen one of the jackals and mistaken it for the goddess somehow. But regardless of Anna's dismissal of what she'd seen, Georgette was sure of one thing: part of Anna believed she'd seen the goddess.

Suddenly, gunshots rang out, ripping violently through the air. One, two, three, each distinct shot a bloodcurdling punctuation mark. Anna and Georgette stared at each other in wordless shock. The shots could only have come from Clara's revolver.

The engine of the truck behind them revved. A moment later, the vehicle shot past. The Berliet could only go thirty kilometers per hour at its top speed, but Eliza was driving as though it were faster than the Napier could ever dream of being. Georgette's blood ran cold. They were running from something. But what?

CHAPTER TWENTY-THREE

Eliza

"What the hell was that?" Eliza yelled. Every hair on her body was standing on end. She pressed her foot so hard against the accelerator she was almost standing. Had the metal been any weaker, she likely would have snapped it in two. She tried to look over her shoulder to see if they were being followed, but the bulky, boxy Berliet obscured everything behind them. She was driving blind.

Clara, leaning as far out of the opposite side of the cab as she could to try to see behind them, replied, "I don't know." Her voice was a pant of fear. Her revolver was held tightly in her hand, ready to fire again.

Eliza's ears were still ringing from the first three shots. Her nerves were on fire, screaming the need to flee. Despite her desperate urging, however, the Berliet could go no faster. It was like a turtle: designed to carry heavy loads, but slow and cumbersome. She smacked the wheel, willing it to go faster anyway.

"Come on, come on, come on," she coaxed. Although she couldn't see behind them, she kept looking out the side of the truck. The danger could come from there too. "Is it following us?"

"If it is, I can't see it."

She growled, willing the truck to accelerate, wishing it was her Jenny. Then they could take flight and leave the desert far behind. She didn't know how far or how fast they had to go to get away. All she knew was that right now, they hadn't done either. She looked meaningfully at Clara's revolver. "Did you hit it?" She didn't want to think about the fact that with three bullets gone, only one more remained.

She shivered, unwillingly remembering the face that had gotten so close to her she could almost have reached out and touched it: long, sharp white teeth like children's fingers; an elongated snout with a foot-long pink tongue like a boot insole; a mouth so wide it could have swallowed her head whole; and to cap it all off, malevolent green eyes with thin black slits for pupils. It wasn't an animal that had attacked them. No animal in the world looked like that. It was a monster.

Clara, head still turned, replied, "No, it was moving too quickly."

Too quickly indeed. Faster than any creature had a right to. The monster had juked nimbly at the first shot, then just as effortlessly at the second. By the third, it had leapt somewhere out of sight, which was when Eliza had finally regained enough of her senses to hit the gas. Unfortunately, while it might have gotten them out of immediate danger, now the monster was at their back, and if it attacked again, they might not see it coming.

Eliza hadn't meant to abandon the other truck, but in the immediate aftermath of the encounter, her only thought had been getting away. Now she remembered it. "Can you see Anna and Georgette?" She hoped they had inferred the presence of danger and hadn't encountered it firsthand like she and Clara had.

"Yes. I see them," Clara said.

"Are they all right?"

"Yes."

Eliza was relieved. She wasn't sure what she would have done otherwise. Even now, her body wasn't entirely hers. The same primal fear and natural instinct toward self-preservation that had taken control of it at Dra' Abu el-Naga' were guiding her now. She wasn't certain she could wrestle control back to turn the truck around if she had to, not knowing that the monster might be there. But since the other truck *was* still behind them, the only thing to do now was to keep running, to press on as hard and as fast as the Berliets would go. And hope the monster couldn't catch up.

Clara dropped back into the cab. Sweat had beaded at her hairline and was running down the side of her face in front of her ears, bringing dirt with it all the way to her neck. "What *was* that?" she asked, repeating Eliza's own question back to her. Her eyes were tiny moons, perfectly round and luminous.

That same question was a constant, howling refrain in Eliza's own mind. "Not anything I've ever seen before." She cast another glance to the side of the truck. And not anything she ever wanted to see again, either.

"Do you think we can outrun it?"

Eliza clenched her jaw, making the muscles flex. Her toes, crammed against the pedal, were cramping. They would outrun the beast if she could help it. And if not, she was already developing a contingency plan. The monster was big, but the Berliet was bigger. She would try to run it over. So long as she didn't tip the truck in the effort, the monster would crush flat as a bug under its tires. Maybe. If they were lucky.

Clara looked anxiously at the faint outline of the road in front of them, unable to sit still. "We need to tell Anna and Georgette. They need to know."

"I ain't slowing down," Eliza growled. "We'll tell them once we're damn certain that thing ain't chasing us anymore." Fleetingly, she thought how Georgette, already terrified of crocodiles, would respond to hearing there was a monster crocodile on the loose. They might have to peel her from the roof of the truck.

Clara didn't argue. She reverted instead to their previous line of conversation, fear making her babble. "You saw it. It wasn't our imagination. It really was there."

Eliza nodded, although even now it was hard to believe the creature that had lunged toward their slowly moving truck had been real. It was too awful, too terrifying to be. But there was no question it had been. She loosened and contracted her fingers on the steering wheel, trying to keep them, too, from cramping. Her heart was still racing, her skin still tingling. "Yeah, I saw it. But I wish I hadn't." She would remember the sight until her dying day. It would come back to her in nightmares.

"Do you think there are more out there like it?"

Eliza hadn't thought about that. In her mind, she had assumed the monster was unique. Now the idea that it was one of many, that the desert could be full of those monsters the same way it was full of snakes and lizards made her shudder. "I hope not."

"Do you—"

"Enough. We'll talk about it later." She didn't want to discuss it anymore. She was agitated enough. "We can ask Anna what it was. She probably knows."

"But—" Eliza gave her a sharp look and Clara fell silent.

For the next ten minutes, they rode without speaking. The cab was electric with their tension. Every creak and groan the truck made, Eliza worried the monster had caught up with them and was crawling over the sides to reach them. But if the creature had given chase, they must have outrun it, because the dreaded second attack never came. When she was finally confident they were safe, she pulled the truck to the side of the road and turned it off. The engine hissed and steamed a little, overloaded by the exertion of traveling flat out under a heavy load.

Moments later, the second truck came to a stop next to them. Anna sprang out and charged toward Eliza and Clara. "What happened? Why were you driving so fast?"

"We were attacked," Clara said. Her revolver was still clutched in her hand. Eliza wouldn't have minded if she didn't holster it again until they were on a steamer sailing away from Egypt.

"What?"

"It looked kind of like a crocodile. It tried to get into the truck. It was awful."

Anna's eyes sharpened. "What do you mean it looked like a crocodile?"

Georgette, who had been a few strides behind Anna, gasped audibly. "Ammit!"

Anna looked queasy. "Don't be ridiculous. Of course it wasn't Ammit. Ammit is a myth. She doesn't exist." She turned back to Eliza and Clara. "Tell me more. What else did it look like?"

"I don't know. Everything happened so quickly. But it was big—the size of a pony."

Eliza unfolded herself from the truck gingerly, her muscles stiff from having been clenched so tightly. "Sound like anything familiar?"

Anna ran her hand through her hair, flustered. "I don't—I don't know. There are no crocodiles in the Western Desert. They don't come west of the Nile."

"Could it have been a lizard? Deserts have lots of lizards, don't they?"

"Yes, but nothing like what you're describing. The biggest can get up to a few feet long, but hardly the size of a pony."

Eliza examined the wood of the truck bed behind her. Long claw marks had been scored several feet across it, the rough cuts half an inch deep. The paw that had made them had been so large that when she set her fingers to the grooves, she could barely reach all five. She swallowed down the saliva that filled her mouth. She and Clara had only escaped the monster by a matter of feet. Had she been even a little slower to hit the accelerator, those same claws might have embedded in her own flesh.

Anna stared at the marks, horrified. "My God, what is that? Did the creature make that?"

Georgette waved her arms at Anna like an agitated bird. "It is Ammit. Anna, it is Ammit, like you said!"

"What's Ammit?" Clara asked.

Anna took a deep breath. Eliza could see determination settle over her like a mantle. She lifted her chin. "It's nothing. Georgette is overwrought." She pointedly avoided looking at her companion. Nevertheless, she shrugged her shoulders uncomfortably, as though redistributing weight across them.

Eliza narrowed her eyes, suspicious. The way Anna was fidgeting nervously suggested that whatever it was, it wasn't "nothing."

"*Who* is Ammit," Georgette clarified, ignoring Anna's curt dismissal. "She eats hearts."

"*What?*" Clara yelped.

By instinct, Eliza and Clara both looked to Anna for an explanation. An unhappy scowl contorted her face. "Ammit is one of the ancient Egyptian gods of the dead. I was telling Georgette about her, but it's ridiculous. Of course an imaginary god didn't attack you. I don't know what animal did, but—"

"But you saw her too," Georgette protested.

"I told you, it was my imagination!" Anna snapped with a viciousness that took Eliza aback. "We were under stress, what with the storm and all. It didn't mean anything. The Egyptian gods aren't real, Georgette! How could you even think it?"

A confrontation was brewing between them. Georgette was puffing up like an angry crow, while Anna was squaring her shoulders defiantly. Eliza didn't understand what was happening, but she was in no mood to sit by and wait for them to finish squabbling. She wanted to get to the bottom of things. She stepped forward and held out her hands between the two of them. "Hold on a minute, hold on. Georgette, why do you think it was this Ammit?" Like Anna, she found the idea that they'd been attacked by an Egyptian god of death more than half crazy, but then again, that monster sure didn't look like it belonged in this world.

"You said it was *un crocodile*. Ammit, she is part *crocodile*, part *lion*, part *hippopotame*. And Anna saw her today during the storm. It was Ammit who attacked you. It must be."

A whisper of cold tickled the base of Eliza's neck. Part crocodile, part lion, part hippopotamus sounded *exactly* like what she'd seen. Now that the animal names had been given to her, she saw once more the creature that had attacked them: a crocodile head that ended in a sparse fringe of wiry hair like a collar. Powerful shoulders that gave way to the catlike paws that

had scratched gouges into the truck. A sloped back that reached to oddly bulky haunches. Eliza saw it all as though it were a photograph in front of her.

But an Egyptian goddess? Eliza didn't even believe in Jehovah and all that. She grasped for an alternative explanation. "Could it be some animal no one's discovered yet?" New species were discovered all the time. Maybe this was one of them.

Georgette made a face at her. "Part *crocodile*, part *lion*? Of course this cannot exist *dans la nature*. One is a reptile, the other a mammal. It can only be her."

She rubbed her forehead. At that moment, all she wanted was to be home. All the gold in the world wasn't worth what they'd been through. "Okay, let's say it *was* Ammit." She could barely say the sentence aloud, it sounded so impossible. "Why..." She faltered. Taking a breath, she tried again. "Why would it—she— attack us?"

"The mummy's curse."

"The mummy's what?" Clara looked dazed.

Eliza shifted to rubbing her temples. At every turn, the conversation seemed to take an even stranger direction.

Georgette explained, "*Le trésor*, it is cursed. Ammit is here because of this curse."

Mystified, Eliza looked to Anna. "What do you mean the treasure is cursed?"

Anna scowled back, frustrated. "It's a story I told Georgette about a man exporting mummies from Alexandria."

"And?"

"It's nothing! A fictional ghost story. It's the twentieth century, for God's sake. How could a demon goddess possibly be running around Egypt now?"

Georgette's nostrils flared. "You did not seem so skeptical of this story before. You said the curse could be true. And how else you can explain what has attacked them, and why you also saw Ammit? I did not believe it either, but now you cannot say it was not Ammit. There can be no other *hypothèse*."

Anna flailed her arm. "I don't know! It could be a lost crocodile for all I know. I'm not a zoologist."

Georgette crossed her arms and raised her eyebrows. "Ah *oui*? So far from water? What did it do, walk hundreds of *kilomètres*? Why it would do that?"

Eliza took a few deep breaths to clear her head as Anna and Georgette began to argue in earnest, letting their words flow over her as a meaningless wave of sound. When she felt steadier, she announced, "Whatever it was, it's gone now. Let's get back on the road." They could keep arguing when they got back in their truck, but she didn't feel like sitting around any longer. Not when whatever it was could catch up.

Georgette stared at her, horrified. "*Non*, we cannot keep going, not with *le trésor*."

Eliza blinked. "Why not?"

"The curse, it is too *dangereuse*. Remember what happened to the thieves? They were taken. Maybe it was by Ammit. It is not safe to continue with *le trésor*."

"For God's sake, Georgette—" Anna protested.

"*Non*, listen. What happened to the thief at Dra' Abu el-Naga'? I have asked myself this question. Where did he go? And why he would have left his gun? He could not have run so fast we would not have seen him. But he was gone. *Disparu*. And then the drivers of the trucks. They did not walk away into the desert, but poof, they are gone."

Georgette continued, building steam, "One *coïncidence*, two, maybe we could understand. But *une éclipse solaire* that is not, *un serpent* that kills one of the thieves, the sandstorm when it is not the time for sandstorms, this *monstre* who is Ammit—*non*, this is too much. It is not *an accident*. The curse is *dangereuse*."

Eliza rocked back on her heels, absorbing the argument. It was a lot to take in. Then again, a lot had happened in the last few days. She briefly closed her eyes, trying to regain some calm. They needed to calm down and think things through. There was no use losing their heads. A few unexplained events didn't mean a three-thousand-year-old curse was chasing them. Although maybe it did.

"Okay, let's say it is a curse. What do we do to make it go away?" she asked.

"We must leave *le trésor*."

"Over my dead body," Anna snarled. Her eyes narrowed into angry slits. "That treasure is mine. It's going to Cairo. It belongs in a museum."

"But the curse—"

"There is no curse. It's all rubbish. No more of this. Get in the truck, we're leaving. And I don't want to hear any more talk of curses or Ammit or anything else." She spun on her heel and stalked back to the second truck, dark as a thundercloud.

The three women she'd left in her wake exchanged uneasy glances. Eliza still wasn't entirely convinced they were dealing with some voodoo, magic curse, but there was more than enough question in her mind that she wasn't comfortable continuing on as though nothing had happened, either. She didn't want another encounter with Ammit or with whatever had captured the truck's original occupants. Anna could throw as much of a tantrum as she liked, but if it came to it, she couldn't force them to continue onward with the treasure. So they were at a crossroads: go with Anna and risk the curse—if it existed—or dump the treasure and endure her wrath.

"Well, what do we do?" Eliza asked.

"If we get in the trucks, we may die," Georgette said. Her mouth was pulled down into a deep expression of unhappiness, the lines accentuated by the sand that was ground deep into the lines of her face. "I think Ammit, she will not give up."

"So we take the treasure out of one of the trucks and drive away? Is that enough to stop the curse?" She avoided thinking about how long unloading would take. Hours.

Georgette shrugged. "I do not know. Maybe. But what about Anna? She will not want to leave *le trésor*."

Clara looked toward their companion, who was sitting at the steering wheel of her truck, staring straight ahead. "I'll talk to her."

At that moment, Eliza saw something in the distance that sent chills down her arms. "You better talk fast. The jackals are back."

CHAPTER TWENTY-FOUR

Anna

"Anna?"

Clara's hand came to rest gently on Anna's forearm, but she didn't feel it. She barely even registered that Clara had gotten into the truck and was sitting next to her, although their thighs were almost touching. She had shut everything out around her, and that included Clara. The entire world had telescoped down to a single point: Cairo. She had to get to Cairo. She would deal with everything else after they brought the treasure to the museum there, but Cairo came first.

"Anna…" Clara began. "Something is wrong, isn't it? It really was Ammit who attacked us, wasn't it?"

Years. She'd spent years—half a lifetime, even—in the desert digging, scraping through tons of dirt and rock looking for even a hint of the gold of Egypt's pharaohs. It had been thankless, brutal work, and it had cost her so much more than she would even admit to herself. But now she had proof that none of it was in vain. She had five tons of Egypt's finest treasures mere feet away from her, sparkling gold and jewels that rivaled any royal treasury in Europe. When she brought it all back to Cairo, it would be an immediate international sensation. Ahmose's treasure would make the paltry trinkets of Tut's tomb look like shabby knockoffs.

She would take her place among Egypt's greatest archaeologists. It would make all the hardship and trouble worth it. Who would remember Carter and his water boy when Anna Baring had chased antiquities thieves across Egypt in the greatest treasure hunt in history? It was delicious, righteous vindication. Carter would be as obscure and forgotten as Tutankhamun himself. But it could only happen if the treasure made it to Cairo.

"If Georgette is right, it may not be safe to keep going with the treasure. We don't know what might happen," Clara said.

She grazed her fingertips across the ridge of Anna's cheek and cupped her jaw in her hand. Under other circumstances, Anna would have leaned into the touch, nuzzling deeper into the other woman's soft flesh. Instead, she turned her head, rejecting Clara's effort to reach her. She started the truck. Over the rumble of the engine, she growled, "Georgette is wrong."

"What if Ammit attacks again? We can't stop her."

Anna clenched her jaw, fighting to avoid thinking about the monstrous, reptilian face she'd seen in the storm and the claw marks on the other truck. "We'll drive fast. She won't be able to catch us." She shifted the truck into gear, still refusing to look at Clara. In her mind, Ammit was fixed at a single location in the desert, kilometers back. All they needed to do was put enough distance between them and her and everything would be all right. She couldn't reach them. The danger would pass.

Clara moved her hand to rest on top of Anna's. "What if it's not just Ammit? What if there's another sandstorm, or something worse? Think about Eliza and Georgette."

Anna's hand tightened against the gearshift so hard it shook. The effort of blocking everything out, of maintaining single-minded determination and focus in the face of Clara's fear, was taking all her strength. "This is my life's work, *everything* I've worked for. I'm not leaving these artifacts." If she had to, she'd hand carry every single piece to make sure they made it to the museum.

"I know. But—"

Anna glowered at her, closing the door on any further discussion. There was no curse. Ammit would not attack. They would reach Mersa Matruh safely and from there Alexandria, then Cairo.

Clara gazed out at the horizon sadly. "The jackals are back." Her voice was toneless.

Despite herself, Anna stiffened. She scanned the horizon for the familiar shapes, dreading seeing the creatures while at the same time not surprised by their return. She saw them in the distance, their long, triangular ears unmistakable. They watched, waiting with supernatural patience.

"They're part of this too, aren't they? There's no way they could have followed us this far. They're not normal animals. What are they?"

With pointed intention, Anna made herself look away. She ground her teeth. So what if Anubis, protector of tombs, was a jackal? So what if the jackals had followed them for dozens of kilometers more than any normal jackal would? It was coincidence, nothing more. The Egyptian gods weren't real. No gods were. She pressed down on the accelerator. "There's no such thing as curses."

Since there were no curses, there was no danger. Anna would *never* put the women in harm's way. She cared deeply about them and their safety. She was bringing them home, and the treasure too. She was doing what any reasonable person would under the circumstances. It would be absurd to cast aside the pharaoh's priceless artifacts out of a silly superstition.

As the truck pulled itself forward, Clara drew her gun once more. For a second, Anna thought Clara might use it to force her to stop the truck, but she didn't. Instead, she set it on her lap. Although she didn't say anything, the expression on her face was full of unhappiness and frustration.

Trying to lighten the mood, Anna said, "You won't need that. It will be a quiet ride the rest of the way back. You'll see."

Clara said nothing. A moment later, the sound of the second truck sputtering to life told Anna that the other women had abandoned their mutiny and were following. They didn't want to be left alone in the desert. She nodded grimly to herself. Good. Her guests might be angry with her now, but later, when they saw the treasure displayed in its full glory in the museum, they would agree it was for the best. They would thank her. Later.

* * *

For the next half hour, the drive was uneventful, although to Anna's chagrin the jackals continued following them with their relentless, eerie perseverance. When the road finally turned northeast, she knew only a few kilometers remained until they reached Mersa Matruh. The tension coiled around her stomach easing, she reached out to stroke the back of Clara's neck. But Clara, who had been silent the whole ride, shrugged her off, wriggling farther away from her on the short bench seat to avoid her touch.

"What is it?" Anna asked, dismayed by the rejection.

Clara didn't respond. She had holstered her gun long ago, but her right hand was still resting upon it, ready to draw at any time. Her body was closed off and tense, her mouth a dissatisfied wrinkle.

Anna grimaced and withdrew her hand to the rattling gearshift. "Is this about the bloody curse still? There is no curse. How many times do I have to say it?" Despite everything she had seen and Clara and Eliza had experienced, she was starting to convince herself that everything really had been a figment of their imagination.

Clara's face drew together, a sour, bitter expression. "All you care about is that treasure. It's all you've ever cared about."

"Of course I care about it! These artifacts are the discovery of the millennium."

Clara crossed her arms and turned her face away. "Why did you invite us to Egypt? If all you wanted was an audience, weren't there people here who could have clapped and told you how wonderful you were? Why did it have to be us?"

Anna recoiled, taken aback. "What do you mean? You know why I invited you. This is a great moment for the Lady Adventurers Club—or at least, it was meant to be. I wanted to share it with you all."

"A made-up club no one else knows about," Clara scoffed.

"But they will—"

"Not if we don't make it home!" The words came out an anguished cry.

Anna ground her teeth together, then took a breath. "We're almost to Mersa Matruh." The quiet drive confirmed she had made the right decision to push forward. They were safe. There was no reason to worry anymore.

Clara shook her head. "And then what? Ammit finds us there? You saw her too. Do you really want to open your eyes in the middle of the night and find her staring back? Or for one of us to? I thought you cared about us."

Anna was appalled by the charge. "I do!" She wasn't a monster. How could Clara even think that about her?

"You said it yourself: you care about the treasure. We're just...props."

"I can care about both things," Anna protested. "And I *am* worried about—about Ammit." Even as Clara glared at her reproachfully, it was difficult to admit. She rallied, piqued by hurt. "And I don't see you as props. That's ridiculous." Then she realized what Clara was really saying. "Is this about us? Do you think I've been using you? That all this has been a fun little romp and I'll happily see you off at the end of it?"

Clara didn't answer, but by her face, Anna could see the thought had more than crossed her mind.

"Well, I haven't, and it's not. I would like you to stay here with me in Egypt. We can live in my apartment in Cairo while I see the artifacts settled at the museum. No one will look twice at two woman companions, and Karim would never tell anyone."

"I don't belong here," Clara said, dismissing the idea. "What would I do?"

The melancholy had returned to her face, but Anna dismissed the question with a flick of her wrist. "I don't know, be my bodyguard?" She was thinking of the chase through Khan el-Khalili, when Clara had barreled after the shooter in her defense. She smiled warmly at Clara, trying to dispel her concern. Finding something for her to do in Egypt was an insignificant concern. Cairo was a growing city. There would always be work, if she wanted it. The important thing was that she agree to stay.

Clara's response was a bloodcurdling scream.

"*Stop!*"

Anna had been looking at Clara, all of her attention on trying to assuage her concerns and win back some of her trust. This effort had come, however, at the expense of watching the road. At the other woman's cry, she jerked her eyes back. A line of jackals stretched across it, a sort of living barrier. Without thinking, she slammed her foot against the brake. The truck issued a high-pitched screech of resistance, fighting against the command to decelerate. Its tires dragged through the thin layer of sand covering the road as it grudgingly responded.

Then the brakes locked. Anna felt a flash of terror. She had lost control of the vehicle. Still, the road was straight. There was no risk of driving off it.

The truck slid forward, unresponsive to Anna's frantic efforts but slowing nevertheless. By some miracle, it came to a stop a few meters in front of the jackals. Anna's body strained forward for another second, still carried by the vehicle's momentum, then rocked back. Her heart was pounding, her nerves screaming. The animals, which hadn't so much as twitched while the truck bore down on them, watched for a second, then trotted away on light paws as though they had never been in danger.

Anna breathed heavily, trying to regain her composure. She was certain the jackals hadn't been there a few seconds ago. They couldn't have. For hours, they had been trailing the trucks; she would have seen if they had raced ahead to pass. What were they doing on the road like that anyway?

Before she could think any more about it, the ground around them began to tremble. The sand vibrated and shifted on the road in front of them. The truck vibrated on its chassis, creaking. Even the gearshift beneath Anna's hand shivered. A low-pitched rumble filled the air. *Earthquake!* Adrenaline flushed her body as tremors rolled through her from the soles of her feet to the top of her head.

With a loud crack, the land to the left of the truck divided in half like an eggshell breaking. Quickly, what started as a narrow seam turned into a gaping maw. It grew by the second, stretching both longer and wider. Earth and sand fell into it like a waterfall. The chasm's edge raced toward the truck, dissolving the earth between them as it went. In seconds, it would reach them. Anna was spellbound. It was both horrific and amazing at once.

"Drive!" Clara squealed.

Her shout brought Anna to her senses. She stomped on the accelerator, intent on racing away from the abyss and to safety, but to her horror, the truck didn't budge. The engine roared belligerently, a cacophonous crescendo of sound, but the wheels didn't turn. Her mind went blank with panic. She slammed the pedal again and again, but with the same result. She didn't know what was wrong. She shook the steering wheel, helpless.

"Anna? Go! We have to go." Clara's voice, full of panic, was barely audible over the snarl of the engine. She bounced on the seat as though trying to impart to the truck her energy.

Go. Go. Go. The words slammed like hammer blows inside Anna's head. If the truck didn't move, they would have to abandon it and run to the other truck, but if they waited too long, the sinkhole would catch them. She had to decide immediately. Desperate, she slammed the heel of her palm against the gearshift, a final effort to do *something* before they bailed out and left it. Anna was certain she had never taken the truck out of gear, but somehow the gearshift moved forward anyway. The truck clicked into gear like a key turning a lock. She mashed the accelerator again and the Berliet heaved itself into motion just as Eliza and Georgette passed on the other side, watching Anna's struggle with concern.

"Go!" she yelled to them, although they needed no encouragement.

The two trucks raced forward side by side, trying to get away from the sinkhole before it devoured them. Lightning raced along Anna's skin. Her breath came short and fast, her chest tight. She couldn't see what was happening behind them. If the imploding ground caught them, she would only know when she felt the pull of the back tires slipping into the abyss, and then it would be too late.

Suddenly, a new sinkhole appeared ahead and to their right. The ground fragmented into a spiderweb of thick cracks that radiated toward the road. In the blink of an eye, the center of the web collapsed into a hole the size of a camel.

"Anna!" Clara cried, pointing.

Anna gripped the steering wheel harder. "I see it."

Eliza and Georgette were closest to the developing pit, gaining on it by the second. Anna jerked the steering wheel hard to the left, pulling her truck off the road to give them room to swerve around it. She had to fight to maintain control of the wheel as the truck bounced off the road and onto the low sand dunes. It was dangerous driving like this. If she didn't return to the road soon, she would have to reduce her speed. If a tire was punctured or blown out, the truck would be crippled. They would have to abandon it. But even a flat tire was better than being swallowed whole.

Anna held her breath. The cracks stretched all the way across the road. If the earth crumbled beneath it, Georgette and Eliza would be lost. There was no guarantee she and Clara wouldn't be too.

But the ground held. The two trucks raced past moments before the body of the sinkhole reached the edge of the road. They had avoided catastrophe once again by the skin of their teeth. Anna started to sweat in earnest, and not from the heat. Egypt experienced occasional earthquakes, but almost always in the east, near the Sinai, not in the Western Desert.

A few moments later, when Eliza slowed a little, she accelerated to return to the road and take the lead. Her mouth was dry. Her nerves were still on fire from their close call. Regardless of what she'd been telling herself about curses, it was clear these sinkholes were no natural phenomenon. It was beyond the possibility of coincidence that the chasms had opened up just where the women had been driving. The sinkholes were *chasing* them. And if they were being chased, then it was likely only a matter of time until the next one appeared.

She glanced at Clara. Her companion was gripping the dashboard, her legs spread wide to keep her from being thrown from the cab. Her face was bloodless. When she caught Anna looking at her, she shouted, "I told you it wasn't safe to keep the treasure! We have to get rid of it!"

Anna's heart wrenched. Her selfish lies had come back to her. She had done an unforgivable thing and knowingly put her friends in mortal danger. She had let her pride and greed override all else. The artifacts in the trucks were her legacy. They represented everything she was, the only imprint she would ever leave on the world. But the choice to stop or go on was out of her hands. If they kept going, that same treasure would be the death of all of them.

She stopped the truck. Eliza pulled up beside her. "What are you doing?" She looked around anxiously. "We gotta keep moving. What if more of those holes open up?"

Anna flinched. The words wanted to stick in her throat. She had to force them out. "Georgette was right. We can't keep the treasure. It's too dangerous. We'll have to leave it."

"We close enough to Mersa Matruh to walk?"

She winced. "It will be a long walk. I don't know how many kilometers exactly."

Her head knew she must do what was right, but even so, her heart was rebelling, begging to keep the artifacts. She wasn't a tomb robber, she was an archaeologist. Surely the curse should be able to differentiate between the two. It wasn't fair!

"So we just leave the trucks?"

She nodded.

To her shock, Georgette exclaimed, "*Non!* We cannot do that."

Anna frowned at her, surprised. "Why not?"

"If we leave the trucks, someone else will find them. They will not know about the curse. It will be *dangereux* for them.

Maybe even they will be killed. We must dump *le trésor* into *l'océan*. It is the only way to stop the curse. Like in the story you told me."

"You want us to keep going?" Clara was alarmed. "But what if there are more sinkholes? Or Ammit comes back?"

Anna agreed. Now that she had made the decision to dump the treasure, she had no desire to keep it a second longer.

"*L'océan* is close. I have seen a few birds in the sky. They are a species that live by water. I believe we can make it."

Anna pondered Georgette's argument. If she had seen a gull, the coast could be only a few kilometers due north. From there, they could walk east to find Mersa Matruh. But there was no telling exactly how far away either were, and the curse might catch them first. Every moment in the trucks increased the chance of something terrible happening.

Eliza looked as ready to protest as Anna and Clara. "I don't think—"

Georgette said something to her, so low Anna couldn't hear it. The two argued for a moment, then Eliza sighed. She returned her attention to Anna. "Do you think we can make it?"

Anna licked her parched lips. A wrong answer could have catastrophic consequences. "Maybe." She had no way of knowing. It was a complete guess.

The path forward with the treasure was a question of responsibility. What did they owe someone who might find the trucks in the future? Anna's priority was keeping the other women safe, which she could only do by abandoning the treasure immediately. But there was, as Georgette had pointed out, an argument to be made about the ethics of leaving it to endanger the first unsuspecting stranger who found it. What if it was Berbers like Gwafa? They didn't deserve to be cursed.

Eliza eyed Georgette with misgiving, then gave a curt nod. "All right, we can try to get it to the ocean. But anything else happens and we're leaving these trucks and it doesn't matter who finds them."

Anna looked to Clara. This time, unlike the last, they all needed to agree on what to do with the treasure. She was determined that if their fourth member refused to go a step farther with it, they would leave it and walk, no matter the distance.

Clara surveyed the desert around them. For now, it was quiet. There were no more sinkholes. Reluctantly, she said, "Okay. Let's try."

CHAPTER TWENTY-FIVE

Anna

To reach the sea, they had to head north, forsaking the road for the featureless, lumpy desert. Anna pushed the Berliet as fast as she dared, racing against whatever forces were behind the curse. It was an uncomfortable, bone-rattling ride, but she was willing to exchange this temporary discomfort for the hope that they would reach the ocean before the next attack came.

Clara's hand found her thigh and pressed lightly. "I'm sorry."

Anna didn't dare take her eyes off the sand in front of them to look at her. Any moment, a new sinkhole could open up. Or if not that, it could be jackals, crocodiles, or who knew what else? By now she was willing to believe anything might appear. The curse had turned all of nature itself against them.

Clara continued, "I know how hard this is for you."

Anna said nothing. If she did, the glue that was barely holding her together might dissolve and she would shatter into pieces. Hard? Hard was watching Carter erase her from her own life. There was no word to describe what this was. She had lost everything. Nothing of her life or her career remained anymore. It was all gone. And at her lowest point, she had even almost sacrificed her companions.

As though reading her mind, Clara said, "I know it doesn't seem like it now, but you haven't lost everything. You found the tomb. You're a fantastic archaeologist. And you'll discover other things in the future."

No, she wouldn't. Finding Ahmose's tomb had been one in a million. She could never do it a second time. Nor did she have the heart to try, not when the next tomb could be cursed too. She never wanted to go through this again. Her days as an archaeologist were over.

"No. I'm done for in the valley."

Her answer surprised Clara. "Then what will you do?"

"I don't know."

Now was not the time to think about it. Later, once the treasure was disposed of and she was back in Cairo, she could consider how to rebuild her life. All she knew for now was that the future she had envisioned for herself was no longer possible, not to mention any kind of life with Clara, who might never forgive her for what she'd done. But there was no future at all if they didn't survive the next few hours.

"I hear Constantinople is nice this time of year."

Anna was so astonished by the shy suggestion she risked a glance at Clara. Clara was staring at the tops of her boots. Carefully, as though choosing each word, she said, "I don't know if I can leave America forever to live with you in Egypt. America is all I've ever known. It's my home. But I know I would like to spend more time with you. To maybe…see…how things could be."

It was no solid commitment, but given how recklessly Anna had behaved over the last few days, it was the best she could have hoped for. Clara wasn't closing the door on the idea of a future together, she was merely asking for more time. Anna could give her that. And assuming they made it out of this mess, a trip to Constantinople would take her mind off what she had lost in Egypt.

Heart swelling, she curled her fingers around Clara's, then brought her hand up to kiss her knuckles, not caring about the dirt and sand ground into them. "I'm certain Constantinople will be gorgeous. I can't imagine anything I'd like more."

A flush of pink wicked up Clara's neck. A small, bashful smile spread across her delicate lips. Anna was so caught up in the moment that she didn't notice the engine shutting off. It was only moments later, when the truck was bouncing decidedly less vigorously over the sand, that she realized they were losing momentum. She pushed on the accelerator, frowning, but the truck didn't respond. Letting go of Clara's hand, she brought the gearshift to neutral and tried turning the key several times to restart the engine. Still nothing. Slowly, despite her increasingly frantic efforts to prevent it, the truck rolled to a halt.

"What's happening?" Clara asked uneasily.

Panic stirred in the pit of Anna's stomach. "I don't know." But it couldn't be anything good.

She gave up battling the ignition and got out of the cab. The second truck had pulled up behind them, so she called back to Eliza and Georgette, "The truck stopped."

"Ours too," Eliza replied. "Engine won't crank."

The feeling of dread moved to from Anna's stomach to her chest, squeezing it tight. It was hard to breathe. With both trucks disabled, they were sitting ducks. The four women met midway between the still vehicles.

"I don't like this," Eliza said. "It doesn't feel right."

"I don't either," Anna agreed. Her senses tingled. At any moment, she knew, the attack would come."

"Could the engines be overheated?"

The question was no sooner out of Clara's mouth than the ground began to tremble. Anna felt a thrill of panic. No! Not another sinkhole! The shiver turned into a rolling quake that threatened to send the women sprawling to their hands and knees. She grasped the wooden slats of the truck bed, clinging to them to keep from falling. Fire raced up her arms and down to her toes. They had to get away before the coming hole sucked them down.

Too late. The ground in front of them cracked open like a clam shell. Sand began to slide into the hungry crevasse. Their only option was to forsake the trucks and flee—and hope they could outrun the vast and terrible power of nature. But Anna's legs wouldn't move. Frozen, all she could do was watch.

There was something different about this sinkhole, however. Unlike the others, it didn't continue to grow after the first crack. No network of smaller fissures appeared. The earth stilled, and for a brief moment, Anna experienced a flash of hope. Perhaps there was still time to get away.

Then a figure appeared from the black gash in the earth, stepping over the sinking sand as though it were nothing.

It was a woman. Or rather, her shape was that of a woman. But she couldn't be mistaken for a human. Her skin was golden and scaled like a snake. Her almond eyes were completely black. She wore a red sheath dress that reached to her ankles, hugging every curve of her long, lithe body. Golden armlets set with lapis lazuli rested over each biceps. Atop her thick, black, shoulder-length hair, she wore an elaborate golden circlet. At its center, sitting against her forehead, was a jeweled cobra. From its sides sprouted long, curved horns that held a red circle between them, balanced on the top of her head.

Anna gasped. She had seen this woman before. She had seen her a hundred if not a thousand times on tomb walls and in temples. (Or a variant of her at least. The Egyptians tended to draw their deities the same.)

The goddess spoke. "Behold, I am She Who Burns. I am the sword of the risen god, king of the dead. I have smitten his foes and chased evil from the earth. Look upon me and tremble in fear."

At least, Anna guessed that's what she'd said. Since Egyptian hadn't been spoken since the fourth century, no one knew exactly what it sounded like. Anna was reasonably sure she recognized some words from the "Coming Forth by Day" invocation in the *Book of the Dead*, but the others she was inferring. In any case, it was clear the goddess wasn't giving a friendly greeting.

Clara, who was standing beside the cab of their truck, gripping the frame, whispered, "Who is that? And what did she say?"

The sun glimmered off the goddess's metallic scales as she advanced toward them, her body moving like a candle flame in a draft. Behind her, she left no footprints. Anna couldn't swallow. Her mouth was too dry. She Who Burns was the title of the goddess Wepset. But if this was indeed Wepset before them, they were in trouble. A personification of vengeance, she wasn't the type to show up for a friendly chat about the weather.

The goddess's head swiveled as she scrutinized the humans, her eyes unblinking. Her tongue flickered from her lips, long and black and forked at the end. It fluttered in the air before retracting. Anna cleared her throat, trying to find her voice. Speaking loudly for Eliza and Georgette to hear, she answered Clara. "She's a goddess from the Egyptian pantheon. And she said to fear her."

"She doesn't have to tell me to fear her," Eliza said, voice low. "She came out of that ground like she was coming up straight from Hell. What's she gonna do to us?"

Anna felt it best not to answer. The goddess wasn't called She Who Burns for no reason.

Wepset spoke again and this time, to Anna's surprise, the words were in English, as though the goddess had recognized the language of the humans in front of her and had adapted accordingly. "Cursed be those who disturb the rest of a pharaoh. They that break the seal of his tomb shall meet death by the hands of the defenders of Osiris. They shall find no refuge, either on land or sea. Their lives shall be forfeit."

The goddess's voice was older than time. It rumbled like the minor earthquake that had preceded her appearance. It sapped any remaining strength from Anna's legs. Even nature blanched in her presence. The color was draining from the sky around them, the bright blue fading to gray. The sun burned an anemic white as the clouds bleached to a pale pewter.

Clara discreetly inched closer to Anna. "What do we do?" she whispered.

Anna didn't know. Clearly, running wasn't an option. But how did one placate a goddess whose sole purpose was retribution?

The ground began to tremble one more beneath their feet. Anna's heart skipped a beat, dread filling her like cold water in a cup. Wepset raised her arms, their bent shape mirroring the curved horns on her circlet, and tilted her face to the sky.

"Desecrators of the pharaohs, violators of that which is sacred and holy, thieves of the relics of the king, prepare to face judgment in the underworld."

The ball of red above her head began to glow, pulsing red like a carnelian. Red-orange flames emerged to lick around the edges. Scholars had always assumed the red circle in drawings of the goddess was merely a pictorial symbolization of the Eye of Ra, a sort of literary embellishment. Seeing it in person, Anna understood it was something much less figurative and much, much more like a weapon.

She closed her eyes. It was over. They were dead.

"Wait!" Georgette cried.

Anna opened her eyes. Wepset's fierce gaze turned to the audacious human, searing through her with such heat Anna was amazed Georgette didn't wither on the spot, but Georgette didn't back down. "We did not break the seal of *le tombeau*. It was already broken when we arrived. It had been opened for many days, in fact."

Wepset hissed, the sound a cross between tearing paper and an ocean wave breaking. It made the hair on Anna's arms and the back of her neck stand on end. "Liesssss. The body of the pharaoh and his treasure lie behind you. You cannot deny your crime." She stared at the trucks as though she could see through the wood, metal, and canvas to the coffins and priceless artifacts inside.

Anna had never wished anything more in her life than that she'd never found Ahmose's tomb. She wished she'd never thought to dig in Dra' Abu el-Naga' or invite her companions to come to the tomb's opening. Had she known this would be the outcome, she would have never returned to Luxor after Carter's betrayal.

Georgette was not cowed, however. She raised her chin, defying the goddess's accusation. "We did not steal *le trésor*. We have taken it back from the real thieves."

Wepset tilted her head and lowered her arms as she absorbed this claim. Her tongue flickered out again, tasting the air—and perhaps Georgette's words. Anna realized with surprise that the goddess didn't know the women hadn't stolen the treasure. It must have been some other deity, likely Ammit, who had taken the real thieves. Wepset, whose purpose in the pantheon was to carry out revenge, only knew to follow the treasure. Her ignorance of the true circumstances behind its theft left them a small window of hope to plead for their lives.

"It's true," Anna said, rallying her courage. "We were taking the treasure to a museum, to go on exhibit."

Wepset hissed softly. "The body of the king and his possessions are not trophies." Her voice was full of such smoldering anger it could have burned a house down.

Anna didn't know how the Egyptian pantheon worked. Perhaps the gods had gone dormant when they ceased to be worshipped, or perhaps Wepset had never been particularly interested in what happened in the land of mortals. In any case, she seemed to be a little out of touch with the modern world. She clearly didn't know that in 1923, many artifacts belonging to Egypt's pharaohs were on display in museums around the world.

"Not trophies. As a form of reverence," Anna hastened to explain. How did one describe to an out-of-touch deity the purpose of a museum?

When Wepset narrowed her eyes, the thick line of kohl around them turned into a single, long black slit. "No." The finality in the goddess's voice made every bone in Anna's body shiver with fear. It was a voice that could destroy armies, a voice that *had* destroyed armies. "The treasure you carry is not for the hungry eyes of mortals, nor is the body of the pharaoh to be made a spectacle."

"We'll put it all back," Anna offered desperately. She could tell the goddess was running out of patience based on the renewed throbbing of the red orb above her. "We'll return it to the tomb and reseal it. No one will make an exhibit of any of it."

"No. What has been discovered once can be found again. The king and his possessions may not return to his tomb."

Anna was at a loss. Then where did Wepset want everything to go? The answer came immediately. "From the earth of Egypt the pharaoh has come. To it he shall return."

The words were cryptic, but Anna didn't have long to wonder what they meant. Wepset raised her arms once more. The red ball blazed. The ground began to rock so violently that Anna was flung to her knees. Cracks appeared beneath the trucks, growing like long black spider legs, enlarging by the second. She scrambled on her hands and knees away from them, desperate to avoid the sinkhole she knew was coming.

Clara found her a few meters later and the two clung to each other as the cracks crumbled into a single, rapidly growing crevasse. Beside them, safe for now, Georgette and Eliza watched in equally open-mouthed horror. First the ground disintegrated beneath the front right tire of Anna's truck, then the back tire. For a moment, the vehicle listed precariously, its undercarriage scraping the earth like a broken teeter-totter. The metal made an anguished squeal as the truck's weight shifted. Then, in the blink of an eye, it was gone.

Now it was the second truck's turn. Its front tires hooked over the advancing chasm edge. As the hole continued to grow, the entire cab sloped downward, headlights staring blankly into the bottomless abyss. For several breaths, the weight of the bed full of treasure kept the truck from sliding in. Then the ground beneath it disappeared. The truck dropped straight down, soundlessly swallowed by the earth.

Anna stared at the place where the trucks had been, barely able to comprehend what had just happened. In seconds, the pharaoh and the treasure he was meant to take with him to the afterlife were gone. Not a trace remained, not even the tiniest scrap of metal or rubber. The train from Luxor, the drive from Alexandria…all of it had been for nothing. The tomb and its contents might as well never have existed.

There was no time to mourn the loss, however. Anna knew the hole could easily consume them too. If the goddess desired their deaths, there would be no outrunning the yawning pit. She grabbed Clara's hand, bracing for whatever was to come. But instead of continuing to grow, the hole shrank. The edges of the black void quietly knit themselves back together, the rift dwindling first to a small fissure and then to a thin crack a few meters long. Within a minute, the sinkhole was entirely gone. The sand shifted and was smooth once more. If Anna hadn't seen it with her own eyes, she never would have believed any of it.

She forced herself to look at Wepset. Their fate still lay in her hands. Sinkholes weren't the only way to die. But the orb had dimmed. The sky was lightening to blue again, color returning to the world.

"Justice is done," the goddess announced, lowering her arms. "The pharaoh will lie in peace once more. He is avenged." Her gaze swept over the cowering women, brutally inhuman. "I judge you innocent. By the mercy of Osiris, you are spared. Thus has spoken She Who Burns."

Her verdict issued, she turned her back to the women and began to walk away. With each printless step, she became more transparent, the sunlight piercing through her as though she were made of smoke. After the fifth step, she was gone entirely. Nothing remained to indicate she had ever been there.

Anna was too stunned to process what had just happened. In the space of mere minutes, they had come face-to-face with an actual goddess, lost the treasure and the trucks, and barely escaped with their lives. It didn't feel real. Later, it would all hit her with the weight of a mountain, but for now, all she could do was feel relief that they had survived. She collapsed against the sand, exhausted. She couldn't have moved if she'd wanted to. She had no more strength left in her body. Clara lay down beside her, entwining their hands together so their shoulders touched.

After a moment of silence, Eliza asked, "Is it over?"

"I think so," Anna replied. The treasure was gone, and that meant the curse was too.

"What happens now?" Georgette asked.

"We've got a long walk ahead of us."

Clara sat up. She squinted at the horizon, then shaded her eyes to see better. "Are those camels?"

Surprised, Anna sat up too and followed her gaze. Coming toward them was another camel train. In the heat of the desert, the animals' long legs bent and waved like they were a mirage. It wasn't Gwafa of course, but likely another Berber on a similar path back to the Siwa Oasis. What were the odds?

"We are dead," Georgette moaned. "I am in Hell."

CHAPTER TWENTY-SIX

December 19, 1923
Alexandria, Egypt

The waves lapped gently against the hull of the steamship. The warm air carried the tang of salt. Anna leaned forward, her fingers curling around the rough white metal railing, and scanned the city around the harbor. If they didn't know better, a visitor might think they were in Naples or Marseille. But that was Alexandria in a nutshell: a veneer of Europe laid over a land older than time. Scratch the surface, and it was Egyptian through and through. Invading armies had carried new ideas and new religions into Egypt, but it turned out the past was still here, the old gods sleeping or waiting until it was time to rise again. Anna hoped she wouldn't be around when or if that happened.

Arms wrapped around her waist as a body pressed into the clean white linen of her shirt. A head came to rest lightly on her shoulder. She leaned backward, enjoying the contact. After everything that had happened, she didn't take it for granted.

"I almost can't believe we're leaving," Clara said. "I feel like we only just got here."

Anna nodded. In total, Clara, Eliza, and Georgette had only been in Egypt for just over two weeks. When she had invited them to come, she had planned for them to stay for at least a month. She had wanted to show them so much more of the country. Now, she never would.

Clara nestled her cheek in more tightly to Anna's neck and tightened her arms. "Are you sad to be leaving?"

Anna watched a steamer sail for the open ocean as she considered the question. Professionally, there was nothing to miss. Upon their return to Alexandria, she had immediately sent word to Ali to brick up the entrance to Ahmose's tomb. No one else, in Luxor or elsewhere, was to know it had ever been found. If anyone ever asked about the closed tomb—including the Department guards who had been placed over it when the women departed Luxor—they were to be told it had been the tomb of one of Ahmose's wives and that it had already been looted. Among those who knew the truth, the tomb's treasure was to be considered lost to the antiquities thieves. These lies were the only way she could be certain no one else would try to steal from the tomb and receive another visit from Wepset.

With the closing of the tomb, her work as an Egyptologist was finished, forever. After decades of excavating in Egypt, it had turned out to be surprisingly easy to tie everything off in a small, neat bow. There was no use even returning to Luxor to collect her picks and shovels; let Ali give them to the next archaeologist who came to the valley seeking fame and reputation.

Personally, she felt more ambivalent about her departure from Egypt, temporary as it was meant to be. Two weeks ago, she had proudly led the other women through Cairo. It was her city, her country. Now her future was unclear. If she wasn't digging in Luxor, where did she belong? What place was there for her in Egypt, which would soon be in the hands of the nationalists? For the first time, she felt like an anachronism.

The answers to these questions could only be unraveled in time, however, with great thought and introspection. She did not need to weigh Clara down with their weight. She put her hands over Clara's and smiled for her benefit, although the other woman couldn't see it. "No, not sad to leave it." It was not a lie, but it was not the full truth either.

She turned her head and kissed Clara on the cheek. "Perhaps I've been overdue in striking out from Egypt. The world is only getting bigger, not smaller. It's high time I see more of it."

Clara was silent for a minute. Then she said, "But it's still home."

Anna felt a pang in her chest. "Egypt has been my home since I was a girl. But perhaps I can find a new home."

* * *

In the comfortable silence that followed, Clara gazed out over the deep blue waters of the Mediterranean. Around them, dozens of steamers lay at anchor, flags from around the world flapping from their sterns. She remembered how awed she'd been standing at the docks in New York City, staring at the massive transatlantic steamships, how small she'd felt. Women like her didn't travel to Egypt. They didn't sail up the Nile by private steamer or stay at the Winter Palace in Luxor. And they certainly didn't go to Constantinople. Or at least, that's what she'd believed a few months ago.

But she had done it. Not only that, she had found that it hadn't been so hard after all. Maybe she hadn't been the woman she'd thought she was, or maybe she had become someone else. However it had happened, this was who she was now. Once, she had spent so much time worrying about where she fit into in the world; now she realized she belonged anywhere she wanted to be.

She closed her eyes and breathed the sea air in deeply, enjoying the way the brine hit the back of her throat. "I feel sometimes like this has all been a dream. I can't decide if I'd be less surprised if Ammit and Wepset appeared on the deck, or if I woke up and found I'd never left Iowa."

"Hmmm, there's an idea." Anna spun in her embrace until their noses were almost touching. Her eyes twinkled with amusement. "If this is all a dream, do you think we'll ever meet in real life?"

Clara entwined her fingers behind Anna's neck. The feeling of being close to her never lost its wonder. "I hope so."

For all the danger they had faced, she was glad none of it was a dream. Spending time with Anna, she had found something in her life she hadn't known she was missing: love. She had meant what she told Anna. She didn't know what the future held for them, but she wanted to see. She couldn't imagine where or how, but she was starting to believe they could find a way to carve out a space for themselves. The world was, as Anna had said, a large place. Surely two women could fit somewhere.

Anna leaned forward. When their lips met, a shiver ran from Clara's mouth to her knees. Anna's hands found her waist to pull her close, carefully avoiding the revolver holstered at her right hip. (Clara had insisted, and after all that had happened, Anna hadn't argued.) Clara's hand sank into Anna's lush hair. After a long moment, during which Clara was increasingly breathless, Anna pulled back. "We've got hours before dinner, you know." Her eyes moved to the cabin door behind them as her hand traced along the waistband of Clara's pants.

Clara's body responded instantly to the invitation with enthusiasm, but before they could take the first step toward their cabin, the black door next to them swung inward.

* * *

"Ah! I am glad to find you are here!" Georgette cried.

And indeed, she was genuinely delighted to see the two women. She had expected to find the deck empty as the passengers settled in, but it was much better to be with her friends. Stepping beside them to the railing, she leaned out to watch the porters push cargo along the docks. At this distance, they looked like a swarm of ants.

If there was such a thing, she already felt a swell of nostalgia for their impending departure. "Leaving *Égypte*, it is like closing a book, *non*? Now the story, it is finished and we start a new one."

She smiled, pleased both by her analogy and the feeling that their experience had come to a neat, complete conclusion. The book of Egypt had been one of action and paranormal suspense. The book of Turkey might be one of adventure and history. The only thing she regretted was that they hadn't been able to see all the treasure before the earth had consumed it. All she'd seen was a few trinkets.

Anna grunted and raised her head from Clara's shoulder. "It's not exactly the story I would have written."

Georgette waggled her head, simultaneously accepting and rejecting her words. It was true they had almost died several times. And true, too, that Anna's career had been ruined. And certainly if *she* had been writing the story, there would have been fewer camels, but she preferred to focus on the positive parts of the experience: although they had ultimately lost the treasure—something for which they couldn't be blamed—on the way they had experienced the adventure of a lifetime. What other mathematician could say they'd chased antiquities thieves across Egypt and faced down ancient Egyptian goddesses? The world might never know what had happened out there in the desert, but the four women would. They truly deserved to be part of the Lady Adventurers Club.

Behind her, Eliza poked her head out of the cabin they shared. "Give those women some privacy, Georgette. Don't you see they want time alone? Go take a walk or something."

Georgette frowned at her. Anna and Clara were on the deck of the steamer, a public place. That hardly suggested they wanted to be left alone. If they had wanted privacy, they would have been in their cabin. She motioned to the harbor around them in explanation. "We are saying *au revoir* to *Égypte*."

Anna sighed and stepped back from Clara. "Go on, Eliza, you might as well come out too. Georgette has a point, I suppose. We may as well bring closure to all this."

* * *

Eliza shrugged and stepped out onto the deck. After their days of caked-on sweat and dust, she finally felt clean and washed. She was wearing a brand-new dress and had tucked her hair beneath her favorite cloche hat, which had miraculously survived through all their train and motorcar rides. Despite Anna's suggestion, she didn't feel she needed closure. Closure was when Wepset threatened to kill them and then the earth swallowed up the trucks, along with all the jewels inside. Nothing more final than that. Besides, she wasn't one for sentimentality. When a thing was done, it was done.

"There, you see?" Georgette said, beaming. "We are all together now—*une famille*."

From acquaintances to friends to family in the space of only a few weeks—danger sure brought people together. Eliza was surprised to find she didn't mind having this new family. The women had grown on her: Georgette, with her earnest sincerity; Clara with her gentle naivety; and even Anna, who had learned a powerful lesson about tampering with cursed treasure. Now Eliza, who had always pictured traveling the world alone, couldn't imagine seeing Constantinople without them.

"Let's make a sort of toast, shall we?" Anna said, although they had nothing in their hands with which to toast. "To Egypt: the friendships we made and the treasure we lost. May we never have to go through anything like it again."

Abruptly, Georgette's face lit up. "Oh! We did not lose all of *le trésor*." She began to rummage in the pocket of her dress. A moment later, she pulled out a small ring on which was set a massive ruby.

Eliza blinked. "Is that—?"

She nodded. "It belonged to *Monsieur* Pearce. I found it in the sand next to his car in *le désert*." Its owner's fate was clearly implied. She handed it to Anna. "It is not *le trésor* of *le pharaon*, but it is *un trésor*. It is for you."

The unimaginable wealth of a pharaoh lost, and this little ring—modern, not ancient, and probably not even made in Egypt—was all that remained. Eliza didn't know whether they should throw it into the ocean or keep it as a reminder of what they'd gone through. Anna held the round gem up to catch the light of the sun. If you squinted, it looked like a miniature version of that dangerous ball on Wepset's head. Eliza shivered at the memory.

Anna smiled. "Do you know what, Georgette? I think it's perfect. Thank you."

The steamer whistled, announcing the raising of the anchor. Around them, cabin doors opened as passengers came out to watch Egypt disappear over the horizon. The women of the Lady Adventurers Club, however, went inside. They had seen quite enough of Egypt.

Bella Books, Inc.

Women. Books. Even Better Together.

P.O. Box 10543
Tallahassee, FL 32302

Phone: 800-729-4992
www.bellabooks.com